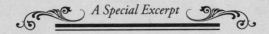

A Special Excerpt

Juliana swallowed. Edouard's warm, callused fingers held hers so gently. Did he clasp every woman's hand with such tenderness? Of course he did. He was a rogue. He'd mastered the nuances of that gallant gesture and knew how to use it to get his way.

Juliana sensed the stares of several esteemed guests nearby. Unease rushed through her. She didn't want to offend Edouard, but she also didn't want to imply interest in a relationship between them. Yet before she could discreetly draw her hand back, he pressed a light kiss to the backs of her fingers. How deliciously warm his lips felt against her skin.

A shiver rippled through her. *Beware this rogue, Juliana.*

"Until our dance, then," he murmured.

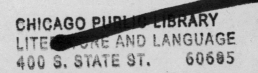

A Knight's Persuasion

CATHERINE KEAN

Medallion Press, Inc.
Printed in USA

DEDICATION

For Mike, who is a hero to me in so many ways. And for Megan, whose beauty and imagination inspire me and make me so very proud to be called "Mom."

Published 2010 by Medallion Press, Inc.

The MEDALLION PRESS LOGO
is a registered trademark of Medallion Press, Inc.

Names, characters, places, and incidents are the products of the author's imagination or are used fictionally. Any resemblance to actual events, locales, or persons, living or dead, is entirely coincidental.

Typeset in Adobe Garamond Pro
Printed in the United States of America

ISBN: 978-160542096-7

10 9 8 7 6 5 4 3 2 1
First Edition

ACKNOWLEDGMENTS

A very special thank-you to my awesome sister, Amanda Caux, who read through a prior draft of this novel. Oodles of thanks, too, to Caroline Phipps, critique partner extraordinaire, for the "midnight line edit." I appreciated your suggestions so much.

CHAPTER

1

Sherstowe Keep, Moydenshire, England

"There she is, at the bottom of the stairs."
Nineteen-year-old Edouard de Lanceau glanced
in the direction his good friend Kaine Northwood had
pointed, toward the wooden staircase descending from
the castle's upper level, the area where Lord de Greyne
and his family resided. Edouard tried to ignore the lurch
of his pulse. Soon he'd see for the first time the young
lady his father, Geoffrey de Lanceau, lord of all of Moydenshire, thought might be a good match for Edouard.

"As you know, Lord de Greyne is one of my most
loyal knights," Edouard's sire had said in a private meeting before this morning's horseback ride to Sherstowe.
"He shares my concerns about King John's rule, above
all, the instability his wars with France and ruthless taxes
have brought to England."

His father had seemed so grave, Edouard had
laughed. "You look as if you have discovered that nasty
past lover of yours—Veronique, I believe she is named?—
is one of King John's advisors."

He'd hoped for a grudging smile. Instead, his sire had looked even more grim. "Do not jest about her, Edouard. If befriending the king would further her ambitions, especially her goal to destroy me, she would find a way to get that alliance."

Edouard had barely resisted a groan. "I was jesting."

"I am not." Anguish touched his sire's gaze. "Until the day I die, I will watch for her and that bastard son she claimed years ago is mine. The unsettled circumstances in England provide the perfect opportunity for her to return and try to wreak her vengeance. Even more reason why I want this alliance."

Veronique hadn't been sighted in these lands for years. She sure as hellfire wasn't going to be a reason for Edouard to marry Juliana de Greyne.

"Listen, Son. King John continues to persecute noblemen he believes are no longer loyal to him, whether his information is true or not. I know of lords whose castles have been seized by the crown or destroyed. One day he may challenge my right to Moydenshire. We need to secure strong allies now, for the day that happens."

"Father—"

Raising a hand, his sire added, "A union by marriage between our household and the de Greyne's would ensure their many relatives will fight for us, as we will for them."

Anger had sucked the breath from Edouard. "You expect me to marry a woman I have never met before in order to protect Moydenshire? You are a rich and powerful lord. You have many allies and command large armies."

"True." A grudging smile tilted his father's mouth. "No bond of loyalty runs deeper, though, than that of families. You are well of an age to wed."

Fury had threatened to choke Edouard. "You cannot ask this of me! I do not want to marry."

"All I ask for now, Son, is that you keep in mind what I have told you and meet the lady."

Edouard strained to see past the noblemen gathered closest to the stairs, while fighting the awful pressure in his throat. He'd rather lick mud from a stone than become betrothed to this woman he considered a stranger.

Kaine's elbow jammed into Edouard's side. "Did you see her?"

"Nay." Edouard resisted a smug grin. Could he possibly go the entire day without meeting Juliana? With the crush of noblemen, women, children, and servants at the feast, it might be possible. If only he could escape outside, but the stairwell into the hall was clogged with arriving guests.

Shoving overlong hair from his eyes, Kaine frowned. "Wait a moment. When the noblemen move, you will see her."

Rolling his eyes, Edouard glanced at the nearby tables. Servants were pushing aside vases brimming over with brightly colored wildflowers to set down earthenware jugs filled with wine or ale. One of the maids was rather fetching; a luscious roundness to her bottom and bosom.

Which reminded him, once again, how he didn't want to be married. Life offered too many exciting, pleasurable adventures for him to be shackled by the responsibilities of a wife. The king hadn't remotely threatened Moydenshire, thus there was no urgency for Edouard to wed.

He'd told his father that during their discussions. His sire, of all indignities, had shaken his graying head of brown hair. "'Tis my honor-bound duty, as lord of Moydenshire, to consider all that might come to pass. I will not fail to protect these lands and the lives of the good folk living under my rule. Or to protect you, Son." Before Edouard could say a word, his sire had smiled. "You would feel differently about marriage if you met the right lady."

"A woman like Mother, you mean?" Nigh everyone in Moydenshire knew of Geoffrey de Lanceau and Lady Elizabeth's love, in part from *chansons* telling of the pivotal battle for Wode years ago that his sire, driven by vengeance for past misdeeds, had fought and won. He'd survived a mortal crossbow wound from the fight because of his lady love's devoted care.

Yet Edouard knew enough married lords who were so miserable they took courtesans to their beds, to know his parents' loving relationship was exceptional. Moreover, their relationship had no bearing on the matter of Edouard's betrothal—and that, too, he'd told his sire.

Still smiling, his father had spread his hands wide. "Come with me to Sherstowe to meet Juliana. One afternoon. Surely 'tis not too much to ask of you?"

And so, here he was, wearing his finest wool mantle, tunic, and hose, wishing to be anywhere but this noisy hall garlanded with enough wildflowers to color a meadow.

"Now your Juliana is walking to the left of the dais."

"She's not *my*—"

Kaine whistled. "Beautiful."

Edouard muttered an oath. His friend had a wicked sense of humor. She might well resemble the whiskered fish they caught in the lake.

With an impatient huff, Kaine jabbed Edouard again. "Look. She is wearing a dark green gown. That girl behind her is her younger sister."

With a reluctant sigh, Edouard looked. He caught a glimpse of a woman through the gap in the throng heading to the dais to pay their respects to their host, Lord de Greyne. Her dark brown hair, swept up around her pretty, oval face, was cleverly tied with a green ribbon in a style that accentuated her fair skin and fine-boned features. He stared, entranced for one awed breath, before a nobleman walked in front of her and she was again lost to Edouard's view.

She was lovely, aye, but . . . His pulse did a peculiar kick against his ribs, as though the emotional chains binding him to this visit and his looming responsibility tightened by a link.

How he hated the sense of entrapment. More than ever, he wanted to retreat outside.

"Come on," Kaine said.

Before Edouard could protest, his friend shoved him forward, almost knocking him into an elderly lady shuffling toward one of the tables.

"My apologies." Edouard bowed to the frowning woman before striding past. He glared at Kaine, strutting a few paces ahead. "Do not do that again. If you were not my friend, I would wallop you."

Kaine grinned. "I did not realize that old crone would be in the way." He winked. "I know you want to meet your lady."

Edouard's jaw tightened. "In truth, I would rather—"

"Kiss her, aye. You shall have more chance of that after the meal. Mayhap during the dancing."

"I do not want to kiss her. Would you listen to me? I—"

The pretty maidservant rushed into the space between Edouard and a table.

Catching her gaze, he winked in the brazen way he'd been taught by the stable hand at Branton Keep, who'd given him several blunt lessons on seducing women.

The girl blushed and smiled before she resumed her duties.

"Hurry!" Kaine called, darting back to grab Edouard's sleeve.

Enough.

Edouard turned on Kaine and propelled him back against the stone wall, close to a tapestry depicting a Norman battle. As Kaine's back hit the stone, his flailing arm knocked a garland of wildflowers draping from an iron sconce beside the tapestry. Edouard caught the earthy tang of daisies. He fought a sneeze.

When he clenched his fist into the front of Kaine's tunic, Kaine laughed and held up his hands in surrender. "All right. We will meet her when you wish."

"Good." Edouard's grip tightened. "You will stop your talk about kissing."

Mischief glinted in Kaine's eyes. "Why? Are you afraid to kiss Lady Juliana?"

"Of course not."

Hearty chuckles rippled from a nearby crowd. Although he knew the laughter wasn't directed at him, Edouard scowled.

"I think you *are* afraid." Kaine glanced past Edouard as though to find Juliana and catch her attention. "I *dare* you to kiss her."

Edouard ground his teeth. Why was Kaine so persistent?

"On the lips."

"Wait just a . . ." As Edouard glowered at his grinning friend, a sudden sense of understanding crept over him. Kaine was getting Edouard back for their bet several weeks ago, which Edouard won; Kaine had to relinquish his favorite dagger as well as a nighttime stroll with the busty, blond kitchen maid they both lusted after.

"If you leave today without kissing Juliana"— Kaine's grin turned sly—"you owe me that nice leather knife belt the village tanner made for you. You will also return my dagger."

Edouard snorted. "I do not have to heed you."

"True. The dare, though, has already been offered. If you refuse to accept . . ." Kaine shrugged. "Our friends will enjoy hearing how you were too much of a coward for a kiss. And from your almost betrothed."

Anger brought a hot flush crawling up Edouard's neck. The blatant challenge, combined with his sire's reasons for Edouard to attend this feast, seemed to weigh down upon him like a monstrous boulder. How Edouard yearned to haul Kaine down to a quiet part of the bailey and wrestle him into the dirt until they were both panting, exhausted, and ready to settle a truce over a pint of ale.

But that wouldn't resolve the matter of the dare.

A kiss? Fine. He'd kissed many young women; he counted himself fairly skilled at such. But he'd have to be sure there were no witnesses, apart from Kaine. If Edouard was caught kissing Juliana, others could interpret that as his promise to marry her.

One quick brush of his lips, bestowed upon Juliana in private, and he'd have met Kaine's challenge. He'd also get to keep the knife belt, which the tanner had made exactly as Edouard desired.

Kaine's gaze bored into Edouard. "Well?"

Edouard managed a reckless grin. "I accept your dare. If I win, I get sole rights to that maid for the next month."

Kaine's mouth gaped.

"What is wrong, my friend? Are *you* a coward?"

A bawdy chuckle broke from Kaine. "Very well. I agree to your terms."

"Good." Edouard loosened his hand from Kaine's tunic. "Now—"

"Get ready for that kiss, Edouard." Kaine pushed away from the wall while running his hands over his tunic. "Lady Juliana is headed our way."

Weaving through the throng, Juliana suppressed a sigh. If only her sixteen-year-old sister Nara, gliding close behind, would stop chattering like an anxious bird; she'd twittered on and on for days about Geoffrey and Edouard de Lanceau's visit. Most exhausting.

While Nara had fussed, preened, swooned, succumbed to fits of tears, and drunk calming infusions whilst lying abed and mopping her face with cool cloths, Juliana had worked with the cook and servants to coordinate the hall decorations, seven-course meal, and entertainment. She'd planned every detail to culminate in a celebration worthy of a visit from Moydenshire's famous lord.

How Juliana wished she could have arranged the festivities with her mother, who loved to be part of such events, but Mother was very ill from her last stillbirth. Responsibility for the feast had fallen entirely to Juliana. She hadn't objected; 'twas important for Mama to focus on resting and regaining her strength, so she'd be well again.

Juliana looked for her father among the guests. She hoped he was pleased with the arrangements. Later she must find Mayda, her dearest friend, who'd recently become betrothed and who'd be attending with her sire—

A sharp tug almost tore Juliana's sleeve. "Are you listening to me? I said the de Lanceaus arrived a short while ago."

God's teeth, Nara. "You have told me that three times now," Juliana said over her shoulder, and then smiled at a noblewoman she recognized from a feast last winter.

"The two of them are in this hall somewhere. I have enormous goose bumps *all* over my arms. The lumps are as big as gooseberries!" Nara tittered. "Oh, how exciting."

For you, mayhap, chirpy nuisance of a sister. For me—?

"I cannot wait to meet Edouard de Lanceau. He may soon be one of our relations." Nara sighed with enough theatrics to draw the curious gazes of the nearby noblewomen. "Oh, Juliana! How incredible, that he is considering *you*, of all women, to be his wife."

"Mmm." Juliana wiped her brow, throbbing from the noise in the hall, and desperately wished for a respite. Some of the cook's soothing mint tea would be wondrous right now. Glancing through a gap in the crowd, she looked over the trestle tables—what she could see of them, anyway—arranged to accommodate the guests for the meal. All the preparations seemed to be to plan. The wine and ale were flowing, the meal's first course would be served soon, and then—

Another pull on her sleeve. "Do you remember what Father said about Edouard de Lanceau? What color is his hair? What about his eyes? Is he handsome? Is he tall, or—?"

Juliana spun around. Wide-eyed, Nara halted. Her embroidered yellow gown, designed to accentuate her small waist and slender figure, floated to stillness about her ankles.

"Nara, will you stop? Please?"

Nara's gaze slid to a point behind Juliana. "But . . ."

A daisy petal drifted from the wildflowers in the nearby sconce and Juliana flicked it away. "At this moment, I do not wish to be reminded of Edouard de Lanceau."

Nara's mouth dropped open. Her hand fluttered to her throat. "Juliana."

"Neither do I wish to be reminded of my possible betrothal. I do not care that he is here. I do not want to get married, to him or anyone else. As far as I am concerned, he can—

"Good day to you, fair ladies."

Dread skittered down Juliana's spine as, snapping her mouth shut, she turned to see two young men standing less than three paces away. The shorter one with sparkling eyes and light brown hair dropped into a chivalrous bow. The other, slightly taller and broader of shoulder, smiled before he also bent at the waist while sweeping aside his black mantle.

The way the man moved . . . Her breath fluttered in her rib cage, for she'd never before seen such controlled elegance. Controlled in the manner of a clever warrior who knew his weapons, including those of sexual seduction; the kind of man Mama had warned her to beware. Elegant in a way that bespoke noble breeding and years of cultured tutoring. The combination made her faintly giddy, for 'twas appealing in a most dangerous, exciting way.

How shocked Mama would be if she knew Juliana's thoughts.

Juliana tried to look away but couldn't. Light from the wall torches flickered on his silky, shoulder-length brown hair. As he slowly rose from his bow, sweat dampened the soles of her feet, suddenly leaden in her best leather shoes. Oh, God. Oh, *good* God. Surely he was not—

"Kaine Northwood," the shorter man said before gesturing to his companion. "May I introduce my friend, Edouard de Lanceau?"

Nara squealed and clapped her hands to her cheeks.

Heat swept across Julienas face. Fighting the odd trembling deep within her, she dropped into an elegant curtsey fit for the highest courts, just as she'd been taught from girlhood.

She sensed the men's stares upon her, traveling over her in lazy assessment. Were they deciding if she was worthy of a great lord's son? Especially after overhearing her words to Nara?

Oh, Mother of God, they were probably ogling her cleavage, displayed to shocking advantage by the low-cut gown her father and Nara had insisted she wear. The fitted bodice made her breasts look enormous. Face burning, she pressed a hand to her breast and rose as swiftly as etiquette allowed.

"Lord de Lanceau," Nara said with breathless delight. "Lord Northwood. What a pleasure to meet both of you."

When Juliana straightened, her gaze came level with Edouard's tanned throat. Even that bit of him looked enticing. Torchlight caught the embroidery along his blue tunic's neckline. Magnificent work. But of course, 'twould be; his sire owned the largest and most profitable cloth empire in England. Some said Geoffrey de Lanceau was richer even than King John.

The weight of Edouard's stare forced her to look up. Their gazes met. His eyes were a bright, piercing blue and shadowed by thick lashes. The glint in his eyes . . . A jolt of unfamiliar sensation ran through her, and that wicked sense of danger stirred again. Her lungs suddenly felt impossibly tight, and she could scarcely draw a breath. She prayed she wasn't going to gasp like a landed trout.

As though attuned to her discomfort, his smile broadened, accenting his strong cheekbones. He looked even more the handsome rogue who only compromised when he knew 'twas to his benefit to do so. The careless tilt of his wide, full lips—a beautiful mouth—suggested he didn't have to compromise very often, because he knew just how to coax a woman to do exactly as he wanted—

Juliana blinked. God above, she *must* get control of her thoughts.

"Oh, Lord de Lanceau." Nara shoved past Juliana in a rustle of silk. "We are very honored to meet you. When Father told us you would be visiting our humble keep, Juliana and I were *so* thrilled. We could not stop talking about it, for we have admired your sire's many accomplishments in these lands. That you are visiting us today is, well," she giggled, "almost too exciting to believe."

"Indeed."

Juliana bit her lip. Even Edouard's voice was beautiful. Smooth and rich like a sumptuous confection.

She clasped her sweaty hands together and wondered how to excuse herself and slip away. Quite apart from being mortified, she had matters to attend—such as tasting the sauce to be served with the roasted quail, since the cook sometimes made it too spicy.

"—and we worked many long, tiring hours on this magnificent celebration planned for you today," Nara was saying. "A delicious feast, some fine musicians." Her voice raised on a flirtatious laugh. "There will be dancing later."

"I love to dance," Edouard said with a lop-sided smile. "And you, Lady Juliana?"

Struggling to quell her rising anger—how could Nara claim credit for the work without a glimmer of guilt?—Juliana glanced at Edouard and, somehow, roused a smile. "I enjoy dancing."

"May I request a dance with you?"

An invitation to dance. Was it a prelude to a betrothal? If so, how did she graciously decline?

Before Juliana could reply, Nara said, "She would be delighted to dance with you."

Edouard's eyes narrowed a fraction. "I am pleased to hear such. Lady Juliana?"

After a sharp glance at Nara, beaming like a giddy fool, Juliana met his gaze again. She tried to formulate an appropriate reply that wouldn't encourage his courtship. "I would—"

"Milady." A petite maidservant curtsied at Juliana's side. With a twinge of alarm, she recognized the young woman she'd assigned to care for her mother that day.

Juliana faced the maidservant. "What is wrong?"

"Yer mama is suffering pains. I have summoned the healer, but I thought ye should know."

Juliana touched the woman's arm. "Thank you."

With a hesitant smile and curtsey, the maidservant hurried away.

A frown creased Nara's brow. "Of all moments for Mama to be unwell."

Juliana clenched her hands, barely holding down the fiery words filling her mouth. How could Nara be so insensitive? Would her sister ever think of aught but herself?

Blinking away the sting of angry tears, Juliana dropped into a curtsey before Edouard. "Please excuse me, milord. I must see to my mother."

As she rose, he caught her right hand.

"Oh!" Nara gasped, and then giggled.

Juliana swallowed. Edouard's warm, callused fingers held hers so gently. Did he clasp every woman's hand with such tenderness? Of course he did. He was a rogue. He'd mastered the nuances of that gallant gesture and knew how to use it to get his way.

Juliana sensed the stares of several esteemed guests nearby. Unease rushed through her. She didn't want to offend Edouard, but she also didn't want to imply interest in a relationship between them. Yet before she could discreetly draw her hand back, he pressed a light kiss to the backs of her fingers. How deliciously warm his lips felt against her skin.

A shiver rippled through her. *Beware this rogue, Juliana.*

"Until our dance, then," he murmured.

Edouard stood at the edge of the raised dais, sipping a goblet of red wine. Bracing his hip against the lord's table, already cleared of the meal's leftovers, he looked over the merry folk in the hall who waited for the last few tables to be moved away to make room for dancing.

"Do you see Juliana?" He glanced at Kaine, also leaning against the table and watching the crowd, no doubt deciding which young woman to ask to dance first.

Kaine shook his head. "I see many lovely ladies, but she is not among them."

The image of Juliana bloomed again in Edouard's thoughts: fair, dewy skin; a willowy figure; wide eyes that assessed all around her with both intelligence and sensitivity. And her breasts . . . A silent growl tickled his throat. He'd never been so tempted by a luscious, well-displayed bosom. The fact she'd been so shy about her feminine beauty made her all the more intriguing, for, if he guessed correctly, she'd had little experience with men. He'd be the first to kiss her on the lips.

Near the hearth, the musicians tuned their instruments, playing a few strains of a familiar song that wove through the chatter and laughter. Edouard took another sip of the fine Bordeaux, welcoming the resolve burning in his gut. His chance to kiss Juliana would soon be upon him. If he didn't seize his opportunity, he'd lose the bet.

Losing wasn't in Edouard's nature—or, he vowed, in the heart of any de Lanceau.

Where was Juliana? Had she run off, anxious about his request for a dance?

When the maidservant had brought word of her mother's discomfort, Edouard had wondered if Juliana's responsibilities would keep her from the celebrations. She'd returned to the hall, however, just before the meal started, to take her assigned chair on the right side of the lord's table beside her father and Nara—to Lord de Greyne's obvious relief.

Edouard and his father sat on Lord de Greyne's left side. The formal seating arrangement made it impossible to converse with Juliana, but he caught glimpses of her during the meal, putting bread into her mouth, nibbling pieces of venison from her eating dagger, and drinking her wine. Several times he had to remind himself not to stare.

Glancing over the hall again, Edouard downed more wine. Whatever Juliana's reasons for vanishing, he wouldn't be denied so easily. He'd find her and woo her into a meeting with him where, with Kaine as witness, Edouard would bestow upon her a kiss she'd never forget.

Kaine tsked. "What a shame Juliana is not here. I think you will lose our bet, my friend."

"The day is not done yet." Edouard spied Nara a short distance from the musicians, talking to two other ladies who looked of similar age.

They glanced his way, gasped, and their faces turned red.

Who better to ask about Juliana than her sister, even if speaking to Nara made him want to rip out his own hair?

He smiled warmly at Nara, brushed past Kaine to step down from the dais, and strode to Nara's side. Ignoring the young ladies' breathless squeals, he said, "I am sorry to interrupt, but have you seen Juliana?"

Nara's pretty face clouded with a frown before she looked to the servants clearing away the last table. "She is not here in the hall?"

"Nay."

"She may be with Mother." A hard glint touched Nara's eyes. "She had best not be outside sketching in that wretched book of hers. Father will be furious."

Aware of Kaine's keen stare, Edouard said, "Where, outside, might I find her?"

Nara smoothed her hand over her fitted bodice that looked a fraction too tight. "The fish pond. But milord, mayhap you would prefer to stay with us? Juliana might return to the hall later. We can dance. Talk. Become better acquainted." Her lashes fluttered. "Please, will you not stay?"

"I will return soon." He winked. "Will you ladies reserve a dance for me?"

Nara's friends sighed with delight.

Her gaze shone with pleasure. "Of course, milord. We anxiously await your return."

Leaving the ladies' excited chattering behind, he wove through the crowd, hurried into the torch-lit forebuilding, and pounded down the stairs to the sun-washed bailey. Servants of the noble guests, most of them drunk, were lounging on parked wagons and empty barrels, drinking and talking; some were swaying to the music drifting from the hall. Only a couple of the commoners looked his way.

No sooner had he started toward the pond glint-ing a short distance past the slate-roofed kitchens, than Juliana stepped out of the kitchen doorway, carrying a wooden tray laden with food and an earthenware mug. Held tight under the silken drape of her left arm was a leather-bound book. Her face taut with concentration, she started toward the keep, seemingly oblivious to the other people in the bailey. Including him.

As she approached the large well, situated between the kitchens at the keep, he cleared his throat.

Her gaze flew up. She blinked, then tried to drop into a curtsey. "Milor—"

The tray tilted. The mug slid sideways, threatening to pitch its contents onto the ground. She squawked, scrambling to right the tray. He rushed forward and snatched up the vessel.

She blushed. "Thank you. I am glad it did not spill."

Her sweet lavender fragrance, distinct from the well's earthy odor, teased him. He savored her scent before looking at the green liquid in the mug. An unappetizing-looking brew. "What is it?"

"An herbal infusion for Mother."

So her responsibilities, not a fit of nerves, had kept her away from the dancing. Triumph began to simmer inside him, even as he strategized how to garner her trust and arrange the meeting for the kiss. "Is your mother still in pain?" He hoped he sounded concerned.

Juliana nodded and looked down at the tray. He followed her gaze to the wheat bread, sliced fowl, and jam tart. A meager repast, compared to the feast. He tried to tamp down inconvenient remorse.

"I did not expect you to be in the bailey, milord." While flawlessly polite, her tone conveyed her suspicions as to how he happened to be nearby at just the right moment to save her mother's healing drink.

"I became concerned when I could not find you in the hall." Unable to resist, he added, "I thought you were avoiding me and the dance you promised me."

A hint of defiance sparked in Juliana's eyes. "Mother

refused the meal the maidservant brought her. I hope she will feel well enough now to eat a little of this for me."

Edouard set the mug back on the tray. "'Tis kind of you."

"She is my mother."

The protectiveness in Juliana's voice made him smile. He admired such loyalty to one's family; he was very close to his parents and younger sister. If and when he married, he'd like that quality in a wife.

He suddenly became aware of footsteps a short distance away, accompanied by an astonished chuckle. Kaine.

Go on, fool! Kiss her right here, in Kaine's view, coaxed a mischievous voice inside his head. *Press your lips to hers and win the bet.*

A tempting thought. The drunken servants were farther down the bailey and caught up in their revelry; they wouldn't notice the kiss. The kitchen door was open, but the folk inside would be dealing with the leftover food, not watching the well. His sire would never know . . .

What are you thinking? a more rational voice intruded. *Have you, the firstborn son of a famous knight, forgotten how to be chivalrous? Stand down from your bet, out of respect for her.*

At that moment, Juliana looked past him and dipped her head in a gracious nod to Kaine. Edouard sensed her preparing to say good-bye to go and see her mother. Sunlight swept her profile, turning her skin to the hue of virgin snow. Her lips looked the color of the trellised roses growing in Branton Keep's gardens.

He swallowed, stunned by the realization forming in his mind. He wanted Lady Juliana de Greyne's kiss. Not merely to win the bet, but because he *wished* to kiss her.

She started to turn away. Purely on instinct, he touched her right arm; his fingers rubbed over her silk sleeve, noting the warmth of the skin beneath.

Juliana jumped and then twisted free, skirts rasping against the well's stonework; the mortared side was level with her lower thigh. Wide-eyed, she said, "Milord, I . . . must be on my way."

How loudly his pulse was drumming. "When you have visited your mother, will you grant me our dance?"

Her breathing quickened. He glanced at her luscious bosom outlined by the shimmering silk—he couldn't help himself— then raised his gaze to meet hers.

"I . . . Mayhap, milord."

The unguarded insolence in her tone should annoy him; he was, after all, the son of the most powerful man in Moydenshire. But he found himself even more captivated. He hadn't yet met a woman who didn't giggle and swoon when he wooed them. Juliana, however, still seemed immune to his attempts to charm her.

He clearly hadn't found the right means of persuasion.

Aye, 'tis the right of it, the mischievous voice coaxed. *You must lure her in, convince her she's the only lady you've ever desired, and then claim your kiss.*

"Please, Juliana." Edouard smiled as though he found her the most ravishing of women and dared to close the slight distance between them. "Surely you will not deny me one dance? I would be honored to have that memory of this day."

She gnawed her lip and glanced about the bailey, obviously unsure. Before she could move away, he closed his hands over hers, still holding the tray.

"Milord!"

She trembled in his grasp. How soft her skin felt against his. The yearning inside him strengthened.

Hurry! Kiss her.

He sensed Kaine edging nearer for a better view.

"Juliana," Edouard murmured, leaning forward, the tray pressing against his belly. He didn't care. His mind shut out all but her, very close now. Instinct told him he had an excellent chance of succeeding in his kiss. And he craved it. *How* he craved it.

"Milord." Her gaze locked on his mouth. "What—?"

"You are beautiful, Juliana."

A shivered sigh broke from her. "I . . . am?"

"I want to kiss you," he whispered.

"Kiss?" Her gaze darted away, as though searching for Kaine.

Did she fear him witnessing their kiss and then telling their sires? She might think he and Edouard were trying to trap her into a betrothal; she couldn't possibly know about the bet.

"Kaine will tell no one," he said softly, trying to think past the anticipation humming in his blood. "'Twill be our secret. I promise."

He lifted his hands from hers, readying to trail his fingers along her jaw and tilt her face up for his kiss. Juliana's lavender scent flooded his senses. Mmm . . . He could almost *taste* the sweetness of her lips.

Just as he reached for her, stomped footfalls approached.

"Juliana!" Nara shrieked.

"Nara?" Kaine called. "What are you—?"

Before Edouard could glance her way, Nara plowed into her sister. A deliberate attempt to thwart the kiss.

Juliana gasped. Stumbled sideways.

Forcing down a curse, Edouard caught the younger lady's arm and hauled her away from Juliana. Giggling, Nara spun against him and slid her arm around his neck. "I am tired of waiting for our dance. Return to the hall with me."

Scowling, he pushed her toward a shocked-looking Kaine and turned back to Juliana. She'd almost regained balance of the tray, but it teetered. An object hit the rim of the well, then landed with a *slap*.

"My sketchbook!" Juliana cried.

Edouard looked at the tome, lying partway over the well's opening. The parchment pages, secured to the cover by a strip of leather, had fallen open to reveal a rough sketch of a man's face.

His face.

Surprise rippled through him, while, with a low moan, Juliana scrambled to retrieve the book. Trying to help, he grabbed for it, and his elbow knocked the tray.

As it crashed onto the rim, the mug shattered. The bread and fowl fell into the well, while the jam tart landed sticky side down near Juliana's sketchbook.

Edouard groaned. "I am sorry."

Moving in behind him, Nara tsked. "Now look what you have done, Juliana." How horribly smug she sounded.

"What *Juliana* has done?" Kaine snorted.

Edouard glared at Nara. What a nasty, deceitful little—

"Why, 'twas not *your* fault, milord." With a blinding smile, the young woman blinked up at him and squeezed her way in between him and Juliana. "Let me get that sketchbook."

"Nay!" Juliana grabbed for the tome. Her shaking fingers tried to grasp hold of the sliding book, spattered with green droplets.

With a rasp, the book slid closer to the well's opening.

"Careful!" Edouard snapped.

Just as he reached past Nara to snatch hold of the book, she poked out a finger . . . and shoved it off the edge. Pages turned as it tumbled down into the darkness.

"Nay!" he roared.

With a choked cry, Juliana lurched forward. She fell to her stomach on the well's rim and made a frantic downward grab.

Nara sniffed, a sound of disdain. "Forget those foolish sketches."

"Go away, Nara." Anguish thickened Juliana's voice. "You have done quite enough."

Edouard's gut clenched. If Juliana leaned any farther into the well, she might fall in.

He pushed Nara out of the way. Now that he stood beside Juliana, he leaned forward to hold her waist.

A swift kick knocked his right foot, causing his boot's sole to skid on the dirt. *Nara's doing.* He roared, even as he tried to regain his balance. Losing his foothold, he pitched toward Juliana.

"God's teeth," Kaine shouted.

Edouard fell against her. With a shrill scream, she hurtled forward.

Her hands flailed, trying to grab the opposite side of the rim. Her legs thrashed. Kicking up a froth of silk, she continued to slide forward.

Worry and rage threatened to choke Edouard. She could be badly injured falling into the well. She could die. Grabbing for Juliana's skirts, he yelled, "Hold still!"

"I am falling!" she shrieked.

Edouard caught rising voices somewhere nearby. Others about the castle were aware of the crisis. Soon, all would know. Including his father.

He couldn't think of such now. "Do not worry," he called to her. "I will pull you out."

"Edouard!" Kaine, too, caught part of Juliana's gown. The fragile silk tore.

"Juliana!" Edouard cried, lunging for her arm.

She screamed again and plummeted head first into the depths.

CHAPTER

3

The scream seared the back of Juliana's throat as she fell in the inky dankness. She scrambled to catch hold of the stones passing by, to find a handhold and stop her descent. Impossible. She was falling too fast.

The wooden bucket for drawing water loomed ahead. She twisted her body, tried to grab for the bucket, but missed.

Down she plunged, for what seemed an eternity, until she splashed feet first into icy water. Before she could draw a shocked gasp, she submerged; the water dragged her into its depths. She shoved out with her arms, forced her body upward. When she broke through the surface, she hauled air into her lungs. The sound echoed back to her, ghastly and hollow.

Kicking her feet, she fought to stay afloat.

"Help!" she yelled to the circle of sunlight far above. "Help!"

"Juliana!" Edouard called down to her, while Kaine and Nara leaned in beside him. Edouard sounded anxious. Worried, no doubt, that he'd be in trouble for what had happened. Well, he deserved to be punished for shoving her into this hellish pit!

"Help me!" she shrilled. The darkness was so intense, she couldn't even see her arms moving in the water. She'd been told Sherstowe's well was wider and deeper than most; a long-ago lord had ordered it built that way, so if necessary, the castle could withstand months of siege.

If she didn't leave these depths soon, she could suffer a severe chill or drown.

"Oh, God," she moaned.

"Hold on," Edouard said. "I promise, Juliana, we will get you out."

An eerie whisper echoed—her silk gown, floating on the water's surface. She couldn't see it, but fabric bobbed against her skin, a sensation akin to the nudging of a submerged creature.

Something else bumped against her. A bit of wood? A lost toy? A monstrous toad who was lord of this underworld? Smothering a hysterical giggle, she dared to reach out and touch the object and found her floating, waterlogged sketchbook.

Tears stung her eyes as she drew the book close. It squelched as she pressed it tight to her chest, the odor of soggy parchment sharp in her nostrils. Her book was ruined. She'd know for certain when she'd got it into the light, but she doubted her sketches had survived.

How kind of you, Nara, a bitter voice cried inside Juliana. *Are you pleased you managed to push my sketchbook into the water? Was destroying my drawings—something so important to me—your way of showing off for Edouard?*

Juliana's teeth chattered. The coldness seeped to her bones. Why wasn't Edouard lowering the bucket to pull her out? Or, if that wouldn't work, sending down a rope?

Frantic activity seemed to be taking place at the surface: heated discussion, a squeaking noise, shouts. Panic shivered through her as she continued to tread water. She must stay calm. Be patient. But what if the pulley for the bucket was broken? Father had planned to replace it, because it kept jamming. That might have happened now. How, then, would she get out?

She didn't want to die. Not today. Not when Mother needed her help to recover.

Not like *this*.

"Help m-me." Juliana drew upon all fear coalescing inside her. "*Help. Meee!*"

"Juliana!" Edouard shouted down.

"Get m-me out!" she screamed, not caring if she sounded like a frightened child. Terror pounded at her temples. She didn't want to die. She didn't want to die!

"Stay calm," Edouard said, his soothing voice floating down to her. "I imagine 'tis dark and frightening—"

"Aye!"

"But we will rescue you. We will not leave you down there, I promise. I give you my word."

The word of a rogue who'd tempted her with a kiss and pushed her into this dangerous place? She didn't want his help. Yet he seemed to be leading efforts to get her out. "W-what is wrong? Why is it t-taking so l-long?"

"The pulley was stuck, but we fixed it. Listen, now. We are going to lower the bucket. 'Twill be easier than you trying to hold on to a rope while we draw you all the way to the surface. Stand in the bucket. We will pull you up."

What if the pulley jammed again? What if the bucket couldn't hold her weight and broke? She might perish before they could find another way rescue her. "Edouard!"

"I am here, Juliana. You will be all right," he said. "Trust me."

A muffled creak came from above. He'd started lowering the bucket.

Hurry. *Hurry!*

She waited, treading with her tiring legs. Her harsh breaths echoed.

"The bucket will reach you soon," Edouard said.

Holding her breath, she tried to discern its arrival. The air stirred close to her face. An object splashed nearby.

She reached out and touched the rough-hewn side of the bucket.

"I have it!" she called, relief soaring inside her. She

reached higher to grab hold of the connecting rope. The bucket shifted, sloshed, but she managed to slide one leg over the side, then the other, and set her feet on the bottom.

"I am in!" she cried.

Tucking her sketchbook under her arm, she held tight to the coarse rope with numb hands. One shuddered breath. Two. The rope tautened under her grip, and then she felt herself slowly rising. A joyous sob rattled in her throat.

Little by little, she rose. The bucket swung gently with each tug from above, while water trickled from her gown, hanging over the bucket's side, to the surface below. Her teeth were still chattering, but hope glowed inside her. Soon, she'd be on solid ground.

Long moments seemed to pass before the sun-lit stones of the well's rim came into view. A crowd of servants and guests had gathered around the opening, many of the men assisting with the rope.

One more tug and her head cleared the well. Edouard and Kaine reached in to catch hold of her arms. They pulled her up to the well's edge.

Clutching her sketchbook before her like a shield, she swung her trembling legs over the well's side and stood.

The crowd cheered and clapped. "Lady Juliana is safe!"

"Well done, milords," one of the men cried.

"What heroes!" another man shouted.

Juliana sucked in a breath of fresh air, all too aware

of the water dripping from her ruined gown to puddle in the dirt. Her bodice stuck to her skin; the wet silk had turned indecently sheer, but at least the sketchbook hid her bosom from the crowd's view.

Most importantly, though, she was safe.

"Thank you," she said to the helpers by the well, to Kaine, and at last, to Edouard.

He no longer looked the arrogant rogue. His expression grim, he dipped his head in reply. Dirt streaked his right cheek and grubby patches marked his tunic. He'd taken off his mantle. It lay in a heap on the well's edge.

As conversation began to spread through the crowd, Edouard touched her arm. "Are you hurt?"

"Nay." Juliana jerked from his gentle grip.

"Are you certain—?"

"I am." She could hardly bear to look at him. He, who'd told her, of all astonishing things, that she was beautiful, almost kissed her, knocked over the tray, pushed her into the well—and then rescued her. She didn't know how to feel about him.

Worst of all, the excitement stirred up by his desire for a kiss still simmered inside her, taunting her with what might have been.

Edouard sighed, a sound heavy with regret. "I am glad you found your sketchbook."

Most likely a ruined sketchbook. Unable to speak past the tightness in her throat, she nodded.

"That . . . drawing of me . . ."

Heat swept Juliana's face. She'd never intended for Edouard to see that foolish, impulsive sketch. Never should she have indulged that curious desire to draw him, and not merely so Mother could see what he looked like.

Fingering wet hair from her cheek, a gesture Juliana hoped might hide her blush, she shivered and glanced toward the keep. Somehow, she must excuse herself, make her way to her chamber, change her garments, and then tend to Mother, all without her sire learning of this mishap.

Of course, he might already know. He'd be very upset to have this incident happen on such a crucial day. She tried not to let her shoulders droop. How she'd wanted this celebration to be perfect.

Nara patted her arm. "Poor Juliana. You must feel rotten, soaked through as you are. What a shame about your new gown. And your sketchbook . . ." She wrinkled her nose. "Is *that* what smells?"

"With careful drying," Juliana said firmly, "the odor will go away."

"Really?" From Nara's tone of voice, she meant, "Not likely."

A tart retort flew to Juliana's tongue. *Nay.* She wouldn't speak so to her sister in front of Edouard and the other guests. Enough dramatics had already occurred, and an argument between her and Nara would only feed gossip. What she needed to say to Nara could wait till later that evening when they were alone.

Looking again at Edouard, Juliana dropped into a stiff but elegant curtsey. "Please excuse me, milord."

His lips parted, indicating he was about to reply. Spinning on her heel, she hurried toward the keep, the torn section of her gown dragging in the dirt.

Before she had taken five steps, footfalls sounded behind her. "Here. This will help to warm you." Edouard matched her strides, and cloth settled about her shoulders. His mantle. As she looked up at him, he reached around and drew the heavy wool about her shoulders. It smelled of horse and sunlight and . . . him. "I wanted to give this to you a moment ago," he said, "but you rushed off."

She wanted to still be annoyed with him, but sympathy filled his gaze. Did he guess how much effort it took for her to maintain her dignity when she was soaked and tired? Did he know how hard she'd fought not to yell at Nara?

"Thank you," Juliana murmured.

Edouard smiled. "'Tis fine English wool." He winked like a mischievous boy. "Comes from the estates of some rich lord. De Lanceau, I believe his name is."

She smiled back. "I feel warmer already."

"Good." His expression sobered. "For all that has happened today, I am truly sorry."

How heartfelt his apology sounded. A secret part of her sighed with pleasure. As she looked up into his handsome face, its angles brushed with sunlight, her sur-roundings seemed to blur away into nothingness, till there was only him.

His gaze, bright with an emotion she couldn't quite pinpoint, held her like a tender touch. Awareness of him ran like a warm drink in her veins. Was this how a lady felt before her gallant hero swept her into his arms? Juliana's pulse fluttered in a wild rhythm, for his stare reminded her of that instant not so long ago, when he'd said he wanted her kiss.

Never before had a man said that to her. Juliana's gaze shifted to Edouard's mouth and, suddenly, she wanted to know exactly what a kiss—*his* kiss—was all about.

Do not be foolish. Have you forgotten he pushed you into the well?

Juliana focused on tugging the mantle closer about her. "Thank you," she managed to say, "for loaning me your garment."

"Keep it as long as you like."

A kind offer. However, others might see him as presenting her with a gift, a token of his affection. A garment as personal as a mantle likely held a certain significance between lovers. She must see the mantle re-turned to him as soon as she'd donned fresh clothes.

"I will get it back to you"—she resumed walking toward the keep—"later today, milord."

"All right."

"Juliana," Nara called. "Does this mean you give up your dance with Edouard?"

Juliana stumbled to a halt, her back to her sister. Dance with Edouard? Was that all Nara cared about? Juliana's grip tightened on the sketchbook until pain shot through her fingers.

A harsh sigh welled inside her as she turned to look at her sister. Right now, the last thing Juliana wanted to do was dance. However, she couldn't very well forfeit her dance with Edouard, one of the most important guests at the festivities, because onlookers could see this as an insult. He'd rescued her. Some would say he'd saved her life. What grateful young woman wouldn't want to dance with her hero?

The day's emotions squeezed down upon Juliana, threatening to crush the last of her courage. She wouldn't yield to tears. Not before all these people. Especially not in front of Edouard.

"At this moment," she said, "I have more pressing concerns than a dance. But thank you, Sister, for reminding me of it."

A sensible, noncommittal answer. Now, to reach the quiet of her chamber; she had no wish to face another dilemma while dripping wet and bedraggled.

"Edouard," Kaine said, somewhere close behind, before a loud slap echoed—the sound of a hand coming down upon a shoulder. "If you ask me, I vow you have lost our bet."

Juliana frowned as she walked. Bet?

"Kaine! For God's sake . . ."

She might have kept on at her steady pace, but for the frustration in Edouard's voice. She turned, wet gown twisting about her legs, and caught the warning glare Edouard threw at his friend an instant before his guilty stare met hers.

"Bet?" Coldness settled in her stomach. "What bet?"

As misgiving clouded Juliana's expression, Edouard fought a groan. He should have known his dealings with Kaine would end in disaster. Now he might have to answer to the folly. And to the woman who, in a very short time, had become more to him than a fleeting challenge.

"What bet?" Juliana repeated, while her poignant gaze bored into Edouard. He felt that stare as though it reached inside him and wrenched his soul. Shame licked through him, becoming more intense when her attention refused to waver.

"Ah . . ." Kaine chortled and threw his hands wide. "'Twas but a private jest between lads. Not a lady's concern."

That's right, a voice inside Edouard said. *Take Kaine's example and lie. You don't have to admit your foolishness. Why hurt Juliana? She's endured enough already.*

That wouldn't be honorable, an equally strong voice broke in. *If you respect her, care for her, you'll be honest. Even if it means you must accept blame.*

Still holding Juliana's stare, Edouard dragged his hand over his jaw. He wanted to make the right decision. If his sire learned of the bet, though, he wouldn't be at all pleased. Just thinking about his father's disapproval made sweat break out on Edouard's forehead.

"Not a lady's concern?" Juliana's eyes narrowed. "Why then, Kaine, do you look so guilty?"

"Do I?" He laughed, even as his face turned red. "Well, I—"

"And you, Edouard. You have not answered me." Her fingers tightened on her sketchbook, a gesture that drew his gaze to her bluish nails. "Do I guess correctly? This bet *does* concern me?"

"Oh, nay," Kaine cut in. "Of course not. Right, milord?"

Another, silent groan broke inside Edouard. "Be quiet, Kaine."

"I am only trying to help."

Edouard barely resisted a snort. Kaine was only trying to save his wretched arse. But like a loyal friend, he'd tried to cover for Edouard, too.

Aware their conversation had drawn the attention of curious observers, Edouard smiled at Juliana. Instead of lying, or admitting the truth, he'd press his charm on her and convince her to drop the matter for now. If she insisted on the truth, he'd divulge it later, when fewer were in earshot, and when no one who overheard would take the news to his father.

Gesturing to her soaked clothes, he said, "Please, Juliana, go and put on dry garments. Then I will be pleased to—"

"I want to know now."

She looked so miserable, he longed to cross to her, draw her into his arms, and hug her, as he'd comfort his younger sister. However, that would certainly set tongues a-wagging.

As the silence persisted, Juliana's chin tilted higher. She wasn't going to give in. Would she stand there, cold and dripping, until she caught a severe chill?

Her chin was quivering.

"Juliana . . ."

"Why will you not tell me? That is most puzzling of all."

Another groan bubbled up within him, for he felt his resolve weakening. He couldn't lie to her; he didn't *want* to lie. In this instance, lying seemed akin to cowardice.

He closed the distance between them, ignoring Kaine shuffling a short distance behind. "Juliana," Edouard said, near enough to her that he could lower his voice and keep their words private. "You are right. We did make a bet."

Kaine cursed and kicked at the dirt.

"We—"

"—bet that my sketchbook would end up in the well?" she said in an anguished tone. Her gaze shifted beyond him to Nara and he remembered the younger woman's eagerness to shove the book into the depths. Did Juliana believe he and Kaine had conspired against her with Nara? Ugh. What a distressing thought.

"Nay, Juliana. We meant no harm to you or your drawings. We—"

"Aye?"

He cleared his throat. "Made a bet as to whether or not I"—*God's blood*—"would win your kiss."

Shock, then hurt, darkened Juliana's eyes. "Kiss?"

Her hissed reply was just loud enough to draw stares, though he suspected the onlookers were too far away to make out what she said. He raised his hands, palm up, trying to tamp down his rising apprehension and regret. "I admit, at first, I went along with the bet. Stupid, I know, but 'twas a challenge between me and Kaine, and I . . . wanted to win."

"Challenge." She shook her head. Tears welled in her eyes, and her lips parted on a sob.

"Juliana . . ."

"'Tis all I was . . . am . . . to you? A *challenge*? Another lady for you to count among your conquests?"

"Damnation." Edouard hauled his fingers through his hair. He hated to see tears streaming down her face. Yet he dared not reach for her. Not when so many gazes were upon them.

Juliana stepped backward, putting distance between them. The pain in her expression faded to stony remoteness.

A dull ache squeezed his innards, for he sensed she was lost to him. Naught he said or did now would likely change her opinion of him. Yet he truly did want her to hold him in high regard. "I did not mean to hurt you, Juliana. Neither, I am certain, did Kaine."

"Hurt me? *Hurt* me, milord? Did you once consider my feelings before you tried to trick me into a kiss?"

"Wait a—"

"Did you feel *any* guilt at all while you attempted to seduce me? What about when you knocked over the food for my mother? Was that mishap part of your ploy?"

Anger began to weave through Edouard. He'd told her the truth about the bet; she'd thanked him by attacking his honor. Did she really believe he'd deliberately knock over a meal intended for an ill woman? Or, in her frayed emotional state, had Juliana just blurted the first words that came to her mind?

He sensed the accusing gazes of the encroaching spectators, condemning him without even knowing all the circumstances. He wasn't a beast. Neither was he a witless peasant, to be shrieked at by Juliana as though he and everyone within earshot were deaf. "Tipping the tray was an accident," he said, struggling for calm. "You must know that. I never intended—"

"And when you pushed me down into the well?"

Shocked murmurs rippled through the crowd.

"Lord de Lanceau rescued her," someone in the throng said. "Did he not?"

"Was that a trick?" another person asked.

Edouard balled his hands into fists. He hadn't pushed Juliana into the well. Nara had done that, by dislodging his foot and causing him to fall against Juliana.

But here, in the bailey of the de Greyne castle, he couldn't point an accusing finger at the wicked little sister. Where was the gallantry in such an act? He'd only come off looking more of a monster, especially when Nara denied his claim, burst into tears, and went running to her father. Not a good idea, to be guilty of offending both of his host's daughters in one afternoon.

Juliana's lips were blue with cold, but she was clearly waiting for some kind of reply from him. An admission of guilt? Never. "I did not mean for aught to happen to you," he said, doubting his words would make any difference. "I realize you are angry, but you must believe me."

She shook her head. Damp tendrils of hair slipped against her cheek and ran into her tears. "I cannot."

Those two words bore into him. He shuddered, as though fighting the pain of a knife.

"All that happened between us today," she said tonelessly, "was part of your deceit. So you could win the bet."

"*Not* all that happened." He locked gazes with her,

about to insist how wrong her words were, but his focus was shattered by the tramp of approaching footfalls. Daring a glance, he saw his father walking alongside Lord de Greyne, their long cloaks swaying with each stride. Neither man looked pleased. In fact, his sire's mouth flattened into a disapproving line.

"Juliana?" Her father's frown deepened. "How in God's name . . . ?"

She glared at Edouard. The fury in her eyes . . . It snatched the air from his lungs. Reaching to her shoulders, she hauled off his mantle and threw it at him. He caught it a moment before it landed in the dirt.

"Juliana!" Lord de Greyne shouted. "What are you doing?"

"Milords," Edouard said, stepping forward and bowing. "If I may explain?"

"Explain. Good," she said, each word brittle. Clutching her sketchbook against her bosom, she said, "Tell them all, Edouard. 'Tis indeed a fascinating tale. One that shows just how unsuitable you and I are for a betrothal, now or ever."

Close behind Edouard, Kaine whistled.

Edouard heaved in a furious breath. Better that she'd have slapped his face in front of all these witnesses. But nay. She chose to outright reject him, in a very humiliating spectacle that would be gossiped about for months to come.

Well, he would not stand for it! "Betrothal?" he growled back. "I have no wish to be betrothed. Especially not to you!"

A collective gasp rose from the onlookers.

"Edouard," his father snapped.

Juliana's tear-streaked face whitened. She stumbled backward. For all of two breaths, he regretted his words, until she dropped into curtsey so stiff, he vowed her spine would snap. "Good day to you, Father, Lord de Lanceau," she said as she rose. "To you, Edouard, I bid *good-bye*."

Juliana shuddered and snuggled into the solar's wide bed, next to her mother. Telling all that had happened—the important details, at least—had left Juliana exhausted. "I am sorry, Mama, for not coming to you sooner. Truly, I am."

Her last words dissolved on a sniffle. The bed ropes creaked as her mother shifted against a mound of pillows; her frail arm slid around Juliana to draw her in close. Mama smelled as Juliana remembered from childhood—of sun-dried linens, sweet almond oil, and comfort.

"There, now." Lady de Greyne kissed Juliana's brow; soft, gray hair brushed against Juliana's face. "No more crying."

Juliana noisily blew her nose on a linen handkerchief,

while strains of a favorite *chanson*, borne on the afternoon breeze, floated in through the solar's open window. She rubbed her cheek against Mama's shoulder and listened, becoming aware of the wheezy quality of her mother's breathing. There was another sound, too. A steady pulse on the bedding—Mama, lightly tapping her fingers in time to the melody. She began to hum.

A sense of discordance, of un-rightness, pushed its way into Juliana's contentment. Beyond the cocoon of this chamber, the revelry went on, regardless of her mother's infirmity and the incident at the well.

What more, though, could Juliana expect? Her father couldn't neglect his invited guests. Not when many of them, including the de Lanceau's, had traveled a fair distance.

Why, then, did that ugly knot inside Juliana twist another notch?

Because of *him*.

She scowled and her fingers clenched around the handkerchief. Before that bet-making knave had come to Sherstowe, her life was pleasant. Uncomplicated. Now? She could scarcely think past the turmoil churning inside her.

Down in the music-filled hall, Edouard de Lanceau was probably dancing with a pretty, young noblewoman. He'd woo that lady to near swooning with his clever words and handsome smile.

That girl in his arms might be Nara.

Juliana groaned.

Her mother's cool, blue-veined hand touched Juliana's cheek. "Hush, my sweet child. All will be well."

"I think not, Mother." Juliana dabbed at her eyes.

"Why do you not go back to the celebration? You look lovely in that honey-colored silk and you worked many days to bring about this day. Go enjoy yourself. Chat with Mayda. Dance . . . with some handsome lads." Her mother sighed, clearly remembering happier times.

Juliana fought more tears. In time, Mama would be well enough to join festivities at the keep; she'd dance again with Father, smiling and laughing as before. But for Juliana to return to the hall? Feel she *must* dance with Edouard? She shook her head. "I cannot leave you now, Mama. Not when you have refused to eat today. The maidservant I sent away a short while ago will be bringing you a tray soon."

"Oh, Juliana." Resignation darkened Mama's voice.

Juliana fought a tug of dread and clung to the promise she'd made to help Mama get better. "You must try to eat, even a small amount." Juliana managed a shrug. "Besides, I do not feel like reveling."

"Because of . . . your sketchbook?" Her mother expelled a short breath, one that seemed tinged with pain.

Sitting up, Juliana looked at her mother. Mama's face relaxed from a grimace, but her chalky skin looked more ashen than usual. "Mama, are you all right?" Juliana pressed her palm to her mother's brow to check for fever. "How selfish of me, to be thinking of myself, when—"

With a feeble touch, Mama batted Juliana's hand away. "Do not worry about me. Your sketchbook might be fine, once dried. If not"—she drew another sharp breath—"you should ask your father for another."

"I shall." Juliana sniffled. "He does not appreciate my drawings as you do, though. He does not say such, but I sense he wishes I would work harder to be a lady."

Her mother chuckled, a sound like brittle leaves. "You *are* a lady. And one, I am certain, who could win the heart of any young lord in our hall."

Juliana blushed. "Mama!"

A tender, sad smile tilted her mother's lips. "Do you know why your father was so pleased to have Edouard de Lanceau here? I know your sire can be difficult at times, but he wants a good marriage for you."

Juliana frowned. "Edouard pushed me into the well."

"That must have been an accident. He did rescue you, aye?"

Juliana barely stifled a gasp. Was Mama taking Edouard's side over her own daughter's? "But . . ."

"He was probably trying to impress you, and—"

"He made a bet with his friend, Mama, that he would win my kiss."

"I see." Her mother winced and slid farther back into the pillows. "Did Edouard win? Did he . . . kiss you?"

50

"Nay! Neither will he have another chance. I do not wish to see him ever again."

Juliana waited for her mother's nod of approval. Instead, the sorrow in her gaze was shadowed with regret. "Are you certain, Juliana, you feel that way?"

Juliana plucked at a loose thread on the bedding, while the tangled emotions of the afternoon burgeoned up inside her again. "I do not know what I feel, Mama. When Edouard told me I was beautiful, when he looked at me as though I were the only maiden in this land, I felt such gladness. It seemed as though part of my heart . . . glowed."

"Mmm," Mama murmured, sounding as though she understood.

"My body felt strange, too, soaring and yet weighty at the same time. I could scarcely breathe. Oh, Mama, I have never felt such odd sensations."

"Imagine how you would have felt if he had kissed you." Mama smiled in a most curious, knowing way.

"I do not care to imagine," Juliana said firmly. "I am glad I discovered what a deceitful rogue he is before that happened."

As Mama's smile faded, the sense of un-rightness weighed deeper, and Juliana looked over at her sketchbook, propped open against the window's iron grille. A precarious position, but she wanted the tome to dry quickly.

The parchment pages had buckled. The leather was ruined. But she'd try anything—anything!—to preserve the drawings she'd rendered with such care. Some, like the sketch she'd done of her stillborn baby brother a few weeks ago, before she'd washed and wrapped his body for burial, she could never replace.

She rose, crossed to the window, and reached out to straighten a wet page that had folded over on itself. Did she dare look at what was left of her brother's drawing?

"Tell me more about Edouard."

Juliana glanced over her shoulder. Mama lay with her eyes shut, upturned hands lying like lilies against the bedding.

"Describe this young man to me," Mama said softly, "who sought your kiss."

Returning her attention to her sketchbook, Juliana sighed. She didn't want to discuss Edouard. However, if Mama wished it . . . "He is, without question, the most arrogant, sly of tongued—"

Mama chuckled, before her laughter faded to a tight wheeze. "'Tis what I thought of your father, when I first met him." A faint pause. "Is Edouard . . . handsome?"

Oh, aye. Did Juliana want to admit, however, that her fickle heart had been wooed by his beauty?

"He is attractive enough." Her finger, somehow, settled near the middle pages of her sketchbook where she'd drawn him. "His hair is dark, his face finely formed. I vow most women would be thrilled to have his kiss."

How strained her mother's breathing sounded.

Glancing back at her, Juliana hoped the maidservant would arrive with the ordered meal. Did Mama also need more healing herbs?

Mama's damp eyes opened. "Juliana," she whispered, pleading. About to tell Juliana, no doubt, she should rethink her opinion of the great lord Geoffrey de Lanceau's son and heir.

Juliana stared out the window, barely able to choke down a frustrated cry. "I know what you are about to say, Mama. You believe I should not judge Edouard by what happened at the well, and that I should be happy he wished to kiss me. But he is not like Father. Edouard and I would not suit."

Mama moaned.

"Mayhap one day, I will meet a lord's son and become betrothed. Right now, I do not care to marry any man."

A rattled sigh came from the bed. A sigh of disappointment? Juliana swallowed hard, for she didn't ever want to disappoint her mother. However, marriage was not a matter to take lightly. "If I wed, I would have to leave Sherstowe. How could I leave behind all I know?" Her finger slid along her sketchbook. "How could I leave you, Mama?"

Silence.

"Mama?" Juliana turned. Her mother lay with her eyes shut, her lips slightly parted. The odd slackness of her jaw, the sudden feeling of being alone, sent Juliana rushing to the bedside.

Shaking, she caught her mother's hand. Limp. Lifeless.

"M-mama?" Juliana gently shook her mother's shoulder. Mama's eyes didn't open. Neither was she breathing.

"Mama!"

Her mother's head lolled against the pillow, as boneless as a cloth doll's.

"Oh, God," Juliana sobbed.

Rowdy laughter rose from the bailey below. Life continued with its relentless momentum, while her mother . . .

"Mama, please. Come back." Juliana sniffled and touched her mother's cheek. Was it selfish to want her mother to keep living? Now, at least, she'd be free of pain.

A soft knock on the door. "Milady."

Juliana slowly rose, uncaring of the tears dripping onto her bodice. She opened the panel.

The maidservant, holding a laden tray, said, "The fare—"

"Please find my father," Juliana said quietly. "Tell him my mother is dead."

CHAPTER 4

Englestowe Keep, Moydenshire
Summer, 1213

*E*douard, you are a wretched coward.

Boisterous music, clapping, and cheering—celebration of the marriage between Landon Ferchante and his bride, Mayda—drifted from Englestowe Keep's great hall as Edouard staggered through the forebuilding's open door and out into the night. Sidestepping several sots sprawled unconscious on the ground, he heaved in breaths of cool summer air.

His head reeled. "Damnation," he said, then grimaced. He shouldn't have downed so much wine. Yet in honor of Mayda's marriage, her proud father, lord of Englestowe, had provided an excellent red imported from France.

Moreover, in past months, discontent amongst Edouard's sire's allies over the king's injustices had strengthened. In secret, many lords vowed rebellion was inevitable. Among them, Edouard's father.

For one night, 'twas good just to drown in the pleasure of now.

And God help him, *she* was here.

Juliana.

Edouard stumbled away from the weak light coming out of the forebuilding and toward the keep's wall. Earlier that day, he and Kaine, along with Dominic de Terre, Edouard's father's closest friend, had arrived at Englestowe to attend the wedding. When still boys, Kaine and Edouard had gone to live at Dominic's keep to serve as pages and to be trained as squires. In due time, they'd earn their spurs and become knights.

After Edouard greeted his parents and Lord de Greyne, he'd turned to counter a remark from Kaine—and had spied Juliana. His words had shattered on his tongue.

Edouard hadn't seen her since that day at Sherstowe. He'd heard from friends that soon after her mother's death, Juliana had gone to live with Mayda, her best friend, and that she planned to move to Waddesford Keep after the wedding to be Mayda's lady-in-waiting. He'd written a letter to Juliana expressing his condolences for her mother's death a few months ago but hadn't received a reply. Mayhap she never received the letter. More likely, she hadn't cared to respond.

When he spied her, she was walking toward the forebuilding with several other ladies. She hadn't seen him. Not surprising, since the keep's bailey was crowded with arriving guests. The instant he saw her, though, with her hair bound in a shiny braid down her back and her buttercup yellow gown drifting at her ankles, the world around him seemed to freeze. Silence enveloped him, one so intense, he heard the choked gurgle of his swallow. Laughing at something her friends said, she'd disappeared into the forebuilding.

He'd known then that he *had* to speak to her. Every day since their disagreement at Sherstowe, he'd thought of her and that kiss they'd almost shared. He couldn't change the past, but he'd like to know she'd at least acknowledge him again.

Finding that opportunity to talk to her? A challenge all day.

His shoulder bumped the keep's wall. He cursed, turned his back to the wall, and slowly slid down it to a squat. He shouldn't care so much about regaining her favor. It shouldn't eat at his pride that months ago she'd said good-bye in a tone that implied she despised him.

But it did.

"Juliana," he said on a groan. His muddled thoughts drifted to earlier that eve when she'd realized he was in the hall. Her elegant head turned, as though she sensed him nearby. Her posture had stiffened, and, when their gazes had locked, her eyes had become huge. Then she'd whirled around and disappeared into the crowd.

During the lavish meal, where she'd sat one table away, she hadn't once looked at him, although Nara, sitting farther behind, had caught his gaze and wiggled her fingers at him with annoying frequency. Later when the dancing and revelry had begun, Juliana had stayed close to her friends and Mayda and managed to be dancing whenever he thought to approach her.

Coward, Edouard. You should walk back into that hall and demand to speak with her. Refuse to let her elude you. You are, after all, Geoffrey de Lanceau's son and heir. She owes you respect.

Aye. 'Tis what he should do. Would do.

When he wasn't quite as drunk.

He sucked in another breath of night air, blinking as his head spun. God's teeth, he shouldn't have snatched up the challenge of that last drinking contest with Kaine and several other friends, but he hadn't wanted to look a fool.

He blew out a sigh. "Juliana," he said softly.

"Not Juliana," a feminine voice said from the darkness, "but I hope you do not mind, milord."

Nara.

He swallowed down an oath. How had he not heard her approach? Regardless of how he felt about her, his father wanted to keep good relations between their families, especially after the mishap at Sherstowe.

Edouard rose on an awkward lurch, his woolen tunic scraping the stones behind him. To steady himself, he pressed back against the wall.

Nara's silk gown rustled as she stepped from the nearby darkness, another young lady at her side. Nara cupped her hand, whispered in her friend's ear, and the young woman curtsied shyly to Edouard and then walked back to the forebuilding.

"Hello, Nara," he said, hoping he didn't slur his words. He blinked to clear his bleary gaze, for her gown, exquisitely fashionable, plunged a little too low in front. The night air, or arousal, had caused her nipples to bead against the fabric.

Unwelcome desire stirred. Nara might be a pretty creature, delightfully formed, but even tonight she didn't compare to his memories of Juliana.

"Good evening, milord." Smiling, Nara strolled closer, her hips swaying more than was appropriate for a maiden. "'Tis a pleasure to see you. You are looking as handsome as ever."

He managed a grin. "Thank you."

Her gaze traveled over him and he wondered, as his fuzzy mind sharpened slightly, what she intended by following him outside. Her being here in the dark with him, without a chaperone, wasn't proper.

Before he could ask what she wanted, she said, "Why are you out here all alone, milord?"

"'Twas warm in the great hall, and I wanted some fresh air." He raised his brows. "You should be inside, showing the young lads how well you can dance."

She laughed, a flirtatious sound. "The only lord I want to dance with is here before me."

Ugh. A sound must have escaped him, for her smile softened into a pout. "We never got our dance at the feast at Sherstowe. I regret that. Very much."

"As I recall, a great deal happened that day."

"Especially with Juliana. I heard you speak her name." Nara raised her brows at him in coy accusation, while her slender fingers swept along her neckline, as though to draw attention to her cleavage.

Shrugging, he looked out across the darkness. He didn't have to explain himself to Nara. Caution tingled through his sluggish mind, for he didn't doubt she was deliberately enticing him. He'd be wise to return to his friends as soon as he could.

He glanced at the light streaming out from the fore-building, a beacon leading him back to Juliana. "'Twas a pleasure chatting with you, but—"

Nara stepped nearer. She stood so close, he could touch her if he wanted. He didn't. He kept his hands firmly by his sides, wishing he'd had the sense to put distance between him and the wall behind him. "Nara—"

"Have you spoken to Juliana tonight?" she asked.

"Not yet. I will as soon as I reach the hall."

Nara tsked and rolled her eyes. "May luck be with you."

He tried to ignore a pinch of misgiving. "Why do you say that?"

"She cannot bear to even hear your name. Did you realize she was so upset after what happened at Sherstowe, she left?" Sympathy crept into Nara's stare. "I doubt she will ever forgive you for pushing her into the well."

"*You* caused that to happen."

Nara smiled. "Me, milord?"

"Aye." He forced enough menace into the word that her eyes widened. "You kicked my foot. You made me fall against Juliana, and that caused her to go into the well."

With a careless shrug, Nara said, "An accident."

"Nay." Emotions of that day simmered again inside Edouard. "That act was deliberate. You could have killed Juliana."

"Mayhap." Nara's hand slowly slipped down her throat, drawing his attention to the plumpness of her bosom enhanced by tight silk. "But all turned out well. Except for our dance."

He dragged his gaze from her enticing breasts but not before she saw. She grinned, caught her lip between her teeth, and closed the gap between them.

"Nara." Cursing the way his blood heated with interest, he scrambled sideways along the wall, his clumsy legs slow to follow.

Her arms slid around his neck. Pressing her supple body against him, she cooed, "Kiss me, Edouard. The way you were going to kiss Juliana by the well."

His drunken body responded to her enticing feminine scent; his loins stirred to her breathy plea. *What are you doing?* his mind cried. *Shove her away, or you are doomed.*

"Stop, Nara." His voice emerged a rasp.

Her lips brushed his chin. "I am the one you want. I will make you forget my sister."

Edouard shuddered as her fingers caressed the hairs at his nape. He didn't want to forget Juliana. He needed to go inside, speak with her . . .

Ah, God, he had to make Nara cease.

"Nay," he said. Hands on her waist, he began to push her away.

Her hot, wet, hungry mouth crushed to his.

"Come on." Eyes bright with excitement, Mayda snatched up Juliana's hand and pulled her through the noisy crowd toward the forebuilding.

"Mayda, wait!" Juliana dug in her heels, but her new shoes, bought to go with her gown for the wedding celebration, skidded on the freshly strewn rushes and herbs on the floorboards. With a helpless squawk, she stumbled along after her friend.

Mayda whirled around, her finest silk gown, chosen to be her wedding dress, floating about her slender figure. Leaning in close, she murmured, "Do not be silly and protest, Juliana. We both saw Edouard go into the forebuilding. 'Tis the perfect chance for you to find and speak with him, now he is no longer amongst his friends."

Giddy anticipation swirled up inside Juliana. She did want to speak with him, but what was she going to say? What if he was still annoyed and didn't wish to speak with her? Terror rushed up in a daunting wave. "I do not think . . ."

Mayda narrowed her eyes. With a firm hold, she drew Juliana away from the singing, clapping throng to a quieter section of the hall. "You have been miserable every day since the incident at Sherstowe," she said, not letting go of Juliana's hand. "You know 'tis long overdue for you two to reconcile."

"True, but . . ."

Mayda huffed. "Still, you protest. How many times have you told me of that kiss he almost bestowed upon you? The way he admired your beauty?" Her eyes shone with her impassioned words. "Are you not curious to know if he wants to kiss you again? If the feelings you hold for him are still worth cherishing?"

"Mayda," Juliana said softly. "He wooed me to win the bet. I do not know if he truly cared for me."

Mayda squeezed Juliana's fingers. "What man could not care for you?"

Tears pricked Juliana's eyes.

With the swish of silk, Mayda hugged Juliana. "I want you to be happy," she whispered. "I want you to have a husband as charming as Landon. That man could well be Edouard." Drawing away, she wiped at her lower lashes. "You must speak with him, Juliana. Tonight, before your opportunity is lost."

"All right." Juliana smiled. Hand in hand with Mayda, she hurried to the forebuilding.

Mayda led the way down the torch lit stairs, and then they were out into the dark bailey beyond. The cool night air touched Juliana's face, but her cheeks felt hot and tingly. Oh, God, she dared not yield to the happiness bubbling up inside her. If she became too overwrought, she'd not be able to say one sensible word to Edouard. She did *not* want to ruin this chance.

"Where might he be?" Juliana's breath caught. "Mayda, can you feel how I am trembling?"

"Keep a lookout," her friend said, still in front, glancing to and fro in the shadows while she drew Juliana forward.

Mayda came to an abrupt halt.

Juliana bumped into her. As Mayda's head turned, expression filled with shock and dismay, movement in the shadows claimed Juliana's attention.

"Nara," a male voice said with a groan.

Blinking hard, Juliana discerned a man and woman pressed against the wall, engaged in lusty kissing: her sister and . . .

Edouard!

A gasp lodged in Juliana's throat.

As though suddenly becoming aware of spectators,

Edouard tore his mouth from Nara's. His gaze, dazed at first, cleared and widened with astonishment. "Juliana," he said, breathing hard.

At the same moment, Nara looked over her shoulder, met Juliana's stare, and smiled smugly.

"I am sorry, Juliana," Mayda said shakily. "I did not know."

Tears blurred Juliana's vision. Drawing her hand from Mayda's, she stepped back, away, heart pounding so ferociously in her chest, she could scarcely breathe. What a fool she'd been!

"Juliana," Edouard called. "Wait." His steps unsteady, he started toward her.

Somehow Juliana managed to lift her chin and hold his gaze. How could he still look so handsome to her? Why did the agony inside her make her want to weep over this wretched rogue?

"I was about to return to the hall and speak with you," he said, tone rough. Looking at frowning Mayda, now standing beside Juliana, he dragged his hands through his mussed hair. "Look, I know how this must appear."

Juliana struggled to hold back the anguish almost choking her. Had he and Kaine made a bet tonight? Since Edouard couldn't have Juliana's kiss, he'd win her sister's? She did *not* care. "You do not owe me an explanation, milord."

Silk rustled as Nara approached his side. "Indeed, he does not. You made it quite clear at Sherstowe you did not want to be betrothed to him. You never wanted to see him again."

A frown darkened Edouard's face. "Juliana, I never intended to kiss Nara."

Disbelieving laughter broke past Juliana's lips. "It just happened?"

Nara winked at Edouard and giggled. "Milord, you give the most pleasing kisses."

Juliana forced down a sob. To know her sister had enjoyed Edouard's affections, to see her sister gloating . . . Refusing to let them see her pain, Juliana spun to face the forebuilding. Sorrow in her eyes, Mayda slid an arm around her, and they began walking toward the light.

"Do not go!" Edouard called.

Glancing back, Juliana fixed Edouard with a glare. "Tonight has further proven what I realized months ago, milord. You could never be my husband, for when a man kisses me"—her voice wobbled—"I want it to be meaningful. I want it to prove the wondrous love between us. I want it to reinforce that we were destined, out of all the men and women in this vast country, to be together."

He loosed a sound akin to a groan. "Juliana."

"What she said about a kiss?" Nara brushed up against Edouard. "'Tis how I felt when you kissed me, milord. I vow you were never destined to wed her. Our fathers will have the alliance they desire, for you will marry me."

CHAPTER 5

Waddesford Keep, Moydenshire
Late spring, 1214

From the muzzy depths of sleep, Juliana heard a baby wailing.

She snuggled deeper into downy softness—the pillows on Mama's bed? She'd been dreaming of Mama. They sat together in the bed in Sherstowe's solar, turning the pages of Juliana's sketchbook, while talking about the drawings: her father's favorite horse; the stillborn baby boy; and . . . the face of Edouard de Lanceau.

Why, tonight, had she dreamed of *Edouard?* Why, after all that had taken place between them, couldn't she forget him?

The baby's cry came again, shriller this time. This infant wasn't part of her dream.

Wake up, Juliana! her conscience urged. *Little Rosemary is hungry.*

Trying to rouse her sleepy mind, Juliana rubbed her eyes. Her lashes were wet, as they were every time she thought of Mama. When she opened her eyes to

67

darkness, her senses wakened, and she recognized the faintly musty smell of her straw pallet in the antechamber of Waddesford Keep's solar. She'd slept in the small, adjoining room from the day she became Mayda's lady-in-waiting, to be close by whenever her friend needed her.

Why wasn't Mayda putting her babe to her breast? At just over a week old, Rosemary needed her mother's milk.

Mayhap, like Juliana, Mayda was only just rousing to the baby's cry. Lying motionless, Juliana waited to hear the *creak* of the large rope bed as Mayda slipped from it, crooning to her child.

The only sound, apart from Rosemary's crying, was the faint crackle of the fire.

Unease tingled through Juliana. Was Mayda all right? She'd been restless and weepy earlier that eve, but had assured Juliana she was merely tired from being wakened often in the night to nurse Rosemary. A reasonable explanation. In most circumstances Juliana might have accepted it. However, the arguments between Landon and Mayda had become more frequent over past weeks. The birth of the little girl, when his lordship had wanted a son and heir, had added to the strain.

Juliana pushed aside her blankets, trying not to heed the other suspicions sifting into her mind. But they wouldn't be ignored. They shoved to the forefront, as demanding as that wretched woman who'd arrived as a guest a short while ago and quickly settled in: Veronique

Desjardin. Her rogue of a son, Tye, who looked close to Juliana's twenty years of age, had also moved into the keep.

When Juliana set her feet on the icy floorboards, her right foot knocked an object in the dark, sending it sliding away with a *hiss*: her current sketchbook. She'd set it beside the bed before snuffing the candle to sleep. Groping in the blackness, she found the book, and then tucked it under her pallet. She didn't want to slip on the tome again, especially if she returned to the antechamber carrying Rosemary.

As Juliana walked into the solar, her eyes began to adjust to the shadows, tinged with a reddish glow from the hearth's embers. Her gaze went to the rope bed. Empty. The bedding on Mayda's side had been pushed to one side, suggesting she'd left the bed for some reason and hadn't yet returned. The blankets on Landon's side appeared undisturbed.

How many nights, now, had he slept somewhere other than the solar?

And with whom?

Juliana's heart squeezed, for she'd seen the scorching glances between Veronique and Landon—looks that went far beyond a lord being attentive to a guest. Not wanting to upset Mayda, Juliana had kept her suspicions of his infidelity to herself. That had become a kind of punishment, for she'd wondered if she *should* tell Mayda?

Juliana, though, had no definite proof, and it would

be all too easy for Landon to deny all and order Juliana to leave Waddesford; then, Mayda would have no one close to her to help her. In the end, Juliana had chosen to stay silent, while hoping Mayda would discover the affair for herself.

No doubt, that was why Mayda wasn't here. She'd gone looking for her husband.

Juliana hurried across the plank floor to the wooden cradle, trying to ignore the unease racing through her. Mayda had placed Rosemary's bed at the edge of the hearth tiles, hoping to keep the baby warm through the night, but a draft swept through the room.

Juliana shivered, and not just from the cold. Mayda adored Rosemary. She'd never let her get so hungry.

From when they were young girls, Mayda had talked in a dreamy voice about becoming a wife and mother. Despite the difficult pregnancy and ordeal of birthing Rosemary, the joy that lit Mayda's face whenever she looked at the newborn with a tuft of wispy brown hair and blue eyes was unmistakable.

"There, now," Juliana murmured, leaning over the cradle. She slid her hands under the bawling Rosemary and the woolen blanket wrapped around her and picked her up. Humming a lullaby, Juliana tucked the baby into the crook of her arm and gently rocked her.

Rosemary kept crying.

"All right," Juliana soothed. She must find Mayda;

if she couldn't be found swiftly, then a nursemaid who could feed Rosemary.

As Juliana started toward the solar doorway, her gaze slid over the long trestle table along the opposite wall. Gold glinted. She crossed to see what the object was: Mayda's wedding ring.

A violent tremor snaked through Juliana. At the same moment, a memory flashed into her mind, of Mayda's tearful, whispered words when she lay against bedsheets smeared with blood from Rosemary's birth. *"If aught should happen to me, you must keep the baby safe. Promise me that, Juliana."*

Sitting on the bed's edge, watching over Mayda till maidservants returned with clean sheets and the healer brought another pain-dulling tonic, Juliana touched her friend's hand. "Do not worry. The healer says you will be fine. So will the babe."

"A girl." *Mayda's lips trembled while she glanced at the infant, sleeping in its cradle beside the bed; Mayda's gaze looked almost . . . terrified.*

"She is beautiful," Juliana said. "Perfect, in every way. Tiny, round nose. Chubby fingers—"

"But not a son."

Landon's wish for a boy was well known to everyone at Waddesford. Juliana forced a comforting smile. "Nay, but—"

Mayda's fingers curled into Juliana's in a tight, almost crushing, grip.

Juliana fought not to wince. Her friend didn't seem like herself, and probably didn't realize her grasp was so strong. "Landon will love her," Juliana murmured. "Why would he not?"

How clearly she remembered her mother weeping over her dead son, a baby she'd desperately wanted, whether 'twas a boy or girl. Surely, no father would reject the miracle of his own healthy child, especially one with such a sweet countenance? "One look at his daughter's face," Juliana added, "and Landon will adore her. I vow he will be so proud, he will want to show her off to all within the keep."

She hoped so. Mayhap this little girl would bring an end to the terrible arguments and unite the Ferchantes as a family. Mayda deserved to be happy.

Mayda shook her head against the pillow. How defeated she seemed. "Listen, Juliana. I must tell you before the others return. I have hidden a bag of jewelry—"

"Mayda." Juliana struggled against rising worry. Her friend was beginning to sound completely out of her wits. Surely, Mayda didn't fear for her and Rosemary's lives?

"If I come to . . . harm," Mayda rasped, "you will take what's hidden and flee far from here with Rosemary. Sell the jewels—"

"Hush, Mayda—!"

"—You will have enough coin to provide for both of you for years." Her tone sharpened. "Promise me."

Unnerved by her friend's wild-eyed stare, Juliana

looked to the door, hoping to see the panel open and the healer step inside. Mayhap his lordship would be with her, eager to see his child for the first time.

"Promise, Juliana."

Agree to steal a lord's daughter and valuable jewelry? Swear to commit crimes that could see her imprisoned for the rest of her life? "I—"

"Juliana!"

Mayda's gaze held such haunted fear, Juliana couldn't help but nod. "All right. I promise. I will do as you ask." *After all, how likely was it that Mayda would come to the harm she feared?*

Rosemary's wail snapped Juliana from her memories. "There, there," she said as she continued toward the door. When Juliana drew near, she realized the door was slightly ajar; the chilling draft blew in from around it.

Wishing she'd taken the time to pull on a woolen wrap, but not wanting to delay Rosemary's feeding any longer, Juliana drew open the door and stepped out into the hallway lit by flaming wall torches. The draft whispered across the passageway's stone floor; it seemed to be coming from the stairwell farther along, the one leading to a door that opened onto the wind-scoured wall walk.

Over the sputter of the nearby torches, she heard voices. A man and a woman, arguing. The harsh quarrel drew Juliana toward the stairwell. Some of the words carried down to her on the gusting wind. She recognized

Mayda's voice, shrilled by bitterness. The sound of her friend's torment . . . Unbearable.

Juliana hugged Rosemary closer. The baby sniffled, then whimpered, as though about to cry again. Curling her finger, Juliana rubbed it against Rosemary's toothless gums. Turning her head to follow Juliana's knuckle, Rosemary began to suck.

Juliana hesitated at the bottom of the stairwell, caught between eavesdropping or walking away. In truth, she had no right to listen. Landon and Mayda, as lord and lady of this keep, deserved their privacy. But remembering the fear in her friend's expression and her earlier promise, Juliana forced herself to step into the close stairwell, shivering at the coldness of the stone beneath her bare feet.

"—do I mean to you? Do you love me? Care for me at all?" A wrenched sob. "I wish to know, Landon."

"Cease."

Partway up the stairwell, Juliana froze. How could Landon speak to Mayda in that manner? His tone was little more than a snarl. He'd speak that way to a murderous traitor chained in his dungeon. His wife, the mother of his babe, deserved far more respect.

Regret pierced Juliana, for less than a year ago, Mayda and Landon had seemed so much in love, in the way they'd smiled at each other, exchanged coy words, touched hands, and kissed. Just observing them had stirred yearnings within Juliana, for she'd hoped one day to have a marriage equally as wonderful. But all the trust and happiness between Landon and Mayda seemed to have vanished. For their relationship to have come to this was nothing less than tragic.

"Do not turn your back on me. I want an answer," Mayda shrieked.

"How you tire me," Landon growled, followed by the *rap* of footfalls on stone. The sound implied he'd moved away from her.

More sobbing came from above, and Juliana bit down on her lip. The cruelty of Landon's tone was truly frightening.

Was Mayda in danger? Would Landon harm her, as she'd suggested days ago?

The atmosphere, indeed, seemed ripe for violence. If Juliana dared to interrupt, though, saying the babe had woken and needed feeding, that would give Mayda a reason to return to the solar. She'd be safe then. If she and Landon had more to discuss, they'd do so later, when they'd both had time to calm their tempers.

Aye. That was the best solution. Yet putting herself in the midst of the disagreement . . . Juliana pressed back against the stone wall and fought a twinge of alarm.

Don't be foolish, Juliana. You are friends with Landon. He will not harm you, especially when you have his daughter in your arms. If you care for Mayda and little Rosemary, you will find the strength to act for them.

Shifting Rosemary closer to her shoulder, to shield her from the wind swirling down into the stairwell, Juliana pressed on.

"You say I tire you." Mayda's words shattered on an angry wail. "I never see you. Day and night, you are always gone. Do you think I am a fool, Landon? Do you believe I do not know of the servants' gossip? Of the rumors you—"

"I told you before. Cease!"

"I will *not*! I am your *wife*."

Weak moonlight touched the stairs ahead; it came through the open doorway leading onto the wall walk.

As though becoming aware of her mother's nearness, Rosemary warbled.

"I warn you, Mayda. If you do not be quiet—"

The brutal fierceness of Landon's voice . . . Mere steps away from the open door, Juliana hesitated. A frightened moan scratched her throat, but she forced the sound down. She thrust her finger against Rosemary's mouth to soothe her hungry snuffles.

"You will not make a fool of me any longer!" Mayda shouted. "I want the truth—"

"Veronique excites me."

A shuddered gasp. "S-she—?"

"—pleasures me. Whenever I wish. However I wish. Are you happy now, *wife*?"

Juliana squeezed her eyes shut. *Oh, Mayda. I*

am sorry. To be rejected with such indifference must be heartbreaking.

Hoarse sobs broke from Mayda, each one swollen with helplessness and rage. The sounds pierced deep inside Juliana, for she'd cried that way after her mother had died. She'd wept until every last tear had dried up, and she'd been too exhausted to cry any longer.

"You *bastard.*" Mayda's weeping roughened, while Juliana climbed the last stairs. "How could you betray my love? And to *her*? Did you not think—?"

A scraped footfall. A grisly crack: the sound of a fist hitting flesh.

Mayda groaned, a sound of excruciating pain.

Oh, God. Oh, God!

Rosemary struggled, her little legs kicking against the blanket, as Juliana forced herself through the doorway and onto the battlements.

Landon and Mayda were some distance down the wall walk, their figures limned in moon glow. The eerie light, cutting through patches of inky shadow, skimmed the squared stone merlons and the gaps between them that overlooked the moat, almost dry from months with little rain.

Glaring at Mayda, Landon flexed his right fingers, doubtless easing discomfort from the blow, then swept his palm over the front of the brown woolen tunic that reached to his thighs. The lazy gesture, executed with a faint measure of disgust, heightened the warning buzzing inside Juliana.

"Mayda," she said. Fear muffled her voice; the wind snatched the sound.

Landon was dressed in garments fit for a cool spring night, while Mayda wore only her linen night rail, covered by a cloak she'd thrown about her shoulders but hadn't fastened. Her unbound blond hair snarled in the breeze as she stood with her head bowed to the side, one hand pressed to her cheek, clearly still stunned by the blow. As Juliana hurried forward, her friend straightened. Her hands lowering to clench at her sides, Mayda faced her husband.

"How dare you hit me? Did you think that would silence me?" she screeched, before she winced and cradled her face again with her hand. "How I *hate you!*"

Juliana shivered as a gust whipped at her; yet her chill went beyond physical discomfort. Perilous emotions flowed between Landon and Mayda. Anger and bitterness seemed to cocoon them from all else, for they still hadn't noticed her or heard the babe's fussing.

"Mayda," Juliana called again, louder this time. If only she were nearer! Still, her friend didn't hear her.

"Listen well, Landon." Mayda trembled. "Our marriage is ended. I cannot wait to tell my parents, who *so* admired you, how you—"

Landon's face contorted in a sneer. His arm

whipped up, no doubt to strike again. Mayda threw up her hands—to hit back or plead with him—even as Juliana cried, "Mayda!"

Her friend's head swiveled. When Mayda's gaze fell upon Juliana and Rosemary, her teary eyes widened. Pain and terror etching her expression, Mayda opened her mouth, clearly about to speak.

Landon's fist slammed into her head.

"Nay!" Juliana screamed. "Mayda!"

Eyes rolling, Mayda keeled sideways, then backward. Toward the gaping space between the merlons.

Juliana hurried forward, trying not to jostle Rosemary, heedless of the wind buffeting her and slowing her down. "Mayda," she shrieked. "Beware!"

Mayda bumped against a merlon, then staggered. Her hands flew wide, a frantic attempt to regain her balance. "Juliana—" she groaned.

Landon lunged forward and shoved her. Hard.

Mayda's hands flailed, grasping for a handhold. Seizing only air.

"*Mayda!*" Juliana shrieked.

With a shrill cry, her friend fell backward over the side. Her scream carried, and then . . . abrupt silence.

Several yards from Landon, Juliana stumbled to a standstill. Horror pounded inside her. Her whole body shook as she looked from Landon, his seething stare upon her, to the dark, vacant space where Mayda had disappeared.

Rosemary bawled.

The wind hissed, cold and . . . empty.

"Mayda," Juliana whispered, pressing her arm across her churning stomach. "Oh, God!"

Over Rosemary's cries, Juliana heard shouts somewhere down the wall walk. Castle folk were investigating the scream. At the same moment, Landon glanced over the battlement, as if to see what had become of his wife.

Could she have survived such a fall? Not likely. Not when the almost dry moat was strewn with rocks.

Mayda was dead. A demise she'd feared days ago.

Even as bile stung the back of Juliana's mouth, another, more deadly thought snared her focus. She was the only one to see what happened. A witness to a lady's murder.

Landon would no doubt convince any curious folk that what took place was an unfortunate accident. He was lord of Waddesford; his statement wouldn't be questioned. Hers, however . . .

She took a shaky step back. He'd murdered once tonight. Would he kill her this eve, to silence her? Then would he do away with his daughter, whom he'd never wanted?

As he tugged down his sleeves and faced her, Juliana scrambled backward toward the doorway. She'd whirl around and run—

Movement on the wall walk snared her gaze. A slender figure emerged from the shadows close to Landon. *Veronique.* Raising her hands, she started clapping.

Merciful God!

As she strolled into the pale moonshine, light swept over her waist-length red tresses that brushed against her long black cloak. The vibrant, reddish hue, unnatural for a woman her age, looked even more eerie in the moonlight. Not only was Veronique applauding, but smiling as though she'd witnessed a superb performance.

"Well done, Landon." Each of Veronique's words sang with triumph.

"Well done?" Juliana choked out while forcing her shocked body to continue backward. *Get to the doorway,* her mind screamed. *Save yourself. Protect Rosemary, as you promised. Hurry!*

"I killed my wife." Landon sounded stunned. Did he not believe what he had done?

"You did what was necessary." At his side, Veronique reached up a hand, turned his face so he looked at her, and kissed him full on the lips. Pressing up against him, she said, "Now you are free. No one will separate us."

Juliana swallowed. There could be but five steps left till she reached the doorway.

"Aye." Landon exhaled a sharp breath. "But—"
Four.

"You had no other choice," Veronique murmured. "Do not worry. We will ensure her death is considered no more than an accident." Veronique's gaze fixed on Juliana. "Starting with her."

Run!

Juliana spun and bolted into the stairwell.

Her bare feet skidded on the rough stones. Rosemary, bouncing in her arms, shrieked. Her cry echoed in the passageway, the sound mirroring the frantic scream rising inside Juliana.

"She cannot get away," Veronique snapped from the wall walk.

"I know," Landon said. "Guards!" he yelled. "Guards!"

Juliana heaved in a breath. She must get out of the castle. How?

No time to retrieve Mayda's hidden jewels. Juliana would have to—

Footfalls pounded on the stairs behind her.

She reached the torch lit passage. Holding tight to crying Rosemary, she raced toward the wooden landing that led down into the great hall. Most of the castle folk would be asleep there; she'd weave through the rows of straw pallets, dash into the forebuilding, and down to the bailey. From there. . .

Then what?

"Juliana!" Landon roared, close behind.

With an agonized gasp, she tried to run faster. Her lungs burned.

Shouts and tramped footfalls carried from behind her—and the landing ahead.

Oh, God. She was trapped.

A sharp tug on her hair yanked her head back. Pain spread through her scalp, while the passageway's ceiling became a blur. She stumbled, almost dropping Rosemary.

"Got you," Landon snarled.

She screamed with all the breath left in her lungs. Landon slammed her back against the passage wall. Rosemary jounced in her arms, even as Juliana twisted against his bruising grip on her upper arms.

"Let me go!" she choked.

Rosemary's gulping cries rang off the stone; Landon didn't seem to notice or care.

"Quiet." Breathing hard, his grasp as tight as manacles, he glared down at Juliana. He smelled of drink, night air, and . . . danger. Juliana shuddered. Would he kill her now?

"Do as I say." Landon clearly expected her obedience.

"Killer!" she cried. How she wanted to spit in his face! "Mayda loved you! How could you—?"

Armed men crowded in from the landing. Not Landon's men-at-arms, most of whom she knew by name, but mercenaries. Veronique's hired thugs.

Oh, God. *Oh, God!*

"Lady de Greyne has gone mad," Landon called, loudly enough for all to hear.

"Liar! You—"

"She means to harm the babe," he cut in, drowning her voice with his own. "She—"

Juliana threw her body's weight to one side. He tightened his grip. She kicked and struggled.

Behind her, metal rasped. The sound of a sword being drawn.

Terror whipped through Juliana, a moment before Veronique sauntered out of the stairwell to block that way out. Crossing her arms, she smiled.

"Someone help me!" Juliana sobbed. "Lady Ferchante was murdered. I saw! I swear—"

Landon pulled her away from the wall. "Take her."

Two of the mercenaries grabbed her arms, restrained her, as Landon stepped away.

"Give me a sword," Landon commanded.

She was going to die! "Please, listen!" Juliana shrieked. "He—"

Lips drawn back from his teeth, Landon raised the blade. One swift slash, and she'd be dead. So, most likely, would Rosemary. Sobbing, Juliana cradled the baby tighter.

A curse broke from Landon. Daring to glance up, she saw him standing as though frozen, his sword ready for its killing strike. For an instant, their gazes met; in his eyes, she saw remorse.

"Please," she whispered. "Landon, I beg you—"

"Turn her around," he growled. She tried to struggle, but the thugs spun her so her back faced Landon.

Whack! Stunning pain crashed through the back of Juliana's head. Her teeth cracked together, while her upper body jolted forward. *Do not . . . drop Rosemary,* Juliana told herself through the blinding agony.

Oh, God. So . . . dizzy.

She couldn't stand up . . . any longer.

Juliana's legs wobbled. The passageway floor swirled into a muddy blend of grays and browns.

Mayda, I am sorry. So sorry.

The cloying tang of rosewater stung her nostrils. *Veronique.* Juliana tried to open her mouth, to speak, but her jaw refused to work. She could only groan as Veronique pulled Rosemary from her arms. "Kill her," Veronique muttered, shoving the wailing baby at a mercenary.

Mayda, I am sorry . . .

Juliana collapsed to her knees. Head . . . spinning. Men . . . still holding her arms. She fought to lift her head.

Fight. Save Rosemary, her mind screamed, even as the agonizing pain sapped the strength from her limbs.

Her groggy mind barely registered the masculine grunt behind her. The whistle of the sword through the air—

Whack!

Blackness.

Veronique stretched out atop the bed in the candlelit solar, propping her head up on her hand. As she tugged at her bodice to reveal more of her cleavage, her gaze settled upon Landon, standing before the hearth with his back to her.

The orange-yellow firelight licked over the front of his body, etching shadows over his legs braced slightly apart, broad arms hanging listless by his sides, face bowed to the flames. He'd stood that way for long moments, tense and silent, as though his mind was elsewhere.

Back on the wall-walk with his shrieking wife, no doubt.

Veronique stifled a sigh of disgust. Was he battling with his morals? Condemning himself for what he'd done? How she despised a man who couldn't subjugate his own conscience.

She'd sensed the turmoil inside him when he'd aimed to run Juliana through with the sword. He couldn't do it; his sense of chivalry got in the way. Instead, he'd ordered her turned around—sparing himself from the condemnation in her eyes—and then hit her twice at the back of the head, rendering her senseless.

"I will finish her off," Veronique had said, taking a sword from one of her mercenaries. How sweetly the pleasure of killing had run in her veins, urging her to plunge the sword into Juliana's pretty flesh.

Landon, however, had stayed Veronique with a hand on her arm. "No need. I hit her hard enough to cause death."

Had he? Or did he not care to see his wife's best friend slashed while he looked on? The true reason no longer mattered, for Veronique had made certain of

Juliana's death. Even if Juliana somehow survived her wound, she'd die from drowning, for two of Veronique's loyal mercenaries were carrying her limp body to the river to throw her in.

The thoughts brought a smug smile to Veronique's lips. The unfortunate Lady Juliana, who saw what really transpired on the wall walk, was safely eliminated. No one would dispute that Lady Ferchante committed suicide by throwing herself over the edge. If, for some reason, any of the castle folk questioned Landon's account of what happened, Veronique's mercenaries would discreetly eradicate them.

All in all, the perfect ending to the night's developments that left Landon completely in her hands. A vulnerable, but necessary puppet in her plot to crush his wretched lordship, Geoffrey de Lanceau. The only man she'd ever loved.

Just thinking her former lover's name caused anguished rage to sear through her breast. How she would make him suffer! Now, though, was not a wise moment to indulge in her hatred of him; now, she must ensure Landon was firmly in her control.

Catching a strand of her hair—its natural, graying color dyed red with henna she'd bought from a merchant in France—she began to twirl it around one of her fingers. "Landon," she said with a petulant sigh. "Come to bed."

CATHERINE KEAN

His head lifted a fraction, causing his light brown hair to glint in the firelight. Yet he didn't glance her way or attempt to speak.

The anger in Veronique's blood deepened. No one ignored her. He should know that by now. He *owed* her respect, for she'd helped rid him of his wife and the babe he never wanted. She'd *freed* him.

"Landon," she said again, more forcefully.

He stirred then, straightening to his full height while he plowed a hand through his hair. The movement caused the wool of his tunic to draw taut over his broad shoulders, outlining indents and swells of firm muscle.

A lustful growl scratched her throat, for while he might annoy her, he was, indeed, an attractive man. Half her age, he'd proven again and again how thoroughly he could pleasure her, and, in his ramblings, proved how useful he could be in furthering her ambitions.

"Why do you not heed me?" She drew out her words with a petulant purr. "You should be abed. With me."

"I cannot," he rasped, still not facing her.

"You are not tired?" A lusty giggle slipped from her. "'Twill be a challenge, then, for me to render you sweaty and sated."

His arm fell back to his side. Tension marked the set of his shoulders. "I killed my wife tonight, Veronique." His voice shook. "I killed her."

Before she could catch it, a fierce breath broke from

88

her. "Landon—"

He spun then, the soles of his boots squeaking on the glazed hearth tiles. A gasp—quickly forced down— scalded her throat at the redness of his eyes and the moisture glistening at his lower lashes. His expression bespoke barely leashed anguish.

Her disgust for him hardened. The sooner she twisted his torment to her desires, the better. A delicate kind of manipulation, but she'd practiced on countless other lords. Years ago, before he became lord of Moydenshire, she'd even manipulated the great Geoffrey de Lanceau, turning his vengeful anger over his father's killing into a scorching passion unlike aught she'd ever experienced before. Or since.

Anger hummed again at the memory of Geoffrey. She forced all thoughts of him aside and, softening her expression into one of concern, pushed up to sitting on the bed. "All is taken care of, Landon, as I promised. Do not fret."

While she held his gaze, she tilted her head and swept her hair to the side, causing it to tumble away from her tightly laced bosom to reveal all of her bountiful cleavage. Since Tye's birth, she'd taken good care of her body, splurging on creams, lotions, and ghastly tasting brews that scoured her innards with painful efficiency but kept her slim. The result was well worth every bit of coin she'd coaxed from her hapless lovers, for her breasts were still smooth and enticing enough to lure men as young and virile as Landon. As she eased a pucker in her bodice, his gaze followed the movement of her finger, and she fought a triumphant little grin.

"Do not fret," he said, before spitting a curse. He looked away, at the far wall. "I was so angry with her, I could scarcely think."

Still, he was dwelling upon his dead wife. Veronique would have to use more effective persuasion. She slid her legs over the side of the bed, stood, and strolled toward him, her fine silk gown brushing at her ankles. "I know you were angry," she soothed. "How could you not be? I saw how your wife provoked you. Bitter word after bitter word."

Landon's watery gaze shifted back to her.

"She was cruel. Relentless." Veronique halted before him and cupped her hand against his cheek. "I vow she planned to enrage you, to make you strike out at her—"

"You do?"

Veronique nodded. "She wanted you to wound her, so she could win sympathy from the folk of this castle. What better way to turn your loyal subjects against you?"

Landon's throat moved with a swallow. "She meant to manipulate me, then."

"Exactly. You wanted a son and heir, as is your right as lord. She birthed you a daughter." Veronique stroked her thumb across his mouth. "She failed you, Landon. *She* is to blame for all that happened tonight. Not you."

Sensing the emotional barrier around him wavering, Veronique dared to press flush against him and loop her arms around his neck. He tensed, but she placed a line of kisses down his cheek. "How foolish she was to turn against you," she murmured against his skin. "You made her the lady of a fine castle. You gave her all she could ever want. Yet still she wasn't satisfied."

Landon shuddered. "I killed her."

"She killed herself." Veronique slid her tongue along his stubbled jaw line, tasting the rough salt of his skin. "Remember that, my love. She committed suicide."

His head turned, and she followed his gaze to the gold ring lying on the trestle table near the pots and grooming essentials she'd brought to the solar. How tempted she'd been to slip that bit of jewelry into her gown, to claim it had gone missing. Before she took the ring, though, she'd wanted to be sure 'twas the one he'd spoken of nights ago, as they lay in each other's arms after coupling—the ring he'd been given by Geoffrey de Lanceau to show he could be entrusted with the most secret of information by Geoffrey's spies and warriors.

Trying not to give away her excitement, she said, "The ring. I noticed it earlier. 'Tis yours?"

"Nay. Mayda's wedding ring." A groan broke past his lips. "She chose it herself—"

"Shh." Veronique used the pressure of her fingers to turn his head back to face her.

"Veronique—"

"*She* is to blame. Remember." Veronique pressed her open mouth to his and forced his lips apart with her tongue, coaxing him to kiss her back.

How unyielding his posture felt—as though he might shove her away. She couldn't allow that. Not when she hadn't yet got hold of the special ring. Not when he had so much more to offer her and Tye in their goal—nurtured for long, *long* years—to destroy Geoffrey and all he cherished.

Even as she sensed Landon rallying a protest, she moved her hand to the back of his head, to tangle into the hair at his nape. While she intensified the kiss, her other hand slipped between them, to the belt of his hose, and then lower, to cup his maleness. Flaccid at the moment. But she knew how to make him hard.

"Veronique," he choked out, against her mouth.

"Let me ease your torment," she whispered, while her fingers dipped inside his hose and closed around his manhood. She rubbed him with gentle strokes. "I know what you like. Let me pleasure you, Landon."

He groaned against her lips. "I . . . cannot . . ."

"Hush, my love. You can." As he trembled, and she felt him thrust against her palm, she indulged in a silent, gleeful laugh. She'd won him over as she knew she could. While she rewarded him with a shattering climax, she'd savor his grunts, gasps, and groans. For with him under her sway, she was ever closer to the day she vanquished Geoffrey.

CHAPTER

6

Edouard lifted a hand from his horse's reins, shooed away a fly that had landed on his mantle's sleeve, and squinted against the morning sunlight. The dirt road he, Kaine, and three men-at-arms traveled ran alongside the slow-moving river to their right that continued through the village a short distance ahead, built close to Waddesford Keep.

His gaze rose to the stone fortress ruled by Landon Ferchante. Memories drifted into Edouard's mind of the wedding celebration at Englestowe. What a night that had been, one that had forever changed him. He struggled with the resentment that flared whenever he thought of his regrettable betrothal to Nara. However, he'd never dishonor his family by forsaking the code of honor that formed the mortar of his life and bound him to her from the moment they'd kissed. Theirs would be a marriage of duty, never love. Stifling bitter regret, he tried to shove the recollections aside.

Not long now until he and his men reached the castle, and he must conduct the crucial meeting on his father's behalf.

Not long, also, before he might see Juliana again. Anticipation wove through him, for he'd heard she still lived there as lady-in-waiting to Lady Ferchante. With him arriving at the keep as his sire's representative, Juliana might at least make an appearance to greet him. 'Twould lift his spirits to see her lovely countenance. Most likely, though, she'd do all she could to avoid him, as she had since his betrothal was announced last summer.

The resentment inside him became a dull ache in his chest. Nara might have succeeded in getting a betrothal, but he hadn't stayed around to be shown off like a coveted bauble. He'd returned to Dominic's keep, focused on his duties, and honed his fighting skills. By accepting every assignment Dominic offered to him, he'd managed to delay the wedding. But by the end of May—mere weeks away—he'd be a married man.

Edouard sighed and lowered his arm to rest it upon his thigh. When he persuaded his sire to let him ride to Waddesford, never had he imagined he'd be this unsettled. Neither had he planned to journey to the keep, but while Edouard was visiting his parents, his sire fell ill.

"You cannot ride to Waddesford," Edouard had insisted when he'd come upon his sire seated at the lord's table in the great hall, scrutinizing the accounts ledger spread out before him. His father had refused to rest, despite his lady wife's protestations and the fever burning his brow.

"I will go as planned." Edouard's sire hadn't looked up from the ledger. "I intended to pay a surprise visit to Landon's keep soon anyway to confirm all is as I expect, as I do of all of my estates now and again. I will also take the blanket your mother embroidered as a gift to celebrate the babe's birth." His voice softened. "But as you know, I aim to discuss another matter with him, and I—"

"—should be abed," Edouard said. Words his worried mother had insisted he work into the conversation somewhere.

His sire, rubbing his sweat-beaded brow with one palm, sighed. "God's teeth." As he wiped perspiration from his flushed cheek, his hand shook.

"You look wretched, Father."

"As I feel." He tossed the quill on the table, splattering black ink, then dropped his head into his hands. "I cannot even stand the taste of wine. The mere smell makes me want to vomit."

"Then you will not be able to raise your goblet in a toast when Lord Ferchante agrees to join your rebellion. One more reason why I must take your place."

His sire, looking weary, shook his head. "I would not ask such of you. 'Tis too dangerous. If aught went wrong—"

"'Twill not. Trust me."

His father had thrust his palm up in clear refusal to discuss the matter any further. "I will contact Dominic."

With effort, Edouard had reined in his disappointment. Dominic would undertake the mission if Edouard's sire asked, but Edouard was capable of the task. Last autumn, after he helped to drive murderous thieves from a forest on Dominic's lands, Dominic ensured Edouard was knighted. The prestige of knighthood proved Edouard was a skilled warrior and could be entrusted with important duties.

Edouard's father, always overprotective because of the remote chance Veronique could resurface in Moydenshire, might be reluctant to put his son in danger, but Edouard was ready for difficult responsibilities. Even a mission as treacherous as privately asking Lord Ferchante if he'd join other lords in trying to reinstate a charter created over one hundred years ago by King Henry I, a document that would set limits upon King John's powers and help curtail his corruption.

"Father," Edouard had said, "with all due respect, sending a missive to Dominic and awaiting his reply will take several days. I can ride to Waddesford on the morrow."

A faint smile touched his sire's mouth. "I appreciate your offer, Son. But you are not yet a lord. 'Tis not your battle."

Edouard pushed his shoulders back and refused to heed the awkward feeling he got every time he challenged his sire. "I believe 'tis my battle, Father. One day, I will inherit the honored title of Lord of Moydenshire from you. If I undertake and succeed in this vital mission, surely that better prepares me for my future responsibilities?"

Edouard's insistence had succeeded, for, with a grudging laugh, his sire had relented and assigned him the mission. Thank God. Thinking of the upcoming meeting with Landon Ferchante wasn't what made Edouard's stomach cinch into a knot. Thinking of Juliana, though . . .

"Oy! Edouard. Any chance we can stop for a piss?" Kaine called from behind him.

Another of the three warriors escorting Edouard grunted in agreement.

"Of course," Edouard said over his shoulder. He looked back at the bank sloping down to the shallows, where some industrious folk—fishermen, mayhap—had cleared away a section of the tall reeds that grew along the water's edge. "'Tis a good spot, also, to water the horses."

"Quite picturesque, really," Kaine said. "Good for all kinds of pleasurable pursuits."

Edouard snorted a laugh and, with a nudge of his heels, steered his horse down toward the river. Kaine seemed to think of naught else these days but seducing women. A pang of regret ran through Edouard, for he could only imagine what his best friend was enduring after his young wife's death last winter from a virulent sickness. Kaine had loved her, and losing her had deeply wounded him.

The closest Edouard had come to love were his feelings for Juliana. Somehow, no other woman compared to his memories of her. Whether she was truly as exceptional as he recalled, or whether his recollections of her had distorted since last year, he'd soon find out, when he met her again.

Today.

His gut tightened another notch as he halted his horse and slid from the saddle. Holding the reins in one hand, he led his mount forward, his leather boots sinking into the mud as he strode into the shallows. Small fish scattered like tiny arrows in the water, while he inhaled the heady scents of moist earth and vegetation. When his horse lowered its head to drink, Edouard turned his face up to the sunlight. How good the sunshine felt on his skin.

Water trickled close by. "Ah," Kaine said, a sound of intense relief.

Edouard chuckled. As he relaxed his shoulders and glanced downriver, a pale object in the reeds snared his gaze. Frowning, he stepped farther into the depths to discern exactly what he saw.

A bare foot.

The muddy hem of a garment, swaying in the stirred-up waves.

He dropped the reins and crashed toward the reeds.

"What is wrong?" Kaine called.

The water grew deeper, soaking Edouard's fine

leather boots to the knee and the lower part of his mantle, but he forged on, hand upon his sword hilt. As he neared the portion of reeds crushed by the body, he slowed to assess the poignant scene before him.

The young woman lay on her left side. Her long, dark brown hair splayed in a grimy tangle across her face, hiding her features from his view. The ends of her tresses had tangled up in the reeds' stems. As he edged nearer, he saw her head was resting on her left arm; it stretched up as though to grab a handhold in the muddy bank. Her right hand, fingers pale as scoured bone, looked about to plunge into the muck and lever her farther out of the water. To safety.

"Edouard?" Kaine shouted again, followed by splashed footfalls.

Edouard caught his breath as he slowly crouched, ignoring the tug of his mantle as it soaked up more water. Her grubby garment looked to be one used as sleeping attire, or a chemise usually worn under a gown. Not a coarsely woven piece of clothing, as a peasant might wear. But judging by the border of tiny, embroidered flowers along her sleeve, one of superior quality.

Foreboding buzzed through his mind, even as he reached out to gently move the hair from her face. He hoped she was still alive. She could tell him who she was, and what had befallen her.

Small waves lapped against her body as Kaine crashed

closer to Edouard. "What have you—? God's blood!"

"Aye," Edouard said grimly.

"Is she alive?"

"I am not certain." Edouard's fingertips slid against her temple, easing the matted hair downward. At first touch, her flesh seemed deathly cold, but then . . . He sensed the faintest pulse of life's blood. As the mud-knotted skeins slid away, they revealed her closed eyes and sweep of thick lashes, the smooth slope of her cheek, and elegant jaw line.

He froze. He *knew* her.

She looked older than he remembered, her features those of a woman rather than a maiden.

Kaine sucked in a sharp breath.

Dismay and anger, suppressed from months ago, broke free on a flood of memories. Edouard trembled at their force, while shock raced through him to settle like a cruel iron band around his heart. "God's blood," He whispered. "Juliana."

Darkness blanketed her mind. Blackness so thick and limitless, she was lost in it.

Lost . . .

She tried to draw together the fragments of her thoughts, to find herself, but the inkiness shifted. It wrapped around her consciousness, squeezing tighter and tighter, until the fragments disappeared. The darkness settled back into a vast swath of nothingness.

So . . . cold.

So . . . alone.

Pain throbbed somewhere in the muzzy reaches of her mind. Sounds—muffled, distorted—sifted down to her. They brushed against her thoughts, taunting her, with all that she couldn't comprehend.

A tiny part of her began to struggle. To fight its way toward the origin of those sounds.

I am here. In the dark. Find me!

But the pain . . . It slashed down upon her, crushing her with its ruthless, invisible grip. Agony screamed within the huddled reaches of her being. How well the pain echoed the greater ache trapped inside her. An anguish that hinted at something . . . ghastly.

I am here. In the dark. Lost!

The inkiness began to press in upon her.

She *had* to find her way out of the darkness. *Had to!* If only she knew why.

Unable to stop himself from shaking, Edouard smoothed his fingers down Juliana's cheek. "Juliana, can you hear me?" He stared down at her ashen face, hoping his question got a response from her. However, he saw not the slightest sign that she'd heard him.

"Juliana!" he cried, his tone hoarsening. The horror of finding her like this churned within him. How he longed to slam his fist into something solid, to channel his ferocious turmoil. Losing his temper wouldn't help revive her, though, or assure her she was among friends. With a strangled groan, he caressed her face again.

"Why is she lying in the river?" Shock tautened Kaine's voice. "What could have happened to her?"

"I do not know. But I will find out."

Juliana had to live. She *had* to.

Pressing his lips together, Edouard looked at the reeds crowding at her back, deciding the best way to take her from the water. His gaze fell upon a dark stain between her shoulders. With sickening dread, he realized what he saw wasn't mud, but blood.

The chill from the water seeped into his bones as he leaned over to examine the hair at her nape. Blood matted the strands together. A lot of blood. It had dried along her hairline and the neckline of her chemise. As his fingers eased aside the hair, an ugly, purplish mass came into view.

His stomach lurched.

"Someone hit her. Hard," he said. "With a heavy object."

Kaine exhaled a ragged breath. "What you mean is they aimed to . . . kill her?"

"Aye." Rage and confusion burned inside Edouard. Who would want to murder her? Did they dump her here, in the river? Who'd dare to consider her life to be as worthless as a sack of refuse?

God above, he would know the truth!

"She was living with the Ferchantes, was she not?" Kaine asked. "Do you think his lordship knows of this incident?"

A very good question. One of many that, God help him, sped into Edouard's thoughts. "Landon Ferchante may indeed have some answers. Right now, though, we need to ensure she survives. We must get her dry and warm. She needs a healer."

"There must be one in the village. Shall I ride ahead and find out?"

"I will send one of the others. If she wakes, she will know us. That may be a comfort to her." Or, mayhap not, considering their disastrous prior encounters. She might tell him to get his wretched hands off her and never touch her again. He'd be delighted if she roused with the strength to scorn him.

Reaching down into the murky water, Edouard slid one arm under her upper body, gently tilted her toward him, and then slid his other arm under her knees. He lifted her into his arms. As he rose, water streamed from her gown and ran into his garments, soaking through to his skin. Her limp body slumped against him, her head falling to rest against his shoulder.

He looked down at her, wondering if by moving her he'd encouraged her to wake. Hoping, *hoping*, that he had. Her eyes remained closed. His heart squeezed at the pitiful blankness of her features.

When his gaze flicked down the rest of her body, a breath lodged in his throat, for he hadn't anticipated how intimately her garment would reveal her feminine form. The muddy linen stuck to her body, defining the generous swell of her breasts, the outline of her nipples, and the curve of her hips. The thought of any other man seeing her this way, almost nude . . .

He glanced up, to see Kaine's attention lift from Juliana. Jealous rage flashed through Edouard, so savagely hot, he almost choked on it. "Fetch my saddle blanket," he ground out.

A flush darkened Kaine's cheekbones. "A wise idea. I will bring mine, too."

"Send one of the men into the village to find the healer." Turning Juliana away from Kaine's view, Edouard said, "I will wait here. The others cannot see her until she is covered."

Water sloshed as Kaine plodded back to the bank. Edouard tightened his hold on Juliana, pressing her body even closer to his, hoping his body's warmth might help revive her.

Hurry, Kaine. Hurry!

"What did his lordship find?" one of his men-at-arms

said from the bank.

"A lady, wounded and near death. Later, there will be time for explanations," Kaine said. "'Tis urgent we see to this woman's well-being." More conversation, less distinct, took place, and then Edouard heard the clatter of hooves as one of the men raced off.

Kaine returned to Edouard, two blankets tucked under his arm. "All is as you ordered."

"Thank you." Edouard slowly faced his friend. "I realize I will need your help to enwrap her . . ."

Kaine's gaze steadily held his. "I am glad to assist." Clearly doing his best not to look at Juliana's bosom, he opened up Edouard's blanket. Together, maneuvering her in Edouard's arms, they managed to get the woolen covering all the way around her. Then Kaine unfolded his blanket partway and stretched it out over her.

"She must be warmer now," he said.

"Warm enough, at least, till we can set her in a hot bath by a warm fire." A shiver ran through Edouard, for his feet were turning numb inside his water-encased boots. But he wouldn't think about his discomfort. All that mattered was saving Juliana.

With Kaine at his side, he headed toward the bank, taking care not to kick up waves and get water on the blankets. Her head shifted against him and her lips parted a fraction, revealing the even line of her front teeth. But she made no sound. Not the slightest cry or pained sigh.

"You are safe now, Juliana," he murmured, willing her to hear him. "I swear, upon my soul, no one will hurt you like this again."

Fear pressed in on him. Would she live, or was she so close to death her spirit would just slip away without him knowing? On the faintest breath . . . gone?

Nay. She wouldn't perish that way. Such a strong, kind, beautiful woman deserved justice for the grievance done to her. If he could do naught else for her, he'd see her assailant captured and held accountable for the heinous crime.

As Edouard neared the water's edge, his waiting men-at-arms exchanged glances. "Milord," one of them called. "What are your orders?"

"Prepare to ride. The healer cannot be far from here." Edouard's boots met firm ground and, when he accidentally jostled Juliana, he cursed. He glanced back at Kaine. "Help me get Juliana onto my horse."

"Shall we help?" another of the warriors asked.

Edouard shook his head. Juliana's body might be well concealed, and they were trustworthy men, but the thought of others touching her in any manner . . . *Nay*.

Halting before his grazing horse, Edouard eased Juliana into Kaine's waiting arms. Edouard mounted his steed, then, with his friend pushing her from below, pulled her up onto the saddle in front of him. He shifted her legs so she sat across his lap, settled the second blanket over her, then slid one arm around her body to draw her against him.

When he took up the reins, her wet head shifted into the crook between his head and shoulder. Edouard paid no heed to the water dripping down his neckline; he'd change his damp garments and dry off once she was in the healer's care.

The faint puff of her breath tickled his skin. How intimate their posture must look from below—as though they were lovers. A notion he'd dispel if anyone made the assumption. He might resent his betrothal to Nara, but, being an honorable man, he'd never abandon his commitment to her.

A long-ago memory of Juliana standing before him by the well, tresses aglow with sunlight, flitted through his mind. How vibrant she'd looked that day. What he would give to see even a glimmer of that spirited woman now.

Find that strength of will, Juliana. Fight to open your eyes. Fight to live.

Edouard glanced down at Kaine, preparing to climb up onto his mount. Hope lit his friend's eyes. "Did she stir?"

"Nay."

Kaine's mouth flattened. He nodded once before he gathered up the reins and swung onto his horse's back.

With the men-at-arms close behind, Edouard spurred his mount in the direction of the village. With each sway of his horse, Juliana rocked against him. Did the motion of the horse cause her pain? He hoped not.

Thatch-roofed cottages, some surrounded by wooden fences, came into view along the roadside. Closer to the village outskirts, hoofbeats, growing louder by the moment, reached them. Narrowing his eyes against the sun's brightness, Edouard looked to the approaching rider: his man-at-arms Kaine had sent to find the healer.

When the man drew near, Edouard called, "What did you learn?"

"The healer's cottage is on the opposite side of the village, milord. According to the merchant I spoke to, though, she is not there."

"Why not?" Frustration turned Edouard's voice to a growl.

Disquiet flickered in the rider's eyes. "She is at Waddesford Keep and has been for the past sennight. Apparently, she went to help Lady Ferchante give birth and has not returned."

Edouard's gaze again slid down to Juliana. A gut feeling told him the healer's situation and Juliana's were connected. How, exactly, he didn't yet know.

As though attuned to the flow of his thoughts, the rider added, "She has folk in the village who depend upon her herbs and ointments to ease their ailments. She has never abandoned their care before."

"Then we must find out what is delaying her."

The village gates loomed ahead. Edouard rode

through them into the main street, shaded by stone buildings and filled with townsfolk, animals, and rumbling carts. He blinked against the churned-up dust, even as worry and impatience chafed at him. So many unanswered questions.

The barest change in Juliana's breath against his neck, the faint shifting of her weight, snapped Edouard's gaze back to her face.

Her eyes were open.

CHAPTER
7

Sounds and smells rushed into the darkness filling her thoughts. Her groggy mind struggled to identify them, even as an onslaught of pain forced her consciousness up, up, into the brightness, like a bubble soaring up from the bottom of a river to pop on the surface.

Her eyes opened. A blur of colors careened before her. She blinked, and, as her perceptions slowly focused, recognized the sweet scent of horse, the metallic tinkle of metal, and the brush of cloth against her cheek.

"Juliana."

The voice rumbled beneath her ear. A man's voice, reassuring as it spoke the woman's name. A glimmer of insight skated at the farthest edge of her thoughts. Something about the voice . . . She tried to chase the intuition, to mentally catch hold of it.

While she did so, she realized she was held in strong arms, upon a horse. She rested against the broad body of the man who'd spoken.

Misgiving skittered through her, heightening her sense of disorientation. How had she come to be upon a horse? Who was this man? Should she trust him, or fear him?

Her stomach clenched on a wave of agony. The ache within her skull threatened to obscure all else, to crush into nothingness the fragile hope blossoming inside her. But she couldn't let it. These new sensations spoke to the loneliness inside her; they promised that at last, she'd been found.

Fighting her pain, swallowing down the bile rising to the back of her mouth, she tilted her head to look up at him.

Her gaze touched first his jaw dusted with stubble, then the taut plane of his cheek. Unable to resist the demand of his stare, she met his gaze. Concern shone in his thickly lashed blue eyes framed by dark, strong brows. Her heart lurched, a hard wallop against her breastbone, for this stranger had the most handsome countenance.

He looked upon her, however, as if he . . . knew her.

As though he *cared* for her.

A startled cry parted her lips. Panic whipped through her like hot sparks, and she tried to struggle, but . . . She couldn't move her arms; they seemed to be trapped at her sides. And the pain—

"Juliana," he said again, more urgently. "Please, do not be afraid. You are safe."

Juliana? Why did he call her such? *Oh, God.*

"You remember me," he urged. "'Tis Edouard. Edouard de Lanceau."

The smallest tingle of acknowledgment brushed the fear and agony clouding her mind. Yet as soon as the sensation surfaced, it was sucked back down into the blackness trying to envelop her. Another hint of insight submerged. *Lost.*

"You remember me," the man named Edouard went on, a plea now in his eyes. "We met for the first time last spring at the feast at your sire's castle. Sherstowe Keep."

Feast. Sherstowe.

A rough sound of discomfort grated in Edouard's throat. "I rescued you from the well."

His words tumbled into her mind, rousing her loneliness. She didn't remember.

His gaze shadowed with disappointment. "Surely you recall what happened . . . with Nara."

She knew no one by that name.

Or did she? She didn't remember. Not him. Not Juliana. Not the feast.

Naught.

A rasping noise broke into her racing thoughts. The sound of her own breathing.

Noises swooped in upon her: voices; dogs barking; the squeaked rattle of passing carts. The sounds crowded one atop another, tangled together, until the cacophony raging inside her head threatened to split her apart.

The darkness coaxed.

"Juliana," Edouard yelled, even as the creeping shadows began to dim the color around her and stifle the noises. How soothing, to fall back into the numbing inkiness . . .

I am here. In the dark. Find me! a voice inside her shrilled.

And then, all went black.

"Nay!" Edouard choked, bending his head close to Juliana's. "Stay awake. Please, Juliana!"

Her head lolled against his arm.

"She is too weak," Kaine murmured.

Edouard's eyes smarted as he studied her wan, expressionless features. A wisp of hair had slipped from the blanket to trail across her fine-boned cheek; it looked gut-wrenchingly stark against her pale skin, and he gently swept it away.

How he wished she'd open her eyes again, look up at him, and prove she wanted to fight the injury that sapped her strength. In that moment before her consciousness slipped away, though, he'd seen doubt in her eyes, and a raw sense of hopelessness.

"She did not tell us who wounded her," he said quietly. "I should have asked her right away. Yet I wanted

114

her to know she was among friends, for she seemed—"

"Frightened," Kaine said.

Edouard nodded. Fear, however, didn't quite en-compass the emotions he'd glimpsed in her eyes. "As you no doubt noticed, she did not seem to recognize me, or even her own name."

"The blow to the head." Kaine sighed. "I have heard of such happening. It may be some time before her memory returns. Days. Weeks."

Clenching his jaw, Edouard looked at his men. "We do not have weeks. I want to know what happened to her. I will not rest till I do." He fixed his gaze upon the rider who'd gone to find the healer's cottage. "You. Ride ahead to Waddesford Keep. Tell Lord Ferchante I will arrive shortly with Lady de Greyne, who urgently needs to be seen by the healer. I also have matters of estate to discuss with him, as an appointed representative for my father."

"Aye, milord." The man turned his horse and rode away into the crowd.

Edouard's gaze settled upon the other two men-at-arms. Tipping his head to the closest one, he said, "You will return to Branton Keep and report to my sire. He should know of these unusual circumstances, as should Lord de Greyne."

The man nodded, then rode past them, back toward the village gates.

Kaine raised his eyebrows. "That leaves only two of

us to protect you, Edouard."

"Me and Juliana." Edouard brushed aside a curious tingle of unease; he, Kaine, and his fellow warrior were all capable fighters. "Is that too great a responsibility for you, my friend?"

Mirth lit Kaine's gaze before he shrugged. "I will do my very best to protect your wretched arse. And Juliana's pretty one, of course."

How in hellfire did Kaine know Juliana had a pretty arse? Scowling, Edouard spurred his horse forward. "Enough. We ride to Waddesford Keep."

Standing before the trestle table in Waddesford Keep's sun-washed solar, Veronique swept a rosewater-dampened comb through her tresses, as she did every morning. The ivory comb whispered as it fulfilled the ritual she never neglected. Her perfumed, vibrant red hair, when trailed over eager, naked male flesh, had seduced many a lover. Including Landon.

A gloating smile edged up the corner of her mouth. Last eve, despite his reluctance, she'd not only wrested sweaty, gasping control of his body, but after fornicating, he'd fallen asleep in her arms.

Landon needed her. His emotions were hers to manipulate as she desired. That was most satisfying of all. If all went as she planned today, she'd finally have possession of the ring he'd been awarded for his trust and loyalty by Geoffrey de Lanceau.

A ring that, slipped onto her son's finger, would let Tye into his lordship's most trusted elite. Her grin broadened. What a perfect moment for Tye to run Geoffrey through with his sword. To at last destroy the Great Lord of Moydenshire.

"Oh, Geoffrey," she murmured, "if only you knew what lay ahead." For long, long years she'd waited to crush him—the one man, in all her life, who'd cast her aside. She'd never met a man as strong willed as Geoffrey until she birthed Tye. At last, Fate was leading her to triumph. With a throaty laugh, she smoothed a hand over her breasts, then down the front of her green silk gown to her belly, where lusty tremors clenched her womb.

Just as her hand eased lower, footfalls sounded in the corridor outside. She recognized that gait; Landon walked like a plodding ox. She ran her comb through her hair one last time and, as the chamber door creaked open, faced him, resting her hip against the table to accentuate her body's curves.

"Landon," she cooed, before realizing another person approached as well.

Tye.

Determination blazed in his eyes as he strode in after his lordship, his shoulder-length brown hair tied back from his face with a leather thong and a sword belt buckled over his light gray tunic and black hose.

Naughty boy. Tye hadn't even asked permission to enter the solar. Later, she'd warn him not to repeat that mistake. But right now—

"A rider arrived at the gates moments ago," Landon blurted. Sweat shone on his forehead—almost as much sweat as she'd roused from him during coupling. How disgusting.

Veronique waved a dismissive hand. "Surely you can deal with him."

"Mother—"

"A messenger"—Landon's voice hoarsened—"sent by Edouard de Lanceau."

Shock tightened her grip to crushing force on the comb. "*What*?" Edouard, Geoffrey's firstborn son. His heir, destined to inherit a rich, flourishing empire. Hatred flared inside her, for she loathed every de Lanceau. *Loathed* them.

"Edouard is on his way here," Tye said, his voice steady and cold.

"With Juliana." Landon groaned. "He asked for the healer to tend her wound."

Veronique hissed a breath. "Juliana is *alive*?"

"I do not want to believe it, either. How could she have survived?" Shoving his hair back with his fingers, Landon began to pace. "That injury should have killed her. I should have made certain. Left no doubt." His unruly gaze locked with hers. "You assured me she was dead. 'Tis your fault."

Rage whipped through her. "How *dare*—?"

"If she wasn't dead by the time your mercenaries reached the river . . ."

"They believed she was. They would not have disobeyed me." How unwise of Landon to blame her for this unforeseen complication. If he wasn't of such use to her, she'd grab her knife and slice his flesh until he begged an apology. Still, she'd find those two mercenaries who'd taken Juliana away and, after questioning, would see them killed, for no one failed to do what she ordered of them.

Landon's boots scraped on the planks as he continued to pace. "De Lanceau must have heard of Mayda's death. He doubts she killed herself. 'Tis why Edouard has come."

Veronique snorted. "I do not think so."

"Why else would Edouard be visiting my keep? The messenger mentioned matters of estate, but . . ."

Shutting out the annoying drone of Landon's voice, Veronique set her comb down on the trestle table and swept her hair back over her shoulders. Landon's insecurities didn't matter. Neither did Edouard's reasons for visiting Waddesford Keep.

"Mother."

CATHERINE KEAN

Tye's tone of voice compelled her to look at him.

"Edouard is riding here." He spoke each word as if 'twas forced between his teeth, and pride kindled in her breast. She'd raised him well. He might have de Lanceau blood running in his veins, but he, too, shared her hatred of them all.

"'Tis an opportunity we cannot ignore," Veronique answered, while her thoughts began to fashion a new plan. *Edouard, Geoffrey's beloved son, so close by. Easily within her grasp.* Her breath caught, suspended by the enticing promise of vengeance. She'd have tremendous leverage over Geoffrey, if she owned his son's life.

"Veronique," Landon groused. He clearly didn't like being ignored.

Her attention slid to him, while laughter bubbled within her; it broke free on a shrill cackle.

Landon threw out his hands. "You *laugh*? Why in hellfire . . . ?"

Warning tingled in the back of her mind. She mustn't lose his cooperation. Not till she had that ring. Softening her laugh, she crossed to him. "Do not be angry with me, Landon. In truth, Edouard's visit could not be more perfect."

He squinted at her as though she was mad. "We will turn him away at the gates. I will order my men to tell him I cannot speak with him, because . . . I am away."

"Oh, come now. 'Twould not be very hospitable."

Tilting her head to one side, Veronique glanced at Tye. She nodded once.

The corner of his mouth tilted in a smirk. He turned, strode to the door, and closed it behind him.

Landon scowled. "Where is he going? I did not give him orders."

Her hips swaying, gown rustling like a cruel whisper, Veronique strolled to Landon. "Tye will make arrangements for Edouard." With a breathy sigh, she slid her hand up under his tunic and stroked his sweaty chest.

Landon caught her hand, stilling it with a fierce grip. Sensual excitement rushed through her as he said, close to her cheek, "I want Edouard sent away."

Did Landon really believe the keep was still in his control? That what he said or thought made any difference? Steeling the disgust from her expression, she lowered her lashes on a provocative flutter. "We would be wise to find out why he has ridden here. Also, we must know what Juliana told him. That is, before we murder her." Veronique nuzzled his cheek and then kissed him. "Aye?"

"How will we kill her? Edouard will know—"

Veronique pressed her fingers to Landon's lips, silencing him. By the time Juliana died, Edouard would be in no position to save her pathetic life, or his own. But Landon didn't need to know any details of what was to come. "We shall say poor Juliana perished from her wound." A credible tale. Even witless Landon would agree.

"If you . . . think 'tis best."

Anticipation throbbed inside Veronique, for now was the ideal moment to mention the ring. "I vow, Landon, you should also be wearing the jewel de Lanceau gave you. Edouard will expect to see it. We do not want to arouse his suspicions."

"A-all right." Drawing away, he strode to his wooden chest shoved against the wall by the bed, opened it, and rummaged inside. He drew out a leather bag and tipped the contents onto the chest's closed lid.

Veronique's fingers curled into fists. At last. *At last!*

Landon went very still, before a strangled cry broke from him.

"What is wrong?" Veronique snapped.

Disillusionment shivered across his face. "The ring. 'Tis gone."

Her jaw clamped so tightly that pain lanced through her cheek. "Are you *certain* 'tis not there?"

"Aye. Many other jewels are missing, too. Cloak pins, gemstone rings inherited from my sire." He shook his head. "A chain with a gold cross—"

"Did you put these jewels somewhere else, for safekeeping?"

"Nay. I—" His expression hardened. "Mayda. She took them!"

A likely possibility, considering their bitter fights

in the days before she died. Trying to control her rage, Veronique said, "Your wife confided in Juliana, did she not? They were the closest of friends."

"Aye."

Welcoming the malice burning within her, Veronique smiled. "Let Edouard ride straight through the castle gates. We will be waiting."

CHAPTER 8

The dirt road curved out of a stand of trees, guiding Edouard and his men into open sunlight and the approach to Waddesford Keep. The stone fortress sprawled across the land ahead, with guards visible above the gatehouse and along the battlements.

As his gaze fell upon the lowered drawbridge and raised portcullis, Edouard blew out a sigh of relief. His messenger had reached the keep. They were expected.

Gently squeezing Juliana's limp body, he murmured, "Help is moments away, I promise." She hadn't stirred since waking in the village. Worry for her left a gnawing ache in his gut, but soon, she'd have the care she needed.

Ah, God, he'd sell his fine horse, even the prized dagger belted at his hip, if the healer needed money to purchase special herbs or ointments to save Juliana.

When he neared the keep, Kaine and the other man-at-arms riding a few paces behind, he sensed many gazes upon him. He was used to drawing awed stares, being the son of Moydenshire's lord. Holding his head high, he tamped down a pinch of nervousness over the meeting he'd promised he'd have with Ferchante, one that now must include blunt questions as to why Juliana was found near dead in the river. Not an easy matter to discuss, but one that mustn't be ignored.

Aware of the onlookers on the wall walk, Edouard briefly savored the honor of visiting on behalf of his respected father. One day, this castle's lord would owe allegiance to him. One day, these folk would be his.

Foreboding suddenly pierced the glow inside him, and his gaze shifted back to the gatehouse. For a moment, he sensed . . . malevolence.

Surely not. His sire and Lord Ferchante weren't enemies, but friends and allies. His taxed nerves must be playing tricks upon his mind.

Mentally shoving aside his unease, he guided his horse onto the drawbridge crossing the moat that looked nearly dry. The scent of stagnant water wafted up to him as the animal's hoofbeats sounded on the wood. A moment later, Edouard heard the other horses walk onto the drawbridge behind him. The escalating clatter of well-trained mounts, handled by skilled, loyal men, sent reassurance flowing through him.

The guards at the end of the drawbridge—heavily armed, tough-looking men—bowed as he rode under the wooden teeth of the portcullis into the shadows of the gatehouse. The sun-brightened inner walls of the bailey came into view. A small crowd had gathered in the bailey, an array of castle folk and servants who'd left their daily duties to get a glimpse of him. They were separated from him by warriors, lined up in two opposite rows to form a corridor, a sign of respect when greeting honored guests.

The warriors dipped their heads as he rode past, and Edouard nodded back while keeping a secure hold upon Juliana. When his gaze skimmed the bailey, he saw Lord Ferchante striding out of the forebuilding's doorway. He looked much the same as the last time Edouard saw him, at a Christmas feast last year. Ferchante smoothed a hand over the front of his tunic, clearly wanting to make the very best impression.

"Lord Ferchante," Edouard called and reined in his horse. Kaine and the men-at-arms halted their horses a short distance behind him, as they'd been trained to do. They'd keep a look out for danger. A formality, really, when they were on friendly ground.

"An honor to see you, Lord de Lanceau." Ferchante dropped into an elegant bow.

"Please, call me Edouard."

"If you will call me Landon, milord."

Edouard smiled. "Agreed. Thank you for opening your gates to us and preparing for our visit."

Landon smiled back. Somehow, though, his expression seemed strained; 'twas even more evident when he looked at Juliana. His hand swept over his face and, for a moment, alarm gleamed in his eyes.

Disquiet tingled anew in Edouard's blood. Was Landon worried about Juliana's condition? She had, after all, been Mayda's closest friend. Or, was he more concerned he'd suffer punishment for what had befallen Juliana, since she resided at his keep? Questions to be dwelled upon later.

"Landon," he said, "as you can see, Juliana is badly hurt. The man-at-arms I sent on ahead was to request the healer. We were told she is here."

"She is," Landon said. "We have readied for Juliana's care."

"Good."

Landon's gaze darted to the crowd, and then back. A nervous gesture that suggested he wanted to be certain all was in order for this initial meeting.

Yet someone standing within this bailey must know who'd attacked Juliana. Edouard's sire wouldn't have let an opportunity pass to coax out a witness; Edouard mustn't, either. "Lady de Greyne was living at this keep, was she not?" His arm tightened a protective notch around her. "Do you know how she came to be injured? It appears someone tried to murder her."

"Murder?" Landon seemed to grow tense. Doubtless he was shocked by the thought that someone in his household may have committed such a heinous deed.

"Did she . . . tell you such?"

"Nay. She only roused once on our journey here, and only for a moment. Let it be known"—Edouard raised his voice to carry across the bailey—"I offer a reward to anyone who saw what happened to her."

A murmur rippled through the throng.

"Please, Edouard." Landon thrust a hand toward the keep. "Come inside with your men. Refresh yourselves. As you ordered, we must get Juliana to the healer."

Indeed, the sooner her wound was treated, the better. The unsteadiness of Landon's tone, though, made Edouard pause.

"My men will see to your horses," Landon went on. "They—"

"One moment."

"Aye?" Landon's hand skimmed over his sweaty face again. A hand that bore only one ring, and it wasn't the one given to him by Edouard's sire.

Edouard forced his lips into a genial smile. "My father has certain ways he likes matters to be conducted between his loyal lords. If you would show me what he gave you. A sign, as you will, of the trust between us."

A curious silence fell upon the crowd, as though all the others, too, awaited that confirmation from Landon. "The ring, you mean." Landon's face crumpled on a wry laugh. "I fear I was so busy making arrangements for your visit, I forgot to fetch it from my chamber."

A fair explanation. Still . . .

"Surely, Edouard, you do not need such proof to know you can trust me?"

A chill crawled through Edouard. He did, indeed, want proof. Why didn't Landon offer to fetch the ring and prove his loyalty?

Just as he tightened his hold on his horse's reins to wheel it around, Kaine's mount nudged alongside his. "Something is wrong," Kaine said between his teeth. "There are too few guards on the battlements, and that man by the stable . . ."

As Edouard began to turn his horse, he risked a glance. His gaze locked with the unwavering stare of a dark-haired warrior who looked about his age. His hair, tied back with a strip of leather, was long enough to touch between his shoulder blades. He had the physique of a seasoned knight. His obvious fighting strength, however, didn't cause dread to slam through Edouard.

The man's face . . .

Familiar.

He looked like Edouard's father. A harder, rougher version, but still . . .

Only one man could fit this shocking resemblance: Tye, the bastard son of Edouard's sire and Veronique. A child Edouard's father pointedly refused to acknowledge.

If Tye was here, then his ruthless mother must be also.

"Ride! Now!" Edouard bellowed. He spun his horse

and kicked it toward the gatehouse.

Shouts erupted behind him, along with the hiss of drawn swords, hoofbeats, and running footfalls.

A creak echoed. The sound of the drawbridge rising.

Hellfire! Within moments, they'd be trapped inside these walls.

"Edouard!" Kaine shouted from close behind.

Men swarmed in around Edouard's horse to block his escape. They grabbed for his mount's reins and reached for Juliana. As he struggled to keep hold of her and draw his sword, Edouard kicked the nearest lout, sending his head snapping back with a loud crack.

The force of the blow sent Juliana bumping against Edouard. He gasped and fought to regain his balance. Kicking out again, he caught another warrior full in the chest. The man careened back into the throng.

Cursing under his breath, Edouard abandoned his attempt to free his sword. Yanking his knife from his belt, he slashed out at a man tugging at his left leg, then rammed his heels into his horse's sides. There was still a chance to reach the drawbridge. But tossing its head, the horse merely sidestepped; a mercenary had a firm hold on its bridle.

A coarse laugh carried across the din. "You are trapped."

Edouard's head swiveled. His furious stare locked with that of the dark-haired thug who resembled his sire.

As though he were some kind of god, the sea of men

parted to let him through. His broadsword, pointed at an angle toward the ground, glinted with lethal sharpness. With insolent, swaggering strides, he crossed to Edouard.

"Who are you?" Edouard glared at him, refusing to look away.

A woman's laugh, shrill with glee, floated from near the forebuilding.

Veronique? *Oh, God. Oh, holy God.*

The dark-haired man reached his side. "My name," he said with a cold smile, "is Tye. At last, we meet, *Brother.*"

Edouard glared down at the man who'd dared to call him brother, the bastard who'd suggested, in that one word, that he had a birth right to be part of the revered de Lanceau lineage. The lout grinned, obviously relishing Edouard's hatred.

From what Edouard knew of Tye, he'd been presented, without any forewarning, to his sire in a meadow when a young boy, a pawn in one of Veronique's prior schemes. Edouard's sire had refused to believe he'd fathered Tye. While insistent that the boy was, indeed, of de Lanceau blood, Veronique had offered no definite proof.

When Tye was a child, his developing features might not have been distinct. In the grown man—the shape of Tye's mouth, the boldness of his gaze, the angles of his face—Edouard saw the resemblance to his father.

Their father.

Or a man who looked very much like Geoffrey de Lanceau.

Refusing to break Tye's stare, Edouard tightened his grip on his knife. How diligently his sire had tried to keep this bastard from influencing any part of his life. He'd striven to spare the family from the anguish of his past liaison with Veronique, an ambitious, French-born commoner who believed herself worthy of the privileges of the noble elite. While they all knew of Veronique and Tye, the two were akin to an unpleasant secret, spoken of only when necessary.

Regardless of the truth of Veronique's claim, Edouard had no doubt Tye's intentions toward him were hostile. He'd never allow himself to be manipulated into a plot to destroy his sire. He *had* to get Juliana away from peril.

"I demand that you withdraw your lackeys. Let me and my men leave," Edouard said, not caring to soften the lashing whip of his voice.

Tye didn't even blink. "Demand." He laughed while he looked to the men around him. They, too, began to chuckle. "Why would I let you go? We only just met. As brothers, we have much in common to discuss."

"I have naught to say to you, whoreson." Edouard glanced over his shoulder. "Landon! Order these men to move aside, or—"

"Ferchante no longer rules this keep." Tye flipped up his sword; the tip rested at Juliana's thigh, atop the blanket wrapped around her. With one thrust, the blade would slice through to her delicate skin and deeper still. He'd leave her crippled. More likely, she'd slowly bleed to death.

"I do not wish to hurt her," Tye said, "especially when she is already so gravely wounded. You must care about her, aye, to have brought her to the healer?"

Edouard glowered. He wasn't going to honor this thug with a response. Tye, though, seemed to read the answer in Edouard's expression, for he smiled.

"Since she is important to you, you will do exactly as I say. Sheath your knife and hand it to me. Unbuckle your sword belt and drop it as well." He motioned to the near-by mercenaries, who edged forward to take the weapons.

Edouard's gaze shot to the drawbridge, almost completely raised. Was there any chance of escape? Any way of getting Juliana away from here?

"There is no escape." Tye's words rang with command. "Do as I say."

Grunts and the scuffling sounds of struggle drew Edouard's gaze to Kaine, trying to fight off mercenaries hauling him down from his mount. Kaine fought well, but there were too many opponents. He vanished beneath a swarm of men.

Tye tsked. Regret flickered across his face before his fingers flexed on his sword, as though readying to plunge it into Juliana's flesh. "I thought you cared for Lady de Greyne, but—"

"All *right*." Edouard slid his dagger back into its leather sheath. Untying it from his belt, he leaned around Juliana to pass it down, even as he watched for a moment of opportunity.

Gaze narrowing, Tye eased his sword back from Juliana's thigh. He didn't step away, but held the weapon at the ready, obviously prepared to inflict the wound he'd promised if his orders weren't obeyed.

Silent, foul oaths burned Edouard's throat as he dropped the dagger and one of the mercenaries caught it. How he wanted to strike out at Tye, to plunge into a ferocious, bloody swordfight. The fighting urge ignited with the same force as his hatred. However, such an assault might endanger Juliana. Here, in this keep where the enemy reigned, he must be her protector. Her survival could depend upon him.

With Tye studying his every movement, Edouard unbuckled his sword belt. It slid away; with a *thud*, it landed on the ground.

"Good." Tye sneered. "Now . . ."

His head tipped to the side. Even as Edouard registered the signal, mercenaries grabbed his left leg. More thugs pulled at his mantle, yanking him down toward the dirt.

"Juliana!" he cried, when her body tumbled from his grasp. A fall from the horse, in her weakened condition, could kill her. Is that what Tye intended? A quick way to be rid of her? Edouard kicked out at the louts dragging him down, lashed out with his fists, but there were too many of them.

He was falling. The ground rushed up to meet him.

Juliana, forgive me.

He landed on his side. His head hit the hard-packed dirt and the crowd of dusty boots within his view became a muddy blur. Groaning, he struggled to focus.

Fight. Save Juliana.

As he hauled himself up on unsteady hands and knees, men snatched the pin securing his cloak and whisked the garment from his shoulders. More mercenaries seized his arms and hefted him to his feet.

His knees threatened to give. Still, he thrashed. He had to break free.

Grab a sword. Rescue Juliana. Fight—

Steel flashed. A sword pressed against his jaw.

Hissing breaths between his teeth, Edouard froze.

"I knew you would struggle." Laughing, Tye walked into Edouard's line of vision while holding the sword. "I expect I would have done the same."

"Juliana—" Edouard croaked.

"There." Tye gestured to two mercenaries, coming into Edouard's view. A crushing ache ripped through him, for they'd stripped the blankets from her body. Ah, God, she was almost naked, before all these men! The louts held Juliana upright between them, her head and shoulders drooping while they gripped her upper arms.

"Did she fall?" Edouard bit out. "Is she—?"

"Alive? Aye. She only fell a short distance. The men caught her."

Rage flared within Edouard. The mercenaries' dirty, callused hands were too close to her breasts. If they dared to molest her, especially when she couldn't protest or fight back . . . Glaring at Tye, he ground out, "If they touch her . . ."

Tye's gaze shifted to the men behind Edouard.

"Damnation!" Edouard yelled. "Do not ignore me."

"Do you have him secured?" Tye said, as though Edouard hadn't spoken.

"Aye."

Tye lowered his sword and shoved it back into its leather scabbard. "I will take her."

"*Nay!*" Edouard struggled, but his captors held him firm. He could only watch as Tye eased Juliana from the mercenaries' grasp and scooped her into his arms. Her cheek pressed against his tunic front, while her silken hair tumbled free.

Edouard shook, barely able to hold back his fury. To see her in that whoreson's arms . . .

Tye turned toward the keep. "This way."

The crowd around them separated, again letting Tye through. The thugs restraining Edouard dragged him forward. Across the sea of warriors, he saw Kaine and

CATHERINE KEAN

his other man-at-arms being hauled away, to be held in a different location, it seemed.

"Hold."

At the curt order, spoken by a woman, his assailants halted. As Edouard's head turned to face forward, he saw a slender, red-haired woman standing beside Landon. Veronique, he guessed. She must be close to his sire's age, but her features were austere, beautiful, and unnaturally youthful. Her crimson, painted lips curved into a triumphant smile as her gaze traveled over his body, from his face right down to his scuffed boots.

"Well done, Tye," she said.

"Thank you, Mother."

Edouard glared. What he would give to wipe that smirk off her gaudy mouth.

"*Tsk, tsk.*" Veronique strolled forward. She smelled of rosewater, a fragrance he vowed to hate for the rest of his life. As her scent filled his nostrils, he exhaled sharply, hating to inhale even the slightest essence of her, the woman who'd devoted her life to destroying his noble sire.

Her smile broadened, suggesting she enjoyed his discomfort. She shifted forward and reached out, as if to wipe dirt from his cheek. He jerked his face away.

"Stubborn," she mused. "Just like your accursed father. But we will change that."

Edouard fought a tremor. What did she mean? The way her eyes gleamed with promise left a foul taste in his mouth.

"Where do you want them, Mother?" Tye asked, shifting Juliana in his arms.

"Veronique." Landon stepped forward, his expression dazed. "I asked moments ago, and you still have not answered me. I demand to know your intentions. To treat Geoffrey de Lanceau's son in this manner—"

"Tye, also, is de Lanceau's son."

Frowning, Landon looked from Tye to Edouard.

"They are half brothers." Veronique's lip curled. "Edouard was born in wedlock; he is considered Geoffrey's first-born and heir. However, but months after Geoffrey cast me aside, I birthed Tye. Who, I wonder, really is the firstborn?"

"There is no proof my sire fathered Tye."

Veronique snorted in disgust. "Is that what your father told you?"

Edouard struggled against an unwelcome tug of doubt. "Even if by some chance your claim is true, Tye is illegitimate," Edouard said through his teeth. "By law, he cannot inherit. He has *no* claim to my sire's estates."

Her gaze sharpened to a cruel glint. "Did you realize your father spurned him when he was but an infant? I gave Geoffrey the opportunity to acknowledge Tye as his flesh and blood; he refused. Clearly, Tye's life was— and still is—worth no more to him than a dog's."

Edouard bit his tongue. She was doing her best to provoke him—and succeeding. He wouldn't dare mention the times he'd come upon his sire, holding one of the gloating missives he'd received from her through the years, that told of Tye's conquests in various fairs and tournaments in Normandy; he'd never forget the haunted regret in his sire's expression, quickly shuttered away when he realized Edouard was nearby. "Do not speak for my father," Edouard growled. "What you say—"

"Is the truth. You will come to know just how true my words are. But for now, we must make you . . . secure."

The way her tongue caressed that last word made him queasy. Did she mean to torture him? Force him, through unbearable agony, to betray his father? He'd fight her and Tye every single moment. Until he died.

"Wait a moment." Landon caught her arm. "I am lord of this keep."

Rage sparked in her eyes; since she faced Edouard, Landon wouldn't see it. Then, as though warning herself not to succumb to anger, she smiled at Landon and set her hand atop his. "'Tis all right. I will deal with this matter, for both of us." Her eyelid dropped in a sly wink. "Trust me."

"Do not!" Edouard shouted. "Where is your loyalty to my father? Veronique is a traitor—"

Edouard glimpsed the mercenary's fist flying in his direction, but couldn't dodge it. The blow sent his head snapping to the side, and he gasped.

When he straightened, jaw sore and burning, he

heard Veronique say, "Have I ever betrayed your trust? Have I given you any reason to doubt me?"

"God's blood, Landon!" Edouard growled. He tried to meet Landon's gaze, to persuade him to reject Veronique's manipulations; his lordship refused to look at Edouard.

"I did not expect Edouard to be harmed." Landon's tone roughened. "We did not discuss—"

"We will," she said. "Later." Sliding her body against his, she kissed him on the lips. The intimacy revealed they knew each other well.

God's blood! Did Mayda know of her husband's infidelity? Edouard thought of the embroidered baby blanket he'd brought with him, the one his mother had lovingly worked on for days, and fought rising hatred. How loathsome for Landon to have betrayed Mayda— especially with a traitorous bitch like Veronique—when Mayda had just birthed his child.

"Go now." Veronique nudged Landon. "Why not return to the solar and look for that ring from de Lanceau? I will join you shortly."

"I do not need the ring now, do I?"

"You do not deserve it," Edouard snarled. "I pray you never find it!"

Landon flinched, even as Veronique murmured, "'Tis best to locate it." She smiled, but Edouard saw the tautness around her mouth. "We—I mean, *you*—may need it in coming days."

Dread trailed through Edouard. Veronique had a purpose for that ring, one no doubt linked to her vengeance against his sire. "Landon," he yelled. "If there is any honor left in you—"

The mercenary's fist slammed into Edouard's belly. He grunted and bent over, hauling in breaths, as his surroundings spun. Heedless of his pain, he forced himself to stand upright.

A hint of doubt lingered in Landon's expression, but he nodded to Veronique, spun on his heel, and strode toward the keep.

Her smile smug, Veronique again faced Edouard. "As you see, he will not help you. Neither, by the way, shall any of the folk in this castle. My mercenaries are making certain of that. This keep is mine now."

"Never," Edouard growled, but she merely laughed.

"Your men are being taken to the dungeon, but you . . ." She curled her fingers, as though caught up in heady excitement. "You are safest in the tower."

"Tower?"

"Landon told me that long ago, a lord of this keep imprisoned the lover of his unfaithful wife. The poor man, chained there year after year, lost his wits. Some folks believe his anguished screams can still be heard." She gestured to the thugs behind him. "Take him. Use the chains. When he is restrained, summon me, and I will search him."

A shudder crawled the length of Edouard's spine. She'd run her wretched hands over him? *Nay!*

"What of Juliana?" Tye looked down at her, still unconscious in his arms.

"She needs to be taken to the healer." Edouard struggled as the men forced him to walk. "Her wound—"

Veronique thrust a crooked finger at him. "You have no say in what happens to her."

How he wished he could snatch that finger in his teeth and bite it hard. 'Twould only make this situation worse, though, and Juliana needed care. "However much you hate me," Edouard said, forcing a plea into his voice, "she has no part in the feud between us. She is an innocent. She deserves to live."

Veronique's gaze shifted to Tye. "Take her to the tower. She will stay there until I wish to see her."

Fury boiled up inside Edouard. "She needs a healer!"

Veronique raised her brows, turned her back on him, and walked away.

She became aware of light, glowing at the edge of the darkness. The brightness coaxed, encouraging her to gather her strength. To push through the fog of pain. To rise up from the abyss of oblivion.

Sounds broke into the shadows. Distorted. Close

by. She mentally grabbed for the noises, hungry to understand them.

A woman's voice. Hard. Unyielding.

A man's, taut with frustration.

Edouard's voice.

Hope fluttered up inside her, fragile and needy. Edouard. She remembered his handsome face. The way sunlight had glinted on his unshaven jaw. His gaze, wide and earnest, when he told her who he was. Such beautiful, honest eyes.

An eager cry welled within her. How she longed to see him.

Her eyelids . . . Heavy as rocks. They wouldn't open.

The shadows stirred. They grasped at her, clawed like talons into her hope, tried to drag her back down into the stifling nothingness.

Nay. She mustn't yield.

I am here, Edouard. I will find my way out of the dark. I will find you.

While the mercenaries propelled Edouard across the bailey and into the keep's forebuilding, he tried to note as many details of the fortress's layout as possible, a strategy that would aid his escape. However, despite his best efforts, his focus kept returning to Juliana several steps ahead, her head pillowed on Tye's arm as he carried her to the tower.

Worry left a stark chill inside Edouard, for he still couldn't grasp Veronique's refusal to see to Juliana's injury. How could a woman—a mother—be so merciless? She'd obviously become so embittered by the past, her compassion had shriveled like a rotting apple till it no longer existed.

The men hauled him through the castle's great hall that smelled of musty rushes and wood smoke, down several dark passageways, and then, after more turns, into a narrow stairwell.

The scents of old stone and unwashed warriors crowded in around him as he was forced up the uneven steps. In the cramped space, squashed between brawny assailants, he could barely breathe. Yet he shut out his discomforts, and silently begged Juliana to find the will-power to stay alive, for he'd get her the care she needed, one way or another.

He'd bribe the lackeys who guarded them. He'd trade his fine boots for a pot of salve, and even his horse for a good chance at escape. Veronique might have wrested control here, but surely, someone could be persuaded to help him.

The stairwell twisted up and up until it ended at a wide area in front of a sturdy wooden door banded with iron.

"Here we are." Tye signaled to one of the mercenaries, who unhooked the key from the ring mortared into the wall. He unlocked the door and the panel swung inward, its hinges groaning with disuse.

Tye entered first, and then Edouard was dragged into the small, rectangular chamber with a plank floor. Light pierced the room's shadows through a window fitted with a wrought iron grille and crooked shutters. The room held little furniture: one battered straw pallet and a wooden stool laced with cobwebs.

More spider webs drifted above the window; they teased down to where dust-covered chains, bolted into the wall, trailed across the floor. The chains looked to run half the length of the pallet; enough to allow a man to sit with his back against the stone wall and wrap his arms around his knees, or lie on the pallet with his hands close to his belly, but no more.

When a rough tug brought Edouard closer to the bed, he saw marks were gouged into the stone above it. Cut by fingernails? Or a spoon, taken by the captive during one of his meals? What had he tried to tell his captors, or those who were to be prisoners after him, as he succumbed to madness?

The chamber's lingering atmosphere of despair brought bile flooding into Edouard's mouth. He didn't want to be chained like an animal, prey to his father's enemies. Thrashing against his captors' hold, he glanced about for any chance of escape. No hope of getting out the window, and the door behind him was blocked by Veronique's lackeys.

"Still, ye struggle," one of the men groused. Before Edouard could twist away, the lout slammed a fist into Edouard's lower back. Gasping, arching his spine, he tried to control the pain flaring through his side, but the mercenaries hurled him forward, slammed him face down on the straw-filled pallet, and grabbed his wrists. Dust whipped into Edouard's mouth and nostrils and he coughed, desperate for fresh air.

"Chain him so he lies on his back," Tye said, while the iron links clanked. "Mother would want him that way."

Edouard clenched his hands, unable to move his head pinned against the mattress by a mercenary's leg. The way they planned to restrain him, he'd be facing the door. Able to see whoever came and went, but unable to defend himself if they mistreated him. A loathsome prospect. He struggled anew, thrashing his legs, even as the mercenary increased the pressure on his head. Edouard's mouth and nostrils stung from the dust, while bits of straw poked into his jaw.

Cold metal clamped around his left wrist. The lock engaged with a click, and then, with a brutal shove, the men pushed him onto his back. A mercenary sat on his stomach, pinning him down. Before he could struggle, the right manacle snapped into place.

The men leapt back.

Spitting an oath, Edouard sat upright. As he shoved snarled hair from his face, iron links banged against his right arm.

Tye grinned. "Comfortable, Brother?"

"Do not call me that."

"We *are* kin."

Edouard glowered and wondered how close Tye had to get to the pallet before he could knock him to his arse and wrap his hands around his throat. Regrettably, Tye—the gloating bastard—was staying well away.

"Two of you will stand watch outside," Tye said to the group of men. "There must always be two guards at this chamber. You are not to respond to any cries or attempts to contact you from the prisoners inside. Understood? Now you may leave."

As the mercenaries turned and headed for the doorway, Tye glanced at Juliana, his gaze lingering far longer than was appropriate on her breasts. "Since you are taken care of now, Brother, I must see to other matters. You will, of course, keep watch on Juliana?" His attention shifted to the nearest wall, as though deciding where to set her down.

"Tye, Juliana needs to be tended by the healer. Will you at least send the woman up here, to look at her wound?"

Tye raised his brows. "And risk Mother's wrath for disobeying her?"

"Surely you have some influence with her. You *are* her son."

Wariness touched Tye's eyes. "You have not seen her when she is angry. She can be truly . . ."

Over the tramp of the men's retreating footfalls, Edouard caught the rustle of cloth.

His gaze flew to Juliana, to see her eyes were open. She peered up at Tye, her expression both puzzled and afraid.

"Juliana!" Edouard called, hoping this time she'd know him. He shoved up to standing.

Her head shifted, and she winced. When she saw him, her face brightened. "Edouard," she whispered. "Oh, Edouard, I found you."

Found him? He didn't understand. But to hear her say his name with such affection was wondrous. "Juliana—"

"At last, you have awakened," Tye drawled. "Mother will be pleased."

CHAPTER
10

Veronique set her fingers on the solar's door handle, the thrill of ordering Edouard to his captivity still hot in her blood. She smiled, for as her coveted bag of fortune-telling bones predicted, events were unfolding that would bring about her revenge against Geoffrey. How she longed for that moment when she saw defeat in his eyes. Could she make him beg for mercy? She would.

She mustn't gloat yet, though. There was still much to be done, especially once she had Landon's ring. Her smile faded as she carefully depressed the handle and eased the door open. Before he sensed her entering the chamber, she'd make certain he was doing as she expected: looking for the jewel. If not, she'd correct that misjudgment on his part—in a way he'd never forget.

As the solar's floorboards came into view, Landon's hushed voice carried to her. "—is very important you tell no one. Trust no one. Do you understand?"

"Aye," a woman answered. Azarel, the healer. Holding

the door still, Veronique listened.

Coins clinked. "Here. When you ride out to buy herbs to tend Juliana, take the missive with you. Use this silver and hire a messenger from the village. Tell him this document must reach Geoffrey de Lanceau."

Veronique sucked in a furious breath. Landon thought to *betray* her?

She shoved the door wide, sending it crashing against the wall. Balling her hands into fists, she glided forward into the chamber.

Whirling away from the trestle table, where candles, an ink pot, and quill rested, Landon faced her. "Veronique."

She narrowed her gaze on Azarel. The young woman's eyes looked enormous as she hastily tucked a rolled object inside her sleeve. When she dipped her head, acknowledging Veronique in the manner she demanded of the castle folk, candlelight winked off her hairpin braided with brown leather, secured in her long, blond hair. The strings of dried mushrooms around her neck shifted.

"Give me the missive, Azarel," Veronique said.

Landon stepped sideways, blocking her way to the healer.

"Step aside." Veronique held his stare, commanding him to yield. Caution flickered across his features before he shoved back his shoulders and remained where he was.

"You are a fool, Landon, to anger me."

"What you are doing to Edouard, the son of my

liege . . . 'Tis wrong."

She'd walked near enough now to smell the hint of fear in his sweat. "Have you still not realized, Landon? All of my actions were meant to protect you." Her attention slid past him to the frightened Azarel. "I thought you wanted your subjects to keep believing you are a just, *honorable* lord, rather than a man who murdered his lady wife."

Landon blanched.

Veronique smiled, savoring the tension in his posture. "Did you do as I asked? Did you find the ring?"

"Why do you keep asking for it? Why is it so important to you?"

Insolent bastard. She didn't have to explain her desires to him. "Did you find it?"

"I did not look. Edouard was right; I do not deserve it. Whatever your reasons for wanting that ring"—his mouth flattened—"you shall not have it."

A coarse laugh broke from her. Did he intend his words as a threat? Ridiculous.

She halted before him, close enough to slap his face if she so desired. "You disappoint me, Landon."

Raising his brows—a clear dismissal of her words—he gestured to Azarel. "Go."

The healer started forward.

But Veronique threw up a hand. "Stay where you are."

Azarel stumbled to a halt.

"Veronique does not command you," Landon growled.

"I do." Her lips turned up in a ruthless smile. "Try to leave, Azarel, and I will have you killed. Then, I will send men into the village to find your lover and gut him alive."

The healer moaned. She didn't move.

Veronique forced coyness into her smile and claimed the gap between her and Landon. When their garments brushed, his familiar scent revived memories of him thrusting between her legs; his hoarse groans when his seed pulsed into her; the many ways he'd sated her lust. She'd miss the pleasure he gave her.

Curling her hand into her right sleeve, she found the opening in the hem and discreetly eased out a small knife.

He'd stepped back, no doubt unnerved by her closeness. Reaching out her left hand, she caressed his cheek. Regret glinted in his eyes before he caught her wrist. "I will not let you destroy de Lanceau."

"You cannot stop me," she said, very gently, "for you see, Juliana will tell me where to find that ring."

He stared down at her, as though suddenly realizing his own insignificance.

She rammed the knife into his stomach. How delicious, to feel his soft flesh splitting apart.

Azarel screamed. "Milord!"

He roared in pain, swiped at Veronique, even as she yanked out the dagger. When he bent at the waist, trying to stem the rush of blood, she slammed the knife into his lower back.

The healer shrieked. "Stop! Please."

Landon wheezed. A dark crimson stain oozed across the front of his garments and, when Veronique stabbed him again, he lunged for her. Giggling, she darted out of his reach. With a gurgled groan, he collapsed on the floorboards.

Sobs breaking from her, the healer knelt beside him. The parchment slid from her sleeve as she lifted his tunic to examine his stomach wound. "Milord," she cried, but the life was dimming from his gaze.

Veronique snatched up the parchment. She crossed to the fire and tossed the document into the blaze. Flames licked over it, devoured it.

She spun, to find Azarel pushing to her feet. Tears streaked her face, and her shaking hands were coated in blood.

"He is dead?" Veronique demanded.

Azarel nodded.

"Good. Now, you will do exactly as I say. You will set the coins he gave you on the table. Then find mercenaries to get rid of this body. Do not try to betray me." Veronique trailed a finger along her bloody knife. "If you disobey me, you jeopardize not only your lover's life, but Edouard's and Juliana's, as well."

Fear tingled across her skin like an unwanted caress when she stared up at the dark-haired man who held her in his arms. The bold way he grinned at her left a chill inside her, for she sensed an element of unruliness about him. In his snug hold, she felt . . . vulnerable.

Somewhere close by, men's voices retreated and then a thud echoed—the sound of a door closing. Merciful God, what had taken place earlier, that she'd be shut in a chamber while in this knave's embrace?

Should she know him? A hint of remembrance skittered across her thoughts, and she tried to probe the blankness wrapped around her mind. The inkiness seemed to shift like a murky sludge, to fill in the attempted intrusion with more blackness.

Dull pain settled in her brow. Dizziness taunted, threatening to snatch her consciousness, and when she'd just found Edouard. The dizziness mustn't triumph. In a moment, her head might quit spinning; then she'd try to squirm out of this man's embrace—

"Juliana," he murmured, his voice deeper than Edouard's. "Are you all right?"

"Of course she is not!" Edouard snapped.

This dark-haired man had called her Juliana, too. That must be her name. How, though, did he know her? "W-who are you?" she whispered to him, trying not to heed her headache or the thudding of her pulse.

The man's expression darkened with suspicion. "You know full well who I am. If you are trying to trick me—"

"Nay!" she croaked.

"Enough, Tye," Edouard growled. "'Tis not a deception."

The man named Tye snorted, a sound rife with scorn. "I should trust *your* explanation?"

"I was with her when she first woke. She did not recognize me, despite us having met before. She has lost her memory. Due, I expect, to the blow to her head."

Lost her memory. That would explain a great deal.

"You know who did this to Juliana." Edouard's tone hardened. "Were *you* the one who struck her?"

"As much as you would like to hear me say 'aye,'" Tye answered, "I did not."

"Who did?"

Tye chuckled, but didn't answer.

Juliana sensed Edouard's intense gaze, and carefully turned her head to look at him, standing in a swath of sunlight. His stare held fierce concern, and, when unexpected tears brimmed along her lashes, his eyes widened. He took a step toward her. Metal clanked, drawing her attention to his wrists.

He was chained. A prisoner!

Shock raced through her. Bracing one hand against Tye's shoulder, she scrambled to sit up. Pain scraped down the back of her skull. Tendrils of agony speared through her forehead and neck, before spots swarmed into her vision.

"Careful!" Edouard cried.

Juliana groaned, fighting an upsurge of nausea.

Her vision swam, and then her cheek met solid

warmth: Tye's arm. She'd fallen back into his hold.

"Juliana." Edouard's worried voice called to her, luring her from the edge of that cozy blanket of oblivion. How easily she could slip into it, but that would mean abandoning him. She couldn't, for she had many questions—among them, why he was a captive. What had happened to put him in jeopardy? And what had happened to her? Warning trailed through her, for she had no doubt his imprisonment meant danger for them both.

By sheer willpower, she forced her eyes to open. To find him again.

As their gazes met, he released a rush of breath, a sound that implied she was important to him. A friend. His lover . . .

His Juliana.

If only she could remember what they meant to one another!

He tried to take another forward step, but his chains snapped taut. His muscles bulged beneath the fabric of his tunic, while he scowled at Tye. "She wishes to be free of you. Put her down."

At the possessiveness in his voice, tiny shivers darted through her. *Why* couldn't she remember their relationship? What else didn't she recall that, for her and Edouard's well-being, she really should?

Tye vowed he hadn't wounded her, but he could have held her down whilst someone else hit her. Had

Tye imprisoned Edouard? Was she to be a captive, too, for reasons she didn't even know? Oh, God, nay. She shoved against Tye, forcing herself to fight through her rising pain. "Edouard is right. Set me down."

Tye tsked. "I doubt you can stand upright."

Her body, indeed, felt weak. She'd rather crumple on the floor, though, than spend another moment in this knave's arms.

"Set me down. Please."

Tye's brows raised. Then he eased his arm out from under her knees and lowered her legs to the floorboards.

Her feet brushed the dusty planks. Her wobbly legs took her full weight for one breath. Two—

Her knees folded.

Just as she plummeted to the floor, Tye's arms slid around her waist from behind. "I have you."

Tye drew her back against him, supporting her quivering body with his strength. Dizzy with the effort of standing, she slumped in his hold. When her head landed against his shoulder, she gasped at the spike of pain. Darkness swirled into her mind, beckoning her to yield.

"Juliana!" Edouard shouted. "Stay awake."

For you, Edouard, I will.

She fought the weightiness of her eyelids, focused on the emotions churning inside her to give her strength. How she loathed being dependent upon Tye. Hated the manner in which he held her. His arms shifted; as one swept higher, touching the underside of her breasts, she shuddered.

"Tye," Edouard growled. His fists clenched, causing his chains to rattle, an eerie echo of the laughter rumbling from Tye.

"I would like to sit," she said quickly, gesturing to the wooden stool. That simple movement sent more dizziness rushing through her head. Edouard spoke again, but his words grew fainter, as though she'd plunged through a hole in the floor.

Dragging up the last of her strength, she concentrated on his voice. On the excitement that raced through her when he looked at her with such fire.

"—is fainting!" she heard Edouard say. "Hurry!"

"Edouard," she managed to rasp. Her eyelids fluttered, while she sensed Tye sliding his arm under her knee once again. A rough scrape—the sound of wood grating across wood—carried before cool roughness touched her calves, and an even colder hardness touched her back and head. When the whirling chaos in her head slowed, she realized Tye had set her on the stool and propped her up against the stone wall.

Opening her eyes, she saw him standing beside her with his hands on his hips, studying her as if to see whether she'd stay upright. Her attention slid past him to Edouard, also watching, his expression a touching blend of relief and anxiety.

Holding on to the stool for added support, she

smiled at Edouard. He smiled in return.

Muffled voices sounded from outside the chamber.

A moment later, metal grated. The panel swung inward.

Two armed guards stepped inside, followed by a woman.

As she strolled farther into the room, the strong scent of rosewater drifted to Juliana. Light slipped over the woman's snug-fitting silk gown and red hair that snaked down to her girlishly small waist. Her hips swayed in blatant enticement; her stride also, somehow, conveyed she had a right to command all those around her. Tall, slender, viewed from the back, she might be mistaken for a much younger woman. Her severe features, however, bore evidence of her years in the faint lines about her eyes and mouth. Most telling were her hands, for her fingers were swollen and bent with age.

"Hello, Mother," Tye said.

Juliana fought light-headedness and a rush of foreboding. This newcomer was Tye's mother. A lady, judging by her gown; 'twould explain her imposing manner.

"All is in order, Tye?" she demanded.

"Aye. I was about to come find you and update you on the situation."

The woman halted several steps from Edouard. As her keen gaze traveled over him, she grinned. "What a pleasure to see you again, Edouard."

Disdain threaded through her words, and Edouard's features tautened. He looked truly formidable. Whoever this lady was, he despised her. "Are my men all right?" he demanded. "Unharmed? Their wounds tended?"

"They are well enough, I expect." Then, as though sensing Juliana's stare, the woman looked right at her.

The force of the lady's piercing, amber gaze made Juliana gasp. Her hands, on either side of the stool, clenched the rough-hewn wood.

"So, Juliana," the woman said. "You are awake."

This woman recognized her. Addressed her by her first name. Juliana's fingers tightened to a painful grip. What relation was this lady to her?

"Juliana roused only moments ago, Mother," Tye said. "I planned to inform you, when I found you."

The older woman's stare sharpened. "What did she tell you?"

"Naught. It appears she has lost her memory."

Panic quickened Juliana's heartbeat, for the lady's expression had turned menacing. Why? What had taken place between Juliana and this woman? Juliana pressed a hand to her throbbing, sweat-beaded brow, for her instincts screamed for her to beware.

Flexing her hands, the woman advanced on Juliana.

"Leave her alone, Veronique!" Edouard bellowed.

This lady was called Veronique? A flicker of alarm sped through Juliana's thoughts, a sense that the name should be important to her. As fast as the warning flared, it dissipated, swallowed by the greater pressure of blankness.

Fear, as icy as a ball of snow, pressed against Juliana's breastbone. Silk rustled as Veronique neared, teeth bared in a smirk. "Juliana is fooling you, Tye, with her expressive eyes and beauty. She remembers *all*." She thrust a gnarled finger in Juliana's face. "As soon as you have the chance, you intend to betray us."

Juliana shook her head, and the room whirled before her. Shoving back against the wall, she tried to stand, but her limbs gave way. She fell back down on the stool.

"Do I frighten you?" Veronique cackled, near enough now for Juliana to see the crimson smear on her silk sleeve. Blood. From what . . . or whom? "You were afraid the last time we spoke," Veronique continued. "You should be terrified now, because—"

"Leave. Her. *Alone*," Edouard roared.

"Patience, Edouard. You shall have your turn with me."

Unshed tears stung Juliana's eyes as she wrenched her gaze from Veronique's bloodstained sleeve. How brave of Edouard to try and spare her from this woman. Yet part of Juliana desperately wanted to know the situation Veronique spoke of.

"Your battle is with me," Edouard went on. "Not her."

"Not true." Veronique smirked. "Go on, Juliana. Tell him, if you have not already."

"I . . . cannot remember." She trembled, but she had to ask the question gnawing inside her. "What *did* happen?"

Veronique's eyes widened, before she loosed a shrill

laugh. "You are either very brave or completely witless."

Tye grunted. "I told you she lost her memory."

"Because of you, no doubt, Veronique." Edouard's chains clattered. "Tye insists he did not injure her. Did you?"

Veronique smiled as she turned around. A giddy breath whooshed from Juliana; she'd won a reprieve for now. When the older woman reached into her sleeve, though, and drew out a knife, Juliana's stomach roiled. Was she going to spill more blood?

Edouard's blood?

"What happened to Juliana is not your concern right now," Veronique said to him.

"Why not?"

She strolled toward him, the dagger in plain view. "I did not come to this chamber to discuss her. Only you."

"Me?" His throat moved with a swallow. He didn't step back, or otherwise acknowledge the threat the older woman posed, but Juliana saw tension creeping into his features.

Veronique halted before Edouard, just beyond his reach. "I looked through your saddlebag but didn't find much of interest. However, as we both know, you would keep your most important possessions close to you." Her gaze wandered over him. "I cannot take the risk you have weapons or documents concealed in your . . ."—her stare focused on his groin—"clothes."

"Hellfire," Edouard growled. "You are *not*—"

"You must be searched. I will undertake the task myself."

CHAPTER
11

Edouard forced down an oath as Veronique's fingers shifted on the dagger's hilt. He could only imagine what her search would entail, the intimate violations she'd force upon him in front of the mercenaries, Tye, and, most importantly, Juliana.

He dared not look at Juliana, although she'd gasped in horror a moment ago. He couldn't risk Veronique glimpsing his fear of humiliation. If she saw, she'd know how to control him; he wouldn't disappoint himself, or his father, by revealing weakness.

"What would Landon say about your searching me? 'Tis his keep. He is responsible for every person within its walls, including prisoners."

"Not any longer." Her mouth twisted in a nasty grin. "He is dead."

"You killed him?" Shock thinned Edouard's voice. He'd thought she depended upon Landon to keep her influence over the servants, but mayhap, if she had enough mercenaries, she no longer needed him. That meant she must also have the ring entrusted to Landon by Edouard's father.

God's blood, Edouard had to know for certain. If she possessed that jewel, she had all she needed to get close to his sire and murder him; she'd kill Edouard, too, and thus remove any impediment to her and Tye controlling Moydenshire. Without doubt, a woman as corrupt as Veronique knew exactly what to offer King John so her and Tye's conquest wouldn't be challenged.

Bracing himself for her gleeful cackle, Edouard asked, "Landon gave you the ring, then?"

Sighing, she shook her head. "He became willful."

Relief coursed through Edouard. Before he left Waddesford, he'd find that ring; she must never get hold of it.

"I will find it myself," Veronique said, before she gestured to her blood-darkened sleeve—blood that wasn't yet dry. "A shame that he tried to send word to your father about your capture. I could not allow it."

Landon had tried to save him. A tremor tore through Edouard, tightening the sickening pressure in his chest. Whatever wrongs Ferchante had committed in recent days, he'd died with some honor.

Would Veronique kill him, also, for her perverse amusement? Or did she need Edouard alive, to bargain with his sire for his life? Either way, she still might mutilate him.

He steeled himself against the revulsion crawling

like invisible ants over his skin. He'd cooperate as long as it took for him to gain an advantage. After that, he'd do all he could to gain his and Juliana's freedom. He'd brought her into this danger; he'd get her safely out.

"Now," Veronique murmured, "to the reason I am here—"

"I hope you will not send me and Juliana away." Tye leaned against the wall near Juliana. "This search could be entertaining."

Only for you, bastard.

A scraping sound drew Edouard's gaze to Juliana. One hand pressed to the wall, she rose on unsteady legs, face ashen. "W-what are you going to do to him?"

"As Mother said, search him."

Fear flickered across Juliana's features. "Why does she have the knife?"

Because she's a cruel bitch, who enjoys inflicting pain.

"To protect herself. You see, Edouard has a violent nature. 'Tis why he is chained."

Edouard snorted. He sensed the bloodlust coursing through Veronique, saw it in the eerie brightness of her eyes. She longed to cut him. She couldn't hurt his sire, thus she'd take out her twisted revenge upon him.

"Edouard does not seem violent." Juliana sounded bewildered—lost, even—and his heart ached for her.

A throaty laugh broke from Veronique before she glanced back at Tye. "How little she knows about

Edouard." She motioned to the pair of mercenaries looking on. "Stay close. I will need your help."

"Aye, milady," the men said.

Milady? She was a bold wench!

"Tye, I want you here, too, in case your brother needs some persuasion." Veronique's gaze slid to Juliana, then back to Tye.

With a lopsided grin, he nodded.

The ghastly tightness within Edouard intensified. If they didn't get what they wanted from him, they'd hurt Juliana? Not if he had any choice in the matter. Fisting his hands, he waited for the assault to begin.

Veronique nodded to the mercenaries. "Hold him."

Metal rasped, the sound of knives being unsheathed. He stepped back, slackening his chains to give him more range of movement, but the mercenaries hastily advanced. He swung at the lout on his right, but the other man darted behind him, wrapped his brawny arm around Edouard's neck, and forced his head back. Pain shot through Edouard's neck, pinned at an unnatural angle, while the back of his head pressed to the mercenary's shoulder.

"Edouard!" Juliana cried.

Knives pressed against his neck: one on the left, the other on the right. Spittle rasped from Edouard's lips. How he wished to break his chains and give these lackeys a proper fight.

"Careful, Edouard." The scent of rosewater threat-ened to choke him as Veronique sidled closer. "Juliana does not want to see you hurt."

Juliana was quietly weeping. Her anguish gouged at his defiance—as, no doubt, Veronique hoped. To think Juliana cared for him that much . . . . He *couldn't* dwell upon that at the moment. He must focus only on the danger.

Forced to look up at the wooden trusses overhead, Edouard struggled to glance sideways at Veronique. Her amber eyes glittered beneath the fall of her lashes as she halted beside him, then breathed out a thoughtful sigh. Her gaze glided from his mouth, to his jaw, to his throat where he felt his pulse leaping in a wild rhythm, then down to his chest.

"Mother," Tye muttered. "Beware."

"He will not hurt me." Veronique's breath warmed Edouard's cheek as she leaned in and trailed the fingers of her left hand along his jaw. "He knows better than to try."

How tempted he was to kick her; his legs, after all, were unfettered. The knives were so close to his skin, though, he'd be cut. Then Veronique might turn her dagger on Juliana, just to spite him.

Refusing to acknowledge Veronique's taunting laugh, he remained still. Remote. Emotionally detached . . .

Her fingers brushed the front of his tunic, over his belly.

He jolted, unable to control the instinctive reaction. One of the knives pierced his skin and he winced; sticky warmth moistened his neck.

"He is bleeding!" Juliana shrieked.

"A small cut. Not deadly." Veronique clucked her tongue. "Look what you have done, Edouard."

"What *you* have done," Edouard snapped.

"Please, stop." Juliana moaned. "Surely there is another way to search him."

"Mmm," Veronique purred, her hand moving again, even as Tye spoke to Juliana, words Edouard couldn't hear. Again Veronique touched his stomach, this time in a probing caress. Was she looking for a weapons belt strapped beneath his tunic? She wouldn't find one.

Her lashes lowered a fraction, and then her palm slipped beneath his tunic to touch his bare skin. A shudder rippled through him, and she smiled. Her palm slid up his belly to the indent between his ribs, then to his shoulders, as though memorizing his physical form.

"You are a strong man," she breathed, while her hand continued to explore. "Such large muscles. You have spent long days practicing swordplay."

Edouard gritted his teeth.

"Your body is akin to your father's, when he was younger."

Did she expect him to respond to that statement? She likely wanted to tell him, in sordid detail, how she'd pleasured his sire when she was his lover. But Edouard had no wish to hear that, or invite more of her taunts. Thus, he kept quiet, despite her fingernails biting into his chest.

Her hand slid out from under his tunic, then grabbed a fistful of it. Leaning forward to nibble his chin, she said, "Let us see just how much you resemble your father."

The straw pallet shifted at Edouard's feet. Veronique disappeared from his view.

She'd dropped down in front of him.

He tensed. What was she planning to do?

The mercenary behind him snickered.

Nausea welled inside Edouard, even as he felt her hands lifting up the hem of his tunic to bare his hose underneath. He fought the urge to flinch. Never had he felt so naked.

"Well, now," Veronique said, and Edouard felt her gaze upon his privates. He swallowed, closed his eyes, anticipated her groping touch—

"Stop," Juliana cried. "What you are doing . . . 'Tis not right!"

"Shut her up, Tye," Veronique snarled.

"I swear to you," Edouard growled, "if he hurts her—"

Juliana shrieked.

If only he could see what was happening!

"You will not hurt him," she sobbed, her voice ragged and desperate. "You will not."

Edouard's gut twisted. "Juliana!"

A scuffle. A gasp.

Silence.

170

"Juliana?" Fear pounded at Edouard's temples.
"Answer me."

On her knees on the pallet, Veronique glared at her son,
standing a few paces from the wooden stool. Her gaze
shifted to Juliana, slumped forward in Tye's arms that
encircled her waist from behind. She looked as boneless—and lifeless—as a toy.

"What has happened to Juliana?" Edouard demanded.

"She just . . . collapsed," Tye said. "When she struggled, and seemed unsteady on her feet, I tried to get her
to sit down—"

Veronique spat a curse. "All I asked was that you keep
her quiet. We need her alive." With Landon dead, Juliana
was the only one who might know the whereabouts
of the jewels Mayda hid, including the gold ring from
Geoffrey—when, that is, Juliana's memories returned.

If she died . . .

Tye huffed, an expression of annoyance. "I did my
best, Mother."

His best. Wretched child. He'd do his best when
he finally killed his father and brought about the life she
expected for them both.

"Fetch the healer," Edouard said. "If you want
Juliana to live, you need to treat her, as soon as possible."

What arrogance, for him to issue orders, especially when he was a prisoner. He was right, though, about Juliana. If she died, that ring might never be found.

Concern tingled through Veronique's mind, even as her focus returned to the tantalizing swells and outlines beneath Edouard's hose. She stifled a frustrated groan and stood, ignoring the pop of her aging joints.

Edouard's gaze locked with hers. Relief shone in his eyes, before they narrowed with hatred.

A mocking chuckle welled in her throat. "Another day, Edouard, I will have my way with you." She looked at the two mercenaries. "Finish searching him. Bring whatever you find to the solar."

"And Juliana?" Edouard asked.

Turning her back on him, she scowled at Tye. "Take her to the solar. Watch over her, while I find Azarel."

Juliana woke slowly. Her foggy mind discerned she lay face down in a shadowed, warm place, cheek resting on downy softness. Trying to sharpen her perceptions, she inhaled a deep breath. She smelled . . . roses.

Her mind raced, memories galloping one after another. The sun-drenched chamber. Edouard in chains. Veronique tormenting him.

Juliana's whole body jolted, and she shoved up on

her forearms, causing whatever she lay upon to creak. Dizziness turned her surroundings into a blur of dark shadows. Blinking several times, she forced her whirling mind to steady.

A skein of hair had tumbled over her cheek. When she slipped her tresses behind her ear, she realized they felt soft, not thick with grime. Drawing a fistful of hair to her face, she inhaled, and caught the hint of lavender.

Unease trailed through her. Someone had washed her hair. Glancing down at her arm, she noted her chemise wasn't mud-stained, but snowy white. Her skin, too, was scrubbed clean.

What else had taken place while she was unconscious?

A lump lodged in her throat as she looked about her surroundings. She reclined on a wide, rope bed in a chamber far larger than the one where Edouard was imprisoned. In the darkness to her left, she saw a doorway to an adjoining room. An antechamber?

A sudden awareness nudged at her consciousness. The antechamber was familiar to her. Why?

The sputter of a candle drew her gaze to the nearby trestle table cluttered with pots and other items. When she glanced farther down the room, she saw the wooden shutters at the window were closed against the daylight, and a low fire glowed in the hearth. Veronique crouched by the flames, poking at the embers to start burning new logs.

When she stood, Juliana dropped her head back down upon the coverlet. Closing her eyes, she feigned sleep.

Silk rasped as Veronique approached the table. A soft thud: she'd dropped a cloth item on the tabletop. Then she muttered under her breath, before a hollow clatter echoed, the sound of small, hard objects landing on the wood.

Juliana dared to open her eyes a little. Vivid red hair flowing down her back, Veronique peered at the tabletop. Muttering again, she ran her hand over the wood to gather up whatever lay upon it.

She stilled, fingers curling into a fist. Her head turned, a gesture that not only implied she sensed Juliana watching, but that she'd expected Juliana to rouse.

"'Tis good to see you awake."

For a fleeting moment, Juliana thought of pretending to still be asleep, but Veronique was too clever to be fooled by such a ruse. Opening her eyes, Juliana pushed up to a sitting position.

"What place is this?" she asked.

"The solar."

"Why have you brought me here? What have you done to Edouard?"

Veronique chuckled. "So many questions."

Questions Juliana wanted answered. The last moment she saw Edouard, he stood with knives against his neck, forced by Veronique into indignity. Ignoring the cautioning cry inside her, Juliana said, "Is he all right? That much you must tell me."

Veronique faced the bed, and the full force of her piercing gaze settled upon Juliana. She scooted toward the edge of the mattress, fighting the spinning in her head and an awful sense of entrapment. As Juliana swung her legs over the edge, Veronique strolled forward, closing the distance between them.

"Calm yourself, Juliana. I will not harm you."

The lump in her throat hardened. "How can I be certain?"

A smile curved Veronique's painted mouth. "I had the healer care for you while you slept. She bathed you, washed your hair, dressed you in a clean chemise, and tended your wound."

"Th-thank you, for arranging such."

"I was glad to do so, for I am not your enemy, Juliana. I am your friend."

Juliana pressed her lips together. She might not remember her past association with Veronique, but she knew, purely by instinct, that this woman wasn't, and never had been, her friend.

As though attuned to Juliana's unease, Veronique said gently, "How is your head?"

"A little better. Thank you." *Liar*, Juliana's conscience shrilled. Indeed, she'd be standing now, on a level with Veronique, if her head didn't pound like a drum.

Still, if Veronique thought her well enough, would

she let her return to Edouard?

"Juliana, do you remember the first time we met?"

"The chamber where Edouard is chained."

Suspicion filtered into Veronique's gaze. "We had met before then."

"I . . ." Juliana struggled to recall. The blankness in her mind refused to yield. "I do not . . . remember." Disquiet coursed through her, for there must be a reason for Veronique's question. "What took place, at our first meeting? I would like to know."

A hard gleam lit Veronique's eyes. "This chamber. Do you remember it?"

"It seems familiar—"

"Aye?" Veronique leaned forward, as though to snatch each word.

"Yet I do not know why."

"You lived here for many months. You were Lady Ferchante's closest friend."

Juliana frowned and took another glance about the room. That explained the sense of familiarity, but not the feeling that something was . . . wrong. "Why is she not here now? May I see her? Mayhap, if I speak with her . . ."

"She is dead."

"Dead," Juliana whispered. Her mind shot back to the blood on Veronique's sleeve. She'd killed the lord of his keep; had she murdered the lady, too?

"Surely you remember the night she perished."

Veronique's words held a distinct edge. "You were there. You saw."

"I did?" Juliana trembled. Her ladyship's death . . . 'Twas clear from Veronique's tone Juliana should remember the crucial event. But she didn't. Oh, God, *she didn't!*

Veronique reached out and smoothed a hand down Juliana's hair. "I did not mean to upset you. I know 'tis difficult, not remembering your past. The healer, however, believes your wound will heal and your memories will return."

Juliana fought the revulsion roused by Veronique's caress. She didn't dare wrench away.

"Since we are friends, Juliana, I will do all I can to help you heal and reclaim your past. I trust, in exchange, you will help me?"

"H-how?"

Veronique's fingers slid under Juliana's chin, tilting it up so their gazes met. "When your memories return, you will tell me right away. Agreed?"

"My memories . . . are important to you?"

"Some of them, aye. They will help forge the days ahead." A cackle broke past her lips and Juliana fought a shudder. What knowledge could she possibly have that would influence the future?

"Agreed?" Veronique said again.

If she said nay, would Veronique refuse to treat her wound? How very much Juliana wanted to remember who she was. To be complete again. "A-all right."

"Good." Veronique's hand dropped from Juliana's face. A muffled clatter, a sound akin to what Juliana had heard earlier, came from the shifting of Veronique's curled fingers. A hard intensity tightened the older woman's features, a look that suggested she saw beyond Juliana's answer to the coming days.

Curiosity nagged, stronger than Juliana's inner warning to beware. "How can you know," she asked carefully, "what might take place in the days ahead?"

Veronique's stare focused when it returned to her. "Circumstances surrounding me and my son Tye have been unfolding for years. Those, I know well. I also have these." She threw out her arm and objects scattered on the coverlet with a soft *tap, tap, tap.*

Bones. Bleached white, polished, and of various sizes. They looked to be the size and shape of . . . Juliana's hand flew to her mouth. Surely not.

"Human bones," Veronique said. "Fingers, cut from prisoners in a French dungeon. They are so beautiful and straight."

"W-why—?" Juliana couldn't find her voice. The nearest bone lay near her hip and she edged sideways, hoping the shifting mattress wouldn't bring the vile object even closer.

"Why were the fingers taken?" Veronique picked up a bone and trailed her bent finger over it in a reverent

caress. "These belonged to criminals, the most treacherous of villains. They would not tell the French king's
warriors what they were entitled to know. So the king's
loyal subjects had no choice but to start cutting off the
prisoners' fingers—one by one—to get the information."

The men were tortured. Juliana could only imagine
the terror and suffering the captives must have endured
as the fingers were severed, which made Veronique's possession of the bones even more grotesque.

"How did you get these bones? W-why would you
want them?"

"Tye and I were living in Normandy, close to the
prison. I knew several of the king's men"—she grinned—
"intimately. When I asked one of them about the finger
bones, he gave me a bag full."

"He—?" Juliana choked down a moan.

"I took them to an old crone who lived outside the
town," Veronique went on, clearly ignoring Juliana's distress. "She cured them and showed me how to interpret
them." Not the slightest remorse touched her expression
as she looked at the haphazard arrangement of bones. "I
ask a question of them. The way they fall reveals to me
what will happen."

"To . . . me?"

Veronique's gaze flickered. "Not just you. Tye.
Edouard. Tell me, what do you know of him?"

Juliana shook her head. "Edouard said we met last

spring. I do not recall." A blush warmed her face. "I intend to ask him, though, what he remembers about me, and who I am."

The impassioned way Edouard looked at her, and the way her heart answered . . . They must have been lovers. They'd kissed, held hands, and made promises of love. That would explain the breathless excitement inside her every time she looked at him.

Veronique began gathering up the bones. "Beware, Juliana, of thinking kindly about Edouard. He will win your trust and then crush it. He is a deceitful bastard, just like his father."

The older woman spat the word "father" with such ferocity, Juliana wondered what had taken place between them. Of all the people she'd met since she woke, though, Edouard seemed the most honest and compassionate. "Edouard seems so gallant," she insisted.

Veronique snorted. "'Tis what he wants you to think. Once he has won your trust, he will ask you to help him escape. He insists he cares for you only because he needs your help."

Could the Edouard she knew be that callous? "Why is Edouard in chains? What crime did he commit?"

Veronique's hand brushed Juliana's hair again. Those same fingers had held and cast the bones of tortured men. Shivering, Juliana turned her head to break the contact.

"There are too many of Edouard's transgressions to recount," the older woman said, picking up more bones and dropping them into her palm. "Above all, he will never accept that his half brother, Tye, is deserving of his father's acknowledgment and riches."

Juliana pressed a hand to her head which had begun to ache anew. Edouard and Tye were siblings? She'd sensed the hatred between the two men, but never had she guessed they were related by blood.

If, that is, Veronique spoke the truth.

Her account, however, was the only insight Juliana had into what was happening at this keep, and her part in all of it; she must find out all she could.

"Edouard is jealous of Tye, then?"

"Exactly. He will do all he can to prevent Tye from one day inheriting what he is due. Did you realize Edouard came here to kill Tye? To eliminate the threat he poses?"

Juliana gasped. "Surely not."

"He planned to murder me, too."

"Why?" Juliana couldn't stifle her shock.

"I am Tye's mother. That alone makes me a threat to Edouard and his despicable family."

"I . . . see." Juliana didn't. Not at all. Surely, Edouard wouldn't kill someone just because they were a bastard child's mother. There must be more to the situation than Veronique wished to divulge. When she had a chance, Juliana would ask Edouard about the older woman's allegations.

"I know 'tis a lot for you to consider, especially when you are wounded. But—"

A knock sounded on the chamber door.

Veronique smiled. "Ah. Enter," she called.

The door opened with a creak, letting in torch-light from the outside passageway. A slim, blond-haired woman, who looked about Juliana's age, stepped in, car-rying a wooden tray. Her waist-length hair, tied back in a loose braid, swayed against the back of her brown woolen gown as she shut the door behind her and then headed toward Veronique.

"Azarel," Veronique said before glancing at Juliana. "The healer."

For the briefest moment, Juliana caught the woman's gaze. "Thank you."

Azarel nodded before her gaze dropped to the floor. Either she was afraid of spilling what was on the tray, or she feared Veronique. As she came close, Juliana tried to make out the design of Azarel's necklace. Not clay beads, but various kinds of dried mushrooms, strung onto twine. Several were the same color as the decora-tive hairpin in Azarel's tresses.

The healer hesitated a few steps from the bed. The objects on the tray were clear to Juliana now: an earth-enware mug, one large and one small covered pot, and a wooden spoon. A peculiar, earthy scent wafted; it reminded Juliana of crushed leaves and wet rocks.

"Did you prepare the potion as I asked?" Veronique demanded.

"A-aye, milady. I brought honey to add sweetness, if needed. I-I also finished the facial cream for you, as you commanded."

"Hand it to me." Veronique took the small pot from the healer and strode to the trestle table. "Set the tray on the coverlet, Azarel. Stay here and wait till Juliana has drunk the potion."

Azarel moved to the bedside and, with a slight tremble to her hands, set the tray beside Juliana.

"What is this drink?" Juliana tried not to sound leery.

"'Tis a calming draught to lessen your pain." Veronique set down the cream pot. After opening up a cloth bag, she poured the bones inside and drew the drawstring. "Go on. Drink it."

Juliana clasped her sweaty hands together. Truth be told, she'd rather endure the pain than ingest that concoction. "I will manage."

"Please, Juliana, do not be difficult," Veronique went on. "Not after Azarel toiled to make that drink for you. What would Edouard say if he knew you refused the healer's care? He was so insistent that you be properly looked after."

Edouard. Juliana's heart constricted and she looked

again at the brew. If it healed her wound, and helped re-vive her memories, she must drink it. She wanted to be well again, for him.

The potion lurked in the mug; the brownish liq-uid reminded Juliana of a brackish pond. She quickly lifted the mug to her lips and sipped. The liquid sluiced onto her tongue. It tasted as it smelled: earthy and raw. Tipping her head back, she downed the rest and, after wiping her lips, set the vessel back on the tray.

"Well done," Veronique murmured. "I expect you will feel better very soon." Setting aside the bone bag, she smoothed her hands over her gown and started toward the bed.

An eerie tingle swept through Juliana. Was she imagining it, or were her fingers starting to feel numb? She flexed them. "What herbs are used in that brew?" Juliana gestured to Azarel's mushrooms. "Did you use any of those in—?"

The shadows in the room were growing fuzzy. She blinked. The inkiness was starting to creep in upon her.

"Why . . . ?" Juliana managed to say, before her tongue became . . . heavy, akin to a . . . small pillow in her mouth. Her mind, too . . . was sluggish. Stagnant.

"Take her other arm," Veronique said, sounding far away.

Hands . . . upon her. Pressing . . . her onto the bed.

Juliana groaned. And then, the shadows rushed in upon her.

CHAPTER 12

Veronique leaned over Juliana, lying on her side on the bed. The young woman slept deeply, eyelids still, jaw relaxed. A grin curved Veronique's lips. Azarel had done exactly as asked.

But of course she would have. Azarel was a gentle soul. The threat of harm to Edouard and especially her friend Juliana—although Juliana, because of her memory loss, no longer recognized Azarel—was more than enough to convince the healer to make the pain potion a higher potency than normal.

"You may go," Veronique said, not bothering to look at Azarel. "Take the tray."

"Of course, milady."

Veronique continued to hover, waiting until the chamber door closed. Then she exhaled a slow breath as she stretched out a gnarled hand and swept it down Juliana's glossy tresses, drawing out strands to play over the coverlet. Years ago, when Veronique was younger and Geoffrey's courtesan, she'd had hair that beautiful. Geoffrey had enjoyed running his fingers through it and for her to wear it loose and flowing.

Her jaw hardened on a stab of resentment as she studied Juliana's face. Smooth, dewy skin. A delicate nose. Full mouth. Her gaze moved down Juliana's slender neck to the swell of her firm breasts, then lower, to her belly and hips. The loose chemise didn't conceal her beauty. No wonder Edouard desired her. Oh, aye, there was no doubt of it. She'd seen the yearning in his eyes, even though she'd heard he was betrothed to Juliana's younger sister.

Tye, also, lusted for Juliana. This unexpected complication made her fate even more interesting. For two brothers who hated each other to want the same woman made for fascinating sport.

Tye, however, mustn't lose his focus. Naught must interfere with his destiny to kill his sire and seize the de Lanceau empire. Edouard? Veronique smirked. Despite his noble breeding, he was still a man with carnal needs. If offered the right persuasion—a clean, beautiful, sweetly scented Juliana—he might not be able to resist her.

Imagine the dishonor that would befall his respected family, if he, the heir of Moydenshire's lord and a soon-to-be-married man, ruined the sister of his betrothed while being held captive. Even if Veronique ended up killing Edouard, she had ways to make sure that the scandal was well known.

How disappointed Geoffrey would be in Edouard. And the anguish the disgrace would cause the de Lanceau family? Wondrous!

Veronique trailed her fingertip down Juliana's cheek. "If only you knew what lay ahead—"

"Mother."

Veronique started. She whirled to squint at Tye, standing barely three steps away. She looked past him to the chamber door. Closed. That meant he'd entered and crossed the planks without her hearing. "When did you come in?" Veronique scowled. "Did you knock?"

Tye grinned. "As Azarel left, I stepped inside. You were so engrossed, I decided not to interrupt. We both know you do not like your concentration disturbed."

True. The boy did have some sense, after all.

Walking to the bedside, Tye frowned. "Is she all right?"

Veronique smothered a smile. How quaint, that he was concerned. "She is sleeping."

Tye snorted. "You drugged her."

"To help with her healing."

"Rather ironic that you are determined to save her, when days ago you wanted her dead."

Veronique's lips tightened at the derision in his tone. Did he believe he'd won the right to challenge her decisions? He hadn't.

"As you well know, circumstances have changed

since days ago," she said. "We need her to survive, at least long enough to recall where Mayda stowed those jewels. I searched the solar myself earlier and could not find them. We do not have much coin left, you and I," Veronique added. "I plan to sell the jewels left in Landon's belongings, but with him dead, we need that money to pay the mercenaries to keep our position here secure."

Tye nodded. "A wise strategy."

"Once we have Mayda's jewels, we can hire more mercenaries. You will need an army of warriors to fight at your side you when you conquer your sire's holdings. With Landon's ring in our possession—"

"We will devise a plan for me to kill my father, so I can seize power in Moydenshire."

"Exactly." Veronique winked. "How well you learn."

A tautness crept into Tye's features. "Does that mean, then, we do not need Edouard alive? If we get the ring and lure Father into a trap . . ."

"Edouard cannot die yet." Veronique plucked a fallen, red hair from her sleeve. "I want Geoffrey to suffer. I want him to know the life of his beloved heir is *mine*, to do with as I please. That Edouard is as worthless to me as you are to your father." She giggled, barely able to hold back her delight. "I have already sent a missive to Branton Keep, detailing that Edouard is my hostage and Geoffrey must surrender all to us. He will be devastated."

"Will he?" Tye didn't look convinced. "Father's

spies will soon alert him we can be found at Waddesford, if they have not done so already. He will not negotiate; he will send his army to crush us."

Veronique rolled her eyes, as if she spoke with a dim-witted child. "If so, our mercenaries will defend us. In truth, 'tis all the better if he comes here. We will kill Edouard while Geoffrey watches, helpless to stop us. You"—she patted Tye's cheek—"will then cut down your sire."

"I will still have the gold ring," Tye said, clearly following the progression of her thoughts. "'Twill win me audiences with the loyal knights and lords who paid fealty to him, allowing me to murder them, too." He paused, and his gaze slid to Juliana, still slumbering. "If all unfolds as planned."

"Why would it not?" Veronique held his gaze, excitement seething inside her like a murky brew. "All that we need to succeed is within our grasp. I promise, you will have your long awaited chance to kill your father."

He stood silent a moment.

She waited, ready to crush his hesitation if he didn't seem convinced.

But his lips curved into a dark smile. "When I slay my sire, he will see the loathing on my face." Rage glinted in Tye's eyes. "He will know how much I resented his cruel rejection of me years ago. By my sword, I will *take* my right to be a de Lanceau."

"You will."

Tye growled. "Tell me of the day he spurned me."

She waved a dismissive hand. "I have told you often enough—"

"Tell me again. Now," Tye demanded. His fisted hands shook.

Touching her face, Veronique hid an elated grin. For him to be this rankled proved he would, indeed, pursue the destiny she'd prepared him for since he was a squalling babe. "That day took place years ago, when you were a little boy," she said, her thoughts slipping back to the past. "I wanted your father to know about you, but since I was not sure how he would react to the news, I arranged a meeting in a meadow where he could not launch a surprise assault. He arrived with armed men. He looked coldly upon me, holding you in my arms. Even when I told him you were his son, proof of the passion we had enjoyed in his bed at Branton Keep, he remained unmoved."

Tye scowled.

"He did not believe me," she went on, bitterness souring her tone. "He said another of my lovers was as likely to be your father."

The fury in Tye's gaze intensified. "Not once did he convey the slightest doubt."

For a fleeting instant, he did, before he regained control of his emotions. "Nay," she answered.

"Yet you are certain Geoffrey de Lanceau is my father."

"I am. I was faithful to him. After he cast me aside, I did not take a lover for many days." She pressed a gnarled hand to her bosom. "I tried to make him listen, Tye, but he accused me of attempting to manipulate him. He ordered me to put you down and surrender to him, to be punished for my past crimes." She managed to bring tears to her eyes. "I sensed he meant to murder us both. Then he'd no longer have to explain us to his noble family or think about his responsibility to you."

Tye cursed, a frightening sound. "I never imagined him a man to slaughter a child."

In truth, your gallant father was concerned you might be harmed, a voice inside her answered. *But you need not know that.*

"I refused to heed him," she said firmly.

Instead, Tye, I goaded him with promises you'd grow up to destroy him.

"I refused to put you down and lose you forever," she insisted.

Why would I, when your body shielded me from his warriors' weapons?

"Protecting your life was all that was important to me."

Because, Tye, you are destined to succeed where I failed. You will kill Geoffrey de Lanceau and bring a new legacy to Moydenshire.

"I am surprised, Mother, you were able to elude my

father that day."

She touched her son's arm, feeling hard, corded muscles through the fabric of his sleeve. How keenly she felt the anger toward his father seething within him. *Good.* Just as she wanted.

"'Twas not easy to get away," she said quietly, "but I had paid mercenaries to protect us. They fought your sire and his men while we escaped."

I held the knife at your throat, Tye, and threatened to hurt you. That allowed us to get away.

"I thank you, Mother, for risking your life to save me. Without you"—Tye's visage hardened with loathing—"I might not be alive. How much I look forward to slaying my wretched father."

She smiled. "*Naught* will stand in the way of our conquest of Moydenshire."

Tye's blazing gaze returned to the bed. "Naught, that is, but the lovely Juliana."

The lovely Juliana, a voice inside her mocked. It didn't matter if Tye admired her beauty. Juliana was but a means to their victory; once she'd helped them find the hidden jewels, Veronique would have her killed. Whether Tye agreed or not.

"What is to happen to Juliana now?" Tye asked. "Will she stay here in the solar?"

A wicked laugh broke from Veronique. "Your brother must be lonely by now. Take her to the tower.

Mayhap he can help awaken her memories."

His boots firmly planted into the pallet, Edouard yanked on the chain attached to his right wrist. With a metallic clink, the links jerked taut, jolting his shoulder and sending white-hot pain through the tendons of his arm. Ignoring the metal biting into his wrist, he glanced back down to the chain's end, secured to an iron ring bolted into the wall; a little more grit floated down to the planks, but the bolts held firm.

He groaned, rubbed his throbbing shoulder, and let his arm fall to his side. How many times had he tried to free the chain? Ten? Fifteen? He'd thought—hoped—that he'd be able to loosen it from the aging stonework. Anger at his captivity and worry for Juliana had driven him to fight for that freedom. However, he'd made no progress. The day was passing, and, unless he came up with another strategy, he'd still be a prisoner by nightfall.

Releasing a harsh sigh, he rubbed his sweaty face. He *had* to get free. He *had* to get Juliana and his men away from here and warn his father that his vilest enemies were in Moydenshire. Ah, God, if only he knew how Juliana fared. Veronique had said she'd locate the healer for Juliana; he hoped she had. What if Juliana perished, and he never saw her again? He could not bear that, especially when he was responsible for bringing her to Waddesford.

Sweat dripped from his brow, stinging his eyes, and he squeezed them shut, giving in to the ache in his heart. *Fight, Juliana. Live! I need you to live.*

He eased himself down and pressed his back against the wall. He'd rest a short while, then tackle the chain again. Mayhap he could rip open the pallet—with his teeth, if need be—and see if there was aught in the straw filling he could use to wear the stone away from around the bolts.

As he dropped his hands into his lap, the metal around his wrists weighed upon him, a silent, physical taunt. How he loathed being chained, enslaved to another's will. Or so Veronique thought. He'd show her how much she'd underestimated the proud de Lanceau spirit.

Along with his fury, he tasted shame. He rammed his fingers into his hair, tightened his grip until he pulled at the roots. How he'd wanted to make his sire proud. He'd wanted so much to succeed in his mission, to prove himself to be worthy of the de Lanceau legacy and capable of one day taking on his father's responsibilities.

Instead, he'd led his men into a trap. If Veronique and Tye succeeded in the poisoned scheme they were crafting with Edouard as their hostage, doubtless he and his father would be murdered. Moydenshire would be racked with chaos. Many innocent folk could die. How easy, then, for the king to bring in his armies, ally with

Veronique and Tye in a false show of heroically restoring peace, and take control of lands and riches Edouard's father had worked hard to keep from the king's influence.

A groan tore from Edouard's throat. That terrible outcome would be his fault. *His*, for being taken prisoner and becoming a pawn to the treachery. He'd handed his sire's enemies every advantage. Veronique had murdered Landon, and, fettered as Edouard was, he couldn't do one wretched thing to fix the situation.

He could only pray that the man-at-arms he'd sent to Branton Keep, after they found Juliana in the river, reached his sire. His father might send more warriors out to investigate.

However, it could take days for them to reach Waddesford, and they might well receive the same welcome at the castle as he and his companions.

He couldn't wait days. His father, in this situation, wouldn't have done so. His sire would have fought to escape. So would he.

Shifting on the pallet, he ran his hands over it, studying each dip and bump beneath the covering. There must be a weak patch somewhere . . .

Male voices—belonging to the guards, Edouard guessed—sounded from beyond the door. Veronique likely had returned to taunt him further.

Edouard rose to a crouch and watched the doorway.

The key sounded in the lock and the door swung

inward, causing a draft to whip over the planks. Dust swirled into Edouard's eyes, and he blinked.

Grunts and the rustle of straw preceded two mercenaries lugging a pallet between them. They hauled the bed across the chamber and, taking care to stay out of his reach, dumped it against the wall closest to him, rousing more dust. Edouard wiped his watering eyes with the back of his hand.

"'Avin a wee cry, are ye?" the graying-haired mercenary said.

Edouard glared at him. "Who will be sleeping on that pallet?"

The other man wiped his running nose on his sleeve and grinned. "Well, ye see—"

"Come on," the older mercenary said. "We still 'ave ta bring up what's at the bottom o' the stairs." He executed a mocking bow. "Yer lordship."

Snickering, the two men retreated out the door. The panel quickly closed and the lock engaged.

Edouard looked over the pallet, as lumpy and grimy as his own. He was going to be sharing this cell. With whom? One of his men? Or . . . Juliana?

Anticipation raced through him at the thought. 'Twould be completely inappropriate, especially when he was to marry her sister, but true to Veronique's depraved character. He and Juliana, imprisoned together, a prospect both exciting and mortifying, for they'd be intimately aware of each other's every moment. Each breath, sound, and whisper would be shared.

'Twould be its own kind of torture.

More voices came from outside the door, the cadence of the tones indicating one man was giving orders. Then the lock turned again, and the door opened to admit Tye, holding Juliana in his arms.

Dismay plowed through Edouard; he'd correctly guessed Veronique's intentions. However, Juliana lay with her eyes shut and appeared as unresponsive as when Tye had carried her out of this chamber earlier. She was clothed in a clean chemise, and her skin and hair looked freshly washed, indicating someone had bathed her. Yet her arms curled toward Tye's chest in a gesture of entreaty.

Edouard shoved to his feet. "What have you done to her?"

Tye's boots thumped on the planks.

"Why is she still unconscious? She was to see the healer—"

"—and she did. She is resting now. Sleep is good for curing ailments, is it not?"

"I tell you," Edouard said firmly, "she does not look well. I demand—"

Tye laughed before halting by the empty pallet. "You are a brave fool, Brother, to speak in that manner to me."

Beware, a voice inside Edouard shrilled. *Do not be*

foolish and jeopardize Juliana's well-being.

Trying to keep the force from his words, he asked, "Why have you brought her here?"

"Mother decided she will stay with you." Tye winked. "She thought you might like a companion." He dropped to his knees, lowered Juliana to the pallet, and stepped away. She lay with her left arm curved over her waist. Her right arm stretched away from her body, fingers slightly spread and accentuating the slenderness of her hands.

He'd put her on her right side facing Edouard rather than flat on her back, a small kindness that kept pressure from her head wound.

Kindness? Nay. That sentiment had no bearing with Tye.

Edouard met his brother's gloating stare. "You know this arrangement is not proper."

"Proper?" Tye shrugged and straightened his tunic.

"I am betrothed to her sister. If that is not significant enough, Juliana is a titled noblewoman. Most likely a virgin."

"Ah. Your chivalrous morals are screaming in protest."

Edouard silently cursed and struggled to rein in his rising temper.

"'Twill not be of consequence," Tye said. "Unless, that is, you intend to defile her?"

"Of course not!" Edouard roared.

Tye grinned, obviously pleased by Edouard's outburst. "You would not want to give in to temptation and upset not only your future bride, but *Father*, would you?"

What a vile taunt. Through the red haze clouding his mind, Edouard realized Tye had called their sire "Father." An even more grave insult.

"He is not your father," Edouard bit out.

"By blood, he is."

"When I explain I had no choice in sharing my imprisonment with Juliana," Edouard went on, tone harshening, "he will understand. That does not concern me half as much as ruining Juliana's reputation."

Tye raised his brows. "What an honorable man you are."

"I think also of her well-being. This chamber is draughty. It has no hearth to provide warmth. In her weakened condition . . ."

Tye smiled, a wry tilt of his lips. "Fine reasoning, but she is to stay here. Mother's orders." His gaze turned cold. "In all honesty, Brother, you two are not likely to leave Waddesford alive. Why torment yourself about morality and matters you cannot control?"

Edouard stifled his biting retort. He *would* leave here alive, and so would Juliana.

He glanced at her, hoping for a sign she was reviving. Her bosom rose and fell on slow, steady breaths, a sign of deep slumber. If she slept through his and Tye's conversation, she might not wake for some time.

Footfalls sounded in the stairwell outside the still-open door.

"At last, they return," Tye muttered.

The mercenaries who'd brought the pallet walked in, sweat streaming down their faces.

"Yer piss bucket, milord." The gray-haired mercenary set it on the floor then shoved it with his booted foot toward Edouard.

"And yer foin beddin'." The other man threw a woolen blanket at Edouard before tossing one at Juliana. It landed on her bare feet.

Edouard caught his blanket before it hit his chest. Chain links batted his side as he shook out the worn covering. A bit thin, but 'twould still give some warmth when night fell.

When he looked up, Tye held his stare and smirked. "You have all you need, then."

"Juliana does not. I would like to speak with Veronique about these arrangements."

A rough chuckle rumbled from Tye. "When she wishes to see you, she will. Until then"—his gaze roved over Juliana, lingering, for a moment, upon her breasts swelling against her sheer garment—"you are on your own."

A gritty rasp edged into Juliana's sleepy consciousness. A rhythmic sound, she slowly realized. *Rasp, rasp, rasp.* Pause. *Rasp, rasp, rasp.*

She tried to rouse to full alertness. Her groggy mind resisted; it felt unnaturally dense, dominated by blackness heavier than she'd experienced before.

Wake, Juliana. Find Edouard. You must be certain he is all right.

She became aware of an earthy smell rising from beneath her cheek. She was lying on her side. A prickly roughness scratched her arm, while across her legs, a softer, yet also prickly, sensation persisted.

Juliana swallowed, for an earthy taste clung to her mouth. An unpleasant flavor. If only she had some water or ale to swill the essence away. Indeed, any drink would do.

Drink . . . The last thing she'd downed was the brew the healer had made for her at Veronique's bidding. Juliana tried to steady her nerves. Was she still in the solar? Was Veronique using those gruesome bones to make that gritty noise?

Rasp, rasp, rasp, came again. A shiver crawled through Juliana as she forced her eyes open.

When the muddied browns, golds, and grays within her view gradually focused, she realized she stared at a stone wall across a wood-floored chamber. The tower, where Edouard was chained?

Raising her head, she glanced toward the fading, orange-tinged light spilling in through the window. Edouard squatted with his back to her, gaze trained on the section of wall, cast in shadow, closest to him. He was examining the mortared stone to which his chains were bolted.

Giddiness bubbled up inside her. He was all right. Oh, how wondrous to see him again. She tried not to allow her gaze to skim over his torn and dirt-scuffed tunic, or note the way the woolen fabric stretched over his shoulder and back muscles, but her mind refused to heed her maidenly request to stop. The hem of his tunic swept his buttocks. Pulled taut from his crouched posture, the dark cloth defined the swells and indents of his thigh muscles. Well-honed muscles, from what she saw.

Her gaze slid lower, to his bare feet pressed into the pallet; his boots were propped upside down against the wall a few yards away from him, mayhap to dry them out. Unable to stop her stare from returning to his arse, she caught her bottom lip with her teeth and hoped he wouldn't suddenly glance her way and catch her ogling.

His posture shifted slightly as the fingers of his left hand skated over the rough stone. The gentle touch, somehow, reminded her of a caress. An odd, tantalizing tremor ran through her.

Movement drew her attention to his right hand, clasped around a small object. Before she could figure out what he held, he raised his hand to the iron ring. *Rasp, rasp, rasp.* The sound of a hard item scraping stone.

"Come on," he said under his breath.

As he dipped his head to check his progress, his hair shifted to trail against his neck and shoulder, defining even more the hard set of his jaw. His uncompromising expression snuffed the excitement inside her, for he did indeed look threatening enough to be a murderer.

Was he truly the man Veronique had described him to be? If so, why was Juliana alone in this chamber with him?

Juliana must have sighed, moved slightly, or made some instinctive sound, for Edouard spun to face her. The chains clanked in a startling cacophony.

Juliana flinched and scrambled back, away from the noise, putting more distance between them.

As her side bumped against the wall, he said, "Sorry. I did not mean to frighten you."

"You—" She groaned, and her hand flew up to her aching head.

"I was beginning to worry and . . . 'Tis good to see you awake."

"Have I slept for long?" she asked.

"All afternoon."

She rubbed her brow, and realized her stomach hurt, too. The aftereffects of that drink?

"'Twill soon be nightfall," Edouard went on, clearly determined to keep her attention now she was roused. "I will keep working until the light fades."

"You hope to dig out the bolts?"

He nodded. "I fear, though, I am making slow progress. 'Twould go much faster with a knife." When he opened his palm, a sheepish grin tilted his mouth.

"This pebble is not much of a tool."

Veronique and Tye wouldn't have left him any item that might be used as a weapon; a pebble could cause harm if thrown at close range. "Where did you find it?"

He gestured to the pallet. "I broke through the cloth covering—chewed it, actually—and felt around inside the straw. At first, I found only a twig, which I tried on the wall but it broke. Then, on my second hunt around, I found this small rock."

"I do not see any straw on the floor."

A faint grin touched his lips. How heart-wrenchingly handsome he looked. "I swept it all under the pallet. I do not want Veronique or Tye knowing what I have done." He winked. "You will not tell, Juliana, will you?"

"O-of course not."

He squinted at her, an unrelenting look that sent unease tingling down her spine. She pushed up to a sitting position against the wall, ignoring the tug of her hair caught on the stone. "W-what?"

"You hesitated. Why do you look at me as though I am a criminal?" Looking down at the pebble in his hand, he clenched it in his fist, implying he had to refocus his rising emotions.

"I do not mean to upset you," she said, choosing her words carefully, "but . . . apart from the past day, I do not remember you at all. I have no idea what kind of a man . . . you really are."

He lifted his head to hold her gaze. His bold, unapologetic stare made her insides quiver, while a grating laugh parted his lips. "What kind of man did Veronique and Tye make me out to be?"

She moistened her lips. "Well . . ."

"Let me guess. I like to rape nuns."

She couldn't hold back a shocked laugh. Dropping her gaze, she studied her hands, entwined in her lap. "Veronique did not say that."

"She told you I was a killer, though, or an equally brutal man."

Misgiving tightened like a knot between Juliana's breasts. She didn't want to make him angry; how would he react? He might be charming most of the time, but prone to a vicious temper. Hadn't Tye said Edouard was chained because of his violent tendencies?

Even while she rationalized, part of her protested. *You know, in your heart, that you can trust him, and he would never hurt you.*

"Tell me what happened when they took you from here," Edouard said, his voice surprisingly gentle. His tone coaxed her to share her most recent memories, to take him beyond the confines of this dreary chamber to what she'd experienced.

"I awoke in a large chamber. I was lying on a bed." How distinctly she recalled the room's details; the dark planes of shadow; the tight weave of the coverlet; the candlelight glimmering on the wooden table. Curious, how she itched to replicate what she'd seen in some way, to understand—to *know*—all the different forms and textures. Blinking aside the perplexing thoughts, she added, "Veronique told me 'twas the solar."

Still crouching, Edouard leaned forward. "Did you wake alone in the bed?"

He'd practically spat out the question. Her face warmed, for she didn't like the implications of that query.

No doubt noting her blush, his expression tautened. "I must know, Juliana. Was someone in the bed with you? A man?"

"Nay!" She threw up a hand. "I was lying *on* the bedcover, not *inside* the bedding."

"Ah—"

"Veronique came to the bedside when I woke. The solar seems to be her chamber, although she said I had lived there, too, at one time."

A curse broke from Edouard. "How like her to assume the role of lady of the keep, especially now Landon is dead."

"Veronique started to explain . . ." *what a dangerous man you are, Edouard.*

Looking again at her hands, she tried to find a less blunt manner to describe Veronique's words.

"Juliana."

"I-I needed to catch my breath."

"Juliana." Her name rolled from his tongue; his husky tone caressed each consonant and syllable, making her name seem exotic and . . . beautiful. "I want to know. What did she say about me?"

She drew in a measured breath, grappling for focus. He might have a delicious voice, but that didn't change the fact she must tell him foul news. "All right." She tipped her chin higher. "I will tell you. But you must promise not to get angry."

He raised his brows. "Her words were that favorable, then?"

Juliana huffed. "Promise."

With a dismissive flick of his hand, he said, "I promise. Why not?"

He sounded bitter. He didn't like being coerced. But she'd achieved her aims and wouldn't delay his answer.

"Veronique said you are heartless," Juliana began.

Edouard grunted.

"A killer—"

"What trained warrior is not?"

"—and that you came to this keep to murder her and Tye, because—"

"Because?" Edouard echoed.

"You are jealous of Tye, your half brother, and do not want him to inherit from your sire, even though he is entitled."

Shaking his head, Edouard laughed. His laughter

faded onto a growl. "Well. She certainly did her best to keep you from trusting me."

Juliana flexed her numbing fingers. "She said you would try to win my trust, so I would help you escape. That 'tis the only reason you care . . . about me."

His sharpened gaze locked with hers. "'Tis not true, Juliana. Not at all. Truth be told, I vow most of what she has told you is a lie."

A tiny part of Juliana's heart sang with gladness. Still, she said, "How so?"

Chains clanked as he dropped to the pallet, then braced his arms upon his bent knees. "To begin, I do not consider myself heartless. Aye, I have killed in my lifetime—I will not lie to you about such—but the men I struck down were enemies of my father or the lords who owe fealty to him. I fought in skirmishes waged to preserve justice and harmony in these lands, as is expected of me and all the honorable warriors of this realm."

"I . . . see."

"Juliana, I did not travel to Waddesford Keep with the intention of killing Veronique and Tye; I came to speak with Lord Ferchante, on my father's behalf. I did not realize, until too late, they were at this castle. If I had known, I would not have brought you here to have your wound healed."

How she ached at the self-condemnation in his words. "Edouard—"

He held up a hand. "Let me finish. I want you to

hear it all, Juliana, for Veronique and Tye are my sire's longtime enemies. My sire has been hunting them for years, because they have sworn to destroy him and take over the lands he has ruled in peace. Tye may or may not be my half brother; that has not been proven. Even if we are related, he is bastard-born and has no right to inherit. I, however, am my father's heir. 'Tis one of the reasons Veronique is so eager to keep me hostage and to stop you from helping me. If I do not escape"—he paused, expression stark—"they will kill me."

"You cannot be certain," Juliana whispered.

"I am. I have no doubt my death will be painful and in a manner to cause my sire great anguish." He dropped his head on a weary sigh.

The finality in Edouard's tone left her cold. She hardly dared to ask, and yet she must. "Do they mean to kill me, too?"

He slowly raised his head. Remorse flickered in his eyes. "I will not lie to you, Juliana. I expect so."

She crossed her arms and hugged herself tight. An awful sense of disorientation swirled through her. "Oh, God, I do not want to die. Not when I do not even remember who I am!"

"Juliana, listen to me. I will not let them hurt you. I will do all I can to protect you. That is why we must escape, as soon as we can. Whatever treachery they are plotting, we must warn my sire. We *must* stop them."

Again Edouard spoke of escape together, as though they were united in their fight against Veronique and Tye. Juliana tried not to dwell upon the conversation in the solar, but the older woman's warning crept into her thoughts: *Beware, Juliana, of thinking kindly about Edouard.*

Sensing his attention upon her again, Juliana looked across the chamber, unable to stop her body from trembling.

"Are you all right?" he asked quietly.

He insists he cares for you only because he needs your help.

She shrugged.

"I am sorry you are caught up in this crisis. Please believe I never intended to bring you into danger."

He is a deceitful bastard, just like his father.

She closed her eyes and, bracing her elbows on her knees, pressed her palms to her forehead. If only she could calm the chaos in her head, all the reasonings and explanations spinning around that she needed to evaluate. What was the truth? What wasn't?

"What else did Veronique tell you about me?" Edouard asked.

Juliana opened her eyes, tilting her head to look at him. Goosebumps shot down her arms, for his stare bored into her, demanding she divulge the remainder of Veronique's cryptic words. "She said you will win my trust, and then you will crush it."

CHAPTER 13

Frustration gnawed at Edouard while he held Juliana's moist gaze. He sensed her turmoil, her confusion as to what she should believe and what was designed to mislead her. She shivered, no doubt from overwrought nerves. How he wished he could go to her, draw her into his arms, and ease her fears with the acknowledgment she wasn't—and never would be—alone during this tumultuous time.

As their gazes held, the ache inside him became keener. After months of her pointedly avoiding him, of living with the turmoil of his unfortunate betrothal, he was finally facing her again. She might not recall him, but, by God, he craved her, for she was even more comely than the maiden in his memories.

What he would give to slide his fingers down her soft cheek, ease her chin up, and smile down at her before he bent his head and kissed her, slowly, thoroughly, skillfully enough to draw from her a pleasured moan. The way he'd longed to kiss her by Sherstowe's well. He'd imagined that so many times as he lay restless and alone on his pallet at Dominic's keep.

He shuddered, fighting a stirring of desire.

She said you will win my trust, and then you will crush it.

Still holding her stare, Edouard's throat tightened. He longed to scorn Veronique's words. However, they were true. He'd won Juliana's trust at Sherstowe Keep and shattered it that same day with the bet to win her kiss. He'd destroyed it with his regrettable kiss with Nara.

You are not that same reckless man any longer; you are a knight, his heart cried. *You cannot woo her, since you are honor-bound to wed Nara, but you can fight to earn her respect.*

Aye, he would.

"I cannot tell you what to believe," he said. "I do not blame you for being wary. I wonder, though, what Veronique told you about yourself."

Juliana's head raised a notch, causing long, silky hair to tumble around her shoulders. "She told me I once stayed in the solar. And—" She frowned. "'Twas all."

Edouard couldn't resist a grin. "I can tell you far more."

"I would like that. I would especially like to know . . . my full name."

"Lady Juliana de Greyne."

"Lady." A slight frown creased her brow. "I did not realize I was of the noble class."

He nodded. "You lived here at Waddesford at the

invitation of Lady Mayda Ferchante. You were her closest friend and lady-in-waiting."

When he'd said "Lady Ferchante," her expression sharpened with intense concentration. "Do you remember Mayda?" Mayhap her name had prompted a return of memories?

"I thought, for a moment . . . " With a heavy sigh, Juliana shook her head. "You may have told me before, but what is your full name?"

"Edouard, the firstborn son of Geoffrey de Lanceau. My father is lord of all of Moydenshire."

Awe swept her features. "I see." She gnawed her bottom lip, as though she considered his words. "You are a valuable captive, then, to Veronique."

"Until I no longer have a use in her schemes. By the way, your father, who is lord of Sherstowe Keep, is one of my sire's trusted knights. He has served my father for many years." He brushed dust from his hose. "Do you remember when you first met my sire?"

Edouard waited, holding his breath, watching the emotions flicker in her eyes. He saw uncertainty, frustration, but not, as he dreaded, remembrance, for if she recalled that day at Sherstowe, they wouldn't be speaking pleasantly any longer. She'd be banging her fists on the door to be as far away from him as possible

Juliana fingered hair behind her ear; he tried not to watch the sheer linen tighten across her generous bosom.

Shaking her head, she said, "I do not recall your sire. Our families know each other well, then?"

Well enough to have wanted to unite their families through marriage. But he didn't wish to bring up that matter yet. "Reasonably well."

A grin curved her mouth. "More than reasonably, I vow."

The smile softened her features and cast a warm glow in her eyes. He inhaled on a renewed tingle of desire. "Why do you say such?" he asked, hoping he didn't sound witless.

To her astonishment, a blush pinkened her face. She dropped her gaze and looked across the floorboards. "Well . . ."

"Aye?" God's teeth, but he was intrigued.

"Each time . . . I look at you," she said with half a shrug, "I get this . . . *feeling* in my breast—"

His gaze fell upon her bosom, then snapped away.

"—a sensation so strong, I cannot ignore it."

"Tell me more." He barely recognized his own voice.

Her gaze slowly lifted to hold his. "'Tis the most powerful sensation I have ever felt. I do not mean to speak boldly, but I believe we know each other well. Very well." Her blush deepened. "'Tis the only explanation."

How beautiful she looked, expression shy but yearning, luscious mouth partly opened on an eager breath. Even as he held her urgent gaze, though, his desire plummeted. She felt strongly about him because of the past between them. The sensation wasn't attraction, but hatred.

How did he explain it, when she'd no recollection of why she despised him?

He searched for a suitable answer. "Juliana . . ."

Her pallet rustled as she scooted toward him on her knees, chemise brushing the planks. "I know why you must be cautious, Edouard," she said in a low voice. "If you identify me as your . . . lover, that would put me in greater danger. You are trying to protect me."

"Protect you," Edouard murmured, as she came even closer. God's holy bones, but he couldn't look away. Sunlight spilled over her, casting her hair and slender body in washes of gold. Her faint, lavender scent wafted to him, and he suddenly remembered she'd smelled of lavender years ago, when he'd almost kissed her by the well, when he'd realized he *wanted* her kiss.

He drew in a breath, hungry for her essence. She smelled of promise, of possibilities, of *freedom*, not of the musty straw and old stone of imprisonment.

"'Tis safest for us both if we do not admit our relationship." She was beside him now, gaze imploring, face flushed and eager. "'Tis why you have kept our relationship a secret. Tell me I am right."

As he took in her excitement, anguish kindled inside him. How wretched that he must disappoint her. He owed her the truth, though. He must admit they were naught to each other.

But she was temptingly close. His wicked hands yearned to reach out and slide into her hair, to feel its shiny softness. All his concern for her over the past day suddenly welled up inside him, mingling into sinful yearning. What he would give to hold her close and kiss her on those rose-red lips—at last, have that kiss he'd desired years ago.

Take it, a voice inside him urged. *Kiss her! Nara will never know.*

He'd know. The dishonor of that act would eat at his conscience. Moreover, 'twould not be fair to let Juliana imagine more between them than there was.

While waiting for his answer, Juliana had clasped her hands and settled back on her heels. Her chemise flowed in a gossamer swath around her. Never had he seen a more alluring woman.

"Edouard?"

Silence, as hideous as a gargoyle, pressed into the quietness between them. He struggled against his inner torment. As his sire always insisted, honorable men told the truth, no matter how difficult that might be.

"I will be honest, Juliana." Edouard said with care. "You and I were—"

Mumbled voices came from outside the door.

Her smile vanished. Her body tensed, while her gaze flew to her bed. She cringed, the movement clearly too fast with her wound, and she cradled her head in one hand.

"Hurry," he whispered. "Return to your pallet."

Dismay shadowed her features. When the key scraped in the lock, though, she nodded and hurried to sit back against the wall, then brushed the dust from the hem of her chemise with a few flicks of one hand.

Edouard sucked in a calming breath, pressed his back to the stonework, and refused to heed the unease churning in his gut. What unpleasantness did Veronique plan for him now? Realizing the pebble lay in plain sight, he snatched it and shoved it under the pallet's edge.

The door began to open, and he stole a sidelong glance at Juliana. Gone was the smiling, desirous maiden. Wariness defined her features. Did she worry that she'd made a fool of herself with him? Or was she as unnerved about what might happen next as he was?

Tye strode in first, followed by Veronique. A blond-haired woman followed a few steps behind them, carrying a wooden tray. It bore bread, a jug of drink, several cloths, and an earthenware pot.

"Tye," Veronique said. "Shut the door. Keep watch."

"Aye, Mother." He shoved the panel closed, then leaned one arm against it, while his hand rested on his sword hilt.

Veronique's sharp gaze slid to Juliana, then Edouard.

A lusty chuckle broke from her. "Edouard, you must be growing *hungry* by now."

Coming from her lips, those innocent words sounded

like an invitation to fornicate right there on the dirty, musty pallet. Trying not to recall her hands on him earlier that day, he scowled. "I have no appetite for what you might offer me."

Her smile turned sly. "You will not be stubborn and refuse the fare I have generously brought. Will you?"

He fought to hold back a snide retort. Knowing her, she'd tainted the food. He wouldn't eat one bite.

With the rustle of silk, Veronique approached Juliana. "How are you feeling?"

"All right, th-thank you." Juliana smiled, but Veronique must have sensed hesitancy in her expression, for her brows quirked.

"I trust Azarel's potion was helpful?"

Behind Veronique, the young woman stiffened. She appeared to brace herself for a wallop, and Edouard fought a stab of pity. Veronique had a firm hold over Azarel. Her chains were invisible, but they were no less real than his iron fetters. Who or what did Veronique use to keep this poor woman under her will?

"The drink helped me a great deal, I am certain," Juliana was saying. Her words sounded rushed; she clearly tried to spare the healer from punishment. An admirable kindness.

Veronique smiled. "We all want you to recover and once again have your memories. Is that not right, Edouard?"

Eyes narrowing, she glanced at him. He tried not to

acknowledge the disquiet clawing at his innards. What was she about? Was she trying to talk him into some kind of verbal trap? To distort this conversation to suit a purpose he didn't yet know?

"Of course I want Juliana to recover," he said.

"Then in this matter we are not enemies, aye? We agree she must eat and drink and regain her strength. That, in turn, will help her memories come back."

Her words made sense. He had to wonder, though, why she was so interested in Juliana regaining her memories.

Veronique signaled Azarel to step forward. The healer crossed to Juliana, dropped down on her knees, and set the tray beside the pallet. Azarel's attention remained fixed upon her hands, folded in her lap; she made no attempt to look at Juliana, or steal a glance at Edouard. Had Veronique warned her not to make any contact with them? What cruel threat had she made, to make this woman seem so remote?

"Ah, look, Edouard. The food is beyond your reach," Veronique murmured, sounding smug. "If you want to eat, you will have to ask Juliana for some fare."

His mouth flattened. He was forced to be dependent on Juliana for a most basic need: sustenance. No doubt Veronique wanted to reinforce his helplessness. Disillusion him, humiliate him, by forcing him, a lord's son, to ask for what should be granted him without restrictions.

"I will gladly share," Juliana said.

Refusing to yield to the annoyance Veronique had roused within him, Edouard shrugged. "I am not hungry."

"*Tsk, tsk*, Edouard. If you refuse to eat, you discourage Juliana from doing the same. However, if you partake of the fare, she will follow your example." Veronique smirked. "You *must* eat. We are, after all, allies in our wish to see her recover."

Allies. Edouard almost laughed. How cleverly she had planned this twisted game of hers. He stared her down, funneling all of his hatred for her into his gaze.

She didn't look away.

"Do as I ask"—Veronique's eyes sparked with malice—"and you might be alive to see your sire ride through the gates of the keep."

"Enough," Edouard growled, still holding her stare. He wouldn't tolerate goading that involved his father.

"Alive to know he tried to rescue you."

"Veronique—"

She cackled, the sound shrill with gloating. "Alive to watch him *die*."

A roar of pure, hot fury boiled up inside Edouard. His hands shook, for he wanted to lunge to his feet and bellow in her pitiless, painted face. With immense effort, he forced the roar into submission. Yelling at Veronique would accomplish naught, especially when Tye looked eager to use his sword. Far wiser for Edouard to hold his tongue and use his fury to help him escape.

221

But in one matter, he would not yield. He wouldn't be the first to look away.

Veronique grinned, as though deciding she'd won that battle. Then, with a lazy dip of her lashes, she looked at Azarel, still kneeling by Juliana's pallet with her gaze downcast. "Begin, Azarel," she said. "Do as I told you. Tye and I will be watching."

When Azarel reached for the pot on the tray, Juliana tried to meet her gaze, but the healer averted her eyes. Disquiet gnawed at Juliana. If only she could find some way to communicate with Azarel; find a way, mayhap, for the healer to send a message to Edouard's father for help.

"Turn your back to me and look down, milady," Azarel said in a strong yet compassionate voice. "'Twill be easiest for me to care for your wound." Lifting the lid off the pot, she released the brisk, herbal scent of the ointment inside.

Azarel was doing no more than tending Juliana as Veronique commanded. However, a curious tension seemed to emanate from the young woman, a stifled sense of anticipation. Taking care not to give away the fact she was aware of Azarel's tension, Juliana did as bade. Anchoring her left hand into her hair, she drew it aside to more fully expose the wound.

While she stared down at the pallet's grubby covering, Juliana heard Tye murmur to Veronique. Words not
meant for others to hear. She sensed Veronique's assessing stare sweep over Azarel and herself, but kept her gaze
locked on the pallet.

The healer's sleeve batted Juliana's hair as she rose
up on her knees and gently probed the lump at Juliana's
nape. Pain and nausea tore through Juliana. Pressing
her arm across her stomach, she drew a ragged breath.

"Lady de Greyne," the healer said, so quietly, Juliana
almost didn't think she'd spoken.

Squinting through the agony, Juliana turned her
head a fraction.

"Do not look at me," the healer whispered. "Focus
on your pain. Otherwise, they will be suspicious."

Juliana rubbed at her aching brow and squeezed her
eyes shut.

"Do you remember me?" Azarel asked.

Juliana slowly turned her head to one side, then
the other.

The piquant scent of herbs wafted before a feeling of
dampness. As Azarel applied the ointment, a fresh flood of
agony seared through Juliana's skull, and she stifled a groan.

"We used to know each other well. I cannot say much
more," the healer said, voice barely audible, "but I wanted
you to know, for when your memories come back—"

Veronique's voice crested on a muffled laugh.

"The babe is safe, in the village."

Juliana's partly inhaled breath froze in her chest. Babe? Whose babe?

Had *she* given birth to a child? An infant she couldn't recall? Was that why she sensed such an undeniable connection to Edouard, because he was the father of her son or daughter? If, as she suspected, he was trying to protect her from danger, he wouldn't have wanted to remind her of the babe; 'twas his way of keeping it safe.

If they'd conceived a child together, though, shouldn't they be married? More questions filled her pain-fogged mind. If only she could think properly. If only she dared to ask Azarel to share more details.

Shifting the hand holding up her hair, she stole a sidelong glance at the healer. But Azarel was pushing the lid back onto the pot and wiping her fingers on a cloth. Naught in her countenance indicated she'd spoken to Juliana. Neither did she acknowledge Juliana's glance.

Frustration urged Juliana to softly whisper, "What babe? Please—"

"How is the wound?" Veronique asked, her voice drowning out Juliana's.

"'Tis healing well, milady," Azarel answered.

"Good."

Juliana swallowed. Had Veronique seen or heard her speak to the healer? Not likely. Still, Juliana must beware. She mustn't jeopardize Azarel's safety.

"Thank you for your help, Azarel," Juliana said loudly enough for all to hear.

Not looking up, the healer nodded once, then set the cloth and pot back on the tray, movements controlled and efficient. Her hands, though, were shaking.

She rose. Her lashes flicked up, and, for the briefest instant, her fearful gaze met Juliana's, before she looked back at the floorboards and faced Veronique and Tye.

The older woman's attention fixed on Azarel. "How much longer till Juliana's memories return?"

"I cannot say, milady."

Edouard rolled his eyes. "She cannot be expected to know that."

"Silence, Edouard." Veronique looked down at Juliana. "Azarel, what can you do"—she flexed her misshapen fingers—"to quicken the process for Juliana? A stronger potion?"

Juliana's stomach rebelled at the thought of another vile drink. "I do not think—"

"We do not expect you to think, with a head wound," Veronique cut in. "Azarel, I expect you to have an answer on the morrow."

The healer's shoulders stiffened, but she said, "Aye, milady."

Chains clanked as Edouard leaned forward, face set in a frown. "Why are you so interested in Juliana regaining her memories? What does it matter to you?"

A very good question. Hands clasped in her lap, Juliana waited for Veronique's reply.

The older woman smiled—a sly, secretive turn of her lips—and motioned for Tye to open the door.

"What does she want from me?"

Juliana's voice reached Edouard over the grating of the pebble on the wall. The daylight was fading, casting an intense, orange-red glow into the chamber. He had precious little time left to make progress on their escape.

Wiping perspiration from his nose, he looked at Juliana, sitting on her pallet, with her arms looped around her knees. How forlorn she looked. He fought a renewed pang of guilt that he'd brought her into Veronique's dangerous realm.

"I do not know what she wants," he said. "I *do* know, however, she intends to profit from what you remember."

"I wonder . . ." Juliana sighed, as though greatly troubled. "Edouard, there is something I must ask you."

He scraped the pebble again. "Mmm?"

"Do we . . . have a baby?"

Shock jolted through him, almost causing him to fall forward against the wall. Of all the things he expected her to ask, that wasn't among them. Why would she imagine they'd made a child together? His mind raced, rousing an unsettling fascination. Did her feelings for him run so deep, she believed they'd shared the pleasure of their bodies?

Did she . . . desire him? Crave him even half as much as he craved her?

A tremor rippled through him as he forced the tantalizing thoughts aside. It didn't matter if Juliana desired him. She was forbidden to him, because of his betrothal to Nara.

While he gathered his wits again, the pebble slid from his fingers, bounced onto the planks, and rattled to a halt a hand's span from the untouched tray of food.

"Why would you believe we have a child?" He didn't mean to sound so astounded, but he simply couldn't help it. As he looked at her, his innards clenched at the bewilderment shimmering in her eyes.

Juliana squared her shoulders; she clearly meant to get the answer she sought. "Azarel whispered to me while she tended me. She said, 'The babe is safe, in the village.' Our babe? If not ours, whose?"

Her earnest expression touched at the yearning for her he'd tried to lock away within himself. How he longed to sweep his mouth over hers, to promise her all would be well, to offer comfort. Turning away from the wall, he faced her and sat down. He wiped dust from his fingers, then took in a careful breath. "Juliana—"

"'Tis *not* a foolish question."

"I agree." He continued to stare at his hands, scraped in a few places from grazing the wall while using the pebble. Refusing to acknowledge a rising sense of awkwardness, he said, "To create a child, a man and woman must . . ."

"Be in love."

"Aye. And—"

"Desire to make a child together."

Oh, aye. Desire certainly helped. Edouard choked down a helpless laugh. Hellfire, he'd just have to say the hot, sweaty, indelicate issue outright. "They must fornicate, Juliana."

He dared to lift his gaze.

Her face had turned scarlet. "Oh. Well," she said, after a long, silent moment. "Does that mean you and I never—?"

"We never fornicated." Although, of all depravities, he couldn't help wondering what 'twould be like to lie with her, run his fingers over her naked flesh, and lazily explore all the delicious permutations of that hot, sweaty, indelicate issue before finding shuddering release in each other's embrace.

His loins warmed. With a silent curse, he willed his lust to dissipate.

Juliana appeared relieved by the fact they'd never coupled, yet somehow also dismayed.

"What child did Azarel speak of, then?" she asked.

"Whose babe would be important to me?"

Edouard started to shake his head, until he recalled the embroidered baby blanket he'd brought to Waddesford in his saddlebag. "The Ferchantes' newborn daughter," he said. "Azarel came here to assist with her birth. You likely helped Mayda care for her."

"In the solar." Juliana's eyes widened. "That would explain why I felt that chamber was familiar."

"Aye. Did you see the babe whilst you were there?"

Juliana frowned. "I saw no sign of a child, or, truth be told, Lady Ferchante. Veronique told me she is dead."

'Twas likely true, especially if Mayda had opposed Landon's affair with Veronique and her growing control of Waddesford. Azarel must have somehow got the babe to safety, before Veronique could slaughter the last of the Ferchante family. Mayhap Veronique kept firm control over Azarel with a threat to snatch and murder the infant.

Grief crushed down upon Edouard. He *had* to get free of this wretched captivity, *had* to undermine Veronique's treachery, before—

The pebble again rattled on the planks. As his gaze focused, he saw it rolling toward him, and Juliana straightening from pushing it his way.

He snatched up the stone, met her gaze, and smiled.

She smiled back, before her lashes dropped in shy hesitation. "There is one more thing I must ask you."

A strange tension threaded together her words. Was

she going to ask him if they'd *almost* fornicated?

"You didn't finish explaining our relationship earlier. Edouard, why do I feel such strong emotions for you?" Her voice softened to a plea. "I realize you may be trying to protect me, but I *must* know. Please. Are you and I lovers?"

Her eyes glistened with the hint of tears. His heart squeezed tight. Fighting the awful pressure in his gut, he said, "Nay, Juliana, we are not lovers. We never can be, for I am betrothed to your sister."

CHAPTER 14

Juliana lay on her right side, head pillowed on her bent arm, staring into the darkness. She saw the same inkiness when she shut her eyes. Yet for some reason, the pervasive blackness made her all the more aware of Edouard lying a short distance away.

"We are not lovers. We never can be, for I am betrothed to your sister."

His words whirled through her exhausted mind. His admission that he was committed to another had shocked the breath from her and left her numb. Shame, too, welled inside her. She might not remember his betrothal to her sister he'd told her was named Nara, but harboring such strong emotions toward him was surely improper.

"I am very happy for you and Nara." She'd bravely forced out the words, while hating the way her voice wobbled.

He must have noticed, for his lips pressed into a line. Before she could ask when the wedding would take place, he'd turned away to attack the wall with the stone. His ferocious assault suggested he didn't want to talk about the matter anymore, so she'd let him to work in silence. He'd toiled until twilight, without saying another word. While he'd made some headway, he hadn't yet managed to loosen the bolts, and his brooding silence had left her unsettled and unbearably lonely.

Odd, how intensely she felt Edouard's presence reaching out of the blackness to her. She sensed his body warmth, heard his rhythmic breathing and the occasional clink of chains, and sensed he, too, was awake and trying to deal with the thoughts racing around in his mind.

Why did she feel this way toward a man who wasn't her lover?

A breeze slipped over her, coming from the open window. Shivering, she drew the thin blanket about her shoulders. Hoping for sleep. Wanting to escape this cell. Longing to finally recall all there was to know about herself, Lady Juliana de Greyne.

While she and Edouard hadn't coupled and produced a child, and he was pledged to her sister, *something* had occurred between them. Her feelings for him wouldn't be so intense or muddled otherwise.

He sighed. Fighting a pinch of guilt, she imagined the broad muscles of his chest expanding and contracting. The parting of his lips—so beautifully sculpted—as air rushed from them.

"Juliana." His voice rumbled through the darkness.

She started. Had he sensed her thinking about him? "A-aye, Edouard?"

"I knew you were awake."

She curled her fingers against the pallet. How unseemly of her, but she found pleasure in the rich timbre of his voice; it roused within her a comforting blend of reassurance and trust. A thrill raced through her, too, to know that he, somehow, had been so aware of her. Smiling, she asked, "How did you know I was not asleep?"

"A feeling. A kind of . . . sensing." Metal scraped and she imagined him shifting on his pallet. "'Tis difficult to put into words."

She knew, though, exactly what he meant. If only she understood what had forged a connection this strong between them.

Another gust swept across the floor, and Juliana shuddered before tugging the blanket all the way up to her chin. The night wind was strengthening.

"Are you all right?" he asked.

"A bit cold." Remorse poked at her, for while she was a captive, she didn't have iron bands clamped around her wrists and could move about as she wished. He must be uncomfortable, trying to sleep while chained. "You must be chilled, too," she murmured. "You are close to the window."

He grunted. "I will manage."

How nonchalant he sounded; she imagined his

shoulder rising in a careless shrug. If she pressed him, he'd probably say he'd spent colder nights sleeping on the ground in midwinter, as part of his warrior training. Yet she discerned he was, indeed, uncomfortable; he likely didn't want to admit such because that would give Veronique a small victory, and he was a proud man who didn't yield easily.

"It must be near midnight," he said.

"Mmm."

"We should try and sleep. When dawn breaks, I will work again on my chains. Mayhap I will have better luck on the morrow."

"There must be another way to escape," she said.

"For you, mayhap. I am here till I break my fetters from the wall or they are unlocked." He growled a sigh. "If only you knew how much I want to be free."

"I can hear it in your voice," she said softly. "I feel your rage and frustration, as if they were my own."

"Really?"

"Really."

"We are one then, in our discontent."

We are one. Three little words that sounded wondrous strung together. Juliana closed her eyes and savored the heady glimmer inside her, ignoring her conscience that insisted she shouldn't indulge such thoughts.

How curious, that she wasn't as cold as moments ago, or as unsettled. She breathed in and slowly exhaled, allowing her muscles to relax for a moment; the constant ache in her head to dim; her mind to calm . . .

Ooooo . . .

Her limbs jerked with the abruptness of her waking. Her heart pounded.

That cry . . . So haunting.

With a shaking hand, she pushed aside hair that had fallen over her cheek while she dozed. Was Edouard moaning because he was in pain? Mayhap he was asleep, enduring a nightmare. Or had she dreamt the noise?

Ooooo . . .

The sound was akin to someone wailing. Not Edouard, though; the noise emanated from outside.

A chill crawled over her skin and she drew the blanket tighter about her. Might she be hearing a spirit? The ghostly presence of a prisoner who'd died in this chamber?

Chains rattled from the darkness. "Juliana?"

When her mind registered Edouard's voice, she also heard short, ragged breaths. Her own.

"What is wrong?" he asked.

"That n-noise." Her voice emerged no more than a croak.

"'Tis the wind blowing past the tower walls."

"It sounds like a person c-crying. A baby's wail . . ." Her teeth chattered. She became aware of cooling wetness on her cheeks: tears.

"'Tis only the wind." His gentle words were no doubt meant to console her. Somehow, though, the anxiety inside her furrowed deeper.

Ooooo . . .

Edouard was right; the night gusts caused the eerie wail. However, the noise tapped into a place inside her that *hurt*. Oh, how she ached. *Why?* What had happened in her past to rouse such a devastating sense of loss?

She squeezed her eyes shut. If only she remembered! She *must* remember, for the anguish threatened to tear her apart.

"Juliana—"

A sob wrenched from her.

"You are crying." Surprise, and a hint of dismay, echoed in his voice.

She dried her eyes on the edge of her blanket. "I d-do not know why." She sniffled. "That s-sound . . ."

Ooooo . . .

Straw crackled in the near darkness. "Come here."

Blinking hard, she glanced in his direction. Foolish. In the inkiness, she couldn't see him. Yet the thought of being close to him during this grim night was very tempting.

"Come to me, Juliana." How tenderly he spoke. "I cannot cross to you."

A shudder rippled its way through her lower body, while she stifled another sob. "I do n-not think . . . You are b-betrothed."

"Aye," he said, tone strained, "but I can still comfort you."

What would it be like to be in his embrace? Part of

her yearned for it; part of her shrilled she'd be wiser avoid temptation and stay where she was. "Edouard . . ."

"I understand your reluctance, but 'tis a cold night. In your weakened state, 'twould be easy for you to succumb to a chill and fall deathly ill."

"T-true." She *didn't* want to die in this miserable cell.

"You must stay well, Juliana, and heal, so your memories will return. Our fate—indeed that of all Moydenshire—may depend upon what you remember."

He was right. Her qualms were nowhere near as important as her survival. "A-all right. I w-will come to you." She pushed to a seated position, letting her blanket slide down to her waist. Then she gathered up the blanket and tucked it under one arm.

"Follow my voice," he said.

Ooooo . . .

Stretching out her hand, she touched the floor. The planks felt as cold as a frozen lake against her palm. Shivering, she tugged her chemise up around her thighs so it wouldn't hinder her progress—he wouldn't see her bared legs in the darkness—then crawled forward on her hands and knees. Listening.

"I am here," Edouard said.

His voice seemed to wash over her, coaxing her on. An unusual excitement flickered within her. How tantalizing, to approach him in this manner. To be in total darkness, but for his voice.

Her chemise bunched at her knees. Pushing the fabric aside again, she said, "Speak again."

"I am here, Juliana." His tone was huskier than before. She imagined him talking to her that way while his lips brushed her cheek, and she fought a wicked tremor.

Stop it, Juliana. He is to marry Nara, remember?

Another crawl forward. Another.

Her fingers bumped the edge of his pallet.

"Almost here," he murmured.

She sensed him very near. He didn't reach for her, or make the slightest move, but his earthy, male scent came from the blackness ahead. Her palms started to sweat. Part of her—the rational, sensible part—screamed, *Turn back, while you still can.*

Nay. She wouldn't retreat. She wanted to survive.

Her fingers slipped onto the pallet. As she edged forward, her hand shifted. Touched warm cloth.

"My left leg," he said.

"Oh." She drew a steadying breath. "Then the rest of you is—"

Metal clanked. His limb shifted beneath her hand; taut muscles and tendons slid beneath the fabric. Icy fingers nudged her, and then his broad hand settled atop hers.

His touch, while cold, sent warmth coursing through her body. Strength, reassurance, the promise of companionship was as inviting as a steaming mug of mulled wine on a winter's eve.

She sighed. His fingers squeezed; heat spread from where their hands touched. Oh, God, even that small contact was wonderful.

"I cannot move any closer," he said gently. "You will have to move nearer to me."

Nearer. Her heart fluttered, as though she were a sparrow perched outside a window, looking in.

"Why do you hesitate?" Edouard's chains rattled again, and she sensed him leaning closer, seeking her out in the darkness.

A thrill hastened down her spine. How breathless, light-headed, she felt, and not from her wound. "I am . . . a bit unsettled," she admitted.

"By me?"

She rubbed her lips together. Him, aye. The odd feelings he roused in her. The fact she felt as she did, when he belonged to her sister . . . The wind moaned again, sending frigid air over her, and she shivered.

"You will no longer be cold," he said softly, "when you are with me."

His hand shifted. With gentle pressure, he slid his palm underneath hers to entwine their fingers and then pulled her toward him.

Her stomach swooped. "Edouard—"

"Come to me, Juliana."

Her arm stretched taut, drawing her torso toward him. Losing her balance, she began to fall toward the pallet. For one panicked moment, she thought to pull away.

With a swift tug, he levered her forward. The breath rushed from her lips as she collided with the broad, solid heat of his chest.

His breath stirred her hair. "You are here," he said. "At last."

Edouard stilled, waiting for Juliana to gain her balance, an instant before her free hand banged into his jaw.

"Oh! I—"

Her fingers were like icicles. Even as he acknowledged their coldness, her hand skated across his cheek, not a deliberate touch, but an instinctive reaction, no doubt, to her body sliding down against his, guided by his embrace.

Not such a bad way to be with a woman.

Her finger jabbed his right eyeball.

"Ah!" His eyelids clamped shut. Just what he needed, to be half blind as well as chained. Of course, she hadn't meant to poke him.

"Sorry. Oh, goodness, w-was that—?"

"My eye." Edouard blinked away moisture.

Her hand bumped against his shoulder. "Did I hurt y-you?"

"Nay."

"Thank the Saints." She laughed, a nervous warble. "This close, and I still c-cannot see you."

Nor I you, his mind answered, while he eased his fingers from hers to allow her to better recline. *But I can hear you breathe, feel the softness of your warm chemise, and smell the perfume of your hair. God above, Juliana, how you entice me.*

Even as he struggled to squash that thought, his hardened loins swelled further. Damnation. He'd vowed to keep control of his desire. He'd offered Juliana comfort, and he meant to honor his words. Either he regained command of his lust, or he'd spend the entire night in aroused agony.

He concentrated on quelling the fire in his groin. Straw shifted as Juliana settled beside him. He guessed she was lying on her side, heard the faint rasp of wool as she covered herself with her blanket. When she fell quiet, he sensed she was looking at where she knew him to be.

A silent growl of pleasure unfurled inside him. He still couldn't see her, but in the small gap separating their bodies, her heat reached out to him like a bonfire beacon in the night. How he longed to bring her flush against him, to feel her supple curves against his hardness . . .

Edouard, you wretched fool! Quit such thoughts, or you will drive yourself mad.

He frowned, determined to conquer his disgraceful weakness. *Be gallant, Edouard, and think about her comfort.* Sliding his hand up the pallet, he found the chain running between them and pushed it closer to him. She needn't lie on it and be uncomfortable. Then he tugged his blanket, barely large enough for one, back up over his waist, painfully aware that even the slightest movement caused the chains to make noise.

"Do they hurt?" she asked.

They. Several answers to this question leapt to mind, the most inappropriate rising to the fore. Managing to keep his tone calm, he asked, "What do you mean?"

"The iron bands around your wrists."

Ah. "A little," he said. "Fetters are not designed to be pleasant. Are you comfortable enough?"

"Aye, but I am still cold."

He settled his cheek upon his bent arm, just as her hand moved, mayhap to adjust her blanket. Her fingers knocked his chin; one fingertip touched his lips.

Purely on instinct, he turned his head and sucked that fingertip into his mouth.

Juliana gasped. "Oh!"

Cease, Edouard! You must! Somehow, though, the shock and delight in her voice held his will captive and forced him on.

Grazing her skin with his teeth, he drew in more of her finger, until his upper lip touched the knuckle bone where her finger joined her hand. He twirled his tongue around her flesh, while savoring her shocked shivers.

Her skin tasted sweet. Deliciously so. He inhaled her alluring scent that reminded him of lavender and honey. Mmm . . . Never had he known a woman to smell so good.

"What"—Juliana breathed—"are you doing?"

He stilled, becoming aware of the merciless throbbing of his groin. What *was* he doing? He certainly wasn't going to seduce her, although, knowing Veronique, 'twas exactly what she'd intended by returning Juliana to the drafty tower after a perfumed bath.

With a wry chuckle, he drew back, releasing her digit. "I was . . . ah . . . warming your finger."

The air stirred between them as she snatched her hand away. "Well, I—"

"'Tis feeling warmer?"

"Aye, but . . . Do you normally warm fingers that way?"

She peered at him. He knew it. How readily he pictured her face, set in a winsome expression of both fascination and uncertainty.

"Not always." He smiled into the darkness. Before he could stop the reckless words, he said, "Shall I continue?"

Her startled squawk brought silent laughter welling up inside him.

"Thank you, but nay. For you to heat up all of my fingers would . . . take a while." She sighed. "There must be better ways to get warm."

Ah, but there were. He knew plenty that weren't

just efficient, but highly pleasurable . . .

No more bawdy thoughts. He hadn't coaxed her over to this pallet to spend a lusty night together, but to offer solace, and, thus, persuade her to trust him. Together, they had a better chance of surviving the ordeals ahead and escaping this tower.

The pallet rustled, and he sensed her yanking on her blanket.

"I know of a way for both of us to get warm," he said.

"I am not sucking on your fingers whilst you do so to mine."

He chuckled. "Nay. I will put my arm around you and draw you close."

"Is that wise?" Her voice sounded muffled by her blanket.

Probably not, considering your arousal, his conscience answered. Ignoring the inner warning, he said, "Of course. By sharing our bodies' heat, we will both become warm. 'Twill grow colder, I vow, before dawn breaks."

She shuddered. Her teeth were still chattering. He rose on his elbow and set his arm around her, just as she wriggled up against him.

As he lowered his head back down onto his forearm, her breath swept against his throat. Her hair glided over his arm at her back, the softness of her tresses a stark contrast to the bite of his restraints.

Did the iron links trailing across her waist bother

her? He hoped not. There wasn't much he could do about the wretched chain.

"I feel warmer already," she murmured.

"Good." Gladness swirled up inside him.

She fitted her body more closely to him, an innocent gesture that, despite the blankets between them, stirred his blood and made his manhood harden all the more. How he *wanted*. If she realized the physical effect she had upon him, though, she'd likely scramble back to her pallet to spend the rest of the night freezing and alone.

Carefully shifting his weight, he raised his arm, moving the right chain up and away from her, and rolled onto his back. The links settled beside him with a muffled *thud*; the chain now trailed along his right arm.

Juliana followed his change of position to rest her head on his shoulder. With a breathy sigh, she snuggled against him. More than one of his lovers had lain that way after a satisfying coupling. He abruptly shoved the inappropriate thought aside.

As she settled to stillness, her hand shifted over the front of his tunic; she was likely trying to find a comfortable resting position for her arm. Edouard savored the warmth of her cheek seeping through his tunic to his skin . . . an instant before her fingers flitted over his groin.

CHAPTER
15

At the feather-light touch, Edouard gasped. Shock whipped through him, and he might have heaved upright, except that Juliana lurched away from him.

Her knees rammed against his leg, while her hand pressed to the center of his chest. He sensed her sitting beside him in the blackness. A groan broke from her, a sound akin to a woman lost in ecstasy.

Before he could clear his mind of astonishment and lust and form a coherent thought, she moaned, "My head. I should not have sat up so quickly, but . . ."

But. Aye. His face burned, and, chains clinking, he dragged a hand over his jaw, very glad at that moment of the darkness. Did she realize she'd touched his privates? Or would he have to answer awkward questions about what, exactly, she'd felt hidden beneath his tunic? God's blood, he'd better have a good explanation as to why he was aroused by her.

"Edouard," she said softly.

"Aye?" He braced himself for the first question.

"What did I . . . touch?"

"My left thigh." *Edouard, you are a rotten liar!*

"Oh. It did not—"

"'Tis a buckled scar," he said hastily. "A wound I got years ago while practicing swordplay." That wasn't entirely a lie. He did have a small scar somewhere on that thigh.

"I did not mean to cause you pain."

A startled grunt scratched his throat. Is that what she'd assumed from his gasp?

"I was trying to get settled. I clearly touched you where it hurt, and I am sorry."

He stifled a curse. He hurt all right, but not in the way she imagined. "'Tis all right, Juliana. Lie back down and get warm."

She didn't move, probably because of his gruffness. He hadn't wanted to sound surly, but his discomfort over the situation had seeped into his tone.

"I really am sorry, Edouard. You have been kind to worry about my well-being, and truly I . . . would never intentionally hurt you." She sounded close to tears, no doubt because of exhaustion.

"Lie down," he urged, patting her hand flattened to his torso. With a breathy sigh, she nestled against him, taking great care, he noted, not to rest any weight on his left leg.

"You cannot imagine how frustrating 'tis not to remember my life." Her voice shook. "When I try to think of my past, I see only a void."

He couldn't bear it if she wept. "Juliana, listen to me—"

"I want to remember, Edouard."

"You will."

She sniffled. "When? I cannot wait to recall every bit of my life. Especially what we were, and are, to one another."

His stomach twisted. He, too, wanted her to regain her memories. When she did, though, she'd be mortified to remember she'd lain in his arms. She might even accuse him of beguiling her while she suffered a weakened mental state.

Thus, he must be honest with her now. "As I told you before, we were not lovers."

He felt her posture stiffen. "Close friends, then?"

"Acquaintances."

"Never! Edouard, my feelings for you . . ."

"There are unresolved matters between us. Important ones you will remember one day."

She fell silent a moment. "Did you reject my affections for another lady's?" A pause. "My sister's?"

The very thought made him want to spit out vile curses. "Nay, Juliana. I never chose Nara over you." He struggled against a surge of ever-present resentment.

"Did you and I have an argument?" she pressed.

"We had . . . disagreements, for which I am entirely to blame."

"Surely we are both partly to blame." Her hand, settled now in the middle of his chest, gently rubbed across his tunic. "And those matters between us? I vow they can be resolved."

"I truly hope so." She might feel differently, however, when she remembered all.

"I sense your torment," she said softly, words muffled against his garment. "Your body grows tense."

He rubbed his brow, ignoring the clink and bump of his chain. Tense didn't encompass what he was feeling now, with shame and remorse churning inside him.

Damnation, but he had to be completely truthful with her. "You hated me, Juliana. 'Tis why you feel strong emotion toward me."

"I could not hate you." She sounded dismayed. "Why would you believe that?"

"'Tis difficult for me to speak of." Purely on instinct, he turned his head toward her. "How I wish—"

Her breath puffed against his lips.

He froze, ensnared by the moment of possibility. Her face was very close. The sweet scent of her skin teased him. Ah, God, if he turned his head the tiniest bit more, their mouths would meet.

At long last, they'd kiss.

Take the kiss! Claim her mouth, as you have wanted.

Yearning seared through him. How he wanted to taste her. To show her how much he cared for her. To answer the need driving through his whole body; the fiery ache for her, the one woman he wanted but could never have.

Edouard, you cannot. Do not prove yourself to be a dishonorable knave.

He sensed her readying to nudge forward, to instinctively seal their kiss. With the last shred of his self-control, he jerked his head away.

Juliana's exhalation blew against his neck.

He swallowed, throat mercilessly tight. His lips burned, as though they really had kissed and the essence of her stayed on his skin.

Desire and regret pulled at him as he stared up at where the roof trusses would be, listening to the wind scrape past the outside walls. He waited, his muscles taut with strain, expecting her to ask what almost happened between them, but she lay quiet, still, and after a long moment, he decided she must have fallen asleep. He shut his eyes.

"Did you . . . almost kiss me?" Her words were a velvety whisper from the blackness.

Aye, his conscience answered. Admitting that, though, wouldn't be fair to her.

He drew deep breaths and pretended to be asleep.

Sunlight on her face brought Juliana from slumber. She stirred, savoring the divine heat against the side of her face and body. A warmth that . . . snored.

She squinted against the morning sunshine, to find herself staring at Edouard's chin, easily within reach if she wished to touch him. Lifting her gaze from the stubble-shadowed line of his jaw, she saw his eyes were still closed. Thick, dark-brown lashes brushed the tanned planes of his cheeks and drew her gaze to his well-defined cheekbones. How arrogant he looked even while sleeping.

A muffled snort broke from him again, and her focus dropped to his lips, slightly parted. Her mouth tingled at the memory of his breath upon her cheek last eve. His face had been very near to hers, and for one thrilling moment, anticipation had burgeoned inside her . . . before he'd abruptly turned his face away.

Had he thought of kissing her and then decided against it? Had he craved her kiss but forced himself to rein in his desire? Nay. He was betrothed to Nara; he'd only want such intimacy with his future wife. Juliana fought a sharp twinge of jealousy, for Nara was lucky to have won the love of a man like Edouard.

For a moment, though, lying beside him, Juliana could secretly dream that he had, indeed, pressed his mouth to hers. The thought of his lips sweeping across hers left a strange, dragging sensation in her lower belly, and she couldn't hold back a shiver.

She indulged her fascination, letting her gaze wander over his muscled physique to the chains snaking along the pallet, and her smile wavered. Last eve she'd hurt him. Accidentally, but his gasp had revealed his discomfort. Now daylight illuminated the chamber, she'd look for that scar he'd spoken of, so she'd be certain not to touch that spot again.

Juliana dared to let her attention drift lower on his body. His left thigh, he'd said. That was close to his man's parts . . .

Oh. She hadn't touched him *there* last night, had she?

A stinging heat spread across her face. Surely he would have told her. Unless, like a gallant hero, he wished to spare her the embarrassment of knowing she'd touched his groin.

She couldn't be sure what to believe. Even more mortifying, his left thigh was trapped beneath her left leg that, during the night, had slid from the blanket and draped over Edouard's legs, likely in her attempts to stay warm.

The sight of their joined limbs stirred a peculiar warmth within her, followed by overwhelming unease. Was she hurting Edouard in the way her leg pressed against him? He didn't appear to be in pain, but he was also sound asleep.

She'd have to move carefully, so she didn't wake or hurt him.

As Juliana slowly pushed up to a seated position, sounds carried from outside the chamber door. Veronique, on a morning visit? What might she do if she discovered them lying together like lovers? At the very least, Veronique might accuse Edouard of all kinds of indiscretions; Juliana couldn't allow that to happen.

She eased her leg from Edouard's and scrambled to sit up, a bit too quickly. Pain and dizziness made the room spin around her, and she froze, silently begging her mind to settle.

That same instant, she sensed Edouard awaken.

The chamber stopped whirling, and she glanced at him, to find his keen gaze upon her. A molten awareness rushed through her, reviving her blush.

Before she could say a word, the key sounded in the lock.

She rushed to rise, but her foot tangled in her blanket. The cloth slipped on the wooden floor. With a choked cry, she dropped back to her former position, bumping against Edouard, who'd just sat up.

"Careful." He steadied her with his hands.

Before she could try to rise again, the door swung inward. Tye walked in, Azarel a few steps behind with a wooden basket on her arm. The door promptly banged shut.

Tye tsked and raised an eyebrow. "Well, well. Slept together, did you?"

Juliana bit her lip.

"We were both cold," Edouard said. "'Twas the best way to keep warm."

"Mmm," Tye said.

"What Edouard said is true." Juliana raised her chin to meet Tye's lewd grin.

Azarel, as before, stood silent with her gaze downward, awaiting orders.

Today, might Juliana be able to ask the healer to contact Edouard's father? Or help them to escape? Juliana would try to speak to her.

"Mother was not able to visit you this morning, as she is seeing to other matters. What will she say, Brother," Tye mused, "when she hears Juliana spent the night in your arms? What would your betrothed think of it?"

An angry hiss broke from Edouard and stirred Juliana's hair. "What choice did we have, but to share this miserable chamber? Whether she slept in my arms or alone on her bed, we would have spent the night together."

Tye grinned. "True."

"Unlike you"—Edouard's voice was almost a snarl—"I am a chivalrous man. Naught inappropriate happened between Juliana and myself. I suffer no shame. Will you, however, force disgrace upon her, by telling tales about us?"

As Edouard spoke, Tye's gaze flicked over her. He stared as though he saw through her chemise and the blanket wrapped around her, and she fought a tremor. "Bold words, Brother." Tye's mouth slid into a lopsided grin. "They make me curious, though. With her loveliness so close to you, were you not once tempted to—"

"Nay," Edouard growled.

Tye's laughter rang in the chamber. "You do not even know what I planned to say."

"I can guess."

With a last chuckle, Tye gestured to Azarel. The healer hurried forward, leather shoes making light taps on the floorboards before she dropped down beside Juliana's pallet. The basket creaked as she rummaged within.

Tye's stare bored into Juliana. "Return to your pallet, so she can tend you." His smile hardened. "You might think that because Mother is not here, 'twill be easy to deceive me. Beware, Juliana. My brother might insist he is an honorable man, but I"—he slowly winked—"am an unscrupulous knave."

Tye didn't, as Edouard had hoped, leave as soon as Azarel had finished seeing to Juliana's wound. Once the healer had completed her work in silence, she picked up her basket, rose, and faced Tye.

"Her injury is much improved from yesterday," she said.

"Mother will want to hear of her progress." Tye

crossed to the panel, knocked on it, and stood guard while the door opened and Azarel hurried out. He exchanged a few words with the men outside—instructions Edouard couldn't make out—then shoved the door closed.

With swaggering strides, he approached Edouard. Leaning back against the nearest wall—beyond Edouard's reach—Tye crossed his arms across his tunic. For some reason, he wasn't wearing his sword belt. Had he tumbled out of a maidservant's bed and hauled his clothes on before coming to the tower, and forgotten his weapons?

A mistake Edouard must try and use to his advantage.

Leather creaked as Tye bent one knee and planted his boot's sole against the stone, an indolent posture that suggested he meant to stay a while. Indeed, as long as he liked.

Ugh. Tye likely intended to taunt him further about his sleeping with Juliana.

Daring a glance at her, Edouard saw she'd scooted back on her pallet and curled her legs beneath her. Her wary expression told him she, too, suspected Tye's intentions.

A smug warmth curled through Edouard; he was glad she disliked the bastard.

Edouard looked back at Tye, to find Tye studying him, narrowed stare thoughtful.

"What do you want?" Edouard demanded in a tone he used only for the most witless of men. Usually it sent the fools scurrying.

Tye smirked. "Tell me about Father."

Edouard scowled, the rise of hatred for Tye instantaneous and fierce. "I told you before. Do not call him such."

Tye's eyes glinted. "He *is* my sire. Do I not deserve to know a little about the man who slaked his lust with Mother and fathered me?"

"For all we know," Edouard shot back, "what Veronique says about your paternity is a lie. She has always been interested in my sire's riches."

Tilting his head, Tye smiled. Then he pointed to his face. "Look at me."

Edouard grimaced. "Must I?"

Tye leaned forward, gaze bright. "Mother says my features favor our sire. Can you not see the resemblance?"

Edouard clenched his jaw. Tye's hair was lighter brown than his sire's, and his skin was more bronzed from the sun. Judging from the shape of Tye's nose, it had been broken several times. Yet his features were similar to Edouard's father. So was Tye's muscular build.

"See?" Tye's tone turned gloating. "You cannot deny I resemble him."

"Looks are your only proof?" Mayhap if Edouard goaded Tye enough, he'd glean more details on Tye and Veronique's schemes. Better still, Edouard might lure the conceited bastard into range of the chains. Then they'd see who was the son of Geoffrey de Lanceau.

"There is the timing of my birth," Tye said. "Mother had no other lover but Geoffrey de Lanceau when she got with child. A fact, I am told, she tried to impress upon him when I was but a young boy, but he refused to believe her."

"I cannot blame him."

Tye's hands slowly curled into fists while he leaned even farther forward. "How many times I have longed to stand before him and demand that he look upon me. *Me*, the bastard son he wishes was never born."

A trace of anguish drove through Tye's words. Edouard steeled himself against any notions of pity. Tye was a clever manipulator, just like his mother. "You will never get close enough to Father for him to look upon you."

Tye pressed back against the wall. A grating laugh rumbled from him. "The day I kill him, I shall."

How Edouard longed to snarl that that wretched day would never come. However, this was a perfect opportunity to lure details from Tye. "What makes you believe you can murder him?"

"You must be aware of the missives Mother sent to Branton Keep. During our many years living in France, I trained with mercenaries who earned a living fighting for the French and English kings, whichever one offered the most coin to fight in a particular battle. I trained hard and, as my skills grew, won tournament after tournament. I am very good with a broadsword."

"Father is better."

"Is he?" Tye grinned. "I look forward to proving you wrong."

"You will never get near to Branton Keep. His men-at-arms and servants—"

"Are honorable and loyal to the death." Tye waved a careless hand. "No matter. I will mingle with our sire's trusted colleagues, find a reason to meet him face to face, and then I will draw my blade." He swung his arm down, mimicking a swift, killing blow. "Ha!"

Juliana gasped.

Edouard sensed her horror but didn't dare look her way, for foreboding stabbed deep inside him. There were very few ways Tye could be accepted into his father's elite circle. He'd succeed, however, if he wore the gold ring entrusted to Landon.

"How quiet you are, Brother," Tye said. "I have shocked you."

Fighting his rising apprehension, Edouard forced an arrogant shrug. He must keep Tye talking. The more he learned, the better he could protect Juliana and destroy the traitorous plans. "I have to say, you are ambitious, but stupid. When, exactly, will you risk this killing?"

"Soon." Tye examined the nails of his left hand. "When circumstances are right."

"When you have Landon's gold ring, you mean."

Tye's gaze lifted on an admiring grin. "How clever

you are, Brother."

"That explains why you and Veronique want Juliana to survive. You suspect she knows where Landon hid the ring. You want it badly enough to take care of her until her memories return."

Juliana gasped again. "Merciful God."

"You have overlooked a critical point, though," Edouard said. "Even if she remembers her identity, she may not know the ring's whereabouts. Landon may never have confided that to her."

"A risk Mother and I are willing to take."

"Because she is the only one alive who might know?" A derisive chuckle grated from Edouard. "What if Juliana doesn't know? Your threat to kill our sire is an idle one, then?"

Edouard held Tye's blazing gaze, hoping the bastard would rise to the goading.

"'Tis not, at all, an idle threat," Tye ground out.

"You talk of slaying him face to face. Brave words. Yet I vow you are a coward." As fury darkened Tye's gaze, Edouard added, "If you really wished my sire dead, you would have confronted him long before now."

"Mother and I—"

"Mother and I," Edouard mocked.

Tye took a step forward, his white-knuckled hands balled at his sides. "Some risks are worth taking; others require money and patience. We will find that ring. When I stand before Father so he can look full upon me, 'twill be with an army of mercenaries to fight at my side."

Edouard snorted.

"Then he will know he is a dead man. Doomed to be slain by his own flesh-and-blood son he cruelly rejected all those years ago." Tye chuckled. "What perfect irony."

God's teeth. Tye spoke in exactly the same manner as Veronique. How well she'd controlled and prepared her son, so he'd fulfill the murderous ambitions she'd not been able to bring to pass years ago.

Surely, though, as a grown man, Tye had a will of his own.

"Your mother hates our sire because he ended their affair years ago. Why, after so many years, she continues to resent him and plot vengeance against him, only she can explain," Edouard said. "You must realize, though, that all she has told you of him is but her opinion?"

"'Tis the only one that matters."

"Have you tried to contact our—my sire—on your own?"

Tye laughed, a sound ripe with bitterness. "Why would I? He has made it very clear he wants naught to do with me. Besides, if I tried to set up a meeting, he would agree only so he could arrest me. Then he would try and use me to capture Mother. As we both know, he has wanted her imprisoned for years for crimes including murder and treason."

True. Tye might be many things, but he wasn't stupid.

CATHERINE KEAN

"On the other hand"—Tye's visage hardened—"he might not even bother to arrest me. He might attack. Once I was overpowered, he would run me through with a sword and leave my corpse for the birds to pick clean. Eliminate me and the threat I pose to him and his heir." Tye pointed. "You."

"My father lives by the code of honor—"

"So you say." Tye's lip curled. "'Tis *your* opinion."

"Look—"

But Tye wasn't listening. "I eagerly await the confrontation to come. 'Twill be a magnificent day when, at last, I make him acknowledge me. I will slay him, seize all that is his, and make it mine."

Ruthless, greedy *bastard*. "You will never defeat him," Edouard growled, yanking on his chains.

"Spoken like a naïve, loving son."

"Father is no fool. By now, he likely knows you are here at Waddesford. He will anticipate your attack, while he plans one of his own."

"We shall see."

Indeed, you arrogant whoreson, we shall. Edouard drew upon all the rage and frustration seething within him. "I will never let you kill my sire—"

Tye laughed.

"—or let you take control of what, as his heir, is rightfully mine."

"You? The helpless son in chains?" Tye chortled.

262

Edouard mentally shoved aside the insult. *Use Tye's ambition to make him angry. Lure him closer, and then you will take the advantage.*

"I might be chained," Edouard said, "but I am worthy of being Geoffrey de Lanceau's son. You are not."

Tye sucked in a slow, deliberate breath. He seemed to grow taller and broader.

"Edouard," Juliana whispered. Fear shone in her eyes as she glanced from him to Tye.

Menace in the slant of his jaw, Tye stepped nearer. "I am not worthy," he said, "because of my birth?"

Edouard managed a thin smile. Let Tye make of that statement what he wished.

As the silence tautened, Tye bared his teeth. He looked furious enough to pummel Edouard into the floorboards.

Good.

"You have spoken unwisely, Brother."

"Have I, you *bastard*?"

Come closer, Tye. Just a little closer . . .

Tye thrust his right fist down in Edouard's face. "One more insult, and—"

Edouard shoved up on his heels and grabbed Tye's wrist. With a stab of dismay, Edouard realized he was almost too slow; his movements, acutely honed in the tilt-yards, were hampered by the added weight of the chains.

Tye yanked back on his hand. "Hell—"

As Tye stumbled and tried to catch his balance,

Edouard tugged him forward, head first toward the pallet.

Twisting as he fell, Tye slammed his left fist into Edouard's jaw. Pain sprayed through Edouard's cheek. Smothering a groan, he shook his head and punched back. The blow bounced off Tye's chest, but on a muffled *clank*, Edouard's chain hit Tye's bent leg. Tye grunted in pain.

With a strong tug, Tye freed his hand. Faster than Edouard expected, another blow flew, this time into his gut.

"Bastard," Edouard choked out, fighting the need to brace his arm against his stomach. Shaking hair from his eyes, he grabbed his chain. When Tye scrambled to rise, Edouard looped it around Tye's neck, forcing him down on his knees.

His back to Edouard, Tye clawed at the chain. His chin tipped up at an awkward angle as he tried to ease the chain's pressure.

Bloodlust pulsed hard in Edouard's veins. Who was helpless now?

"Edouard." Juliana's voice wove into the haze filling his vision. "Edouard, stop."

A choked breath snapped his gaze down to Tye's face. Tye's skin was reddening, while his mouth parted on strangled breaths.

"Now," Edouard said with a smile, "who is the fool?"

Spittle oozed from Tye's mouth. "Kill me, then."

"Edouard, nay!" Juliana cried. Daring a glance, he found her standing dangerously near, hands open and pleading. "Murdering Tye will solve naught."

Tye writhed in Edouard's grasp. Edouard tightened his hold on the chain. A grisly choke rose from his half brother.

"You are a man who lives by honor," Juliana shrilled, "just like your father. "'Tis not your way to—"

"You do not remember me," Edouard bellowed. "How can you say that?"

Her wide-eyed gaze beseeched him. "From all I have known of you recently, I have guessed your true nature." Her hands knotted together. "You know I am right."

He dragged his gaze away from her, lovely and passionate in her desperation. Never had he imagined killing an unarmed opponent, but here, with Tye at his mercy, he had a chance to end Veronique's merciless plotting against his sire once and for all.

Killing Tye just might save his father's life.

And yet Juliana's words gouged into Edouard, running like blood into the parts of him ruled by chivalry between warriors. As much as he hated to admit it, killing Tye in this way held cowardice.

Edouard looked down at his fingers, pale against the taut iron links, and tried to reason with the powerful rage blazing inside him. Glaring down at Tye's sweat-beaded profile, Edouard snarled, "Call the guards. I want the key to my manacles."

Digging his fingers into the chain, Tye glared back.

"Call," Edouard growled. "Now!"

"They will . . . not come. Told them . . . not to . . . heed cries."

"*Do it!*"

"Will have . . . to . . . kill me," Tye rasped.

Edouard stared down into Tye's red-rimmed eyes. In them, Edouard saw a mirror of his own resolve never to yield. "I ask you," Edouard bit out, "once again."

"Please," Juliana whispered, stepping nearer.

"Stay away," Edouard snapped.

Tye's lips quivered into a mocking smile. "Go on. Kill me. If you . . . are man enough."

The haze of anger nearly blinded Edouard. *Man enough—?*

"Do not heed his taunts," Juliana cried.

"Juliana!" Edouard roared.

"Even if you kill him, you will still be chained. How will we defeat the guards outside? How will we escape the keep? We cannot. Please, Edouard"—her tone hoarsened—"if you will not spare him out of honor, spare him because I ask you to."

Blowing aside a skein of hair, Edouard stared at her. God help him, but she was right about killing Tye. It gave them no advantage whatsoever. 'Twould only make their situation even more dire.

Tears trailed down her face. Her bosom rose and fell on anxious breaths. In her eyes, he saw disappointment as well as an urgent plea.

Her disappointment in him hurt worst of all. She'd looked at him that way when she'd found him kissing Nara.

Spitting a foul oath, he loosened his hold on the chain. Tye lurched forward, staggered to his feet, and, inhaling on a gasp, raced to the wall.

The chains clinked as they tumbled back onto the pallet to lie like iron snakes.

A wobbly smile lifted Juliana's lips. "Thank you."

Edouard looked away, trying to control the tremendous pressure building inside him. Now that he'd attacked Tye, would Veronique exact punishment upon him and Juliana?

The scrape of a boot heel on the planks snapped his focus back to Tye. Sucking air between his teeth, Tye flattened his hand against the wall and straightened to his full height. He ran his other hand over his tunic. "I will not forget what you did, Brother." His voice cracked.

"Nor will I forget all you have done," Edouard answered coldly.

"Please," Juliana said. "No more fighting. 'Twill solve naught."

Tye's blazing stare didn't waver. Edouard refused to look away, to back down from the challenge still crackling between him and his bastard brother.

His mouth set in a sneer, Tye turned toward the doorway. At last, he acknowledged he'd lost and was leav—

Tye spun. Before Edouard could lunge aside, Tye's

foot slammed into Edouard's chest, a solid blow between the ribs that propelled him back against the wall. Grunting, he doubled over and tried to get air back into his lungs; each short, sharp breath was agonizing. Hellfire, he should have expected such trickery from Tye—

"Stop!" Juliana shrieked. Footfalls pounded on the floorboards. Edouard raised his head to see Juliana standing between him and Tye, hands fisted, hair a wild tangle down her back. Sunlight poured over her, turning her chemise to the pure white of fresh snow.

Tye's gaze prowled over her. Edouard gritted his teeth, for he knew the sheerness of her garment. Lit at just the right angle, it might become transparent, baring all her innocent beauty to Tye's view.

Stubbornly ignoring his pain, Edouard rose.

Tye didn't cease his lustful inspection that left no doubt what he wanted to do to Juliana. Clearly sensing a physical threat, she raised her fists as though to ward him off.

"Tye," Edouard croaked. His voice was barely audible to his own ears; he drew more gasped breaths and willed strength to return to his words.

"You want to fight me now, fierce little Juliana?" Tye chuckled like the gutter-born rogue he was.

She didn't move, not even the slightest flinch. "I want you to leave Edouard alone."

"Such passionate words."

"Please," she said. "Just go."

How proud Edouard was of Juliana for being so brave. Another part of him, though, resented that she felt she must do battle for him. "Listen to her," he managed to growl. "Leave."

With lazy disdain, Tye's attention shifted from her to Edouard. "This fight between us is not done, Brother."

"I agree," Edouard said. "'Tis not."

Tye smiled. "I vow it has only begun."

CHAPTER
16

As soon as the door slammed behind Tye, Juliana whirled and dashed to Edouard's side. He leaned back against the wall, sitting with his legs bent and his arms braced on his knees. Leaning his head back against the stone, he shut his eyes.

Tears still wet on her cheeks, she dropped down on her knees at his left side, took his face in both hands, and tilted it to her view.

He winced, even as his eyes flew open. "Ah—!"

"What?" Lifting her left fingers, she spied the purpling bruise on his jaw. "Oh. Sorry." Cringing inside, she dropped her hands into her lap. As Edouard carefully flexed his jaw, she asked, "Are you all right?"

"Aye."

"Do you hurt anywhere else?"

Edouard's gaze slid away. He looked mutinous, angry, and she sensed him struggling with an inner torment. Most likely, he didn't want to admit to his other injuries. He doubtless saw himself as a bold, brave warrior, and he'd endure, congratulating himself for suffering in silence.

New tears dampened her eyes while she studied the taut planes of his face. His expression, when he'd held that chain wrapped around Tye's neck . . . Frightening. Her heart had squeezed so tightly within her rib cage, she couldn't breathe, for in that instant, she knew he'd kill Tye if circumstances left him no alternative.

There *had* been a choice, though. Edouard had listened to her. Respected her plea. Spared Tye's life, and for that, Edouard was all the more noble to her.

Tye's kicking of Edouard? Unscrupulous. In a fight governed by chivalry, Tye would have been disqualified and sent off in dishonor. Yet 'twas clear he didn't care about gallantry. He wanted to appear to have won the scuffle, by whatever means he deemed necessary. Another reason why Edouard's actions were even more admirable.

Still looking at a point beyond her, Edouard swallowed; her attention fell to his Adam's apple, moving beneath his tanned skin. How she ached to tell him how grateful she was that he hadn't committed murder. How she wanted to voice the emotions churning inside her: admiration; relief . . . and something wonderful she couldn't quite name.

"Edouard," she whispered, willing him to meet her gaze. He closed his eyes again. He didn't answer.

Juliana fought the dismay gnawing at her. He didn't move, but he was withdrawing from her, taking refuge behind a mental barricade. She shifted on her knees and her breast brushed against his bent knee. An unplanned contact that she felt, with shocking intensity, in places she dared not name.

At her sharp inhalation, his eyes opened. His gaze, smoldering with emotion, settled on her mouth.

Did he want to kiss her, as she'd secretly dreamed? How shameful that she yearned for the intimacy.

"Edouard," she murmured, "I—"

"You should not have confronted Tye."

At last, Edouard spoke to her. Not, however, in the tender manner she'd hoped.

Tamping down a pang of disappointment, she said, "He looked about to kick you again."

"I can defend myself," Edouard gritted, each word edged with frustration.

So he suffered from wounded pride, as well as a battered body. Was being rescued by a woman more distressing to him than his other discomforts?

Gentling her tone, she said, "Of course you can defend yourself. But you are at a disadvantage, being chained as you are."

Edouard's stare bored into her. Was he angered by her honest words? Did he resent her pointing out his infirmity? "Juliana," he growled. "The brazen way he looked at you—"

An icy shiver rippled through her. "Aye, but—"

"But all is well?" Edouard threw his arm wide, causing a dissonant *clank* of the chain. "But he left us alone, so we should simply forget the matter?"

The intensity of Edouard's gaze snatched her next breath. Did she see fury in his eyes, or an emotion even more startling: jealousy? She struggled to speak calmly. "I did not say—"

"I am glad you did not try. For I will *not* forget that insult to you."

Tears again moistened her eyes. For him to speak so fiercely . . . To feel so strongly on her behalf. . . . Had any man ever been so passionate about her?

"Tye will answer for his disrespect, along with all his many other crimes."

She blinked the wetness from her vision, even as a thrill rushed through her to flit like a moth in her stomach. She'd thought Edouard noble before; she now wanted to throw her arms around his neck and kiss him like a giddy fool.

But she wouldn't. Couldn't.

Nara, what a fine husband you have found. I can only hope one day to find a man even half as gallant.

Squashing a flare of jealousy, she said, "Thank you, Edouard."

He nodded once, and then his chains shifted. Before

she guessed his intentions, he slid his fingers into her hair and wound a generous fistful around his hand. At the startling, unexpected entrapment, she tried to pull away, but he tightened his hold a fraction. Gently, but firmly, he pulled her head toward his.

"What . . . ?"

His narrowed gaze locked with hers. Beneath the fall of his lashes, his blue eyes gleamed as though lit with cold fire, and she caught her breath, wary, yet at the same time, enthralled.

"Do *not*," he ground out, "speak so—"

"Edouard—"

"—to Tye again."

She sucked in a quivery breath and tried to wrest her gaze from his. But she couldn't. His blazing stare captured her with its heat, commanded her to obey him. In the corners of his gaze, though, she caught traces of his fear for her, and of his wish to protect her.

"I know you are going to disagree," he said roughly, "but I will not have you come to harm. Not on my behalf."

Juliana frowned, even as his fingers relaxed their grip on her tresses, for her earlier encounter with Tye *had* given her an idea. One that might aid their escape.

As she sat back on her heels and smoothed her hair, Edouard muttered, "I was right. I see it in your eyes. You are going to disagree with me."

"Aye, because you make demands I cannot possibly

keep. How can I not speak to Tye? He will grow suspicious if I refuse to acknowledge or answer him."

Edouard sighed. "Of course you can speak to him. Just do not challenge him."

"Are you asking me to do that, Edouard, or ordering me?"

Concern darkened his expression before he shook his head. "Look, Juliana—"

"I *know* Tye is a dangerous man."

"You cannot imagine. The less you must associate with him, the better, for your own safety. From now on, you will let me—"

"I will *not* promise to never challenge Tye again, Edouard. That may be our way to get free."

Edouard's mouth flattened into an uncompromising line. "What do you mean?"

The enormity of her plan welled up to loom inside her like a grinning specter. However, she wouldn't lose her courage. Not if it meant she could save Edouard and his noble sire and put a stop to whatever cruelty Tye and Veronique were plotting.

"One of us must get out of this chamber and get the key to your shackles," she said with surprising calmness. "Also, the more I see of this castle, the better chance I have of my memories returning. Then, when we escape, I will be able to guide us out of the keep to safety."

Edouard said naught. He was, however, watching her attentively.

She rallied her courage, sensing she walked a precipitous path. "I thought I would try and convince Tye to take me from this room. Only for a short while, of course."

Edouard exhaled through his teeth.

She threw up a hand to stop any protest from him. "I realize 'tis dangerous, but if we do not escape soon, we may both die here." Softening her tone, she added, "Nara is waiting for you to return to her. Do you really want to give up your wedding to her?"

His impassioned gaze glowed even brighter than before. His love for Nara must be true and precious. Juliana struggled with a fresh pang of jealousy.

"How, exactly, will you persuade Tye to take you from this chamber?" Edouard demanded.

Dread coursed through her, even as she said, "I shall entice him."

"Mother."

Tye's voice cut through the clang of swords wielded by two mercenaries dueling in the sun-drenched bailey. What did he want *now*? Biting back an oath, Veronique braced her hands on her thighs and rose from squatting before the woolen mantle she'd stretched out on the dirt. The prime spot not only allowed her to accomplish her fortune telling, but watch the fight and decide which mercenary would be most useful to her.

Now that she was standing, the arrangement of bones upon the mantle looked slightly different, but equally uninformative.

Tye halted beside her and frowned. "Why did you bring those outside? Whose garment—?"

"Edouard's." Veronique gnawed on her fingernail. "I had hoped, by casting my bones upon a garment belonging to him, that I might gain insight into the coming days."

"And?"

"The future remains unclear." She sighed and glanced at the tantalizing display of male prowess close by; her gaze settled on the taller of the bare-chested men, then the stockier one.

Her hand instinctively smoothed over the gown she'd tugged into place a short while ago, after walking, flushed and weak-kneed, out of the stable. Fornicating helped to clear her concentration; she'd insisted upon it before casting her bones. She'd almost torn her skirts in her frantic, gasping, womb-shuddering rut with a young, blond mercenary, a friend of these two warriors who'd given up his turn to fight to lie with her.

Her bodice wasn't quite straight, but Tye might not notice.

His lips broke into a smile that flashed all of his straight, white teeth. He looked at the mercenaries, then back at her. "Accomplishing two desires at once, I see."

"Whatever do you mean?" She arched her eyebrows.

The glint in his eyes warned he knew full well what she'd done.

He laughed. "Do not play coy with me, Mother. The glow of sex still warms your face."

Sometimes she wished he wasn't quite as wretchedly perceptive, but then again, she'd raised him to be so. He had to be quick-witted to defeat and kill his noble sire, the destiny she expected of him. But that didn't give him any right whatsoever to remark on her sexual liaisons.

"That is enough, Tye." With luck, her tone, fit for a disobedient infant, would silence his teasing. However, she silently admitted with a twinge of regret, he was far from a child. His impressive physique proved he was all man; so did the trysts she'd caught him in over the years with serving wenches, courtesans, and even widowed ladies. If he wasn't her own flesh and blood, she'd have lured him to her bed long ago.

Tye's attention shifted to the mercenaries, grunting as their swords locked. The weapons slid together with a shriek before the men sprang apart, faces shiny with sweat. "The question is," Tye said quietly, "have *you* had enough? Or are these two next?"

She wrinkled her nose. A fresh tug of lust, though, wove through her. Her son—wicked and clever boy— might well be right.

The sooner she finished with Tye and sent him away,

the sooner she could focus on other matters, such as the men at hand.

"What do you need of me, Tye?" she demanded. "Did you come merely to pester me, or do you have news?"

A sly gleam lit his eyes. "I do have news."

Veronique drew an excited breath. "Juliana's memories have come back?"

"Not that I know of, Mother." Clearly anticipating her demand for his information, he raised a staying hand. "However, I found her and Edouard lying together this morning."

"Did he deflower her? Do you think . . . ?"

Tye shook his head. "She did not have that look about her."

"Mayhap this eve, then," Veronique said with a wicked cackle.

"That might, indeed, come to pass. You see, Juliana challenged me in the chamber after I kicked Edouard. Clenched her delicate fists and looked about to punch me in the stomach."

A grin curved Veronique's lips. "What a brave but foolish girl. Did she not realize you could have knocked her to the floor with one strike?"

"I believe her emotions were so heightened they diminished her sense of caution."

"Ah. Juliana has developed feelings for Edouard."

"Aye, Mother."

"Feelings," Veronique murmured, caught up in her

evolving thoughts, "she must realize are not at all proper, when Edouard is her sister's betrothed. When I spoke to Azarel earlier, Tye, she did not advise another potion for Juliana. She said Juliana's memories would likely return when prompted by strong emotional reactions: anticipation; fear—"

"Desire?"

Sometimes, Tye could be such a bright boy. A smile burgeoned inside Veronique, born from that ingrained, often inconvenient sense of maternal instinct. Still, she couldn't keep herself from bestowing that affection upon her son as she patted his cheek. "Aye."

Tye smiled back. Mischief glinted in his eyes. "What do you suggest?"

Veronique laughed, a gloating sound that carried across the bailey. The two fighting men paused and looked her way. "We shall tighten our grip on Juliana's fragile emotions. We *must*, after all, find Landon's ring. If what I have in mind works, we will not only revive her memories today, but have her seeking comfort again in Edouard's arms. You, Tye, are just the man to accomplish what needs to be done."

CHAPTER
17

"What do you see?" Edouard asked, his gaze on Juliana standing before the window, peering out.

The ring of swordplay carried up from the bailey. Not enough noise to signal a rescue, but his men might be attempting an escape. Impatience chafed at Edouard. If only he could see for himself! How he hated having even that small freedom denied to him.

"Two men are dueling with swords," Juliana said. "I do not see much else."

"Look to the edges of the bailey." He tried to envision standing before the window's iron grille, looking down, and using all that his warrior training had taught him to analyze the scene before him. "Who else is there with the fighters? Are other armed men standing around? Is anyone lying on the ground, injured? Do you see saddled horses, or—?"

Juliana flicked a hand at him. "Patience. Please."

Tenderness softened her voice. He silently groaned,

for when her memories returned, she'd realize how much she despised him. Would she resent having trusted him enough to sleep beside him? Embarrassed by the thoughts she'd shared about her feelings for him, she might avoid him for the rest of their living days.

A crushing ache pressed upon Edouard. Her laughter, her beauty, the way his heart soared when she smiled at him . . . He'd never care for Nara the way he loved Juliana. He should have listened to his father's wise words years ago and insisted on a betrothal to her. Then neither he nor Juliana would be in this wretched mess now.

As Edouard blinked away his regrets and focused again on Juliana, he noted she'd curled her hands around the grille and risen on tiptoes to lean farther into the embrasure. Standing that way, her body looked even more lithe. Her gown clung to her bottom, emphasizing its enticing roundness. He curled his hands into fists, feeling the pinch of his manacles against his wrist veins, as his desire flamed anew.

"Wait!" She pressed her brow to the grille, tension now in her posture. "I see Veronique."

"What is she doing?"

"Speaking with Tye, who is beside her now."

Just hearing that bastard's name, especially when his blood ran hotter, made Edouard want to slam his hand into the wall. A broken wrist, though, would only be a hindrance in an escape.

"What else?" he asked, shifting his stance on the pallet. He rolled his shoulders, more to tamp down his impatience than because he felt the need. "Are Tye and Veronique holding any objects? Are they speaking with any others?"

"Not that I can tell. The men are continuing their swordfight." She sighed. "I do not believe aught of consequence is happening."

"When Veronique and Tye are together," Edouard said, "aught of consequence is most definitely—"

Veronique's shrill laughter carried up from the bailey.

Juliana glanced his way. "I vow you are right."

"Whatever they intend, we will defeat them." His anxiety sharpened with defiance. "We must escape, Juliana. Today."

Juliana faced him, her expression solemn. "I agree."

"I have tried to think of a sound plan that does not put you in jeopardy, but—"

"There are few options," she finished for him. "'Tis why I must focus on Tye."

Edouard exhaled on a frustrated growl. He couldn't stand to think of her alone with Tye. What he might do to her . . .

"I know you do not like the idea," Juliana rushed on. "However Tye, like Veronique, depends upon my memories returning to find the gold ring. He will not risk harming me. At least not until he has the information he wants."

Bitterness gouged Edouard like an invisible knife. He, the trained warrior, should be protecting Juliana, confronting danger to rescue her, not the other way around. "I have another suggestion. Azarel will likely visit you again today to check on your injury. When she does, you will lure her over to me. I will take her hostage." He regretted using a woman for leverage, especially one who already seemed terrified, but Veronique valued the healer's skills; for all he knew, Veronique might depend upon them.

Juliana frowned. "Azarel is a kind woman. If she was hurt—"

"She won't be. I would make sure of it. Never would I harm a woman."

"You might not, but what of the others?" Juliana rubbed her arms, as though chilled. "We do not know what Veronique might do to prevent you from getting free. She might order Tye or her lackeys to kill Azarel while she is your captive. Then we would have accomplished naught, except the death of a woman devoted to caring for others."

He loosed a silent groan; Juliana was right.

"My plan is the only choice, Edouard." Her determined gaze held his. "I must get my memories back, and if I leave this chamber, that might happen. I will look for anything to aid our escape. A weapon. Keys . . ."

Edouard squeezed his eyelids shut, struggling against the battle waging in his heart. He felt her hand upon his arm, and opened his eyes to look down at her.

"I can save us," Juliana whispered. "I want to try."

"I cannot protect you," he said hoarsely.

She smiled. "When you are free of your chains, you will rescue us all."

Her brave words sent anticipation racing through him, rousing anew his rebelliousness. Aye, he would rescue Waddesford Keep. He'd give Veronique and Tye a fight to make his father proud.

Edouard nodded. "All right. Promise me, though, you will be careful. Promise me—"

A muffled exchange of voices came from beyond the door. An instant later, the rasp of the key.

Juliana's posture stiffened. "If 'tis Tye," she whispered, "I must act now."

Edouard's teeth ground together. Sheer luck only that they didn't break apart in his mouth, but he forced himself to nod.

"'Twill be more convincing"—she darted away—"if you seem reluctant and even . . . jealous."

Pretend to be jealous? If she only knew what raged inside him.

The chamber door opened. Tye sauntered in, one hand on the hilt of his sheathed sword. His other hand clasped what appeared to be a garment, along with a pair of leather shoes.

His gaze fell to Juliana's vacant pallet, before he quickly glanced about the chamber. When he found her by the window, he grinned. "There you are."

She didn't answer, but, facing him, linked her hands together. Sunlight poured in through the window, surrounding her in light.

"Why are you standing there, Juliana?" Tye took a step toward her in that slow, almost predatory way of his.

"I wanted to catch the sun's warmth." Her voice held the faintest waver.

"Leave her be," Edouard snapped, hoping he sounded suitably annoyed.

"I am not speaking to you," Tye shot back, while he moved closer to Juliana. He clearly meant to trap her against the wall with his body.

Edouard cursed. He couldn't reach either of them while chained.

As Tye neared her, his focus slid to the sunlight outside. "Not spying on me, love, were you?"

Her mouth pinched, and he chuckled.

"Do not call me such," she said.

"What?" Tye feigned a gesture of innocent surprise. "Love?"

"Aye. You are not my love. Neither am I yours."

"Ah, Juliana, but you could be."

An image of Tye and Juliana lying naked together,

his hand trailing over her virginal skin, brought an angry red haze to Edouard's vision. *"Pretend to be jealous,"* Juliana had said. Hellfire, he'd show her jealous. "Cease, Tye," he snarled.

Reaching for her, Tye set his hand upon her shoulder. His fingers trailed down her shoulder blade to the swell of her breast in a slow, purposeful caress.

Her back flattened to the wall, Juliana shuddered.

Blinding rage seared through Edouard. "Do not touch her." He sounded jealous all right—just as he felt.

A mocking laugh broke from Tye. He glanced at Edouard. "You want to stop me, Brother? Go ahead." His gaze returned to Juliana as he shoved the garment and shoes at her. "Put these on."

"Why?"

"You are to come with me. We cannot distract the other men in the keep with your"—his lustful gaze skimmed over her—"state of undress, despite how fetching you look."

How dare Tye ogle her as though she was intended for his pleasure! Lunging to the end of his chains, Edouard dragged in a shaky breath. "Where are you taking her?"

Tye stepped away from Juliana. "Not your concern, Brother."

"'Tis indeed my concern. I brought her to Waddesford. Thus I am honor-bound to protect her."

Edouard caught the pride and resolve in Juliana's

gaze before she dropped the shoes on the floor and shook out the garment, a plain, woolen gown. Turning her back to Tye, she drew it over her head and began to smooth it down over her chemise.

"Honor-bound?" Tye's lips curved in a nasty smile. "How pointless, especially when you will soon be dead."

When the door to the tower chamber slammed behind Juliana, she flinched. She squared her shoulders and tried not to heed her thumping pulse while she met the gazes of the two guards, standing with their swords drawn. Any hopes she had, however remote, of racing down the stairs and escaping Tye fizzled like raindrops on a hot stone.

One of the men stepped behind her and, with the jangle of keys, locked the door. Tye brushed past her, close enough to stir the skirt of the gown he'd given her. The coarse fabric scratched her skin through her chemise, but she'd tolerate that discomfort even if she broke out in rash; at last, she was out of the chamber.

Tye paused at the entry to the stairwell and studied her, his face rendered an eerie mask of light and darkness by the burning wall torch nearby. "Do not even think about escape, Juliana. If you so much as try—or I believe you are contemplating it—I will haul you back here and you will never leave this chamber alive again. Understand?"

Fear welled inside her, but she forced it aside and nodded.

A hard grin tilted his mouth. "You might think you can trick me, pretend to obey while you're secretly looking for a way to save yourself and Edouard. I assure you, all of the folk in this keep are loyal to me and Mother. You can trust no one." His lewd gaze ran over her. "Not even me."

Indignation sparked at his glance. "I would not be foolish enough to trust you."

He laughed softly. "So says the willful but innocent little lamb."

The two guards snickered.

Juliana stiffened. "'Tis in my interest, as well as yours, for me to recall my past. I am eager to see as much of the keep as possible." Fighting a nagging trepidation, she gestured to the area enclosing them. "I see naught here that I recognize beyond the past day."

Tye raised his brows. "You have not forgotten your boldness, Juliana."

"What makes you say such?" she asked, but her words were drowned by the tramp of his boots as he took the first few steps down.

"Come," he said.

She had no choice but to follow; no other passage led away from the chamber.

Juliana crossed to the stairwell and started to descend,

pressing one hand against the stone wall to guide her way. *Down into the unknown*, her mind whispered.

Around and down the stairwell went, like an uncoiling serpent. The musty smell of stale air and ancient rock surrounded her. In the farthest reaches of her mind, the darkness stirred, akin to dense fog shifting in a breeze.

Willing the sensation to gather into a memory, she continued her descent. Hope quickened her pulse. How fervently she hoped her recollections returned. Then she'd finally, completely know who she was.

Some distance down, Tye halted several steps below her and glanced back. "Well?"

"Naught yet," she said.

He stared at her for a long, grueling moment, as though debating whether she'd lied to him. Then he turned and continued down the stairs.

When some distance along, they came to a passageway opening off the stairwell, Tye waited for her to catch up to him. "You will go ahead of me." His hand slid along her lower back to nudge her. "That way, I can keep watch upon you."

You already told me I couldn't get away, a voice inside her sniped. *I know your warning was genuine.* She kept silent, though, and did as he bade.

On they went, through the shadowed corridors of the keep, until she saw an iron-banded wooden door on the left.

Somehow, this passageway seemed familiar.

An ominous pressure, very different from the earlier stirring, crawled up from the base of her skull. It slipped into her thoughts and rammed against the void in her mind: a memory, fighting to break free. So strong was the sensation that she stumbled, fingers pressed against her brow.

Closing her eyes, she willed the recollection to materialize.

"What is wrong?" Tye demanded, sounding a distance away.

She thought of lying and saying naught. However, if he grew suspicious, he might send her back to the cell without her being able to experience more. "I sensed . . . something."

Heaving in breaths, she straightened, opened her eyes, and glanced about the corridor, wisped with smoke from the wall torches. Tye stood a few paces away, hands on hips, his hard gaze upon her.

Hot, sharp tension buzzed inside her as she let the emotions of the place sift deeper into her consciousness. A terrible event had happened here. Oh, God, she must remember.

Her head began to pound. "Where are we?" she whispered.

Tye gestured to the door. "The solar."

The solar. Where she'd wakened yesterday and met Veronique. Where Juliana had previously lived and cared for Mayda's babe. She would have traveled this passageway often. No wonder her senses roused. But

CATHERINE KEAN

something—*something!*—awful had taken place here and left its imprint upon her soul.

"What do you see?" Tye urged.

Tears moistened her eyes while she struggled to probe the void in her mind. *Please. She wanted to remember all. She wanted to understand why she felt this way.*

"Juliana?" Anger now darkened Tye's tone.

Frustration broke from her in a sob. "I see naught. I am trying to remember, but . . ." She grimaced. "My head." She touched her throbbing forehead. "It hurts so fiercely." She fought a threatening wave of dizziness, determined not to faint. Not when she seemed so close to remembering.

"The torches are giving off lots of smoke," Tye said. "Mayhap you need fresh air."

She nodded. 'Twould be good to clear her head.

He crossed to her, took her elbow, and propelled her onward to a narrow stairwell. A draft swept over her ankles, indicating an upper door opened to the outside.

As Tye pushed her into the stairs, fear swirled into the emotions churning inside her. She'd climbed these stone steps before. Around the same time the terrible event had occurred?

Edouard, I am horribly frightened.

Thinking of him, though, of mayhap finding a way to free him, gave Juliana the strength to take the last stairs and push through the doorway to the wall walk.

Sunshine lit the squared merlons and rough hewn walkway before her. An armed sentry farther down looked her way, then resumed his watch on the landscape beyond the keep.

As her gaze traveled the wall walk, a monstrous sense of dread swept through her. Something gruesome had transpired here, too. Panic seared her thoughts, urged her to turn around and flee back down the stairs, but Tye was behind her. If he sensed her memories were returning, he wouldn't let her past.

What had happened here? Oh, God, *what*?

Pressing a trembling hand to her forehead, she moved forward. Her inhalation rattled in her throat, for the foreboding pulled at her like a malicious ghost. It dragged her consciousness down, down, as though she were falling into dank, smothering blackness.

Into . . . icy water.

She gasped, eighteen again, the well's coldness swallowing her.

"Juliana."

Edouard's voice, calling down to her from the well's rim? Nay, not his. Tye's.

She realized once again she stood on the wall walk. The breeze stirred her gown and she shivered, hugged herself tight, for she still felt the frigid water sucking her down. The chill seeped into her skin, her heart, her bones . . . *Deathly* coldness.

Beside her now, Tye said, "What is wrong, Juliana?"

She held up a hand, staying Tye before he tried to catch her arm. Her heart pounded wildly in her chest. With each painful beat, she sensed the onslaught of more insight.

The wind gusted through the space between the nearby merlons with a wail.

Like an infant's cry.

An image flashed into her thoughts. *A baby, crying. Struggling in her arms.*

Rosemary!

"You look very pale," Tye said. "Are your memories returning? Do you recall what took place here?"

Beware, Juliana. Tye is a part of what happened.

Rubbing her brow, she forced her lips into a weak smile. "My head aches very badly. 'Tis almost unbearable."

"I will tell Mother, so Azarel can prepare another potion."

"Hopefully after I have breathed the morning air a while, the pain will ease."

His stare sharpened, as though he suspected she wasn't being entirely truthful, but then he nodded and glanced away. While she blew out a relieved breath, she became aware of conversation carrying from down the wall walk. The sentry's head turned as he spoke to someone standing beside him, blocked from Juliana's view.

Darkness suddenly whirled into Juliana's mind, rousing the sense of nighttime. *Raised voices. Landon and Mayda arguing on the wall walk. Mayda cradling her face, as again they fought.*

Juliana swallowed hard. What had she witnessed?

Landon's fist slammed into Mayda's head. She fell against the merlon. Tried to get away, but Landon shoved her. She fell, screaming, over the side. To her death.

"Oh, God," Juliana moaned.

"Juliana," Tye snapped. "If you are lying to me—"

She clawed her hand into her hair. "My . . . head," she managed to say, despite the grief and panic swarming inside her. She mustn't let Tye know she remembered Mayda's murder. If he guessed her memories were start-ing to come back, he and Veronique would force her to reveal the location of the gold ring. Then Edouard would die for certain.

She fought to steady her tattered nerves. But then Veronique strolled from behind the sentry, her hair a gar-ish hue in the sunlight.

"Well?" Veronique called. "Has she remembered anything?"

Juliana froze, captured by the memory of moonglow on Veronique's red locks as she stepped out of the night shadows, applauding Landon's actions. More memo-ries careened, one after another: Veronique blocking the passageway by the solar so Juliana couldn't escape with Rosemary; Veronique smiling while the armed thugs seized Juliana; Veronique grabbing the baby from Juliana's arms and thrusting her at a mercenary to be slaughtered.

Anguish and hatred boiled up inside Juliana. She wanted to scream at Veronique, scratch her painted face, rip out handfuls of red hair. But that would help no one, especially Edouard.

She shook, struggling to keep her emotions from being discovered. She mustn't fail Mayda, Edouard, everyone she cared about.

"Juliana?" Veronique's eyes narrowed.

Oh, God, did Veronique guess? Did she know?

"She claims she has a bad headache," Tye said.

A rasp echoed. The scrape, Juliana vaguely realized, of Tye's heel, but her mind filled with an image of Landon, lip curled, sword aimed at her, while thugs spun her around.

"She is fainting," Veronique shrieked.

In her darkening mind, Juliana saw Landon's sword slam into the back of her head.

CHAPTER
18

Juliana," Edouard said in a gentle voice. Squatting on his pallet, he studied her ashen face, watching for the tiniest response. She lay on her side on her bed, where Tye had left her moments ago.

The sight of her unconscious in Tye's arms had sent fear lancing through Edouard. From the moment she'd left the cell, he'd worried. Tye and Veronique might use any means to get the information they wanted from her, including threats and the infliction of pain. His imagination had refused to give him a moment's rest, and, unable to focus on digging out the bolts, he'd counted the torturous moments until her return.

When the door opened and Tye had carried her in, a lethal roar had torn from Edouard. Rising to his feet, he shouted, "What have you done to her?"

"She collapsed," Tye said, his nonchalance fueling Edouard's rage another notch.

"Why? What torture did you force upon her?" A

vile taste flooded his mouth. "Did you . . . defile her?"

Tye raised his brows and knelt beside Juliana's pallet. Her body slid down on the mattress, while her gown tangled about her legs. Standing again, Tye said, "Your fury is unwarranted, Brother. While we walked the passageway near the solar, she complained of a headache. I took her up to the wall walk in hopes the clear air would ease her discomfort. Whether pain caused her to swoon, or another reason, we will not know till she wakes."

"Summon Azarel. She must examine Juliana's injury again."

Tye had glowered. "Mother is doing that. I will return shortly with the healer." He'd stormed out, and the door slammed and locked behind him.

"Juliana," Edouard said again, then dragged his hand through his hair. She hadn't yet stirred. What if she never woke?

"Oh, God," he muttered, dropping his head into his hands. Guilt squeezed his conscience. If she perished, he was to blame; he couldn't bear to live with that agony. "Please bring her back to me."

A soft inhalation snapped his gaze to her face. Her eyes were still closed, but a frown puckered her brow. A low groan broke from her, and then her eyes flickered open.

"Juliana!"

Her unfocused gaze fixed on him. Her stare sharpened before she pushed up to a seated position, hair falling around her shoulders. Her expression, though, remained filled with uncertainty. Her body began to shake. She still looked unnaturally pale, and, he realized, she avoided looking at him.

The joy within him dimmed. "Are you hurt? Tye said you had a headache."

With a shaking hand, she swept fallen hair from her face. "My head feels a little better."

"Good. Tye will be bringing Azarel here soon to tend you." Trying to keep the roughness from his voice, Edouard asked, "What happened to you? Did Tye and Veronique catch you trying to find a way to free me?"

"Nay." Her gaze slid to his pallet, and a blush stained her face. She seemed to be struggling with an inner dilemma, some kind of awkward memory . . .

And then he knew.

"Look at me, Juliana."

She heaved a breath. Her shoulders stiffened, as though she planned to refuse, but then slowly her head tilted and her stare met his. In her guarded gaze, he saw the Juliana he'd met long ago.

The woman he'd hurt more than once.

He sensed the turmoil battling inside her: the resentment from their past dealings, versus the need to ally with him to escape and survive. How he hoped he hadn't lost the trust he'd earned from her in the past days and that she'd still consider him worthy of friendship.

Before he could venture to break the silence between them, she said, "I remembered, Edouard. Tye took me outside to the wall walk, and all of my memories flooded back."

He managed a smile. "I am glad. I know 'tis what you wanted."

He'd hoped for a hint of a smile in return. Instead, tears slid down her cheeks. "I, too, thought I would be delighted. What I recalled . . ." A tremor shook her. "'Tis too important to keep to myself. You must hear the truth, Edouard, so you can tell it to your lord father."

You will live to tell him yourself, Edouard silently vowed, before he said, "You know who wounded you days ago?"

"Aye, but 'tis only part . . . of what I must tell you."

"Go on," he coaxed.

"Tye took me to the passageway by the solar. I felt on the verge of remembering something horrendous. 'Tis when the headache started. He took me up to the wall walk. I later realized I had used those same stairs the night I was injured. Outside, my memories began rushing back. I saw again"—she paused, as though rallying her strength—"the treachery I had witnessed nights ago. 'Twas awful, Edouard. The horror, the fear, the sense of danger . . . I knew I couldn't let Tye see I had regained my memories, so I pretended my headache was severe. Then Veronique came toward us, and I knew she would see through my ruse. Panic overtook me, and

I . . . fainted."

"Tell me," Edouard said. "What treachery did you see?"

"Mayda's murder."

"God above!" He could only imagine how ghastly it had been for her to see her best friend killed. "I am sorry, Juliana." As she wiped at her eyes, he added tersely, "'Twas Veronique's doing, aye?"

Sorrow etched Juliana's features. "Nay. Landon murdered Mayda."

"*Landon*?" Shock forced Edouard to drop down on his pallet. Surely Landon wasn't corrupt; he'd tried to spare Edouard from Veronique. "How can that be? You and I attended Mayda and Landon's wedding. They seemed very much in love."

"I know." Shaking her head, Juliana said, "Their marriage, happy at first, unraveled over the months. He and Mayda constantly argued. Mayda and I had hoped that the newborn would help to revive their love, but Landon wanted a boy, and Mayda gave birth to a girl. As if that were not unfavorable enough, Landon invited Veronique and Tye to live as guests in the keep. Veronique and Landon soon became lovers."

"That deceitful bitch," Edouard muttered.

"Landon and Mayda fought the night she died," Juliana went on, each word heavy with anguish. "'Twas a terrifying disagreement. When I caught their angry voices coming down from the wall walk, I sensed Mayda was in grave danger. She had feared, since Rosemary's birth, that Landon might try to harm her and the babe. I thought she was imagining that, but when I heard them fighting, heard him say how he desired Veronique, I knew Mayda had spoken the truth. I hurried up to the wall walk with the baby. I tried to call out to Mayda, to bring her back to the solar to nurse Rosemary. But Mayda did not hear me. Landon struck her again—"

"Nay," Edouard whispered. Landon had hit his wife more than once? What kind of beast had Landon become, to hurt a woman?

"—and, just as Mayda saw me, Landon hit her hard enough that she fell against a merlon. She tried to regain her balance, to save herself. In his rage, he shoved her again, and she"—Juliana's voice wobbled—"fell off the battlement. To her death."

His innards twisted with the pain binding together Juliana's account. Damnation, how helpless he felt. How he longed to offer her the comfort of his embrace, but she likely wouldn't accept it. "I am sorry," he finally said. "Truly sorry."

Nodding, Juliana said quietly, "I did not know Veronique was also on the wall walk, until she appeared, gloating over Landon's actions. They had both, however, seen me. In that moment, I realized I was the only other witness to what had befallen Mayda. If I died, the truth about her demise would die, too. So I ran. Oh, Edouard,

I tried to keep my promise to Mayda, to keep Rosemary safe"—a moan tore from her—"but Veronique's thugs trapped me. They grabbed me and forced me to turn my back to Landon. The last thing I remember of that night is the blow of his sword."

Edouard scowled. "They thought you were dead. Until I found you in the river, and, fool that I am, brought you right back here."

Self-condemnation darkened Juliana's expression. "Mayda should never have perished. I should have acted sooner to get her attention. I should have shouted to distract Landon. *Anything*. I failed her, and now she is dead, and Rosemary will grow up without her mother."

"Juliana, I vow you did all you could to save Mayda. Veronique obviously wanted Mayda killed and manipulated Landon so he would accomplish the deed for her. If Landon hadn't succeeded, Veronique would have found another way to have gotten rid of Mayda."

Juliana dried her eyes on the edge of her sleeve. "She was my best friend. I should have—"

"Should have," he cut in. "You cannot allow yourself to believe that. The guilt will eat at your soul, day after day, if you allow it."

Her wet lashes flickered. Anger defined the line of her jaw. Did she not believe he knew of what he spoke?

"I know," he said, drawing on the torment he'd tried to suppress, "because I have lived with guilt ever since that day at Sherstowe, when you fell into the well."

Her eyes sparked. "When you pushed me in!"

Shaking his head, he sighed. "When you leaned forward, trying to rescue your sketchbook, I grabbed hold of your waist. I meant to pull you out, but Nara kicked my boot and dislodged my balance. My falling against you caused you to tumble in."

Shock glistened in her gaze. "You dare to blame the mishap on Nara?"

He refused to break her stare. "I do. Kaine witnessed what happened. Ask him, if you do not believe I am telling the truth. Better yet, ask Nara."

Juliana held Edouard's determined gaze. He didn't look away. Not the slightest trace of guilt stole into his warrior-tough expression, not even when he blinked, and a sickly sensation wended its way through her.

All these months, she'd despised him for being reckless. She'd believed him wholly responsible for the frightening plunge into the well that had endangered her life.

What if he wasn't to blame?

"If you knew Nara had caused me to fall in," she said carefully, "why did you not tell our fathers that day? Why did you choose to keep silent?"

He shrugged and his lips formed a crooked grin. "I

dared not cause offense. My sire made it clear to me he wanted an alliance between our families for important reasons. 'Twas simplest for me to take the blame, especially when the day ended up a disaster."

How noble of him—and true to the character of the man she'd grown to know.

How like selfish Nara to not worry about putting her own sister in jeopardy. She was likely trying to win Edouard's attention.

Fighting rising anger toward her sister, Juliana said, "I truly believed you had put my life in danger. And then, with the bet . . ."

"I would never intentionally put any woman in peril, Juliana. Especially you."

The unevenness of Edouard's tone sent a raw pain racing through her. He looked so solemn, and the honest emotion in his words touched deep in her soul, finding all the secret desires she'd harbored for him, along with the anguish of his betrothal to Nara.

"In the end, my sister's antics came to fruition," Juliana said quietly, memories of that night at Englestowe filling her thoughts. "She got her wish for a betrothal to you."

"Aye. 'Tis my duty to marry her."

He didn't sound at all pleased; in fact, he sounded as though he disliked the commitment. Did he not want to marry Nara? Before Juliana could ask him about it, though, he said, "I am sorry for all the anguish I have caused you. Every moment of it."

Juliana tried to hold back the blush stealing into her face. Did his apology include almost kissing her? Oh, but how she found a secret pleasure in that memory. One to which Nara could never lay claim.

He must have sensed the direction of her thoughts, because he said, "I do not intend to dismiss the issues in our past we have not yet touched upon. However, Azarel and Tye will soon arrive, and there is one vital matter we must discuss."

She frowned. "What matter?"

"You were right to be afraid to let Tye and Veronique know you had regained your memories. 'Tis crucial you keep pretending you do not remember the past. You must act no differently than when you left this cell earlier today."

As Juliana's gaze instinctively flew to the door, she said, "Veronique may already suspect. The way she looked at me before I fainted—"

"Then you must convince her otherwise."

"I know, but—"

"Do you recall when you were in the well, and I called down to you? When I promised to get you out?"

"I do remember." The warmth of that recollection stirred within her. "Your voice was very calm and reassuring."

He grinned. "I am glad to hear you say that. In truth, I was terrified I wouldn't be able to get you out before you drowned. The danger involved seemed to give me strength to accomplish what had to be done. Juliana, I know you have endured a great deal," he said, his voice gentling, "but you are the only one who knows in detail what took place at Waddesford over the past months. You *must* survive, so Veronique can be brought to punishment for her part in Mayda's death and the other atrocities she has committed here. The truth of Landon's involvement, too, must not be forgotten."

"You are right."

He glanced at the door, then back at her, his expression becoming grave. "I realize you may no longer want to be in my arms. However, Tye and Veronique have endeavored to force us together. He will be suspicious if he sees you are not seeking comfort in my embrace."

Oh, God. To be in Edouard's arms now, after all she remembered . . . After recalling how intensely she'd craved his kiss . . .

Nay. Survival, for both of them, was far more important than indulging such thoughts.

Faint voices carried from outside the door.

His lips parted, as though to give a warning, but she was already scrambling across the planks. His left arm slid around her, drawing her against his side. She ignored the crush of her breast against him, his enticing scent, and how part of her rejoiced in once again being close to him.

Just as she tried to control the racing of her pulse, the door opened.

"You are a fool, Tye. Juliana is trying to deceive us."

"Are you certain?"

Releasing a furious breath, Veronique came to an abrupt halt in the bailey and glared at her son, who'd been walking at her side. Was he acting witless apurpose? Or had his senses become befuddled by Juliana's pitiful dramatics earlier?

"I saw the look in her eyes before she fainted," Veronique muttered. "She was afraid, not overcome by pain. I vow she remembered the night of Mayda's murder. Once Juliana wakes, I mean to find out."

Veronique scrutinized the folk working nearby. Where *was* Azarel? None of the servants she'd sent to find her had returned yet. The healer shouldn't be hard to locate.

Still sensing Tye's stare, Veronique scowled at him.

He didn't, as she hoped, take his leave, but said, "Juliana does have a bad wound. What if she did faint because of a headache? Forcing her memories when she is fragile—"

"Is exactly what I will do. I have been more than patient with her. Now I will keep up the relentless

pressure till she has no choice but to surrender the information we want."

Impatience chafed at Veronique. After what transpired on the wall walk, she should be consulting her
bones, not wasting moments with Tye. The bones would
help reveal what would come to pass with Juliana.

Tye was still standing before her. "What is wrong?
Do you no longer want your father's legacy? Has her
beauty weakened you—?"

"Of course not!" He glowered. "You know how
much I want to kill Father."

"Then you will bring Juliana down to the garden,
where she and Mayda spent many afternoons together.
Once I have found Azarel, she will look at Juliana's
wound there." Veronique's gnarled hand curled into a
deformed fist. "Tell Juliana I suspect she remembers all.
If she still will not admit it . . ." She smiled, her palm
heating with the remembered hardness of a knife hilt. "I
will start the killing."

CHAPTER 19

Seated on a stone bench in the garden, Juliana linked her hands together in her lap and tried not to heed the clamminess of her palms. "Why did you bring me here?"

On the opposite bench, Tye sat with his legs parted, elbows braced on his knees, leaning slightly forward. Sunlight bled through the overhead boughs of the apple tree and cast bright splotches over him and the grass stretching like an unruly carpet beneath their feet. His posture, while somewhat relaxed, reminded her of a predator awaiting the right moment to lunge and en-snare. "You spent afternoons here with Mayda," he said, indicating the area with a flick of his hand. "Does this place not rekindle any memories?"

She fought the sickening misgiving that had rooted within her ever since Tye had returned to the tower and told her to come with him. *"You must act no differently than when you left this cell earlier today,"* Edouard had warned. He was right.

How intently Tye had watched her as he escorted her through the castle, out the forebuilding door to the sunlit bailey beyond, past the stables and kitchens, to this part of the keep. Still, she sensed she was being scrutinized, her gestures analyzed for signs that she had, indeed, regained her memories.

Juliana worked to keep her expression of wary disinterest—an expression he'd expect to see from a captive who couldn't remember her past—while her pulse became a hard drumming against her ribs. Daring to tuck a wayward skein of hair back behind her ear, she looked about the overgrown garden enclosed by a low, mortared stone wall.

To her right, the dirt space of the bailey blended into grass thickened with weeds. To the left, shadows and sunlight defined birds flitting in search of insects and straggly beds of flowers, herbs, and vegetables. Her gaze slid farther back to the neglected rosebushes. Mayda had loved to pick the rose blooms and set them in vases about the solar, but toward the end of her difficult pregnancy, she'd been abed more often than not . . .

Beware, Juliana.

Forcing frustration into her sigh, she looked back at Tye. "I wish I did recall this place. 'Tis very peaceful. I can see why I could have come here with Mayda."

"But you do not recall any of your days spent here? Things you and Mayda may have talked about?"

The urge to quickly look away leapt inside Juliana.

She *had* to stay focused. By keeping Tye fooled, she might be able to find a way to free Edouard. Castle folk were going about their duties in the bailey; if she could convince Tye to walk her through the area on the pretense of jostling her memories, she might be able to make contact with one of the servants she considered a friend. She must try.

Discreetly easing the painfully tight clasp of her hands, she slowly broke Tye's stare and took another glance about the area. Recollections, tinged with sadness, teased her senses. Mayda had preferred the bench where Tye sat, because she could see the activity in the bailey. Days before Rosemary's birth, while Mayda rested, Juliana had visited here alone and sketched the empty bench dappled by sunshine. The light had cast a speckled pattern that complemented the peppery surface of the stone . . .

"Juliana?"

She jumped, a purely instinctive reaction. Merciful God, had she betrayed herself?

Forcing down the fluttered breath that had leapt to her throat, she shrugged and looked back at him. "For a moment, I thought a memory was surfacing."

"And?" Suspicion darkened Tye's voice.

"I tried to make it materialize, but . . . I could not." She tried to sound disheartened. "Mayhap, if we wait awhile, 'twill arise."

He shook his head. An unforgiving smile curved his mouth.

Before she could say another word, Tye rose to standing. The air froze in her lungs, and she could only watch as he crossed to her bench and eased down beside her, claiming what small space had separated them.

What was he going to do? Touch her? Force her to accept his lust?

No one would stop him, for he and Veronique ruled Waddesford.

She scooted down the bench, even as his broad hand captured hers. His thumb swept against her left wrist, a movement that chilled rather than warmed her skin.

"What are you doing?" she demanded, her voice unsteady.

"Are you telling me the truth, Juliana?"

Do not let him see the truth! Do not jeopardize Edouard. "I am," she said firmly.

The breeze shifted the boughs overhead, changing the dappled play of light and underscoring the tense silence between them.

"I have told you all I remember," she insisted.

"Have you?" Tye's fingers shifted to entwine with hers, a gesture not of affection, but entrapment. "Mother believes your memories have fully returned."

Oh, God!

Juliana tried to twist her hand free, but his grip tightened. Tye's gaze slid toward the bailey, and then he released a sigh, a sound that stirred dread in the pit of her stomach. "Mother will be here shortly with Azarel. I will be honest with you, Juliana. Mother grows impatient." He paused, a deliberate emphasis. "She plans to force your memories out of you today, including where to find Landon's ring. One way or another."

Juliana's stomach plummeted. "What do you mean?"

"Do you care for Edouard?"

"O-of course!"

Tye smiled. "Then you will do your best to remember. For his sake."

"Veronique means to harm him?"

"Oh, aye. She will likely start with a finger or two—"

Juliana's free hand flew to her mouth. Panic whirled in her mind. "Please," she whispered hoarsely. "I . . ."

Again, Tye glanced toward the bailey. Shouts carried, followed by sounds of a commotion.

"Tye!" Veronique bellowed. "Where is Tye?"

He swiftly rose, drawing Juliana to her feet. "Come." Without waiting for her reply, he strode forward across the grass, hauling her along after him.

"W-what is happening?" Juliana cried. Was Veronique about to begin her torture? Had she dragged Edouard out of the tower to make Juliana and all the other castle folk watch him suffer? She couldn't bear to see him maimed.

Stones skidded beneath her feet. She could hardly

keep up with Tye, and she stumbled, fingers scraping the ground—long enough to snatch up a pebble—before she righted. When they left the tree's shade for the bright bailey, she sensed Tye's pace quickening.

"There you are!" Veronique advanced on him, shaking out a long garment while holding on to her bag of bones. "How dare you take so long to answer my summons?" Her accusing gaze slammed into Juliana before returning to Tye.

He released Juliana's hand. "We were in the garden, Mother, as you ordered of me." He clearly fought for patience. "What is going on?"

"The prisoners in the dungeon are attempting to escape. You are to crush their rebellion."

Excitement surged inside Juliana. Edouard was safe. Oh, how she hoped the escape attempt succeeded.

"A bloody fight?" Tye grinned. "Gladly, Mother."

Tye raced off, and Juliana swallowed hard as the poisoned heat of Veronique's stare fixed upon her. With a sharp thrust of her hand, Veronique signaled over one of the men-at-arms who'd joined the mercenaries gathered outside the dungeon's entrance.

The man bowed before her. "Aye, milady?"

When he rose, she shoved the garment and bone bag into his arms. "Return Juliana to the tower cell. Then deliver these to the solar. Lose even one bone, and I will kill you."

Juliana walked ahead of the man-at-arms, his footfalls and noisy breaths echoing off the passageway's walls. She shifted the pebble in her palm and anticipation fluttered inside her, for on this walk to the tower stairwell, on the return to accursed captivity, she'd decided to escape.

This might be her only opportunity. She'd not let it slip away, especially when Veronique had decided to harm Edouard.

Holding her head high while she walked, Juliana concentrated upon her resolve, coaxing it until it spread like fire within her. Never would Juliana allow Veronique to torture Edouard in order to force her to confess her memories. She'd rather die.

She turned a corner in the passage illuminated by wall torches, and the stairwell leading up to the tower chamber came into view. Eight steps, at most, till they reached it. A nervous jolt ran through her. Soon, very soon, she would act. She steeled herself for the just right moment.

Two careful breaths. One . . .

The guard grunted. "Do not give me trouble now. Up—"

Juliana discreetly tossed the pebble. It clattered away into the shadows.

The man's strides slowed.

"What was that?" She turned partway to face him, pretending surprise.

Light glinted off his drawn sword. His grizzled face clamped into a scowl.

Ignoring a pang of uncertainty, she peered at the stone floor. "Did you drop something?"

"Nay." He thrust his sword in the direction of the stairwell. "Move."

She *had* to distract him. Otherwise, her plan had already failed. "Are you certain the bag of bones is securely tied? If you lost one of them . . ."

He tipped his chin toward the mantle and bag, cradled in his left arm. The bag lay partly concealed in the folded garment. "They are safe."

"For your sake, I hope you are right. We both know how important those bones are to Veronique. If you *did* drop one . . ." Juliana raised her hands, a gesture of dismissal. "But you know best. I will not worry."

The guard leaned closer to her, as though to gauge her expression.

Managing a little smile, she shrugged, turned her back to him, and started toward the stairwell, fighting an awful sense of discouragement. Her ruse hadn't worked. She must think of another—

"Hold."

She hesitated, trembling hands forming fists.

"Turn around."

Her gown whispered as she obeyed.

Leveling his sword at her chest, he said, "Stand against that wall." He nudged his elbow at the one nearest, opposite the stairwell's entrance. "Stand there, where I can see ye."

A nervous flush warmed her face. She mustn't appear anxious, or he'd suspect her of trickery. Narrowing her gaze with what she hoped would appear to be mutinous hatred, she stepped back until her bottom bumped the wall.

He nodded once, suggesting he thought her well enough secured, before his gaze dropped to the floor.

"I think it fell by the torch." Juliana gestured farther down the wall.

The lout glanced where she indicated, before his face cinched into a scowl. Then, keeping his sword trained on her, he took two steps sideways for a better look.

How tempting to lunge at him now. His sword, though, looked deadly sharp. She must be patient.

His full attention shifted to the wall's lowest stones.

"I see it!" she cried. "Right there. 'Tis a bone, aye?"

"What?" His face whitened. Looking away, he dropped into a partial crouch to examine the shadows.

Juliana dashed around the extended sword. As his head swiveled, she rammed her hands into his back and shoved with all her might. Cursing, he pitched toward the wall, while he lashed out with his sword. The lethal steel swung near her with a faint whistle.

The man caught his fall by bracing his palm against the wall. Soon he'd straighten and turn on her. She might be quick, but she was no match for an enraged, sword-wielding warrior.

Rallying her strength, she slammed her whole body against him. He loosed a furious roar. Dropping the garment and bone bag, he swung his burly arm back, grabbing for her, almost catching hold of her sleeve.

"Ye will not get away—"

She dodged his swipe, then kicked the inside of his knee, above the rim of his boot. He grimaced, his leg buckled, and his shoulder banged against the wall.

Before he could raise his sword to her, she shoved him again. With a loud *thwack,* his head hit the stone. He groaned. His knees gave way, and he slumped to the floor, eyes rolling closed. The sword, still in his grasp, settled beside him with a gritty clank.

Triumph raced through Juliana. She'd defeated him! She'd done it.

Stepping back out of his reach, Juliana waited through several agonizing breaths; she must be sure he wasn't trying to fool her. When not a flicker of cognizance crossed his slack face, she crept to him and pried his fingers from the sword. Then, keeping watch on him in case he roused, she picked up the bag of bones. The contents rattled softly, and she choked down a disgusted moan. How she loathed to hold such grimness in her hand, but they might be a useful bargaining tool at some point.

Holding the sword—heavier than she expected—she started toward the tower stairwell. She clung tightly to her excitement, refused to listen to the doubts swirling up inside her. She'd subdued one guard; there was at least one more up by the chamber door. Somehow, she'd find a way to defeat him, too.

As Juliana started up the stairs that were raised and uneven in places, cool air swept over her; it made her all the more aware of the sweaty dampness of her hand gripping the sword. Her arm, unused to the weapon's weight, began to shake. After sliding her hand through the drawstring of the bone bag so it hung from her left wrist, she then pushed the bag down inside her sleeve for safekeeping. Gripping the sword with both hands, she continued on, trying to move as quickly but quietly as possible. If she could surprise the guard—

"Who goes there?" a man called down from above.

Hellfire, as Edouard would say.

Hesitating in the stairwell's shadows, Juliana mulled what to do next. Should she reply? Was it better to stay silent, so mayhap he'd come down and investigate? He'd be suspicious then, which meant she'd have less chance of catching him unaware.

"Kerr, is that you?" the man shouted. When she didn't respond, the guard growled, "Answer me! Who goes there?"

With grudging dismay, she realized her current tactic was likely to fail. That meant she must resort to other, more cunning measures.

"Please," she called back, forcing a wobble into her voice. "Is someone there? Can you help?"

"Help?" From the faint footsteps filtering down to her, she guessed the guard had walked to the opening to the stairs.

Hoping she sounded terrified and helpless, she said, "The man-at-arms who was escorting me . . . Kerr . . . he . . ." She managed a tremulous sob. "Something is wrong."

"What do you mean?"

"He fell to the floor. He has not moved."

A tense silence. "Who are you?"

Of all the questions to ask! She certainly wasn't going to reveal she was the woman he'd guarded in the chamber. Fighting her unease, she said, "A . . . visitor. A friend"—she shuddered at the necessary lie—"of Lady Veronique's. I arrived a short while ago. Will you help this poor man, or must I go find aid elsewhere?"

"There is no one else about?" The guard sounded doubtful.

"Veronique and the others are busy with a prisoner uprising in the bailey." She forced out a frightened moan. "If you will not help me, just say so and I will bother you no more. This man, I mean, Kerr's life is—"

Footsteps carried from above. "Wait there."

The guard was heading down to her. His boot falls grew louder as he neared.

Tightening her grasp on the sword, she quietly continued up the stairs to meet him. Sweat moistened her brow and the curve between her breasts. What she'd do when she faced him, fighter to fighter, she didn't quite know, but . . . she'd make that judgment then.

A huff and loud footfalls reached her. The man was very close. She drew back against the wall, a moment before the guard came into view, his sword raised. As soon as he spied her, his eyes widened. "You!"

Before she said a word, his gaze dropped to the blade clutched in her hands. He chuckled, then stepped down to the next stair, no doubt moving in to attack. "Do you mean to fight me?"

His taunting sent a raw tremor running through her. "If I must." She tried not to let show how much her arm was shaking. "But I was not lying about Kerr. He is hurt."

"Of course he is." Only two steps above her now, the guard grinned and shook his head. "'Tis a heavy weapon for a young woman. You will end up getting hurt. Put the sword down on that stair there, and I will be kind."

What exactly did he mean by "kind?" He wouldn't beat her senseless—or worse—before he threw her into the chamber and locked the door?

His brutishly large fingers shifted on his sword's hilt. "Do as I say. You really do not want to battle me."

A weak groan came from the bottom of the stairs.

"Kerr," Juliana said.

Not breaking her gaze, the guard's expression darkened. "That could be anyone."

"'Tis Kerr."

Uncertainty flickered in the guard's eyes.

"Is he your friend?" she said. "Go and help him."

"And let you get away?" the guard sneered. "Veronique would gut me alive."

Juliana tsked, as though he was a fool. "Where can I go? There is only one route in and out of this stairwell. I doubt you will let me leave these stairs."

"True." The guard's mouth tightened. "Move from this spot, and I will kill you myself." He edged past her and, turning away, started descending the stairwell.

Before he'd taken three steps, she rushed down behind him and kicked him in the back. He lurched forward, foot twisting on an uneven stair. "You wretched—" He swung his sword back in a cutting slash that barely missed her leg.

Before he could catch his balance and attack, she lunged forward and kicked him again. He stumbled. Missed a step. Fell on his arse. His free hand scrambled to break his fall as he tumbled down several more stairs, sword scraping on the stone. He finally came to a stop, facing the wall.

He groaned. Clutching his head, he tried to sit up.

She couldn't let him get away or thwart her efforts to free Edouard. "I am sorry," Juliana said, before she kicked him again. His forehead knocked the wall and he went limp.

She stooped, grabbed his sword, and hefted the weapon. Edouard would need it once she'd freed him.

Up she climbed toward the tower, hoping she wouldn't have to face another guard. She softened her steps, listening. When she approached the entry to the small area before the chamber door, she paused.

Over the sputtering of the torches, she caught a muffled scraping sound. It seemed to emanate from near the door.

Groaning inwardly, she tipped her head back against the rough wall. Was there another guard, after all? Summoning her courage—she must rescue Edouard before the two fallen men roused and warned their colleagues—she dared to peek into the space in front of the chamber.

Empty.

As she hurried forward, she wondered what had made the noise. One of the torches, shifting in its metal bracket? A mouse gnawing on the door? Brushing the thoughts aside, she propped one sword against the wall to free her right hand, snatched the key ring from its hook, pushed the key into the lock, and turned. With a prompt click, the lock released.

Juliana eased the door open. Her gaze fell upon the sunlit planks and the pallet just coming into view. "Ed—"

Before the sound fully formed in her mouth, the door was yanked from her grasp. She gasped, while she was spun and thrust against the wall. The sword was knocked from her hold.

With a splintering crash, the door hit the stone beside her.

A strong hand clamped around her throat.

CHAPTER

20

"E douard," Juliana croaked.

The hand pinning her fell away. She sucked in a breath, pain and dizziness slowly subsiding.

"Juliana, I am sorry. I thought you were a guard." Edouard touched her arm before stepping away to look around the open doorway. His head tilted as though to catch any sounds from beyond. "Are you alone?"

Rubbing at her neck to ease the discomfort, she nodded.

He frowned. "Where are the guards?"

Juliana couldn't help but smile. "One is lying injured at the bottom of the stairs. The other is unconscious partway up the stairwell. They will not, however, be subdued for long."

With each word, Edouard's eyebrows raised higher. "You defeated two armed men?"

"I did." When he whistled softly, pride warmed her breast. Bending down, she picked up her sword. "I brought a weapon for you, too. 'Tis leaning against the outside wall."

Edouard disappeared through the doorway and appeared a moment later holding the sword. Standing in the embrasure, he thrust the weapon and swooped it from side to side, then flexed his fingers to adjust his grip. "Not as fine a weapon as I am used to," he said, "but 'twill do."

She shook her head. "The next time I rescue you, I will attack guards with better quality swords."

Edouard laughed and executed a gallant bow. "Thank you, Juliana, for coming to my rescue."

His roguish grin, the elegant way he bent at the waist, the forward slide of his hair, reminded her of how he'd kissed her hand at Sherstowe last spring. Stifling her regret, she glanced at the pallet where he'd been restrained. The iron links wove across the mattress; the hinged manacles lay open, like the jaws of metallic snakes.

"How . . . ?" she began.

Edouard grinned and held up a hairpin. "Azarel visited while you were with Tye." Holding out his hand, clearly wanting Juliana to cross to him, he added, "The guards sounded reluctant to let her in, I guess because you were not here. She managed to persuade them, though. One of the guards kept watch while she examined my bruised jaw, but she still managed to slip me the hairpin. I sprung the locks on my manacles and was working on the door before you came in."

That explained the noise Juliana had heard.

She reached his side, and he took her left hand in his. "I did not mean to frighten you earlier or hurt you. The sight of you"—his gaze dropped to her lips—"is indeed very welcome."

At his whisper-soft words, a tingling ache dragged through her. God above, she must crush this forbidden yearning. Regardless how she felt about him, he belonged to Nara.

"Edouard," she said, struggling to rein in her emotions, "right now, Kaine and your men are trying to break free from the dungeon. Last I saw of Veronique and Tye, they were going off to quell the attempt."

Edouard's eyes glinted. "My men will need my help in that fight." He squeezed her hand, then released it. As her arm lowered, a muted clatter sounded, and curiosity sharpened his gaze.

"I have Veronique's coveted bag of finger bones." Juliana held out her sleeve to show him. "I took them from a guard. They may be useful in our fight against her."

"As disgusting as those bones are, you may well be right." Edouard motioned her through the doorway. "Come. We must not delay our escape."

Without bothering to soften his footfalls, he hurried into the stairwell, sword at the ready. Either he wasn't concerned about being attacked or he believed he could best whomever they encountered.

She followed, keeping a tight hold on her weapon. A moment later, she heard the muffled scrape of his boots as he halted. After racing down several more stairs, she came upon him squatting beside the man she'd left lying by the wall.

"He is still unconscious," Edouard said. "'Tis an ugly bruise on his head. He will have a rotten headache, and will be looking to get even with you."

"Then we had best be gone from here."

Edouard grinned up at her. "My thoughts exactly." He unfastened the dagger from the guard's belt and slipped it under his tunic. "Come on."

With Edouard in the lead, they hurried down the rest of the stairs and out into the passageway. Glancing to the left and right, Edouard said, "Where is the other guard?"

Juliana looked to where she'd felled the sentry. Dread clutched her innards. "He was there," she pointed to the floor. "I heard him moaning before I attacked the other man." Looking down the passage, she said, "Do you think he has gone to warn the others?"

"Aye." Edouard blew out a breath. "We must hurry. Which way?"

"To the right," Juliana said. "I know of a lesser used stairwell. It leads down to the far corner of bailey."

"Good." He loped forward, and she did her best to keep up with his brisk strides. How keenly she sensed his wish to be free of captivity and do whatever he could to save his sire.

The sword became heavier in her grasp. Her arm muscles ached, but she ignored the discomfort. She wouldn't slow Edouard down or be a burden to him.

When voices carried from a connecting passage, he threw up a hand and urged her to flatten back against the shadowed wall; three men-at-arms strode past the opening. Edouard quietly confirmed the rest of the directions with her, and then, after glancing both ways to ensure the route was clear, forged on.

At last, they came to the dimly lit stairwell. Cobwebs floated from the stone ceiling, while the stench of burning pitch wafted on the faint breeze coming up from below.

He raised a cautioning hand and listened. His fingers flexed on his sword, suggesting he looked forward to the confrontation to free his men.

"What is your plan, once we reach the bailey?" she asked.

He rolled his shoulders, doubtless to ease tension gathered there. She tried not to notice how his tunic stretched taut over his upper torso.

"Do you know the location of the postern?" he asked.

Most castles had an alternate door in the thick, surrounding wall, a means of escape in case of mutiny or siege. "'Tis in the keep's back wall," she said, dropping the tip of her sword to the floor to rest her tired arms.

He glanced back at her, then frowned, as though

realizing her discomfort. Reaching under his tunic, he
withdrew the dagger he'd taken from the guard and offered it to her. "Leave the sword. Take this knife instead."

"Thank you." She set the sword by the wall and unsheathed the dagger.

"Listen well, Juliana. I want you to stay hidden till
'tis safe for you to slip through the postern. Once you
are out, I want you to run from here. Find help. Go
to Branton Keep. Tell my father, if he does not already
know, all that has occurred here."

His harsh tone made her quake inside. "I will. And you?"

"I will fight to free Kaine and the others. Then,
mayhap, we can encourage other folk at this keep to rise
up against Veronique and her lackeys."

Worry pressed against Juliana's breastbone. "'Tis a
risky plan. There are so few of you, while Veronique has
many mercenaries working for her."

"My men are strong and capable." Edouard headed
down into the stairwell. "If we can take Veronique or
Tye captive, we will have more of a chance of gaining the
castle folk's help. They may be too afraid to challenge
her—unless they have the right leadership."

"You," she said, and began to descend the stairs.

Glancing back to meet her gaze, he nodded.

How brave and determined he looked. Yet he could
well be killed.

She didn't dare tell him, the son of a renowned

crusading warrior, not to do battle; 'twas Edouard's destiny. That fighting spirit ran in his blood. Still, she couldn't quell a rush of bone-deep terror. "I am afraid for you, Edouard," she said softly.

He shrugged a little too swiftly. "Fear not. If I fail to win control of the keep, Veronique and her mercenaries will not kill me. I am of no use to them dead."

There were fates worse than death. They might cut his body so badly, he'd long for death. "Edouard, why not come with me to Branton Keep? You will be safe from Veronique and Tye's wickedness. Without you as a valuable hostage . . ."

He halted, three steps below her, and slowly faced her. "I considered it. But my men need me. The good folk at Waddesford Keep need me. My sire would never run from such a fight. I will not, either."

How her heart ached with concern for him, but she mustn't hold him back. She nodded and followed him the last few steps down to the stout oak door.

On the bottom step, he smiled up at her, gaze bold and determined. "Stay safe, Juliana. I will see you anon." He depressed the iron handle, shoved open the door, and stepped through to the bailey beyond.

While she walked in the keep's shadows toward the far

wall, Juliana forced herself to slow her strides. Utter torment. Foreboding tightened her limbs, shortened her breath, and raised goose bumps on her arms. The importance of what she must do, and the consequences for Edouard and so many others if she failed, rendered her light-headed.

Her grip tightened on the handle of the dagger, held straight down at her side. By now the guards she'd fought had likely alerted their fellow mercenaries. At any moment, she might hear shouts, running footfalls, and commands to halt.

Get away as fast as you can. Once you have gone through the postern, you must run. Run!

She reached up to smooth her windblown hair, and the bones in the cloth bag clattered. If Veronique discovered Juliana had stolen her beloved bones . . .

Juliana shoved aside the unfinished musing; she didn't care to guess what punishment the cruel woman might inflict. Yet trailing after that thought, was a glimmer of insight. What might Veronique agree to, if, in desperation she thought she might never see those bones again? Any advantage must be used in a fight against an enemy as evil as Veronique.

Daring to veer from her original plan, Juliana crossed to the garden. Looking over the tangled mess of herbs before her, she spied several large stones, once arranged as a decorative element in the middle bed. Crossing to them, she crouched, lifted one stone partway using the knife for leverage, dug a small cavity beneath, and set the bag in the hole. She dropped the stone back into place and scattered the extra dirt amongst the plants. After brushing her hands on the grass, she picked up her weapon, rose, and resumed her careful stroll toward the postern.

A shout drew her gaze to the wall walk to her left. Several men-at-arms ran along the battlement. One of them shouted again to a warrior farther down. She strained to hear over her footfalls, but she couldn't make out what he said.

He could well be relaying word of her and Edouard's escape.

Get away. Hurry!

She quickened her strides. Not far now. Shutting out the harsh voices floating down to her, she searched the wall a short distance ahead for the gate.

Somewhere behind her, she heard footfalls.

"You will search the entire bailey," Veronique was saying, voice growing louder as she neared. "If you fail to find Edouard and Juliana, I will slice off your ballocks. To start!"

Judging by the footsteps, there were at least five men with Veronique. Fear seized Juliana. With a gasp, she broke into a run. Pain lanced through her head, radiating from her wound, but she kept running.

"There!" Veronique shrieked. "Get her!"

Unable to suppress her panic, Juliana looked back

while she raced on. Veronique, face twisted with fury, pointed a crooked finger at her. Barreling toward Juliana were four burly men, including the guard Juliana had tricked by insisting he'd dropped a bone.

Oh, God! Run, Juliana.

Run!

Squinting against the afternoon sunshine, Edouard glanced about to get his bearings. His gaze, drawn by the clash of swords somewhere to his left, slid past the dove-cotes, kitchens, and stables, toward the gatehouse. The fight, though, was taking place beyond his range of view.

Castle folk crowded into the bailey to watch the skirmish. Some of the women were dabbing at their eyes. The battle sounds made Edouard's muscles tauten, caused the blood to pump faster in his veins. He tasted the fight, its essence akin to a strong liquor on his tongue.

Keeping his back to the keep and trying not to draw attention from the onlookers, Edouard kept walking until the fight came into view. As he took in the grisly scene, the discordant ring of steel sharp in his ears, he choked down an agonized roar.

At least ten mercenaries fought with Tye. Two of Edouard's men—the one he'd sent on ahead to Waddesford Keep to alert them of Juliana's injury, and the warrior who'd ridden with him and Kaine into the keep—lay bloodied and motionless on the ground. They were dead; he knew by the blankness of their eyes.

Kaine was still fighting. Sweat glistening on his face, he bared his teeth and met a brutal strike from Tye. While Kaine struggled, his strength clearly ebbing, Tye's motions appeared lazy and effortless. Like a smug feline toying with a doomed bird.

Light flashed off Tye's sword and he lunged, his blade grazing Kaine's left leg. Gasping, Kaine stumbled back, dodging another close blow from a mercenary. A crimson streak formed on Kaine's woolen hose.

"Soon enough, you will join your friends in death." Tye laughed. "You are one man against eleven."

Several of the mercenaries chortled.

The malevolence in Tye's grin raised Edouard's fury to lethal pitch. Raising his sword, Edouard marched from the shadows, dirt crunching beneath his boots. "You, Tye, are the man to die."

Shock flickered over Kaine's face. "Edouard!"

Tye suddenly appeared taller, more alert, than a moment ago, as his attention focused on Edouard. "Brother." He spoke the greeting as though 'twas a curse.

"I am not your bother," Edouard growled, continuing his relentless pace. Thrusting his sword toward the sky, he shouted: "Hear me, good folk of Waddesford Keep! I am Edouard de Lanceau. I am the loyal son of your liege, Moydenshire's great lord, Geoffrey de Lanceau."

A murmur rippled through the throng by the stables.

"All those who hear my name," Edouard yelled, "stand with me. Fight! Help me rid Waddesford of this *scourge*."

"You are a fool," Tye sneered. "You will not find supporters here."

"Fight with me, good folk," Edouard roared. "I command you, on my lord father's behalf!"

"He speaks true!" Kaine yelled. "He is Lord de Lanceau's son. Fight!"

Edouard sensed movement behind him. He turned to see two stable hands stepping forward from the crowd, wielding pitch forks. Mercenaries left Tye's side to intercept them.

"Fight!" Edouard bellowed again. "The rest of you, join me!"

More murmurs. A few more men walked forward in a show of allegiance. Hope flared within Edouard.

"Dead men, all of them." Tye signaled to the other mercenaries. With wicked grins, all but one stalked toward the crowd. Women screamed.

"Now"—Tye's sword glinted as he adjusted his hold—"to deal with you, Brother." He lunged.

The blade flew toward Edouard, a bright streak of steel. The thrill of the challenge raced through him as he met the assault. *Clang. Clang.* The force of the blows hammered through his bones and muscles, warning him of Tye's impressive skill and strength. Damnation, but Tye would not triumph!

Putting all his weight behind his thrust, he struck again, forcing Tye to take two steps back.

"Milord, beware," Kaine called, before he clashed swords with the mercenary who remained with Tye.

A shrill cackle drifted from across the bailey: Veronique. Ignoring the bitter rage that sound stirred inside him, Edouard kept his gaze on Tye's face. If he could overpower Tye, take him hostage with the onlookers witnessing, more folk would likely take up the fight against the traitors.

Poised for attack, Tye blew away a lock of hair trailing into his face. "You cannot win, Brother. The men who tried to join your cause are finished. You are already defeated."

With a mutinous growl, Edouard lunged.

Tye leapt away, following with a slash that barely missed Edouard's thigh. He tsked. "I am surprised your skill is so inferior to mine. Did Father not ensure you were properly trained?"

Edouard forced himself to ignore the taunt. He watched for an opportunity to attack. No doubt, he'd fight better with the sword specially designed for him, the one stripped from him days ago. But he'd fight well enough with this blade.

"Lean in a little closer, next time you strike," Tye goaded, matching Edouard's wary stance. "You might come close to cutting me then. Or are you not strong enough to put the power behind the steel?"

Edouard scowled. Ah, God, he could not wait to run this blade right through Tye's gut.

A choked cry carried from somewhere behind him: a woman, suffering intense pain.

Juliana? He ground his teeth. Nay. By now, she'd be safely through the postern.

Tye glanced at a point beyond Edouard, then chuckled. "Brother, I think you had best lower your sword and surrender."

"Edouard!" Kaine rasped.

Edouard risked a backward glance. And froze.

Two guards held Juliana between them, pinning her arms behind her back.

A cruel smile on her lips, Veronique held a dagger at Juliana's throat.

chapter
21

Juliana tilted her head against the grimy dungeon wall behind her. When she moved, her cheek brushed her upper arm, bared by her fallen sleeve, and she caught the scent of sunlight still clinging to her garments.

Not a single sliver of sunshine reached into this belowground prison; a few wall torches provided the only light. With her arms stretched above her head, and chains clamped around her wrists and ankles, she awaited the dawn and the grim fate Veronique had promised after the guards had secured Juliana's shackles. "Come daybreak, you will tell me where that gold ring is hidden. I will kill servants, one by one, till you yield that information." Veronique had smiled in that depraved way of hers. "Better still, I will use my knife on Edouard."

Juliana swallowed, her mouth painfully dry. She didn't want to reveal any secrets to Veronique, but she also didn't want Edouard or any castle folk to be harmed. Not because of her.

The faint clink of another prisoner's chains reminded her that Edouard and Kaine were shackled in the same manner as she, and lined up along the wall beside her. The three of them were all that were left of Edouard's supporters. Beside her, Edouard blew out a sigh, and her eyes burned. She fought the desperate need to look at him, to know he was still alert and full of fighting spirit.

But, oh God, she couldn't meet his gaze. Not yet.

How could she, when she'd failed him? Him, Kaine, Lord Geoffrey de Lanceau, and all the other good people who'd hoped for an end to the treachery at Waddesford.

A silent cry broke within Juliana and she dropped her head back to the wall. She ignored the twinge of discomfort from her wound, for the pain was unimportant compared to the slaughter Veronique would carry out. Somehow, tonight, Juliana must think of another way to save Edouard and Kaine, and give Lord de Lanceau an advantage over the traitors.

One of the torches popped, sending flames licking in a greedy spike, and she flinched. The yellowish light flicked over mortared stone smeared by years of God only knew what. In places, she recognized the spread of gray-black mold; the earthy odor of it thickened the stale air. Closer to the door, where two guards stood talking in lowered voices, grooves in the dirt floor showed where a heavy object had been dragged several yards. A torture rack? A coffin? A shudder crawled up from the soles of her feet, as though the souls of those who had died here had come to warn her of doom.

"Are you all right?" Edouard's voice seemed unnaturally loud, and she couldn't stop herself from looking at him.

His blue eyes blazed, a look that reminded her of the fiery torches. "Aye," she whispered. "I am . . . fine."

Edouard's brows raised before he tipped his head toward his chains. "As well as we can be, strung up like puppets on strings."

Kaine snorted, a dismayed sound.

"Edouard," Juliana whispered, "I am sorry."

A sad, wry smile tipped up his mouth. "Do not blame yourself." Metal clinked as he tried to stretch sideways and catch her hand, but the bindings wouldn't allow their limbs to touch. As he shifted back to his original position, his chains grated against the stone.

Do not blame yourself, he'd said in a kind voice. How could she not? Edouard was once again a captive; 'twas her fault they were imprisoned. Moreover, if Edouard hadn't found her lying in the river and resolved to help her, he wouldn't have ended up in the tower. He'd be free and far away from Waddesford's danger.

"I do blame myself. I should have run for the postern the moment we stepped into the bailey."

"Juliana," Edouard said, more firmly.

"You know I am right."

He shook his head. "If you had run, the men on the wall walk would have noticed you right away. You would have had little chance of escape."

His defense of her actions heightened her sense of torment. "I still might have got through the postern."

"The garrison, alerted to your escape attempt, would have sent riders to catch you." Edouard's eyes closed, and a muscle jumped in his jaw. "Nay, Juliana, the fault is mine. I should have been able to defeat Tye and rally the castle folk to my side. My father would have managed to do so."

"Edouard!" Tears slipped from the corners of her eyes.

"I failed in my duties as my father's heir. I failed . . . my sire."

"Edouard," Kaine cut in. "Do not say such."

"You were fighting too many enemies at once," she insisted. "Your father is a great warrior, but I doubt even he—"

"He would have succeeded."

How she wanted to rail against that statement. Yet as she stared at Edouard's taut profile, she sensed her words would go unheeded. His loyalty and sense of responsibility to his sire were too thoroughly ingrained.

In truth, though, she'd want no less than absolute allegiance from her lord's son.

How gallant Edouard looked, emboldened by his belief in his father; a faith that stemmed from his noble family's honorable right to rule these lands on behalf of the king.

Edouard might be chained once again, but he wasn't broken or defeated. His conviction was a weapon all its own. It strengthened Edouard's determination not to fail again; it fueled his hatred for those who stood in his way; and it inspired Juliana to stand with him.

When dawn came, she wouldn't yield to Veronique. She'd fight back, with words, strength of will, and what she knew Veronique would want: the location of the bag of bones.

As though sensing her stare, Edouard glanced at her. Remorse filled his gaze. "Do not be afraid, Juliana. I promise you, I will get us out of here."

In hushed tones, Kaine said, "Do you have an idea, Edouard, how to escape?"

"We shall ask for Azarel; she will help us. She can check Juliana's wound and tend the slash on your leg," Edouard said quietly. "Then—"

Kaine shook his head. "One of the guards already examined my injury. He told me I did not need to see the healer."

"Cruel bastard," Edouard muttered.

Juliana looked over at the guards, still engrossed in whatever they were discussing. "We could distract those men," she suggested in a low voice. "Offer them a bribe, if they set us free."

Edouard's stare sharpened. "You are offering *naught* to those thugs. Not even the promise of a kiss."

A flush heated her face. "I never intended to offer *myself*, but a reward, mayhap a share of the jewels when they are recovered."

"Ah," Edouard murmured. "The ones Mayda hid along with Landon's ring?"

"Aye." Thinking of Mayda brought a fresh tug of distress. Mayda had intended those riches to support Rosemary and Juliana for years. But if she were alive, she'd readily agree some should be bartered to win Juliana, Edouard, and Kaine's freedom. Otherwise, Rosemary would never be found and raised as Mayda had asked of Juliana.

"A good idea," Edouard said, his gaze shifting to the two men. "They may be too afraid of Veronique to consider a bribe, but we must try."

As Juliana's thoughts slipped back to Mayda's frightened account of where she'd put the bag of jewels, she realized in her own way, she was honor-bound to the very same ideals as Edouard. She was the only one who knew where the wealth was hidden; her responsibility, to every living soul in Moydenshire, was to keep Landon's ring from falling into the wrong hands.

If Juliana were to die before she could recover the jewels, what she knew would be lost forever. Landon's ring might never be returned to de Lanceau. The riches would remain hidden, to be found, if not by Veronique, than mayhap by another of his lordship's foes determined to stir up chaos. That must not come to pass.

Even as Edouard cleared his throat, likely about to address the guards, she caught his attention. "Listen," she said softly. "In case aught should happen to me—"

"Juliana!" he growled. "Do not speak so."

"You should know where the jewels are," she rushed on in a whisper, "for your father's sake. No one else must get hold of those riches. You will not find them unless you follow the steps I tell you."

Regret flickered in Edouard's eyes, but he said, "Go on."

"When you enter the solar—"

The guards abruptly stopped talking.

Juliana pressed her lips together, holding back the rest of her sentence. Had the louts overheard her? Is that why they'd gone silent?

A sudden tension swept through the room. The men straightened. Hands on their sword hilts, expressions wary, they looked toward the confined passage that led down into the dungeon.

Muffled footfalls echoed, and then Veronique appeared, silk gown rustling as it brushed the steps. Juliana's breath caught as the older woman's wicked gaze pinned her, then slid to Edouard and Kaine.

Her crimson lips parted on a gleeful cackle as she strolled in their direction. "Do I see concern in your eyes, stubborn, proud Edouard?" She winked. "I will. For I have the most *astonishing* news."

Edouard smothered the bitter reply he longed to spit at Veronique. Provoking her wrath, especially when he stood shackled before her and prey to her perverse whims, would solve naught. And, if she thought he'd pose a problem for the guards, she might post more men in the dungeon, and make it even more difficult to escape.

Still, he held Veronique's bold stare, even when she moved so near her rosewater scent brought a tickle to his throat. He indulged in a noisy cough.

She waited until he'd finished, then said, "You are not interested in what I will tell you?" Her tone resembled a smug purr. Clearly, her news benefited her, not him.

"I vow you will tell me anyway, whether I wish it or not." He did his best to look bored.

Her painted smile widened before she reached into her cleavage to draw out a crumpled, rolled piece of parchment. Part of a broken wax seal showed beneath her thumb. He couldn't quite see the impression in the seal, but when he tried to focus on it, she shoved the parchment in his face. "A reply from your loving father."

Edouard scowled, hoping she sensed the full depth of his hatred for her.

"Shall I read it to you?" She shifted the parchment so it scraped against Edouard's jaw. "I think his mighty lordship's words will shock you. What a shame, for me to have to destroy your admirable sense of loyalty to him—"

"Stop it!" Juliana cried, her chains rattling in protest.

Edouard jerked his face from Veronique's touch. He wouldn't submit to any more of her toying or heed her hateful words. Regrettably, however, Veronique didn't move away. With a gloating laugh, she skimmed the document along the side of his neck to the front of his tunic, leaving a smarting trail across his skin.

"Take your hand," Edouard growled, "away from my neck."

"*Tsk, tsk*. If your chains were long enough"—she fingered aside a sweaty length of his hair—"I vow you would try to strangle me, as you did Tye."

"I would. Without hesitation."

Veronique tittered. "How like Tye you are."

"*Never!*"

"Indeed, you might come to hate your father as much as Tye does," she said softly, "if you knew your sire's answer."

Edouard glared at her.

"There, now." Her lustful gaze fell to his mouth. "Save that rage for your father. Because I fear, Edouard, you are all mine."

"Really?" he ground out.

"Really." She smiled in a way that left a cold knot in his chest. "My demands were simple. He was to grant all rights to his estates and riches to Tye, and recognize

Tye as his heir, in exchange for your life. Your father, however, made it very clear in his missive. He does not intend to save you."

Juliana's chains clanked again. "Edouard, do not listen to her. She is trying to mislead you with her lies."

"Am I, Juliana? You know what the missive says, then?"

"Read it to me," Edouard said.

"How bluntly you ask." Veronique ran her fingernail down the parchment. "I do understand, though, being the mother of an equally ambitious son. The anguish of your father's abandonment is what renders your voice so . . . stark."

"Juliana is right. You are lying. My father would never abandon me."

"But he *has* cast you aside." She shook her head. "Just as he abandoned Tye long ago, and all the years since then."

Foreboding mingled with the hot fury churning inside Edouard. What did Veronique mean? No doubt she was trying to undermine his confidence, but he must hold on to his trust and faith in his sire; these would get him through this crisis.

"Read the missive to me." Edouard couldn't stop his tone from roughening.

Veronique laughed. "*Beg* me."

The guards by the doorway chuckled.

"*What?*" Edouard choked out.

CATHERINE KEAN

"You heard me." Cruelty tightened Veronique's features. "Beg me. Like the lost, rejected son you are."

"Merciful God!" Juliana gasped.

Edouard ground his teeth. Veronique obviously wanted him to suffer, in all the ways in her control. To suffer, though, he had to acknowledge she'd conquered him. *Hellfire.* He wasn't finished fighting her; he'd resist until the moment he died.

He met her gaze, focused all of his hatred into his stare. "I will not beg."

"Is that so? Because—"

"Either read me the missive, or leave me be."

A flash of anger, followed by grudging admiration, brightened Veronique's eyes.

"If my father has indeed abandoned me, and I am to die your prisoner," Edouard added with a snarl, "you might as well read me the letter. A last request, if you will."

Veronique chuckled with genuine pleasure. "All right." She unfurled the parchment, revealing several sparse lines scribed in black ink. "Veronique," she read out in a mocking tone. "If the darkest hours of night never gave way to the light of dawn, my answer to your demands would remain the same: never."

Shock coursed through Edouard. There was no doubt as to his sire's refusal.

The answer, however, was oddly phrased. He almost didn't dare to hope . . .

"Show me 'tis what it says," Edouard said.

Veronique sighed as though losing patience with him. "You do not believe I can read?" She held the parchment up at an angle, close to his face. "Years ago, I could not read one word, but I learned. Lovers are good for a great many things." She raised her brows. "Well, Edouard?"

He managed a terse nod. "It does, indeed, say such. 'Tis my father's signature."

"So, you see, I never lied to you this day. I spoke the truth."

Edouard fought the eerie coldness washing through him. He sensed Juliana and Kaine's concerned gazes upon him, but kept his attention firmly fixed upon Veronique. He couldn't betray his suspicions about the missive. He didn't dare.

Stepping away, Veronique rolled up the parchment with her misshapen hands. "I have given you much to think about. Thinking, by the way, is all I allow of you tonight. If you try and talk to one another in even the tiniest whisper or speak to the guards"—she waved a hand at the two men—"they will silence you. I will not have you planning an escape."

"You are a heartless bitch," Edouard ground out.

Smirking, Veronique tapped the parchment against her palm. "Beware, Edouard. I no longer have any reason to keep you alive. Another reason why Juliana will give me all the details I want at dawn."

CHAPTER
22

At the distant sound of a wooden door crashing against stone, Juliana's head snapped up. She winced at the answering pain lancing down the back of her neck and through her shoulders, stiff from being held immobile by her chains. She could barely feel her hands. When she flexed her numb feet, a sleepy, pained groan welled in her throat.

"Easy," Edouard whispered, beside her.

Juliana forced her weary eyes open. "I cannot believe I slept."

"What else was there to do?" Kaine grumbled, rolling his shoulders as best as he could.

Juliana sighed, for Kaine was right. After Veronique had left the dungeon yesterday, Edouard had dared to address the guards. He'd tried to bribe them with a share of the hidden jewels, but, without answering, they'd walked over to him and plowed their fists into his stomach. He'd collapsed in his chains, head bowed, gasping for breath, while she'd silently wept.

A draft of fresh air swirled down into the dungeon as Juliana watched the entrance stairs across from her. Dread brought a sickly sweat to her brow. Footsteps carried, and, with the rattle of weapons and leather armor, the guards straightened. They stood tall, looking to where faint light touched the upper stairs: the light of dawn.

"Try to stay calm." Edouard's soothing tone reminded her of when they'd lain together to stay warm, before she'd recalled his and Nara's betrothal. "Do not give in to your fear, Juliana. Veronique cannot know for certain your memories have come back. She will try, though, to make you betray yourself and thus confirm her suspicions. You must keep pretending you do not remember. You must keep a clear mind."

Juliana shuddered. "I . . . will." She *must* stay focused. Good folk, mayhap even Edouard, would die this morning unless she could successfully bargain with Veronique for the return of her ghastly bones.

"When the guards come to take you," Edouard added, "do not fight them. Let them take us outside. We have a better chance of defeating them in the bailey, when we are not as well restrained."

"All right."

Stay calm. Keep a clear mind, she told herself, when Veronique glided down into the dungeon. Tye and six armed mercenaries followed, but kept back a few steps.

Veronique's merciless stare settled upon Juliana. "Well? Will you tell me where the ring is hidden?"

"I do not remember." Juliana trembled, hoping she revealed naught in her gaze.

Veronique's lips twisted. "You are a poor liar, Juliana."

"Nay!" Juliana choked. "I promise you."

Veronique signaled to the mercenaries. A hard grin curved her mouth as she glanced at the approaching thugs, several carrying lengths of rope. "Bind them and take them up to the bailey."

"What will happen there?" Juliana asked, unable to stop the words racing past her lips.

"What I told you would take place." Veronique smiled. "The killing shall begin."

"Until I yield?" Juliana said.

"Until I have the jewels, including Landon's ring. How many lives will that be, Juliana?" Her cruel gaze raked over Edouard's body. "Will I have to take his life?"

"Nay." Juliana's mind whirled. The bag of bones. She must try to barter with Veronique. "Wait—!" she cried, but her plea was lost as the mercenaries closed in.

Men reached for her manacles, their groping hands running over her limbs. Panic made her head swim, threatening to cause her legs to fold, but she focused on the rhythm of her breathing. That she could control. As her wrists fell free of the bindings, her upper body sagged, weakened from the strain of being held upright so long. Slumping forward, she groaned.

More mercenaries hauled her up by her numb arms and then tied her hands in front of her, heedless of the welts on her wrists caused by the manacles. For the barest moment, her gaze locked with Edouard's. The heat in his stare roused within her a tangled mix of sadness and hope, but then men stepped between them to bind his wrists, blocking her view.

As she concentrated on her breathing, she welcomed the roughness of the rope against her tender skin and the pinpricks of pain shooting through her arms. The sensations reminded her she was alive, and she'd fight to survive.

When the commotion began to clear, she searched for Veronique, but she was no longer in the dungeon; she'd left with the two dungeon guards. Edouard and Kaine, bound and escorted on either side by mercenaries, were hauled up the stairs to the bailey. Then the men at Juliana's side pulled her toward the stairwell.

"You really will not yield?" Tye said, falling in behind her. "Why not, Juliana? You can save yourself much torment."

"I do not remember," Juliana cried, even as she was forced toward the daylight.

Watery sunlight touched her face. When she reached the bailey, she dragged in a grounding breath of clean air. Veronique couldn't win. She mustn't.

Juliana became aware of the eerie stillness surrounding her. She glanced about to see a silent crowd filled the bailey. The castle folk were herded into groups by mercenaries with drawn swords.

An open space marked the middle of the bailey. Her captors pulled her to this area and forced her to halt. Edouard and Kaine, mercenaries surrounding them, stood a short distance away. Tye moved to stand near them.

"Keep them there," Veronique said to Tye and the men watching Edouard and Kaine. "We do not want any foolish heroics, do we?"

A hideous shiver ran through Juliana as she glanced over the throng of men, women, and children, many of whom she recognized. She couldn't watch any of them die.

Her gaze flew to Edouard. How handsome, proud, and defiant he looked, even in this dreadful moment.

Stay calm. Keep a clear mind . . .

A metallic rasp sounded beside her. Veronique had drawn a knife from its leather sheath. Holding the blade straight out in front of her, she tilted it from left to right, a slow, leisurely examination, as she might admire a coveted new trinket.

"Perfect," Veronique murmured. "Sharpened just as I asked." Was she looking forward to the bloodletting? Did causing others to die give her pleasure?

Clearly attuned to Juliana's horror, Veronique looked up. Her amber gaze sharpened. "I ask one last time, Juliana—"

"Why ask?" Juliana didn't bother to caution her words any longer. "You do not believe me when I say I do not remember. You *want* to start murdering innocent folk."

Shocked cries rippled through the crowd.

"'Tis true," Edouard yelled, obviously eager to stir up unrest. "You are in danger,"—he winced when one of the mercenaries kicked him—"all of you!"

As screams and frantic shouts broke out in the crowd, Veronique's stare on Juliana didn't waver. "The deaths today will be upon your conscience."

Juliana shook her head. "Not mine. Yours."

A brutal smile defined Veronique's lips. "You are trying to delay me." She whirled, facing the closest group of onlookers, mostly maidservants holding tightly to their children; they recoiled in terror. "Now . . ."

Oh, God! "Do you really believe that your killing will prompt my memories?" Juliana shouted. "Did your wretched bag of bones tell you that?"

Veronique's whole body stiffened. Slowly, her head turned. "Strange, you should say that. My bones went missing yesterday."

Juliana raised her chin. *Stay calm. Keep a clear mind . . .*

"So, too, did Azarel. My men have not yet found her. I thought she had taken them." Veronique's eyes snapped into menacing slits. "You know where they are."

"I do."

Rage burned in her eyes. "You stole them?"

"I took them from the guard I rendered unconscious and then hid them. I *do* remember where they are—somewhere you will never find them."

Veronique hissed. "Why, you—"

"Put down the knife. Let me, Edouard, and Kaine go free. Promise you will not hurt any of these folk. In return, I will tell you where to find your bones."

Veronique tapped a finger to her chin, a gesture that implied she pondered Juliana's demands. Then she whirled, red hair snaking out around her. "A tempting offer. Yet mayhap 'tis time I started a whole new collection—"

"Nay—"

"—of fresh bones, cut from the dead!"

"God, *nay*!" Juliana cried, bile stinging her mouth. "Veronique—!"

Horrified screams arose. Folk scrambled to flee as, shrieking a laugh, Veronique snatched a young girl, no more than five or six years old, from the throng and dragged her forward. Sobbing, the girl looked back at a crying woman struggling to reach her; a mercenary kept the mother back.

"Let her go," Juliana pleaded, almost choking on her revulsion.

Veronique anchored her hand into the girl's long braid and twisted. The girl cried out, face crumpling with pain, even as Veronique jerked her head back and set the dagger at the girl's exposed throat.

The terror in the young girl's tear-filled eyes . . . A girl too young to have really lived or loved . . .

Juliana pressed her arm over her stomach and gasped, fighting to draw breaths into constricted lungs. This girl didn't deserve to die. *Couldn't* die. "Veronique," Juliana croaked.

"I *knew* you would give in," Veronique snarled, spittle at the corners of her mouth. "You pathetic, weak—"

A shout echoed from the wall walk above. "Milady!"

"Be *quiet!*" Veronique screeched, and pulled the weeping girl's head back farther.

"Milady! Riders," another man cried from above. "Approaching fast."

Veronique glared up at the battlements. "*What?*"

"How many?" Tye snapped, hand moving to his sword.

Juliana blinked up at the men on the wall walk, then looked at Edouard. Wariness still defined his posture, but he appeared to be . . . grinning.

Catching her gaze, he winked at her.

Winked!

Her pulse thundered, while the guard on the wall walk shouted down, "Two score riders. Likely more."

Veronique spat an oath before her furious gaze snapped to Edouard.

He smiled. "That will be my father."

Edouard laughed, the sound rich and jubilant, as Veronique's face contorted with shocked outrage. That look alone made his heart leap with pleasure. Knowing she'd believed him left to her depravity made this moment all the sweeter.

Today, his sire would wrest Waddesford from her clutches. At last, his father would see her punished for all the pain and treachery she'd caused not only the de Lanceau's, but so many others through the years.

Hope shone in Juliana's eyes. "Are you certain 'tis your sire, Edouard?"

"I am."

"You *knew*!" Veronique shrieked, gaze still upon him even as she shoved the young girl from her grasp. The child stumbled, scrambled to her feet, and ran, crying, to her mother.

Edouard shrugged, as well as he could with his wrists bound and mercenaries at his sides. "I had my suspicions."

The knife shifted in Veronique's white-knuckled hand. "I see now. The missive was strangely worded. You would understand it held a message."

"I told you." Tye stormed to her side, expression dark with fury. "I warned you last night, Mother. I said 'twas too simple, but you refused to heed me—"

Veronique trembled on a violent curse. She turned

on him, knife flashing in the sunlight. "Cease!"

Easily dodging the errant strike, Tye's brows raised. "Swear at me all you wish, Mother. However, I do not intend to become my father's prisoner."

"Neither do I." She thrust her hands at the mercenaries amongst the throng, looking uneasily at one another while still keeping the castle folk corralled. "Give all the menservants weapons," she shouted at them. "They shall fight for us or their families will die. Then you will go to the battlements. Do not let the army get near. Kill anyone who tries to cross the moat. Do you understand?"

The warriors glanced at each other. Some looked disgruntled, an opportunity Edouard mustn't let slip by.

"Obey Veronique, and you will die," he called. "You cannot defeat my sire. Lay down your arms and surrender to him."

"Silence, Edouard," Veronique shrilled. "Win this battle for me, my mercenaries, and I will pay you thrice what I do now!" She pointed to the warriors guarding Edouard and Kaine. "You, too, shall be so rewarded."

"Aye, milady," the mercenaries said, before those in the crowd rushed off to do her bidding.

Veronique gestured to Tye. "Round up the remaining mercenaries. Send them to guard the gatehouse. No one is to enter or leave that way." She thrust a gnarled finger upward. "Then join me there on the wall walk."

Tye's mouth flattened, and his relentless gaze clashed with Edouard's. Fury raced anew through Edouard. Digging his nails into his bonds, he vowed to get free and ensure his bastard brother never escaped this fight. "What of our hostages?" Tye said. "Shall we chain them back in the dungeon?"

"They are to come to the wall walk with me. There, we will not only survive this battle, but negotiate its bloody end to our benefit."

"Mother—"

Annoyance flashed in Veronique's eyes. "Do not make me question your allegiance, Tye. Especially not on the day we will confront your father."

"Why would you? When have I *ever* given you a reason to doubt me?"

"Just do as I told you," Veronique snapped.

Tye growled, then loped away into the crowd.

When Veronique's attention returned to Edouard, he braced for a struggle. She might think she'd haul him up to the battlements, but he'd fight her. The sooner he got free of his bonds, the sooner he'd open the gatehouse to his sire. And his father would win.

First, though, with Tye no longer close at hand, he had to get Juliana away from Veronique. The older woman looked angry enough to kill Juliana out of spite.

A brittle laugh rippled from Veronique. "You are still thinking of escape, Edouard?" Her brazen gaze slid over him. "A pity you waste your stamina on such use-less pursuits. Your life is mine to do with as I please. As"—Veronique turned to face Juliana—"is hers."

"Run!" Edouard shouted, as the malevolence in the older woman's expression crested. Just as Juliana attempted to dash into the throng, Veronique grabbed her arm. Screaming, Juliana tried to wrench free, but with a brutal yank, Veronique unbalanced Juliana and she half fell, skirts dragging across the dirt—enough of a delay for Veronique to shove the knife against Juliana's side.

Alarm, as biting as the flick of a whip, lashed through Edouard. Juliana slowly rose to her feet, her breathing shaky. Did she feel the pinch of the dagger's tip through her gown? Was her flawless skin pierced? He should have tried sooner to get her to safety.

"Now," Veronique said, raising her voice to carry above growing din of battle preparations. "Juliana and I will proceed"—she tipped her head—"to that stairwell. Edouard and Kaine, you will follow. If you refuse, or try to fight the mercenaries escorting you, I will shove my dagger into Juliana's flesh. She can still tell me where the jewels are, while she is bleeding to death. I will not repeat my warning."

Juliana's face paled, but she held her head high.

Stay strong, a voice inside him said. *I will protect you, Juliana. Because I love you.*

"Walk," Veronique ordered.

Juliana started toward the keep, walking as though terrified to misstep.

Edouard scowled. Never again would Juliana suffer at Veronique's hand. Never!

Without waiting for the mercenaries to prod him, Edouard followed, aware of Kaine's limping footsteps close behind. While walking, Edouard continued to work his nails into his bonds. He must undo the knot. He could fight with his hands tied, but if he could get them free, he'd be far more lethal.

The dankness of the stairwell closed in on him. He trudged up the narrow steps and, moments later, emerged on the wall walk. He stepped out onto the windblown stone, caught Veronique's curse, and followed her gaze to the dust cloud churned up by the approaching forces, all the knights and men-at-arms his sire had been able to summon at short notice.

The faint pounding of hooves carried on the wind.

Veronique forced Juliana forward, until she stood almost directly opposite the entrance to the bailey. "Line Edouard and Kaine up alongside her," Veronique said. "I want de Lanceau to see them when he rides in to give his surrender."

Edouard loosed a disparaging snort. "My father will never yield. Not to you. Not to anyone."

Veronique laughed. "Oh, but he will."

CHAPTER
23

The morning breeze stung Juliana's eyes and tore at her garments as she stood on the battlement, held by two mercenaries. Shouts and sounds of weapons being readied for the fight carried up from the bailey below. Her thoughts, however, hardly registered the commotion. All her sharpened senses were held hostage by the odors of her guards: a pungent blend of grubby leather and sweat.

The mercenary to her left obviously hadn't washed in months. Juliana caught her breath and hoped the next wind gust past the castle walls would defray the smell.

Oh, God, 'twas selfish and senseless to focus on the mercenaries' odors, when she—and of course Edouard and Kaine—faced far greater concerns. In truth, though, the very male smells cut sharper edges into her fear. Rebellion might seethe inside her, but the men restraining her were large, strong, and well trained with their weapons.

If, on Veronique's orders, they tried to harm Juliana to prove their intentions to de Lanceau, she'd fight as fiercely as she could. The men, though, already had the advantage. The oaf to her left held her arm in a ruthless grip; he also held a dagger at her throat. The man on her right, grasp equally as bruising, cut circles in the air with his sword, no doubt readying his muscles for the upcoming assault.

A giggle, tinged with hysteria, bubbled inside Juliana. On any day in her life, had she ever imagined herself standing on Waddesford's battlements as a bound captive, an impending sacrifice to Veronique's wickedness? Not likely.

Yet here she was.

How Juliana hated the cold touch of the dagger against her neck; despised the grim sense of helplessness; welcomed the anger churning within her, ready to be summoned to the fore. However the morning's events unfolded, she wouldn't be used to help bring about Geoffrey de Lanceau's downfall—or Edouard's death.

A shout from below drew her gaze through the gap between the closest stone merlons to the bailey. Mercenaries bellowed, ordering servants carrying longbows and arrows to the battlements. Women and children scurried to obey other thugs' shouted commands. In the shadows of the gatehouse, she saw Tye talking to several men, gesturing as he relayed instructions.

A stifling sense of impending catastrophe seemed to

A kNigHT'S pERSUASiON

linger in the air. How many people would die today? With so many men at his command, and having traveled many leagues, de Lanceau wouldn't be denied what he wanted. The thought of the bloodshed to come . . . Oh, God, it made her feel ill.

A grunt sounded beside her, then the crack of a brutal slap.

"Bitch!" Edouard snapped, his focus on Kaine, who'd fallen on one knee. "You know his left leg is injured." From Edouard's lethal expression, he looked ready to break free of the mercenaries holding him and wallop Veronique, but one of the thugs pressed the tip of his sword against Edouard's stomach, forcing him to remain still.

"Kaine will stand," Veronique said, "or I will slay him now."

His face white with agony, Kaine straightened. His left leg trembled, even as he forced a lopsided grin. "No need to kill me."

Juliana offered him a sympathetic smile, for his attempt at humor took a great deal of inner resolve; he was clearly in pain. Edouard exchanged a glance with Kaine, then nodded, before his defiant gaze shifted back to Veronique.

With a smug arch of her eyebrows, she turned her back to him to peer down at the bailey. Standing as she was, the skirts of her dark red gown flapping in the breeze, she resembled a gaudy, deformed bird, waiting to swoop down and snatch unsuspecting victims below.

Juliana shivered and then sensed Edouard's stare upon her. In his blazing eyes, she saw all her own emotions. While their gazes held, her spirit lightened, drawn to his inner strength. Inspired by the warrior force that was integral to who he was, to his father's legacy, and the noble de Lanceaus who'd come before.

In that moment, she wondered how love felt between a man and a woman. Was it as profound as what glowed inside her now? Was it anywhere near as wonderful as her memory of that breathless moment, lying in the darkness, when she'd thought Edouard would kiss her?

Of all her regrets, how she wished she'd experienced love. With him.

As their stares continued to hold, she blinked away the sting of tears. If she had to die today, she'd make her last moments meaningful. She'd fight for Mayda, for little Rosemary, for all she wished she could have experienced with Edouard. To her very last breath, she'd do all in her ability to ensure Edouard and his sire triumphed.

As though guessing her thoughts, his eyes widened slightly, and then his gaze dropped to his bound hands. A deliberate gesture.

A signal?

He'd been working at the rope knot. She'd tried to dig her nails into hers as they climbed the stairwell, but the knot was too tight.

Had he managed to loosen his bonds?

An excited tingle swept over her skin. She forced herself to stare straight ahead again, not wanting to risk what Edouard had divulged.

The armed riders were near. The approaching group had separated into two lines that spread along the perimeter of the castle wall. Not so close that the riders were in range of the mercenaries, but near enough to make a formidable impression.

Once the riders had reached their intended destination, they halted, horses facing the castle. The distant thud of hoof beats lessened. Then stopped.

Sudden silence spread down the wall walk, punctuated only by the whistling of the wind. Even Veronique stood motionless, attention fixed upon the riders; hands splayed into the breeze, as though she sought insight from it.

Juliana curled her fingers against her bonds and dug her nails into the knot. If Edouard had loosened his bindings, she'd try, too.

Beyond the castle, a single rider separated from the neat line of warriors. He wore an iron helm that covered all but the lower third of his face, a flowing black cloak, and a surcoat decorated with embroidery that flashed in the sunlight.

"Geoffrey!" Veronique trembled and smoothed a

hand over her windblown tresses.

Halting several paces ahead of the others, the rider lifted his head. A moment later, Juliana heard a shout, distorted by the wind. Had he ordered the castle to surrender? If so, battle was only moments away. She *had* to get free, so she could fight.

"Aim!" a mercenary bellowed, somewhere down the wall walk.

Veronique's head swiveled. "Wait!" she shrieked. "Let de Lanceau draw closer." The nearest of the mercenary archers, eyes wide with surprise, shouted her order to the other fighters on the battlements.

Clearly unafraid of the mercenaries watching him, de Lanceau urged his horse to a walk. He rode toward the gatehouse, and, as he approached the castle, was blocked from Juliana's view by the exterior stone wall.

Another shout carried. Faint, but distinct. "Veronique." The shout repeated again and again, growing in volume as it blew up on the breeze. Now Juliana heard many men's voices, calling in unison: "Veronique. Veronique."

Setting her hands on the curve of her hips, Veronique cackled. "They are calling my name. *Glorifying* me."

Juliana choked down a stunned laugh. Glorifying? Nay. The repetition of her name was menacing. A warning.

"Veronique. Veronique."

Glancing at Edouard, Juliana whispered, "Why are they chanting?"

"I do not know," he said quietly, his attention on the line of men. "I am sure my father has good reason for ordering it."

Raised voices and a cry drew Juliana's gaze again to the bailey. Drawn sword gleaming in the sunlight, Tye brushed through the crowd and looked up at the wall walk where Veronique stood. "Mother!"

"What?" Veronique threw up her hands in obvious annoyance. "I told you what to do. Why must you distract me?"

Tye's expression hardened. "You said not to let anyone in."

"Then do not!"

"De Lanceau is at the gate. *Alone.* He asked to speak with you."

"What in hellfire?" Edouard muttered.

A gasp burned Juliana's throat. She'd heard tales of his lordship's bravery and cleverness. Surely, though, he realized confronting Veronique on his own put his life—and the lives of many others—in jeopardy. Why would he take such a risk? Did he believe that by speaking privately with Veronique—by reminding her of their long-ago liaison—he could negotiate for Edouard's life?

Alarm whipped through Juliana, for in her mind, the likely sequence of events unfolded. Veronique wouldn't negotiate. She'd kill de Lanceau and Edouard, relishing the gruesome spectacle before these witnesses. Juliana

CATHERINE KEAN

would remain captive until she finally yielded the whereabouts of the important gold ring, whereupon she'd be
murdered. Tye would use the ring's influence to quickly
seize control of Moydenshire and become ruler.

"Oh, God," she whispered.

"Veronique. Veronique."

Running a hand over her indecently tight bodice,
Veronique tittered. "Mayhap, Edouard, your father believes he can save you. He has come to plead with me, to
beg forgiveness for the past cruelties he inflicted upon me.
To surrender to my demands, in hopes of sparing you, his
precious wife, and the daughter he loves so much."

Edouard snorted. "You truly believe that?"

She shot Edouard a smug glare before she called down
to Tye: "You were right to consult me. Lower the drawbridge and let your father in. We will see what he wants."

Tye frowned. "It could be a trap."

"Aye. However, he is on his own."

"Still, Mother—"

"*One* man, who, rumor has it, is still not recovered
from his recent illness." She cackled, drowning out the
rest of Tye's words of protest. "Weakened as Geoffrey
is, he will not have his usual fighting prowess. He will
be easily defeated. Once his men learn he is dead—and
Edouard is doomed to die, too—they may not bother to
stay and finish the fight."

Juliana couldn't stop herself from looking at

Edouard. Hatred and suspicion lined his features. How lonely he seemed, doubtless torn between the shock of all he'd heard and the questions whirling in his mind.

If only she could reach out and take his hand. To let him know he wouldn't face the coming moments alone. She'd be with him, as he'd stayed with her every moment till she was rescued from Sherstowe's well.

"If I let Father in," Tye said, tone gruff, "I want to kill him."

"As I expected." Veronique smiled and flicked her hand at Tye, a gesture of dismissal. "Today, the destiny you deserve will be yours."

Edouard blinked against the buffeting wind. Why was his father on his own at the keep's gates? God's blood, *why*?

Such rashness, from his sire, made no sense. His father wasn't a fool; before every battle, he strategized, calculated, considered all options, as he must have done before deciding to leave the protection of his men and ride alone to confront Veronique.

His sire would never underestimate Veronique's malice. What motive, then, could he have for such a dangerous tactic? Did he count on rousing the folk inside the castle walls to fight against her and her mercenaries, while his warriors besieged the fortress? Had he found a way to sneak some of his men-at-arms inside the keep, who would attack when he gave a signal? A dull ache tightened Edouard's innards as he struggled to figure out the probable course of events.

"Veronique. Veronique," the men beyond the walls continued to chant. Edouard dug his nails into his bonds again and did his best not to reveal his concern over his sire's actions. Yet Veronique seemed to know exactly his turmoil.

"Soon, you will watch your father die." Her face twisted into a grin.

Believe in your father, as he'd expect of you. Prove you will not be swayed by her taunting. Mimicking her grin, Edouard said, "Will I?"

Veronique spread a gnarled hand wide, indicating the surrounding keep. "He thinks to defeat all of us?" She laughed. "Wretched fool."

"He will destroy you," Edouard fired back.

"He is arrogant enough to believe he will succeed." At the grinding squeal of the drawbridge being lowered, Veronique glanced toward the gatehouse. She straightened her gown from breasts to hips, as an eager wench would right her garments before meeting a lover.

"Veronique. Veronique," continued the riders.

She laughed, obviously reveling in the chant. With an indulgent sway of her hips, she moved closer to the merlons, hair drifting in the breeze. "The portcullis is rising. Not long now, till I see him again."

The wood and metal barrier was, indeed, lifting up into the gatehouse. The muffled grating, accompanied by Tye shouting for the crowd in the bailey to stand aside, sent a painful tremor snaking through Edouard.

He forced his stiff fingers into the bonds again.

Father, turn your horse around. Ride back to your men. Protect the future of Moydenshire and the justice in which you believe.

A figure became visible in the murky shadows of the gatehouse. A hush fell over the crowd as Edouard's father emerged in the bailey. Behind him, on Tye's shouted instructions, mercenaries ran to block the way out through the gatehouse.

The tall rider paid no heed to the activities intended to entrap him. With his voluminous cloak sweeping from his shoulders, he looked imposing and formidable. When he continued forward, light glinted off his helm and the embroidered image of a flying hawk on his silk surcoat that covered his chain-mail hauberk. Edouard's mother had embroidered the symbol years ago, conveying her love in each stitch.

What would happen to Edouard's mother if his sire died today? She'd be overcome by grief. That must never come to pass. Not, Edouard vowed, when his sire was here at Waddesford, risking all, because of him.

"Stand aside," Tye and several mercenaries yelled,

as they hurried to walk in front of the rider, swords at the ready. Castle folk bowed as Edouard's sire rode past them. "Make way," Tye shouted, "for the great Geoffrey de Lanceau, lord of all of Moydenshire."

Edouard scowled at the contempt in Tye's voice.

Veronique chortled. "Well done, Tye. Bring your *father* closer. Bring him to his death."

At the word "death," Edouard's sire's head lifted a proud notch. He didn't rein in his horse, though, but kept the onward pace, the *clip-clop* of his destrier's hoof-beats echoing in the tense silence. With a twinge of surprise, Edouard noted the animal wasn't his father's usual horse. Why had he chosen the bay with a white stripe down its muzzle, and not the fast, spirited black that had become his favorite?

Wait. *Was* there such a bay in his father's stable?

As his sire headed to the cleared center of the bailey, in plain view of where Veronique stood, he nodded to castle folk—a gesture of acknowledgment and respect, delivered with a touch of arrogance. Yet something about the dip of his head . . .

Suspicion washed through Edouard. He studied the broadness of his father's shoulders beneath the cloak, and the shape of his chin, not concealed by the helm.

"Milady," a mercenary shouted from the wall walk near the rear of the keep. "Mil—!"

"Silence!" Veronique screeched at him.

He thrust a hand toward the ground. "But—"

She pointed to the mercenary closest to the one who'd shouted. "Kill him. I want no more interruptions, or I will kill you as well."

At that moment, the rider drew in his mount, halting the destrier so he faced Veronique. The horse tossed its head; the bridle chimed, the only sound apart from the steady chanting: "Veronique. Veronique."

"Good morning to you, Geoffrey." Veronique's words of welcome were sharp with gloating.

Edouard waited for the rider to speak. His fingers shifted on his horse's reins, but he didn't respond. Not surprising. Edouard's sire's hatred for Veronique was well known; he obviously didn't care to show her even the slightest respect by granting her a reply.

The rider's helm-covered head turned a fraction, and Edouard sensed him assessing the armed men in the bailey and the castle's defenses. A far more important task than answering Veronique.

Edouard couldn't resist a smile.

Tye's face hardened; he clearly interpreted the insult.

Veronique huffed. "Are you a man without a voice? I demand you acknowledge me, Geoffrey. After all, we know each other well." Her husky laughter carried down to the bailey. "So *very* well, my lusty lordship, you got me with child."

A disgusted snort broke from the rider.

Veronique's posture stiffened. Anger seemed to swirl about her as she glowered down at him. "Have the years made you a fool? You know you are unwise to taunt me." She gestured to the mercenaries awaiting her order to fire upon him. "*I* am the one with all the advantage."

The rider's chin lifted another notch, a silent gesture of disagreement.

"Veronique. Veronique," the men outside the walls chanted.

She moved closer to the gap between the merlons. "Acknowledge me, Geoffrey. Do it now, or I will order a start to the bloodletting. I will begin with your beloved Edouard."

At her vile taunt, the rider pressed his shoulders back, without the slightest sign of fatigue or discomfort. Could Edouard's father have recovered from the old-wound aches triggered by the illness? Not likely. The suspicion inside Edouard rose to a full roar.

"Edouard," his sire grated.

Veronique tittered. "You do speak, after all. Although," her tone turned thoughtful, "your voice sounds different."

"'Tis hoarsened, because I have been ill. Or were you unaware?"

Silent laughter bubbled in Edouard's throat, for that voice was definitely not his father's. It belonged to Dominic de Terre.

"Oh, I knew of your sickness," Veronique said.

"Good. Then you will understand why I wish to end

this conflict as quickly as possible. To begin, you will send Edouard down to me."

"How forceful you are," Veronique said, toying with a strand of her hair. "As demanding as when I spread my legs for you and made you groan—"

"Send Edouard down. Now."

"I think not." Veronique's tone hardened. "You see, his life depends entirely upon you. Do as I command, and he might live. As I said, *might*. To begin, you will acknowledge your other son—your *bastard*—whom you have spurned for nigh twenty years now."

"I have but one son."

How true. Edouard fought not to grin.

"Your other son is beside you." Veronique gestured to Tye, who stood at the horse's head, his sword half raised. Not the pose of a child hoping for a reunion with his father, but of a warrior, readying to strike. Fighting a rush of unease, Edouard worked his fingers again into his bonds, and felt the rope shift against his wrist.

"This man is not my child," the rider said.

"I believe I am, milord." Tye's frosty voice held a determined note.

"He is grown now. Far from the little boy you met at our meeting in the meadow, all those years ago. The day"—Veronique's voice shook with fury—"you so heartlessly rejected him."

"Did I?"

Tye spat an oath, while Veronique recoiled, as though the rider had reached up and slapped her across the face. "You *dare* deny that day took place? How very *gallant*, for a man who vowed to live his life by honor and chivalry."

As she railed at him, the rider raised his free hand, palm up, a very definite attempt to deflect her accusations. Then he reached for his helm.

With a dramatic flourish, he drew it off. Chestnut brown hair, streaked at the temples with silver gray, fell to his shoulders. A stray wisp brushed the corner of his mouth.

Juliana drew in a breath. "Why, 'tis—"

"Dominic de Terre," Edouard said with a chuckle. His hopes soared, for his father and most trusted men must be close by.

"*Dominic?*" Veronique shrieked. "Why, you—"

Tye scowled. "Where in *hellfire* is de Lanceau?"

"Aye. Where *is* your father?" Juliana whispered to Edouard, before her gaze darted back to the bailey.

Edouard smiled. "I expect he will present himself soon."

With a careless grin, Dominic settled his helm on his lap. "For shame, Veronique. You are not delighted to see me? Our acquaintance goes back over twenty years. By the way, I do have a son."

"Geoffrey!" Veronique spluttered. "I demand—"

Dominic rolled his eyes. "Veronique, you never learn. He would not allow himself to be an easy target for you, which is why I am here. I am surprised you did not guess our ploy long ago."

Veronique shrieked. "Where *is* he? If you do not tell me—"

"He hoped to surprise you. I believe he spoke of an alternative way in?" Even as she glanced at the rear battlement, Dominic flicked his hand. "Ah. Here he is now."

With a startled jolt, Edouard noted the mercenaries crumpled on the far wall walk. One of them must be the man Veronique had ordered murdered moments ago; but what of the others? They must have been killed from a distance. Few men had that remarkable skill. Few, that is, except Aldwin Treynarde, one of his sire's most respected knights, whose astonishing expertise with a crossbow was still recounted in local *chansons*.

Brisk footfalls echoed in the bailey below. As the crowd looked at whoever approached, Edouard strained to see.

A group of armed warriors strode into view. In the midst of them he recognized Aldwin, crossbow cocked. There, too, was his father, broadsword unsheathed. And, protected on all sides by the warriors, was Azarel. She must have slipped from the castle yesterday and located his father's forces; she'd probably told him of the postern.

Edouard suddenly realized the men outside had stopped chanting. They no longer needed to; they'd helped Dominic distract Veronique long enough for Edouard's sire to get inside the keep.

"Well done, Father," Edouard murmured. Pride

burned in him as he watched his sire cross to Dominic. His father wore a chain mail hauberk over a pewter gray tunic and hose, garments that wouldn't distinguish him as one of England's most powerful lords. Yet there was no denying the bold authority that defined his strides.

Veronique's hands twitched. "Geoffrey!"

As Edouard's sire halted and looked up at her, sunshine struck his face. Sweat shone on his brow and dampened the sides of his graying, wavy, brown hair. His skin looked ashen, but his gaze held the familiar strength Edouard had always known. And respected.

"I am Geoffrey de Lanceau, Lord of Moydenshire," he roared, his voice easily carrying across the bailey and up to the battlements. "I demand you surrender this keep to me."

Veronique laughed.

"Surrender," he repeated. "Without delay. Or my army will attack." As though sensing Edouard's gaze, his sire looked directly up at him. Frowned.

"Are you all right, Son?" he shouted.

"Aye," Edouard called back, while anchoring his fingernails deeper into his bindings; they loosened a fraction more.

His sire's attention shifted to Veronique. "A good thing Edouard is not harmed. For if he were—"

"An empty threat," Veronique said with a sniff. "Now you are here, Geoffrey"—she glared at Dominic—"and your senseless little game is finished, you will yield

382 ❦

to me."

"Is that so?"

Edouard sensed his father working to keep his temper under control.

"You will put down your weapons and fall to your knees on the dirt," Veronique continued, lips curling. "You, the great lord of Moydenshire, will sign all rights to your estates over to your son."

Edouard's sire raised his brows. "Edouard already is my heir. Years from now, when I am dead, he will have all, as is his birthright."

"Not Edouard," Veronique said through her teeth. "Tye."

"A man I do not recognize."

"You *will*," Veronique sneered.

"Will I? You have undeniable evidence that I sired him?"

Fear edged into Edouard's consciousness. His bastard brother, looking angrier by the moment, stood dangerously close to Dominic and the other men-at-arms; close enough to lunge in an attack.

Beware, Father, for Tye is ready to run you through with his sword.

"Tye is near you." Veronique motioned to him. "Seeing you two together, there is no doubt he looks like you, as he has since he was a young boy. Ask anyone here if they can deny a resemblance. That, Geoffrey, is proof enough."

Edouard's sire glanced at Tye, whose expression held both anguish and loathing.

An odd look flickered over his father's features. Surprise? Recognition?

"Hello, Father," Tye ground out.

Edouard waited for his sire to reply. Silence carried, ominous and strained. Then, without a word, de Lanceau looked back at Veronique. "I told you before, and I will say so again. You have not proven he is my son."

Tye chuckled, a bitter sound. "We expected your refusal." From the front of his tunic, he withdrew a rolled parchment, tied with twine, and thrust it forward.

Eyes narrowed in a scowl, Edouard's sire said, "I will never sign."

"Never? That is a strong word, Father."

Beware, Father. Beware!

"My answer is, and always will be, *never*."

Come on, come on! Edouard silently pleaded as he worked again on his bonds.

The knot loosened further.

"Your reluctance, too, was anticipated," Veronique said with a wicked giggle. "I know we will change your mind." She looked back over her shoulder at Kaine, then Edouard, then, with bright, glittering eyes, Juliana. "Kill her."

CHAPTER

24

Veronique's words slammed into Juliana's mind.

She was going to die.

Now.

Before the horror fully bloomed in Juliana's thoughts, the mercenaries eased aside their weapons to haul her forward, toward the wall walk's edge.

Juliana dug her heels into the rough stone beneath her feet. She twisted her upper body to and fro, trying to break their punishing hold.

"Nay!" Edouard roared behind her. "Take me instead."

"Edouard!" Juliana screamed, while she struggled. But the mercenaries were too strong. With brutal tugs, they brought her to the open space between the merlons, giving her an unhindered view of the steep drop to the ground and the shocked crowd below. The mercenary on her left shoved his knife near her face, a reminder of what was to come.

Sickening shudders ran through her. Her breath

whistled sharply in her throat. She'd vowed not to yield. What more, though, could she do? How did she break free of these thugs and fulfill her vow to fight?

Tears slipped down her cheeks. *Edouard, my chivalrous protector, how I wish we'd never disagreed in the past. How I wish you weren't betrothed to Nara. How I wish we were both free and could begin anew. I weep, in my very soul, that I never had the chance to love you.*

"Release her," Lord de Lanceau bellowed from below.

"Kill her!" Veronique shrieked.

The mercenary at Juliana's right, holding his sword at hip level, wrenched her arm and thereby tugged her body sideways as though to better thrust his blade into her belly. Ignoring the dagger close to her cheek—she'd die anyway, unless she got free—she fought the thugs' hold.

In her mind, she suddenly saw Mayda, poised at the edge of the wall walk, fighting for her life. *Mayda, I am sorry. I failed in all you asked of me.*

The glint of metal warned her of the moving sword. Her tear-blurred gaze fell to Lord de Lanceau, his grim stare fixed upon her. Even as she struggled, her stomach clenched, preparing to feel the weapon's sharp bite.

As though the passing moment had somehow slowed, she saw de Lanceau nod, the barest dip of his head.

The blond man beside him, holding a crossbow, aimed his weapon at her. Fired.

The steel-tipped bolt streaked through the air toward

her. A merciful death. They'd taken the right to her life from Veronique.

Edouard, I am forever lost—

The sword's tip touched her stomach.

Blood splattered across her face and torso. It dripped from her hair, even as she squeezed her eyes shut and awaited agonizing pain.

Through a fog of expectation, Juliana heard the mercenary to her right groan, followed by the clank of metal by her feet.

The mercenary wielding the dagger gasped. Shouts erupted along the battlements. Veronique shrieked, her voice accompanied by the whistle of fired arrows.

Juliana opened one eye to see arrows flying down into the bailey, where servants and warriors had started fighting. The mercenary who'd aimed to plunge his sword into her had crumpled over, clutching at his chest, where the feathered fletching of the bolt poked out. His blood stained her clothes.

Relief and hope raced through her. As the wounded mercenary turned his bloody head to glare at her, and tried to pick up his sword, she brought her leg up and slammed her foot into his thigh. He reeled against the nearby merlon. With a strangled roar, he lost his balance, tripped on uneven stone, and fell over the side, down to the bailey below.

A sharp tug snapped her focus back to the other mercenary. His lips drew back from his blackened teeth, and the knife gleamed as he tilted it, clearly readying to strike. Before she could draw in air to scream, a crossbow bolt spliced through his neck, from throat to nape, with a grisly *fwoop* and crack of bone. Eyes rolling, he fell backward onto the wall walk, the dagger still in his hand.

She was alive. *Alive!*

"Get her!" Veronique shrilled.

Dragging in a breath, Juliana dropped to a crouch before the fallen sword and sliced her bonds. Then she snatched up the weapon. Keeping an eye on Veronique and her lackeys, she glanced over the battlement, to thank de Lanceau's crossbowman who'd saved her. Yet the bailey was a seething battle scene, with castle folk fighting mercenaries, the wounded crying for help, and the dead sprawled on the ground. De Lanceau and the crossbowman were nowhere to be seen.

Neither was Tye.

"Do not let her escape!" Veronique shrieked. Raising the sword, Juliana spun around to face a bald mercenary, one of the men who'd restrained Edouard. A knife flashed in the mercenary's grasp.

She glared at him. Then, quickly, at Veronique. Juliana focused all her hatred and resolve into her stare; never would she allow the murderous woman who'd caused so much grief at the castle win this battle.

Veronique's stare sharpened. "I was right. You remember."

"I do. *Everything.*"

"Get that sword from her," Veronique snapped to the mercenary. "I want her as my hostage. Now!"

The mercenary lunged forward, and Juliana darted back two steps. She dared a glance at Edouard. Pride shone in his gaze, and he winked.

Juliana's pulse fluttered—oh, how she savored that wink—even as she guessed he wanted her to keep this lout distracted. Her arms, though, had started to tremble from the weapon's weight.

The mercenary grinned. "'Ow long, lovey, 'till ye 'ave ta put the sword down?"

She scowled, for Veronique was edging in toward her. She would *not* be Veronique's captive again. At least this time, when facing Veronique, Juliana had a weapon.

A pained grunt, then the clang of falling metal came from behind the bald mercenary. As he spun, knife at the ready, Juliana saw Edouard had thrown aside his bonds. His remaining guard stood with one arm crossed over his belly, his dagger on the stones several yards away.

"Well done, milord!" Kaine struggled against his two captors.

His face dark with fury, Edouard's guard staggered back, then reached into his boot, no doubt for another knife.

Edouard snatched up the fallen dagger and then looked at Juliana. "Bring me the sword."

As the bald mercenary swung back to face her, she

dashed past him, keeping her blade aimed at his gut. He muttered then advanced on her.

Another backward step, and she bumped into Edouard. The touch of their bodies sent bittersweet longing racing through her, but she didn't dare meet his gaze. Not when the battle against Veronique had yet to be won.

Edouard's fingers brushed hers as he exchanged the dagger for her sword.

"What now?" Holding the knife at the ready, she fixed her gaze on the mercenary, who obviously waited for a favorable moment to attack.

"Juliana, head for the doorway into the stairwell."

He spoke calmly, as though he'd asked her to fetch a couple of pints of ale.

"Why—?"

"Find a safe place to hide. Stay there until the fighting is done."

An awful tightness filled her breast; he was sending her away. "I am not leaving—"

"Juliana, you are an important witness to what happened at Waddesford in the past days. I want you out of danger." As though sensing her rising protest, he sighed, a sound of impatience. "Please do not argue. 'Tis my duty, as my father's son, to protect you and to fight for his cause. For this castle."

"Moments ago, I almost died." Juliana glared at Veronique, edging in alongside the mercenary. "To think I might never"—*look upon your handsome face again*—"draw another breath . . ." She shook her head. "Thanks to your father's crossbowman, I have been given another chance to live. I will not waste it."

"Juliana—"

"I shall fight. For my dearest friend who was murdered. For Rosemary, who lost her mother. For all the folk who have suffered or died at this keep because of Veronique."

A chuckle interrupted her last words. "What lovely sentiments," Veronique said, so close Juliana caught her rosewater scent. "However, you should have done as Edouard asked."

Over the gusting wind, Juliana caught sounds of a commotion, emanating from the stairwell. Shouts. The clamor of clashing swords. Pounding footfalls.

"Too late, Juliana." Veronique's words dissolved into a wicked cackle. "Too *late*!"

The mercenary lunged. Edouard stepped forward, sword glinting in a well-executed strike. As the weapons collided, Juliana risked glancing at the stairwell.

Moving backward, his sword slicing the air with a deadly *fwhoop*, Tye emerged from the stairwell. Lord de Lanceau followed, with three of his men-at-arms a few steps behind. Sweat streamed down his lordship's face as he pursued Tye, his sword poised to attack and his expression stony.

More clanging rang out behind Juliana, reminders

of Edouard's ongoing fight, while Tye growled and swung his sword down, aiming for de Lanceau's chest. With a metallic crash, their weapons met. Grunting, the two men glared at each other, swords locked, before Tye spun away.

At the same moment, Dominic hurried out of the stairwell.

"Go, Juliana!" Edouard shouted. "Now!"

"I am not leaving you!" She whirled to face the mercenary and Veronique, to see Edouard had driven the bald fighter several yards back down the wall walk.

And Veronique?

Again, Juliana caught the sweetish tang of rosewater. Fear crawled up Juliana's nape into her scalp. Just as she whirled around, Veronique grabbed her forearm in a crushing grip.

"Too late," the older woman taunted. "Now, tell me where to find the jewels, or—"

"Nay!" Gasping, Juliana twisted her trapped arm which held the knife. She tried to slash with the dagger. Veronique's bruising hold curtailed her movements. As the older woman dug the nails of her free hand into Juliana's flesh, forcing her to let go of the weapon, Juliana kicked out at Veronique. The older woman twisted aside, avoiding the brunt of the blow.

With a triumphant grunt, Veronique snatched the dagger. Her painted lips formed a grin, and she released

392

her grasp.

Juliana heard footfalls thundering toward her.

"Juliana!" Edouard bellowed. "Look—"

Someone slammed into her. A cry broke from her, even as she pitched toward a stone merlon. She threw up a hand, desperate to thwart the imminent contact, when a muscled arm locked around her waist. She was hauled back against a broad man who smelled of sweat and hatred.

Tye.

His breaths seared her temple, even as the sharp blade of a sword came into her sight. "Do not come any closer, Father," Tye growled, his voice rumbling next to her ear, "or I will slice her from ribs to belly."

CHAPTER
25

At the sight of Juliana pinned in Tye's arms, Edouard's fury heightened to a dangerous pitch. She'd endured so much already; more than a lady of her grace and loveliness should ever have to face. This . . . *this* was the last. It ended. Here. Now.

Rage scorched through his body, firing renewed strength into his tired arms. The bald mercenary lunged again, and Edouard thrust up his sword. The blades met, tension jarred through Edouard's torso, and then he pushed with all his strength against the joined swords.

When the mercenary staggered back a step, Edouard lunged forward and swung the blade in a wide arc. The steel sliced the mercenary's upper arm. Blood shot in a crimson streak across the man's leather hauberk.

The mercenary screamed.

"Yield," Edouard said between his teeth, "or I will kill you."

The man's anguished gaze shifted from Edouard to

a point near Tye before he pressed his free hand over the wound, spun on his heel, and hurried away.

"—I will not ask again. Release her," Edouard's sire was saying, as Edouard dried his sweaty brow with his sleeve and faced the others.

"Why should Tye heed you, when you do not even respect his birthright?" Veronique's tone darkened. "Do you have the parchment, Tye?"

"I do."

"Then, Geoffrey, you will sign it. Or Juliana dies."

Edouard marched forward. His boots thundered on the stone, and, as Juliana's sorrowful gaze met his, her eyes widened. Did she sense the lethal edge to his fury? By God, he'd cut Tye to bleeding pieces and—

"Edouard," his sire said.

Blinking through the haze of rage, Edouard glanced at his sire, flanked by three men-at-arms. His father's face was turned to Edouard in profile. Not looking at Edouard, he said, "I have this matter in hand. Free Kaine. Secure this section of wall walk." Brusque orders, yet Edouard was glad of the harshness. It reminded him of what he'd learned from his sire: he must keep firm control of his emotions. In this deadly battle, which his father must win, he couldn't make one mistake. Not when Juliana's life was in peril, and those of many others.

"Aye, Father."

Before Edouard could turn to locate Kaine, Veronique

clucked her tongue. "How very obedient. Is that how you prefer your sons, Geoffrey? Raised to do your bidding, without question? Like loyal hounds?"

Veronique likened him to a trained dog? Edouard's hand tightened on his sword to the point of pain. How he longed to run her through!

"Edouard does as I ask," his sire replied, "because he has been raised with honor and respect. Values that define all that is noble and just."

"Listen to you," Veronique sneered. "Rambling like—"

"A lord who is proud of his legacy? Of his respected family? I am."

"Those values you prize so highly have brought you here. To this grim moment where you have no choice left but to yield to my demands or be responsible for Juliana's death."

"As I told you before, I will never yield to you."

Veronique smiled. "A shame. Did you know Edouard cares for Juliana? They even lay in each other's arms."

"Stop!" Juliana choked.

A muscle leapt in Edouard's father's cheek. "Is this true, Edouard?"

Veronique, you malicious bitch! Hatred for her seethed inside Edouard. After all she'd had done to him, she'd try and dishonor him and Juliana in front of his father. Veronique knew his sire would be furious if he believed Edouard had forsaken his commitment to Nara.

Yet as Edouard stood aware of the many expectant gazes upon him, he welcomed the conviction in his soul, the emotion that had settled there, he realized, the first time he'd seen Juliana. No longer would he ignore it. He'd be speaking with his sire as soon as this battle was over.

"Father," he said, his voice strong and determined, "since Juliana and I were forced to share a cold cell, we had no choice but to sleep together for warmth. However, we were never intimate, as Veronique cruelly implied. I never once acted with dishonor."

"He speaks the truth," Juliana cried. "I swear it, upon my mother's grave."

Edouard's gaze met hers. "'Tis also true that I care for Juliana."

Eyes glistening with tears, she braved a smile. What he would give to be able to sweep her into his arms now and kiss her, to make her *his*.

"What a shame, Edouard, that you were promised to Juliana's sister," Veronique went on, sounding on the verge of laughter. "Denied your true feelings for Juliana, right to your death."

"Enough," Edouard growled.

Veronique chuckled, then reached out and smoothed her fingers through Juliana's hair. As Juliana jerked her head away, her cheek pressing against Tye's tunic, Veronique murmured, "How you must hate your father, Edouard, for not caring to spare her life. A kind of abandonment, is it not? A small taste of the anguish Tye has endured all these years."

Squaring his shoulders, Edouard turned his back on Veronique and Tye. He had to shut her out, deny her the sordid pleasure of squeezing his emotions until they bled.

He'd promised to obey his sire; he'd do his duty.

As he forced himself to stride away, he sensed Juliana's gaze upon him. His heart ached. Walking away, after all he'd admitted and when her expression held such gut-wrenching fear, felt akin to betrayal. Yet if his father insisted the matter was under control, then Edouard must trust 'twas so.

As he walked, he looked to where he'd last seen Kaine, flanked by his guards. They'd moved a short distance down the wall walk. Edouard drew near, and he realized only one mercenary remained with his sword pointed at Kaine, who stood favoring his hurt leg. The other guard, head lolling, collapsed against a merlon, as Dominic stepped away, shaking out his right fist.

Switching his sword to his right hand, Dominic looked at the mercenary beside Kaine. "Now, 'tis your turn."

Sneering, the man adjusted his grip on his weapon, readying to attack.

Edouard strode to Dominic's side. "Allow me." As the mercenary lunged, Edouard swung his blade in a brutal arc. With a clash of metal, his sword met the mercenary's, whose weapon tilted close to Kaine's stomach.

"Oy! Careful!" Kaine hobbled backward. "I hoped you were rescuing me."

Before Veronique's thug could recover his hold on his weapon, Edouard set the tip of his blade against the man's neck.

"Drop the sword," he growled.

Dominic whistled. "Best do as he says. He looks more than ready to slaughter you."

The mercenary's eyes narrowed. Then, with a loud clank, the sword landed by his boots.

"A wise decision." Dominic flexed his fingers. "I do apologize for what I must do now." Drawing his arm back, he slammed his fist into the man's jaw. The oaf fell to his knees, then to his side on the stones.

"A bit dishonorable, that," Dominic said with a wry shrug. "We cannot have these louts sneaking up on us, though, while we tend to other matters." Sympathy crept into his gaze. "Not when we have a fair damsel to rescue."

A flush warmed Edouard's face, and he looked at Kaine. "Are you all right?"

"Apart from my leg." He grimaced. "It hurts like hell-fire. I am not certain how much use I will be in the battle."

"You can guard these mercenaries," Dominic said, bending down to pick up the fallen sword and handing it to Kaine.

"If they wake," Edouard added, "wallop them again."

Kaine grinned. "That, I will be more than pleased to do."

Edouard glanced back at Juliana, his pulse lurching to see her still trapped against Tye. He'd pulled her closer to the battlement's edge, nearer to Veronique.

Juliana's frantic stare locked with Edouard's, and concern, heightened by anger, blazed within him. *Stay brave, Juliana. We will rescue you. This I vow, upon my very soul.*

"Good luck," Edouard said to Kaine, before he pivoted on his heel and headed back to his father, aware of Dominic striding close behind.

When Edouard reached his father's side, he could barely control the rage crackling inside him. Tye had his arm pressed up under Juliana's bosom—a far too intimate hold for Edouard's liking. Moreover, Tye stood with a merlon at his back, and far enough away from the battlement's edge he couldn't be hit by the archers below. A sign Tye had noted Aldwin's abilities.

"At last, you have rejoined us." Veronique adjusted her grip on the knife. "We waited for you, before killing her."

A sigh shivered from Juliana.

Edouard clenched his teeth. "Father?"

"She wanted you to see Juliana perish," his sire said, "although I assured her that would not happen."

Edouard barely choked down a shocked roar. Had his father not promised he had this situation under control? Why, then, was Juliana's life still endangered? Why had his sire not ordered his men-at-arms, standing motionless behind him, to attack Tye and save her?

"Poor Edouard. I see your disappointment." Veronique sneered. "Your beloved father has failed you."

"Nay, Veronique. Look below," Edouard's sire said. "My men-at-arms are winning the battle."

She snorted a laugh. "Geoffrey—"

"My loyal knights and men-at-arms were ordered to take control of his keep, level by level. They will. They are loyal to me, because I earned their respect. Your mercenaries do not care about loyalty. They swore allegiance to you only for the coins you paid them."

"Enough. Tye—"

"They have realized your cause is lost," Edouard's sire continued, "and are escaping while they still can." He waved to the space between the merlons. "Look for yourself. The drawbridge is crowded with people fleeing."

Tye's expression darkened. "Mother?"

Veronique glared at her son. "Your father lies. How like him, to try and undermine us."

"Release Juliana," Edouard's sire commanded. "There is no advantage to killing her."

Tye's gaze narrowed. His fingers tightened on his sword.

"Your lives are all you have *left*," Edouard's sire said. His gaze slid, for the briefest moment, to Dominic, standing at his left side. "And if you wish to leave this wall walk alive . . ."

Realization hummed through Edouard. Left. A secret command.

"He is *right*. Do you not agree, Edouard?" Dominic added.

Tye scowled and, for the barest moment, his gaze flicked toward the gap in the stones.

"Go!" his lordship roared.

Raising his sword, Edouard lunged for Tye's right side. Out of the corner of his eye, he saw Dominic racing for Tye's left. Veronique shrieked and slashed with her dagger, even as Edouard heard brisk footfalls. His sire and the men-at-arms were closing in on her.

Cursing, Tye tried to position his sword, but Dominic shoved his blade's tip against Tye's shoulder blade. "Do not be a fool."

His weapon at the ready, Edouard halted before Tye, near enough to reach out and touch Juliana. The sword Tye still held hovered, a physical barrier separating them. Tears streamed from her eyes. He caught her sweet fragrance, blended with the essence of fear, and his gut twisted. "Let her go," he said quietly.

Tye glowered. "You will kill me, if I refuse?"

"If I must."

"Attack me, and she and I will both die."

"Not necessarily," Edouard said with a growl.

Juliana's mouth quivered.

"She means so much to you, Brother?"

"Aye." The acknowledgment came easily. From his heart.

"Edouard," she whispered.

Tye's face contorted. The bastard was beaten, but still he meant to hurt her? Edouard should have expected no less. Tye had been raised by Veronique.

Edouard loosed a furious cry and brought his sword up.

Tye's arm fell from Juliana's waist.

She raced to Edouard, her soft warmth pressing against him. He kept a firm grip on his sword, even as his other arm wrapped around her.

Through a giddy rush of relief, he caught Dominic's grunt of pain.

Heard the arcing swish of a sword.

Sensed Tye's attack.

Juliana clung to Edouard. Her body shook with terror and exhaustion, even as joy sang like a bright melody within her. Tye had let her go; there was some sense of honor in his treacherous soul, after all.

"Juliana," Edouard gasped.

Then she sensed it. Movement, behind her.

She whirled, at the same instant Edouard shoved her away. Tye, his face twisted with bitterness, slashed his sword down toward Edouard's chest.

Clang. Clang.

Steel sparked, marking the fury of their blows. Hand pressed to her throat, Juliana didn't dare look away as the two brothers struck at each other. Again. And again.

"Bastard!" Edouard snarled.

"Kill me now," Tye mocked. "Do it."

They were only five paces from Veronique. She stood at the wall walk's edge between two merlons, silk gown flapping in the wind, knife lost. Her fingers were raised like claws against de Lanceau and the men-at-arms who'd trapped her.

"Surrender, Veronique," de Lanceau shouted.

"Surrender?" She arched her brows. "I would rather *die* than be your prisoner."

"You have nowhere left to go," his lordship said. "You cannot defeat us. You cannot run."

Veronique's crimson lips parted on raucous laughter.

"*Veronique!*" de Lanceau bellowed. "*Surrender!* If you refuse, I will—"

She spun to look down at the bailey. "Good-bye, Geoffrey."

"Nay—!" De Lanceau grabbed for her.

She jumped.

"God's teeth!" Dominic gasped. Juliana raced with him to side of the battlement, where de Lanceau peered down, shaking his head.

Far down in the bailey, Veronique tried to rise from

where she'd fallen onto several dead servants. Grimacing, her movements slow and her left arm listing at an odd angle, she pushed to her knees.

"She cannot get away," de Lanceau growled and gestured to two of his men-at-arms.

The men ran for the stairwell.

Steel clashed close by, and Juliana again looked at the two brothers, still fighting. Sweat dripped from their faces. Had Edouard suffered any wounds? She hoped not.

"Yield, Tye," de Lanceau bellowed. "The battle is over." He signaled to Edouard. Reluctance tautened Edouard's features, but he stepped away from Tye, his chest rising and falling with ragged breaths. He did not, however, lower his sword.

Juliana forced herself to remain still, although she longed to throw herself in Edouard's arms. A fierce, invisible tension seemed to crackle between the three men.

Tye's gaze sharpened as he looked at Dominic, de Lanceau, and the man-at-arms. Then, at the empty space where Veronique had stood, moments before. "Where—?"

"Your mother leapt over the side," de Lanceau said. "She abandoned you."

"*What?*" Edging sideways, sword ready to deflect any assault, he approached the gap. Bracing his left hand on the merlon beside him, he leaned slightly backward over the edge to glance down; he clearly didn't want to turn his back to his foes. Juliana sensed the moment he saw Veronique. His lips flattened.

"She is wounded," de Lanceau said. "She cannot get far. My men will take her prisoner."

"And?" Tye dared another look at the bailey. The awkward position forced him to strain his body backward. If he lost his balance . . .

"She will be imprisoned in my dungeon. I will see her brought to trial—"

A strangled sound broke from Tye, akin to a curse. His body wavered, as though buffeted by a breeze, and then his sword pitched downward. Even as Juliana wondered why, she realized he'd lost his grip on the merlon.

"Tye!" she and Dominic called in unison. She raced to the wall walk's edge, aware of the man-at-arms following close behind.

Tye's sword clattered on the stone near them.

With a guttural cry, he dropped from view.

"Oh, God," Juliana cried, peering over the edge. Muttering under his breath, de Lanceau elbowed aside the man-at-arms and stood in the windblown gap.

"Tye!" His roar spread down over the bailey.

As Juliana's gaze slid toward the ground, movement and a choked breath snared her attention. She barely held back a horrified moan. Just a short reach away, Tye dangled from the wall walk by one hand.

"Father!" Edouard shouted.

"I see him." Boots scraped as de Lanceau knelt and

reached down. "Give me your hand, Tye," he said roughly. He sounded as though he fought intense emotion.

Sweat streamed from Tye's face. His lips pulled away from his teeth as he said, "Why?"

"I will save you."

A sob jammed in Juliana's throat. *Take the offer of help, Tye. Take it!*

Tye's weight-bearing arm began to tremble. Bitterness contorted his features into a mask of anguish. "Why bother to rescue me? I am *naught* to you. You wish I had never been born. What do you care, Father, if I fall and die?"

An expression close to pain flickered across his lordship's features, before it disappeared behind stern resolve. "Take my hand. I will pull you up."

Do not be a stubborn fool, Tye. Accept his help!

Tye's throat moved with a swallow. "You want to save me because . . . I am your son?"

Torment darkened de Lanceau's eyes, even while his jaw hardened. "I save you because there is honor even between enemies."

Tye's white-knuckled fingers began to slip from the stone.

"Hurry!" de Lanceau yelled. "For God's sake!"

Tye grinned, a hateful, almost sad twist of his lips, and plummeted toward the ground.

CHAPTER

26

"Tye survived the fall," Edouard said, just as his father exhaled a sigh and rose.

"He is injured." Juliana's voice cracked, implying she hated to see Tye hurt, and Edouard struggled to control a flare of jealousy and dismay.

Pain contorted Tye's features as he pushed up from the dirt. He stumbled to his feet, wavering for a moment like a drunkard. Even as Edouard acknowledged his bastard brother's survival, a sense of relief rushed through him. Ridiculous, since he despised Tye. But he couldn't deny that the haunted look in Tye's eyes, in the tense moments before he'd fallen, had affected him.

"Tye and Veronique will try and escape," his sire said, tone rough. "I will not allow it. Dominic."

"Aye, milord?"

"I want both of them captured, bound, and well guarded. Tell the other men fighting in the bailey. I will join you there in a moment."

Dominic nodded, then ran to the stairwell and disappeared inside.

Flexing his hand on his sword, Edouard tried to tamp down a rising sense of misgiving. He should follow Dominic and help secure the bailey; 'tis what was expected of him as a future heir, especially when the din rising from below indicated the battle, while less frenzied than before, was still ongoing.

Heading to the bailey, though, would mean Juliana was out of his sight. He'd almost lost her a short while ago; watching her confront death had nearly ripped his soul from his chest. He couldn't leave her, not with Veronique and Tye still to be captured. Not when he'd come to realize how much he loved her.

"Father," he began, "I—"

His sire, wiping his brow, swayed, as though about to topple over.

"Lord de Lanceau!" Juliana cried.

Lunging forward at the same time as the man-at-arms, Edouard readied to grab his sire's arm and prop him upright if need be. "Father, what is wrong? Were you wounded?"

Refusing assistance with a wave of his hand, de Lanceau steadied himself and drew in a few strong breaths. "I am not injured. Not fully recovered from my illness, 'tis all."

"Father, you should sit for a moment. Regain your strength."

His sire grunted. "Edouard, you sound just like your mother."

"She is a clever woman. And always right." Edouard couldn't resist a grin.

His sire's lips tilted in a grudging smile before he glanced down into the bailey and, frowning, shook his head. "I will not rest. Not before Tye and Veronique are my prisoners. Not before this keep is secured to my satisfaction."

Protest welled inside Edouard. His sire looked exhausted. His reactions could be impeded; he might make a grave error during the fighting and be injured or killed. But even as the words gathered on Edouard's tongue, he forced them to silence. His father was a proud man and far too stubborn to yield to any infirmity. Moreover, his warrior's sense of duty was too tightly woven into his nature, his hatred for Veronique too ingrained, for him to consider quitting the battle now.

How well Edouard knew his father's reasons, for those would be his reasons, too, if he were in his parent's place.

"I will gladly fight alongside you and Dominic, Father," Edouard said, even as he looked at Juliana, "but there is an important matter I vow should be attended to first."

"What matter?" While his sire spoke, he tightened his grip on his broadsword. A muscle jumped in his cheek, a sign he was eager to join the fight.

"Landon Ferchante's gold ring—the one you entrusted

to him—is hidden in the solar. Veronique and Tye wanted to get hold of that ring and use it to gain admittance to your court and then murder you."

His sire's gaze sharpened. "You were right to mention this to me."

"Juliana is the only one who knows where the jewels are hidden," Edouard said.

"Mayda told me days before she died, milord," Juliana said. "Before her lord husband pushed her off the wall walk and killed her."

"*Landon*? God's blood! Are you sure?"

She nodded, grief in her gaze. "I witnessed her murder, milord. That is why I was hit about the head and left for dead in the river."

"What of the newborn? Is she here? Safe?"

"Veronique ordered Rosemary killed. Azarel managed to get her to safety in the village. Milord, there is a great deal more I must tell you, especially concerning Landon's affair with Veronique and her influence at the keep."

"Veronique murdered Landon," Edouard added. "He tried to contact you, Father, after I was taken captive, and she found out."

His sire clenched his free hand into a fist. "Azarel mentioned Landon's killing to me. Yet another crime for which Veronique will be punished. Once this fight is won, I want full accounts from both of you. What you say will be documented, for the day she is brought to trial.

Meanwhile, Juliana, I want you to go to the solar." He pointed to the remaining man-at-arms. "He will escort you, and I will send more warriors to stand guard with him outside the chamber. Lock the door. Do not recover the jewels. Do not open the door, either, till you hear three knocks and either my voice or Edouard's beyond."

"Aye, milord." She dipped in a curtsey.

"Thank you, Lady de Greyne, for all your help," Edouard's father said. Looking over at Kaine, he said, "I will send reinforcements to help you defend the wall walk. Edouard, come with me."

When his sire strode for the stairwell, Edouard loped after him. The thrill of battle licked like greedy fire in his blood, tempered, though, by worry for Juliana. Soon she'd be gone from his sight.

As he brushed past her, he slowed, touched her arm. "Be careful. Promise me." *There is so much I will say to you, Juliana, once this is over.*

Her eyes bright, she whispered, "I promise."

Juliana hurried into the stairwell's shadows. With the man-at-arms leading the way, they proceeded to the solar with the same caution Edouard had taken when they'd escaped from the tower.

How eerily quiet the passageways seemed, almost as

though the keep had been abandoned. A good sign, she decided, as they neared the corridor leading to the solar. Most of the castle folk must be in the bailey, fighting to save Waddesford.

After halting before the iron-banded door of the solar, the man-at-arms leaned close to it and listened. Apart from her own breathing, Juliana heard only the crackle of the passageway torches.

The man thrust up a staying hand, and she nodded, recognizing his order to stay still and silent. They must be careful. Veronique, realizing she was defeated, could have ordered her thugs to gather her belongings and steal whatever else in the chamber was of value. The thick door might be muffling the sounds inside, and thus Juliana would be walking into danger.

Inhaling a steadying breath, she thought how Edouard would enter the solar. The image of him striding out of the shadowed far stairwell into the sunlit bailey, bold, determined, and without the slightest trace of fear, filled her mind. He wouldn't hesitate to barge through the doorway. This warrior would likely do the same.

The man-at-arms pushed down the iron handle and shoved the panel open. It swung wide and, with the jarred squeak of hinges, slammed against the wall. Keeping his back to the panel, hands on his sword, he darted inside, then returned a few moments later and bowed to her. "'Tis deserted, milady."

Deserted except for the scent of Veronique's rosewater. "Thank you," Juliana said. She strode in, pushed the door shut, and locked it, as Lord de Lanceau had commanded.

The stillness of the chamber settled around her like a weighty cloak as she looked about. Mayda's musical laughter, soothing murmurs, and anguished sobs lingered in the shadows along with Rosemary's hungry cries, the essence of these memories intensely poignant. Was it only days ago that Mayda had died?

Eyes stinging, Juliana looked at the rumpled sheets on the bed, silk garments heaped on the floor, and numerous pots and grooming items strewn across the trestle table. Her mouth tightened on a painful flare of rage. How thoroughly Veronique had claimed the space that belonged to the lady of the keep.

"No longer," she said firmly. "Never. Again."

For Mayda, for Rosemary, she'd vanquish every trace of Veronique's presence here.

Juliana walked to the trestle table, then crossed to the bed, grabbed a feather pillow, and yanked off the linen case. Her hands itched to smash into it all those precious pots of creams Veronique coveted, to snap the comb into tiny pieces, to destroy every tool of seduction Veronique had used to manipulate Landon and many other men to her will.

As Juliana turned back to the trestle table, faint sounds of battle carried from the shuttered window.

She moved to it and threw the shutters open, letting in a breeze. While she couldn't see much of the fighting, shouts, hoarse cries, and clashes of metal rose to her. Somewhere, down in the chaos, Edouard was fighting with his sire.

Oh, Edouard. Please say safe. I cannot wait to see you again.

Worry for him crested, and she took herself away from the torment of the cacophony. She must keep busy. Do what she could here to restore peace and order to the castle, and get rid of Veronique's influence.

Upon returning to the table, Juliana opened the pillowcase and began to stuff items inside. Soon, the case bulged, and she fetched another from the bed. Once the tabletop was cleared, she walked about the solar, snatching up any item she didn't recognize as belonging to Landon or Mayda. Later, she must pack up their belongings, as well as her own. The task would have to be done anyway, since a new lord would shortly be appointed to rule Waddesford Keep and he'd be moving into the chamber.

Some moments later, she removed the dirty bedding and dumped it by the door, then dropped the filled pillowcases with the linens. When the battle was over, she'd see all of Veronique's items destroyed. Every last one.

Savoring a heady sense of satisfaction, she walked to the center of the room, set her hands on her hips, and looked about to be sure she hadn't missed anything. As her gaze traveled over the bed, a small object glinted behind one of the rear legs. She crossed to the bed, stooped, and, with a strangled gasp, picked up the silver baby rattle.

Hands shaking, she stood and looked up at the shadowed ceiling. "As soon as I can, I will find Rosemary, Mayda," she whispered. "Wherever we end up living, she will be well cared for. I swear it."

A breeze whispered in through the window. Juliana stilled. She no longer heard the noises of battle. Hope soared within her. Did that mean . . . ?

Three brisk knocks sounded on the door.

CHAPTER
27

With a brutal roar, Edouard plunged his sword into the mercenary's gut. He recognized the thug who'd helped drag him up to the tower and force him into chains. Moments ago, the fool had tried to sneak up and stab him in the back while Edouard was engaged in a swordfight. A deceitful attack.

With a pained grunt, the mercenary tried to lash at Edouard with his dagger, but the blade skated on the chain mail hauberk Edouard had stripped from one of his sire's fallen knights earlier in the battle and donned. Standing firm, breath rasping through his teeth, Edouard held the mercenary's murderous, dulling stare until he began to slide sideways to the ground, dead.

Yanking his sword free of the corpse, Edouard spun on his heel and assessed the fighting around him. Before this mercenary had become separated from his cohorts, he'd been among a protective group encircling Tye and Veronique. Despite her abandonment of Tye on the wall walk, they seemed to have decided that fighting together was their only hope of escape.

A futile hope. They were clearly defeated.

Edouard's father, Dominic, and at least twenty knights surrounded the villains, swords flashing in furious strokes as they fought the mercenaries of the group who remained alive. Tye also wielded a sword he must have taken from one of the dead. Face white with pain, he hobbled on an injured leg, while he slashed the blade at the advancing warriors. He wouldn't be able to keep up his fight for long.

Step by step, the warriors edged forward, tightening the entrapment while forcing the villains back against the bailey wall.

Capturing them, Edouard noted, appeared all that was left before his sire claimed victory. Bodies were scattered across the ground and, in places, slumped over the edge of the wall walk. Near the entrance to the dungeon, prisoners, mainly mercenaries, were being bound and kept in order by Aldwin and more men-at-arms. The drawbridge and entrance to the forebuilding were heavily guarded; Tye and Veronique couldn't get in or out of the castle even if, by remote chance, they escaped the attacking warriors.

"Fight harder, idiots," Veronique shrieked over the din of colliding swords. Agony distorting her features, hair a snarled mess, she cradled her broken arm against her bosom. "Think of the gold I will pay you!"

"Surrender," Edouard's father yelled back. "You cannot escape."

"He lies!" Spittle glistened on Veronique's smeared lips.

"Heed me well," de Lanceau bellowed, his words carrying across the bailey. "My knights control every way in and out of this keep. Lay down your weapons. Yield to my men. Refuse, and you will die."

"Fight!" Veronique screamed, as, with a grisly cry, another of her mercenaries collapsed to the dirt.

Edouard glowered at her, focusing all his hatred of the past days upon her. *You will yield, Veronique, as my father commanded. On my honor, as a knight, I will see it done.* Adjusting his grip on his sword, he crossed the blood-soaked ground to join the fight.

Anticipation humming in his blood, his gaze locked with Tye's. Rage and loathing blazed in Tye's eyes before he spun away, swiftly deflecting a blow from a man-at-arms.

Edouard's sire stepped back from the fray and wiped his brow. His chest rising and falling with exertion, he glanced at Edouard, clearly sensing his approach.

"I have come to fight," Edouard said.

"No need, Son. This battle is already won."

Edouard struggled against his rising frustration. "I want to fight them, Father. After all they have done to me, Juliana, and so many others, I want to see them vanquished. I need to know they can no longer inflict their evil." *Especially upon Juliana.*

"I feel the same way about those two." A bitter smile curved his sire's mouth as his gaze fixed on Veronique. "How many *years* I have waited to capture her. Finally, she will stand trial and be condemned for the crimes she has committed. Finally"—his voice shook—"I will have peace from her madness."

A pained scream rang out, and Edouard dared a glance at the fight. Another mercenary careened to the ground, narrowly missing Veronique as he fell.

"You have fought well for me today," his sire went on, wiping his sweaty face again. "While you may want to see this fight brought to its end, I ask another duty of you. One I would prefer not assign to anyone else."

Surprise, sharpened by a glimmer of pride, ran though Edouard. "What duty?"

"Take five men-at-arms with you to the solar. They will join the others in standing guard outside while Juliana retrieves the hidden jewels. Bring the riches to me."

Edouard nodded and turned on his heel.

"When you return," his sire added, an odd tension in his voice, "there is a very important matter we must discuss."

"You lied to me, Mother."

Snapping her attention from the burly mercenaries shielding her from de Lanceau's men, Veronique glared at Tye. How dare he address her with such contempt, especially in front of their enemies? Fury raged as sharply as the agonizing pain from her broken arm.

Grinding her teeth, she struggled to think beyond her physical distress, to focus on her loathing of Geoffrey that had helped her evade capture in the past and kept her alive.

"Lied?" she demanded, the word drowned by the crash of swords as her mercenaries thwarted a fierce attack. "About your chance to kill your father and seize all from him? Is that what you mean?"

Tye's wan face was slick with sweat. Limping, he lunged at a man-at-arms, deflecting a strike, and his whole body stiffened at the resulting collision. Tye was in great pain. Regret, born from maternal instincts she couldn't seem to suppress, lanced through her; she forced it aside.

A grisly choking noise, accompanied by spraying blood, warned her that one of the mercenaries was mortally wounded. She took an instinctive step back, groaning as she misstepped on the stony ground and jostled her arm. "You *will* defeat your father—"

"Another lie. We are surrounded. Backed against a stone wall." Each of Tye's words shot from his lips like bits of ice. "Why should I believe another word from you, when you lied to me about Father?"

Astonishment plowed through Veronique, turning her innards cold. Anguish underscored his voice, a pain that ran deeper than any physical injury he might have received today.

"*You* left me on the wall walk," Tye went on. "You thought only of saving yourself. You did not care whether I was slain or escaped."

Wretched boy! "You are a champion warrior!" she shrieked. "You can defend yourself."

Tye's burning gaze slammed into her. "Tell me why Father tried to save me from falling from the battlement. He offered me his hand. He *wanted* to save me!"

Veronique swallowed an ugly flare of disquiet. She'd spent years cultivating Tye's hatred and forging him into the brutal warrior she expected him to be. Geoffrey had shown him kindness? A complication she'd crush like a beetle, for she aimed to keep her hold upon Tye. She must, in order to escape.

"Why did he try to rescue me?" Tye demanded. "*Why?*"

Misery strained his features. Did he think there was fatherly generosity behind Geoffrey's gesture? Did Tye presume he might get his sire's acceptance? Fury boiled inside her that Geoffrey had found and preyed upon this weakness in Tye, no doubt intending to turn their son against her. "Your father tried to save you so he could imprison and interrogate you. If you died in the fall, he would never be able to wrest information from you."

"I do not know. In his eyes, I saw—"

"What he wanted you to see," she sneered. "No doubt your sire gilded his offer with false words about his chivalrous intentions. He did not act out of honor; he hoped to manipulate you so you'd be easier to capture. How right you were to refuse his trickery and risk the fall. Our injuries will heal and soon—"

Tye brought his sword arcing down toward a man-at-arms.

A gurgle erupted close by. As a warrior crumpled in her direction, eyes rolling back into his bleeding head, she took another backward step. She sensed the wall looming behind her, less than a hand's span away.

"Listen to me, Tye," she said, her words muffled by the din of fighting. "For years I have protected you from your sire. Even now, I have not failed you. Remember when you told me that you believed the missive from Geoffrey was a trick?"

"Mother—"

"Listen!" she hissed. "I thought well about what you said. The mercenaries your father claimed were fleeing the keep today? Not all of them left because they feared being conquered."

Tye glanced at her, his gaze filled with suspicion.

"I dare not say too much, except that during our trysts, Landon confided secrets that will be of interest to King John. I paid a mercenary to deliver a message for me if Geoffrey decided to attack Waddesford." She indulged in a laugh, grimacing as her arm throbbed. "The king will be most eager to hear what I have to say."

"You will tell him," Tye said with a mirthless grin, "in exchange for our freedom?"

She grinned back. "You will get that opportunity to cut down your sire." As the last mercenary fell and de Lanceau's men-at-arms swarmed in, she said, "We are not vanquished. That is most certain."

At the raps on the solar door, Juliana started.

Three knocks. The signal Lord de Lanceau had described, if accompanied by—

"Juliana," Edouard called from outside.

Unable to hold back a delighted cry, she set the rattle on the table, rushed to the door, and unlocked it. Drawing it open, she saw him standing beyond, grinning, sword sheathed at his side. The chain mail he wore, though, was spattered with blood.

"You are alive!" Before she could think better of it, she threw herself into his arms. Only then did she remember de Lanceau's armed men in the passageway, who exchanged bemused glances.

As her body collided with Edouard's, he grunted. "Of course I am alive." His broad arms wrapped around her, embracing her with the scents of sun-warmed metal, fresh air, and sweaty male. A truly pleasing blend of smells, because he was *alive*! She'd remember his scent always, even when he was gone from Waddesford.

Refusing to acknowledge the sadness chasing that thought, she stepped out of his embrace and smiled at him. "Is the fight won?"

"Aye. Veronique and Tye are trapped in the bailey. My father will soon have them as his prisoners. Their treachery ends today."

"Good. Are you all right?" Her gaze dropped to the blood on his armor. "Were you wounded?"

"A few nicks, but naught of concern." Signaling the men who'd accompanied him to wait outside, he brushed past her into the solar. Once she'd followed him inside, he shut the door.

A wicked thrill shivered through her that she and Edouard were once again alone. *'Tis a senseless thrill,* her conscience answered. With Veronique's tyrannical grip on the keep destroyed, Edouard would be returning to his duties for his father. He'd be marrying Nara.

Juliana's stomach twisted, for on the wall walk he'd admitted he cared for her. Could that make any difference, though, since he was pledged to Nara? How did Juliana manage to say she believed she loved him? That none of the disagreements between them mattered anymore? That if, by some chance, he cared enough to want to marry her instead of her sister, she'd say aye without the slightest delay? She couldn't let him leave the keep without telling him that truth.

His cool, steady, captivating gaze locked with hers. Again, she felt that wondrous surge of joy and anticipation. Could he see in her eyes how she felt? Oh, God, could he see?

He looked away, swallowing hard, obviously fighting a tempest churning within himself. He turned his back to her, hands clenching and unclenching. Her gaze skimmed over him, memorizing the curves, lines, and angles of his masculine beauty as she would before sketching him.

In her mind, she made him hers forever.

Before she could venture to break the silence, he muttered, "I smell rosewater."

"Not for much longer," she managed to say. When he glanced at her, she gestured to the heap by the door. "These are Veronique's belongings. I plan to throw them over the wall walk. Smash them on the rocks, break them, rip them into tiny, worthless pieces . . ."

"I will gladly help." Edouard's lips formed a tight smile. "I cannot wait to rid this castle of all remnants of Veronique."

"Most of them, anyway," Juliana said. They couldn't change the events of the past few days. The memories they both had of Veronique would be with them for the rest of their lives. Her cruel grip on this keep, though, was gone.

Edouard dragged a hand through his mussed hair and faced her, his expression solemn. "Juliana, I know you and I have a great deal to discuss. But I am afraid that conversation must wait. Father wants us to retrieve the jewels and bring them to him."

A great deal to discuss, her mind echoed, while anxiety snaked its way through her. Did Edouard plan to tell her that whatever he'd said on the wall walk, they could never be together? That he'd never meant to raise her hopes?

She pushed the agonizing thoughts aside. Lord de Lanceau had given important orders. They must be obeyed.

"One moment," she said, before hurrying into the antechamber. Reaching beneath her pallet, she pulled out the sketchbook—still, thankfully, where she'd left it—and opened it to one of her drawings of Mayda. The most important one, she silently acknowledged.

When she started toward the trestle table, she sensed Edouard's gaze traveling over her. Not a cursory glance, an intense stare that assessed her from head to toe. A look she might mistake as . . . possessiveness. A wanton excitement raced through her, and she bit down on her lip, using the discomfort to help her refocus on her task.

Edouard's boots thudded on the planks. As she reached the table, he came to stand beside her. She ignored the inconvenient warmth pooling within her, set the sketchbook flat on the table, and smoothed the pages.

"A good likeness of Mayda." Edouard studied the drawing of her ladyship standing before the trestle table, the fingers of her right hand touching the table top just above one of the three large drawers.

"After Mayda told me of the hidden jewels," Juliana said, glad of her steady voice, "I drew this picture of her to help me remember her words." Lifting up the hem of her skirts, she settled on her knees on the floorboards before the table.

"Juliana." Edouard made a small sound, akin to a groan; he obviously couldn't believe she was down on the dusty floor. "Why—?"

"You will see." She patted the planks next to her.

He dropped to a crouch, boots creaking with the movement.

"This table was a gift from Mayda's parents," Juliana said. "Part of her dowry. Now, if I remember what Mayda told me . . ." She pulled open the closest drawer. It slid easily, as though frequently used. Inside, were sheaves of parchment, beeswax candles, a few quills, and sections of twine.

With a brisk tug, Juliana removed the drawer and set it aside. Then, peering into the empty space, she felt around the plain, rough-hewn back panel. "This table was specially commissioned by Mayda's parents," Juliana said, while her fingers explored the wood. "Her father suspected a traitor in their household, so he had this table built. From underneath, the framework all looks the same, but Mayda said there is . . . Ah." A slight shifting of the wood told Juliana she'd found the right spot. She pressed. With a muffled scrape, the wood fell away, revealing a concealed section.

Reaching in, she drew out a cloth bag. The contents inside shifted with a musical clink.

Edouard chuckled. "The ring was within Veronique's reach all along. Judging by the sound, many other jewels, too."

Juliana nodded, doing her best not to reveal how her stomach swooped at his velvety, roguish laughter. "Thankfully, Veronique did not suspect—"

"Wait. There is something else." Edouard brushed against Juliana as he reached inside; the mere drag of his garments against hers caused her to catch her breath. When he straightened, he held out a rolled parchment bound with twine.

"Read it," he said softly. "I suspect 'tis for you. You were the only one, besides Mayda, who knew of this hiding place."

Sudden dread trailed through Juliana as she handed him the jewels, then unfastened the parchment's twine. Metal chimed. Glancing at Edouard, she saw he'd tipped the bag's contents into his palm and was fingering through it, no doubt to make sure Landon's gold ring was there.

"Good," he said under his breath. He must have found it.

When the missive unfurled, Juliana recognized Mayda's elegant handwriting. A shocked cry warbled from her.

"Edouard," she whispered. "Oh, God—"

His broad hand cupped hers. "If you would rather read it later—"

She shook her head. "It may be important." Swallowing hard, she began to read.

My dearest Juliana,

If you are reading this missive, then I am dead. I do not leave this letter to place blame or bemoan the life I might have lived, if circumstances were different. I ask only that you remember me kindly. For you were, to me, the one joy in days that became increasingly bleak. Your loyalty, kindness, and companionship, my dear friend, were more precious to me than all the gold in the bag you likely now hold.

As I vowed before, I give these jewels to you, to care for little Rosemary and to live a life that, I trust, will be filled with happiness. For true love, I realize now, is a most miraculous gift. One that was never mine, but that I wish, with all my heart, for you.

With love,
Mayda

A sob broke from Juliana. As she pressed a hand to her mouth, she caught Edouard's muffled oath. He shifted on the floor beside her, and then his arms were around her, drawing her close. How good it felt to have his strong warmth surrounding her.

"Oh, Mayda," Juliana sobbed.

"May I read the letter?" Edouard's voice rumbled next to her ear. She nodded, and he carefully took the parchment from her fingers. A moment later, he sighed against her hair. "'Tis clear she cared for you very much."

"When the battle is over, I must find Rosemary," Juliana whispered.

"We know she is being well cared for," he soothed. "When 'tis safe to do so, we will find her."

We. Juliana pressed her lips together, fighting the onslaught of emotion carried by that tiny word. What she would give for Mayda's wish for true love to come true. For Edouard to be her true love.

"Come." He gently eased her away, then coaxed her to her feet. "My father awaits."

CHAPTER
28

Edouard led Juliana through the keep to the bailey, the armed men following a few paces behind. With every step, the relentless pressure inside Edouard intensified, for he guessed the matter his sire wished to discuss was the wedding to Nara.

As Edouard entered the forebuilding descending to the bailey, his senses seemed even more attuned, somehow, to Juliana a few steps behind him: the lighter tap of her shoes on the stone; the whisper of her gown; the feeling of her gaze upon him. He'd never felt this acute sense of *knowing* for a woman before, but truth be told, he'd never met one as remarkable as Juliana. Ah, God, how he longed to know her in all the honest, tender, pleasurable ways a man could know a woman.

As he descended the last steps, he remembered the fetching pinkish hue that had warmed her face in the solar. Had she sensed the desire he'd barely managed to keep under control? Had she realized how hard he fought not to shove aside his irksome honor, draw her into his arms, and kiss her until she swooned?

Just thinking about such a lusty kiss made his manhood swell.

He silently groaned. No way in hellfire could he spend his life married to Juliana's sister. If it took every bit of his willpower, he must tell his sire he wasn't following through with the betrothal. He couldn't bear to think about his father's displeasure or the dishonor he'd bring to his family, but breaking his commitment to Nara was the only way he could kiss, touch, and *love* Juliana.

When they stepped into the daylight, he heard her draw a sharp breath. She wasn't used to seeing the gruesome aftermath of battle. Catching her hand, he gently squeezed it, before leading her to the large crowd of men-at-arms guarding Veronique and Tye. The two stood with swords aimed at their throats, backs against the wall. Several warriors held lengths of rope, clearly preparing to bind them.

"Seeing them captured is a wondrous sight," Juliana said.

"I agree."

As though hearing Edouard's voice, Veronique's gaze shifted. Her hard stare locked with his, and shock jolted through him. The cruel bitch didn't look humbled or distressed. Triumph and resolve blazed in her eyes. Did she hold some kind of absurd hope of escaping? His sire would ensure that never happened. So would he.

Edouard scowled at Veronique and looked for his father, who stood with Dominic and several men-at-arms. Judging by his gestures, he was relaying instructions. Still holding Juliana's hand, Edouard drew her forward.

His sire turned, as though alerted to Edouard's approach, and smiled. Then his gaze slid to their entwined hands, and a frown knit his brow.

Edouard felt Juliana tremble as he brought her before his father. Discreetly wriggling her fingers free, she dropped into a curtsey.

"Father," Edouard said, then noticed Dominic pressing a hand over a wound on his arm bandaged with a strip of cloth. "Are you all right?"

"Tye managed to cut me before we grabbed his weapon and subdued him," Dominic said. "I am glad I am not dead. He is an impressive swordsman. He could easily have slashed my ribs instead of my forearm."

Ignoring the unwelcome praise of Tye, Edouard asked, "Are you badly wounded?" Of all his father's friends, he held the greatest respect for Dominic, who'd always treated him like a son.

"I shall live." Dominic waggled his eyebrows. "I am sure my lovely wife will take excellent care of me whilst I recover."

Edouard chuckled, while Dominic's gaze slid to Juliana and lit with a curious sparkle. One that hinted of news Edouard did not yet know. Was it related to the matter his sire wished to discuss?

Impatience gnawed at Edouard, and he settled his gaze on his father. "As you ordered, we found Landon's ring." He held the gold band out to his sire. "Juliana has the other jewels."

"Good." His sire took the ring and slid it onto his finger.

"Mayda left her jewelry to Juliana. She wanted Juliana to sell the jewels to support her and the Ferchantes' babe, if ill befell Mayda."

"I see." His sire frowned again. "Juliana, you witnessed Mayda's killing. It seems she anticipated her husband's murderous rage. Did she sense she might need to also protect her child's life?"

"Aye, milord," Juliana said. "When she gave birth to a daughter, not a son, she was terrified of Landon rejecting the babe."

Edouard's sire exhaled a sigh tinged with disbelief. "As the parent of a beautiful, intelligent daughter, I cannot imagine. Landon clearly became someone other than the lord I believed I knew and could trust." His somber gaze locked with Edouard's. "I am sorry for sending you into a trap. If I had known—"

"Father, I understand."

Relief crept into his sire's features, and then he asked, "What of the duty I asked you to conduct?"

Edouard met his father's gaze, knowing he spoke of the secret meeting to ask Landon to join their rebellion against

King John. No doubt his sire wanted to know if Landon might have told Veronique and Tye about it. "I was unable to fulfill what you asked of me. I was taken captive upon riding into the bailey. 'Tis the only time I saw Landon alive."

His sire nodded, and Edouard sensed his gladness that their ambitions against the king hadn't been revealed. "In coming days, Son, there will be a need for meetings like the one I asked you to conduct with Landon, if you are willing."

"I am."

A smile softened his father's features. "Good. I regret you and Lady de Greyne endured such appalling treatment here, but I am pleased that, in the end, you are unharmed and all has resolved well."

"If I may, milord," Juliana said, her voice wavering, "Rosemary still has to be found. Azarel knows where she is. With your permission, I would like to ride to the village and bring her home."

As shouts carried from where Veronique and Tye were surrounded, his lordship glanced in their direction. Appearing satisfied all was in order, he looked back at Juliana. "With prisoners still to be dealt with in the bailey, I cannot spare men to ready your horse and escort you on that journey. However, I will speak to Azarel about Rosemary's whereabouts."

Disappointment glinted in Juliana's eyes. Edouard sensed the anguish coursing inside her, but she merely smiled. "Thank you, Lord de Lanceau."

Reaching out, Edouard caught her hand. Her fingers were cool and clammy, and he wished he could take her in his arms and give her a comforting hug.

"Geoffrey," Dominic muttered. "For God's sake. Tell him."

Edouard frowned. "Tell me what?"

With a polite but dismissive smile, his sire turned to Juliana. "Will you excuse us a moment, Lady de Greyne?"

"Of course." She curtsied, then strolled in the direction of the forebuilding, where Azarel appeared to be stitching the arm of a wounded knight. The way the sunlight played upon Juliana, accenting her willowy body . . . Edouard silently groaned. He *had* to address the issue of his unwanted betrothal.

Looking back at his sire, he said, "What must you tell me?"

His father, expression grim, shook his head. "I fear there is no easy way to say it."

"Say what?"

"Nara is . . . with child."

All of the air whooshed out of Edouard's lungs. A merciless knot formed in his stomach. "Wait a moment." He hauled in a strangled breath. "I did not . . . Nara and I did not . . . We *never*—"

"I know." His sire's mouth ticked up in a wry grin. "Dominic has confirmed you were living at his keep, fighting to protect his lands, and as celibate as a monk around the time Nara's babe was conceived."

A stunned chuckle broke from Edouard.

"'Tis a great dishonor," his father went on, "for her to have betrayed you in this way."

The odd warmth in his sire's voice made Edouard pause. "Honor, Father, is the reason I was forced into a betrothal to her."

"Aye. Lord de Greyne is most embarrassed about the situation and furious with Nara. As you are aware, he and I desired a blood alliance between our families. We have decided, however, she will marry the father of her babe, who is a man-at-arms in her sire's garrison. You are no longer bound to your betrothal."

Relief rushed up inside Edouard, breaking from him in a roar. "'Tis wondrous news!"

Raising his eyebrows, his sire said, "I am glad you are not too upset."

Heat warmed Edouard's face. Now was the right moment. There couldn't be a *better* one to talk about Juliana. Refusing to break his sire's perceptive stare, he said, "I ask your permission, Father—"

"Permission?" His sire's gaze slid to Dominic.

"I wish to marry Juliana."

"Ah. The sister I believed might be well suited to you?"

Was that teasing mirth in his parent's eyes? Edouard said, "Aye."

His sire studied him a long moment. Sweat slid down Edouard's spine. Did his father expect him to explain why? Divulge what qualities made her the right lady to be his wife? Admit that the thought of spending even one day without her left him empty inside?

"I love her," he finally said. "I want no other woman."

His sire smiled. "Well, you will need her father's approval—"

"I will ask it at my first opportunity—"

"—as well, but since a betrothal between you was favored before . . ."

As well. Edouard barely held down a triumphant whoop. "Do you agree then, Father?" He waited, holding his breath.

"I do." Even while Edouard loosed an elated shout, his sire said, "Although, with Juliana entrusted with caring for Rosemary, you will not just become a husband, but a father. These are great responsibilities. Are you ready for such?"

His father spoke true. The thought of raising a babe was indeed daunting. But Juliana would teach Edouard what he needed to know. Stronger than the uncertainty niggling at him was a tremendous sense of excitement, a knowing that he'd face each day's challenges with her. Together.

Meeting his sire's gaze, he said, "I am ready, Father."

Admiration sparkled in his sire's eyes. "You are. I am proud of you, Son."

"As am I." Dominic smiled.

"Waddesford Keep needs a new lord," his sire went on. "A nobleman who knows his responsibilities. The folk here will support and no doubt welcome you, especially if you marry Juliana."

"You mean . . ." Shock made Edouard's head reel. "*I* am to be appointed lord of this keep?"

His sire grinned. "An early wedding gift. If, that is, you want this fortress?"

"Aye!" He glanced to where Juliana stood beside Azarel, chatting and smiling while helping to fasten a bandage.

"Does she know you will propose marriage?" Dominic asked.

"Not yet. I feel certain, though, she wants to wed, too."

"And you did not even have to push her into a well to convince her."

"Dominic," Edouard's sire muttered, with a hint of laughter.

"Sorry. I could not resist." Wincing as he moved, Dominic shook Edouard's hand. "I am pleased for you. I trust you and Juliana will be very happy together."

"Thank you." Edouard glanced again at Juliana. Love, pride, and excitement coalesced within him like a bright fire.

Go to her. Don't wait another moment to make her yours.

Grinning, he said, "I must speak to Juliana. Before I do, though, Father, may I request a favor of you?"

"Why have you brought me to the garden, Edouard? Azarel needs my help to tend the wounded." Unable to quell her restlessness, Juliana glanced at the bailey. Edouard had waited for her while she helped Azarel care for a wounded knight, but there were many injured. She wanted to be useful, especially when she couldn't leave for the village to get Rosemary.

Seated beside her on the stone bench beneath the tree, Edouard said, "Azarel has quite a few servants helping her. I vow she can manage without you for a few moments. And"—his tone softened—"what I must tell you is too important to wait."

Her heart fluttered, and she met his gaze. Judging by his expression, his sire had told him something momentous, no doubt related to Nara. Juliana braced herself for unfavorable news, even as she said, "Go on."

His attention fell to her hands, clenched in her lap. Turning so his knees bumped her legs, he leaned over and took both her hands in his. The brush of his warm skin, slightly damp with sweat, was almost more than she could bear.

"Edouard—" she pleaded.

"There is . . . something I must say. But I must say it the right way." Before she could try and guess his intentions, he released her hands and dropped to one knee on the grass. Light spilled through the overhead boughs onto him as he took her right hand. He suddenly looked nervous.

Her heart thundered in her breast. Mayhap she'd heard too many romantic *chansons*, but surely he wouldn't be down on one knee unless . . . ?

Shaking his head, he plopped her hand back into her lap. "'Tis not right at all."

"Edouard! What . . . ?"

He reached under the bench and snapped a long blade of grass, then picked up her hand again. Lifting her ring finger, he looped the grass around it several times. Then he tied the ends to form a makeshift ring.

Eyes filling with tears, she stared at him. "How can this be? You are betrothed to Nara."

"Not any longer. She is with child. Not *my* child." Edouard's eyes sparkled. "Another man's."

Shock rushed through Juliana. "I did not know."

"I vow 'tis not yet common knowledge. My sire informed me a short while ago. Because of the circumstances, I am no longer bound to marry Nara."

Juliana's indrawn breath froze in her lungs. "Really?"

"Really." Edouard kissed the grass ring he'd made her. Then he lifted his head to meet her gaze. "Will you be my wife, Juliana?"

Joy raced through her.

"I asked my father for his permission. He agreed."

Looking at his makeshift ring, Edouard said, "'Tis not an appropriate ring for a betrothal, but if you agree . . ."

"Aye."

His gaze flew up. "Aye . . . As in . . . ?"

Turning her hand to weave her fingers through his, she said, "I will be honored to be your wife."

He swallowed, the happiness in his features tinged with anxiety. "You must know . . . I am not asking just . . . because I am no longer betrothed to Nara." He kissed their joined hands. "I love you, Juliana. I believe I have loved you since you told me good-bye at Sherstowe."

Surprise fluttered through her. "Why then?"

Grudging laughter rumbled from him. "You made me acknowledge my flaws. Because of you, I came to realize that even a wealthy lord's son must earn respect— and his lady's love."

How earnestly he spoke. Yet his honest words buoyed the elation inside her. Unable to restrain her gladness any longer, she smiled. "I love you, Edouard de Lanceau. My soon-to-be husband."

He grinned. "Soon to be husband *and* . . ."

The glint in his eyes hinted at astounding news. "And?" she echoed.

"Lord of Waddesford Keep."

"Edouard! Oh—!"

"'Tis all right with you? I know this keep holds many 'ghosts' for both of us."

"Together we shall bring love and happiness to this castle. In Mayda's honor. If, 'tis all right with you?"

"Aye." Edouard smiled and rose to stand before her, tall and beautiful and . . . hers.

The thought left a delicious, tingling burn in her belly as he gently drew her to her feet and slid his arms around her waist, drawing her in close. She fell gently against him, bosom pressed to the front of his hauberk. Love for him soared inside her as she embraced him, washed in shadow and sunlight.

"I am glad you are happy, Lady de Greyne. My soon-to-be wife and lady of this keep."

"I would be even happier," she murmured, hardly recognizing her throaty voice, "if you kissed me."

Desire gleamed in his eyes. "A kiss with meaning?" he said, his mouth tantalizingly close.

An excited shudder raced through Juliana, for he'd remembered her impassioned words from long ago.

"A kiss that proves the love between us?" he added huskily, his eyes glowing with that thrilling blue fire. A roguish grin kicked up his mouth.

"A kiss that proves we were destined to be together," she whispered, while her breath mingled with his.

"We were," he whispered back.

As his arms shifted, squeezing her hips even tighter against his, she slid up on tiptoes and pressed her lips to his.

A ravenous growl broke from him. She inhaled on

CATHERINE KEAN

a gasp as his mouth swept against hers. So tenderly. As though she was extremely precious to him.

Over and over and over their lips met. Tender kisses. Rougher ones. He groaned and his tongue slid into her mouth, deepening the shocking, breathless, wondrous contact. Oh, God. *Oh. God.* The burn within her intensified until every tiny part of her body seemed ablaze with hunger.

Drawing back, she shivered through a gasp. "I never imagined a kiss could be so . . . magnificent."

Edouard winked. "Shall we indulge in another?"

A sound intruded into her bliss. Footfalls, drawing near.

Still in Edouard's arms, Juliana looked to see who approached. Azarel strode into the garden, a baby cradled in her arms.

"Rosemary!" Juliana cried.

Smiling, Azarel nodded. "Lord de Lanceau sent one of his warriors to the village to collect her. A favor, I am told, for his son."

"Edouard, thank you," Juliana cried, stepping from his embrace to take Rosemary into her arms. "She has grown." The little girl warbled. Eyes wide, she stared up at Juliana.

Juliana smiled. How complete she felt. How loved.

Beside her, Edouard chuckled. He slid an arm around her waist and kissed her flushed cheek. "Are you

446

happy, Juliana?"

"I am."

"Good, because I mean to keep you happy for the rest of your living days." He kissed her again, a slow, loving mingling of their mouths.

"That was wonderful," she breathed.

He growled against her ear. "I promise you, 'tis only the beginning of my persuasion."

One More Moment

Check it out! There is a new section on the Medallion Press Web site called "One More Moment." Have you ever gotten to the end of a book and just been crushed that it's over? Aching to know if the star-crossed lovers ever got married? Had kids? With this new section of our Web site, you won't have to wonder anymore! "One More Moment" provides an extension of your favorite book so you can discover what happens after the story.

m e d a l l i o n p r e s s . c o m

A Knight's Vengeance

CATHERINE KEAN

A quest for revenge . . .

Geoffrey de Lanceau is a knight, the son of the man who once ruled Wode. His noble sire died, however, branded as a traitor. But never will Geoffrey believe his father betrayed their king, and swears vengeance against the man who brought his sire down in a siege to take over Wode.

A quest for love . . .

Lady Elizabeth Brackendale dreamed of marrying for love, but is promised by her father to a lecherous old baron. Then she is abducted and held for ransom by a scarred, tormented rogue who turns out to be the very knight who has sworn vengeance against her father.

A quest for truth . . .

The threads of deception sewn eighteen years ago bind the past and present. Only by Geoffrey and Elizabeth championing their forbidden love can the truth - and the lies — be revealed about . . .

A Knight's Vengeance.

ISBN# 978-193281548-1
US $6.99 / CDN $9.99
Historical Romance
Available Now
www.catherinekean.com

A Knight's Reward
CATHERINE KEAN

Assaulted and injured by her abusive husband Ryle, Gisela Anne Balewyne flees with her small son, Ewan. Hiding from Ryle, and working as a tailor in the town of Clovebury, Gisela struggles to save enough money to move north and start a new life. With her latest commission from rich French merchant Crenardieu—sewing garments from luxurious blue silk—she will finally be able to leave and be free of Ryle forever. All goes well until Dominic de Terre, back several years from the Crusade, accepts his lord de Lanceau's mission to find out who has stolen de Lanceau's cloth shipment, worth a fortune.

For Dominic is the father of her son, although he does not know it. And although they discover neither her love, nor his, has ever died, she still cannot tell him the truth. Not yet. Tragically, however, Gisela waits too long.

Dominic discovers not only that Gisela has lied to him about the stolen silks, and has concealed them in her shop, he learns Ewan is his illegitimate son. She has betrayed his trust not once, but twice, and Gisela expects him to arrest her and take Ewan away.

Crenardieu's thugs, however, reach Dominic first, and Gisela realizes there is only one way to save his life. She must go to de Lanceau, admit her crimes, and convince him to let her help him save Dominic. And then she must confront Ryle, the dragon of her nightmares . . .

ISBN# 978-193281599-3
US $7.95 / CDN $9.95
Historical Romance
Available Now
www.catherinekean.com

CATHERINE KEAN
A Knight's Temptation

Aldwin Treynarde, a squire who shot Lord Geoffrey de Lanceau with a crossbow bolt after being deceived by Baron Sedgewick, is ordered to retrieve a stolen ruby pendant before it falls into the Baron and Veronique's hands. Haunted by his guilt over being manipulated by the baron years ago, Aldwin wants to prove his worth to his lord. If he excels in his duty, he might even be awarded knighthood. Such an honor would also help redeem himself to his respected parents who, ashamed by his reckless near-murder of de Lanceau, told him never to return home.

Lady Leona Ransley, in an effort to help her depressed father, only wants to hand over the pendant, collect the reward, and vanish. When she arranges a meeting in a seedy tavern, she never expected to face Aldwin, who almost caused her death twelve years ago when they disturbed a bee's nest during a childhood game. Although Aldwin does not recognize her, he is reminded of Leona and is haunted by his belief that she died from the bee stings from that day twelve years prior. Believing that the woman before him is a courtesan and has information on the conspirators' whereabouts, he takes Leona hostage and spirits her away, meaning to deliver her and the pendant to de Lanceau.

She, however, fights him at every chance. He desires his warrior captive more than any noble woman he has ever met, and when he discovers who she really is, he knows he has one last chance to protect his lady's life. Only by resolving what happened between them and by fighting side by side can Aldwin and Leona defeat the conspirators and surrender to their greatest temptation—love.

ISBN# 978-193383652-2

US $7.95 / CDN $8.95

Historical Romance

Available Now

www.catherinekean.com

Dawn Schiller

The Road Through Wonderland is Dawn Schiller's chilling account of the childhood that molded her so perfectly to fall for the seduction of "the king of porn," John Holmes, and the bizarre twist of fate that brought them together. With painstaking honesty, Dawn uncovers the truth of her relationship with John, her father figure-turned-forbidden lover who hid her away from his porn movie world and welcomed her into his family along with his wife.

Within these pages, Dawn reveals the perilous road John led her down—from drugs and addiction to beatings, arrests, forced prostitution, and being sold to the drug underworld. Surviving the horrific Wonderland murders, this young innocent entered protective custody, ran from the FBI, endured a heart-wrenching escape from John, and ultimately turned him in to the police.

This is the true story of one of the most infamous of public figures and a young girl's struggle to survive unthinkable abuse. Readers will be left shaken but clutching to real hope at the end of this dark journey on *The Road Through Wonderland*.

Also check out the movie *Wonderland* (Lions Gate Entertainment, 2003) for a look into the past of Dawn Schiller and the Wonderland Murders.

ISBN# 978-160542083-7

Trade Paperback / Autobiography

US $15.95 / CDN $17.95

AUGUST 2010

www.dawn-schiller.com

Passion's Blood

Cherif Fortin & Lynn Sanders

Lady Leanna is a flame-haired beauty loved by her betrothed, Prince Emric, desired by his loathsome brother, Prince Bran. Although in love with Emric, Leanna has still not made her peace with the knowledge that this arrangement was forced upon her.

Prince Emric, noble and courageous, rides to war, ignorant of his brother's dark treachery.

In a net of betrayal and violence, the young lovers must preserve their faith, and Leanna must keep Emric alive with her love and the magical powers she herself does not fully understand . . .

"I love this idea . . . I highly recommend this one!"
—**Jennj,** *Night Owl Romance*

". . . a quick-moving, snappy story coupled with absolutely gorgeous illustrations, this is a volume that deserves to be cherished . . ."
—**Marilyn Rondeau, CK2S Kwips and Critiques (February 2009)**

ISBN# 978-160542062-2
Hardcover Adult / Illustrated Romantic Masterpiece
US $25.95 / CDN $28.95
AVAILABLE NOW

There be Dragons
Heather Graham

Illustrated by
Cherif Fortin & *Lynn Sanders*

Bonus CD produced by
Reuven Amiel

Nico d'Or was a kind and gentle man who lived in the age of dragons. Through a simple twist of fate, Nico married the lovely Princess Elisia, and the couple were blessed with a beautiful daughter, Marina. Would they live happily ever after?

Well, not quite. The neighbor's wife, Geovana, was neither sweet nor lovely, but a devious sorceress who spent her time casting dreadful spells, devising vile tricks, and mixing powerful potions with eye of newt and the horn of a toad.

Geovana used one of her favorite spells—strategically hurling rocks through windows to smash into the heads of her victims—tragically killing both Nico and Elisia, and leaving the beautiful Marina all alone. To make matters worse, Geovana became Marina's guardian and, greedy for power, arranged a marriage between Marina and her own evil son, Carlo Baristo.

But Marina was in love with someone else. And as Christmas Day approached, Marina was faced with a terrible choice: save her land and her people, or follow her heart and believe in the magic of Christmas and true love.

ISBN# 978-160542071-4
Hardcover Adult / Illustrated Romantic Masterpiece
(Includes bonus audio CD)
US $25.95 / CDN $28.95
Available Now
w w w . t h e o r i g i n a l h e a t h e r g r a h a m . c o m

Insanity is doing the same thing over and over and expecting different results. If you're not getting the results you want out of life, than it's time to do something different! *MOTIV8N' U* will focus on taking a look at where you are now and how you want to spend the rest of your life—and will teach you how to restructure the beliefs and behaviors that are keeping you running in circles.

If you're not where you want to be, this book will show you how to unleash the spirit of strength and the power of fitness in every area of your life. I will walk you through twelve fundamental keys that will enable you to unlock the life-transforming fitness you've been dreaming of!

There is nothing more empowering than self-discovery, nothing more inspiring than self-direction, and nothing more rewarding than self-discipline—I will equip you to transform your life by motivat8n you in the spirit of strength! The spirit that already resides within you!

MOTIV8N' U is the only book you'll ever need to become the fittest you possible!

ISBN# 978-160542092-9
Trade Paperback / Motivational
US $15.95 / CDN $17.95
DECEMBER 2010
w w w . s t a c i b o y e r . c o m

Helen A Rosburg

Lady Blue

From the independent freedom of the American cattle ranch to the stifling restraint of the prim English parlor, Harmony Simmons loses all she has ever valued after the death of her affluent parents. According to her mother's will, she must remain under the guardianship of her domineering older sister, Agatha, until she turns twenty-one, a crushing blow to her ambitious spirit. Dowdy Agatha is jealous and spiteful, resentful of her attractive sibling. A restricted existence in England promises hell compared to Harmony's former privileged life with her successful father in the heavenly expanse of the West.

When Anthony Allen meets Harmony, he plays the rogue. Kidnapping this beautiful, well-bred angel with the sapphire eyes is a risk he's willing to take to coax her into his arms forever. His Lady Blue. Never has he seen a woman like her. Never will he adore another. Later, however, he introduces himself as suave aristocrat Lord Farmington, a title she suspects is a sophisticated ruse.

Baffled by his duplicity, Harmony cannot determine whether her mysterious lover is a cavalier bandit or an honorable hero of the landed gentry. His secret ignites a fear deep inside, where her passion for him burns. What sinister shadows may lurk in his past? Does he love her as he claims . . . or is he a jewel thief and a criminal predator seeking her inheritance in an elaborate masquerade?

ISBN# 978-160542063-9
Mass Market Paperback/Historical Romance
US $7.95 / CDN $8.95
Available Now
www.helenrosburg.com

EMERALD EMBRACE

SHANNON DRAKE

Devastated over the premature death of her dearest friend, Mary, Lady Martise St. James ventures to foreboding Castle Creeghan in the Scottish Highlands to dispel rumors surrounding the young woman's demise and retrieve a lost emerald. Beneath the stones of this aging mansion lurks a family crypt filled with sinister secrets. Locked within this threatening vault is the answer to the most dangerous question, and the promise of the most horrifying death.

Amid jaded suspicion, underlying threats, and the dreaded approach of All Hallow's Eve in 1865, Martise encounters a witch's coven and meets Lord Bruce Creeghan, the love of her friend's life. Mysterious, yet passionate, Mary's husband elicits a deep desire and a profound fear in the core of her soul. He knows . . . something. And it's up to Martise to reveal what he hides from her prying intrusion.

Lord Creeghan wards off the invasion of his private fortress, yet he cannot resist his magnetic attraction to the beautiful sleuth. As strong as the inevitable pull toward the catacomb beneath their bed, an overwhelming obsession propels them into disheveled sheets of unquenchable hunger and lust. While savoring an affair that cannot be denied, Martise must discover whether her lover is a ruthless murderer or a guardian angel.

ISBN# 978-160542082-0

Mass Market Paperback / Historical Romance

US $7.95 / CDN $8.95

AVAILABLE NOW

www.theoriginalheathergraham.com